BABY GRAND

D1649090

BOB BACHNER

Black Rose Writing | Texas

CH

ISBN: 978-1-68433-302-8
PUBLISHED BY BLACK ROSE WRITING
www.blackrosewriting.com

Printed in the United States of America
Suggested Retail Price (SRP) $19.95

Baby Grand is printed in Chaparral Pro

In memory of my sister, Suzanne B. Samstag,
who deserved much more than she was given.

BABY GRAND

I

Willie bought the piano in 1941 as his wedding present to Lila. There was no question of her going back to the stage after their honeymoon. The best she could have done was the chorus, possibly with a specialty bit thrown in; acceptable for Willie Burke's girlfriend, not for his wife. His pride would have required her to have a starring role, and for that, he would have had to put up all the money, which would have been dumb.

He had to come up with something, though, to keep her from spending too much time with Gloria in Brooklyn. So he decided to make her a singer, the kind that wears an evening gown and sings from her piano in classy nightclubs and cocktail lounges. The piano was the first step: a Steinway baby grand with white lacquer finish and gilt trim.

Lila knew what she was good at, and this was not it. She could sing on time and in key, but that was all, and she wasn't much at the piano. But if Willie said it was right, it must be. She had too much riding on that horse to bet against it now. So she applied herself to her new career.

The preparations lasted four months, followed by weekend spots in Westchester and Long Island. Willie brought in carloads of friends to applaud her, but there were no further bookings. When the war came, she participated in a few shows for the USO, which called for less talent and more leg and enjoyed a modest popularity. But when the war ended, so did her career and the piano came home to stay.

Fifty-plus years later, it looks perfect in the living room of her Palm Beach house, complemented by white and gold draperies, white rugs scattered about and the gilt frames of the paintings. She hasn't played since Willie died fifteen years ago but will have it tuned today as she does every six months. Tuning a piano that nobody plays is an affectation. Lila knows that. So is maintaining a pool that nobody swims in, a tennis court that nobody plays on and a 24-room house with five servants for one old woman.

Lila's manners are affected, too. Born Lina Granatelli in Brooklyn to Italian immigrants, she has adopted the broad vowels of a Boston Brahmin.

Long ago, she chose her name, manner of speech, clothes, her views on art and politics, all in order to become what she had to be, not what she pretended to be, not as hermit crabs remain unchanged inside the deserted shells they assume, but as some insects enter the bodies of others for their own metamorphosis. Lila, too, has had to change into a different creature to survive.

This is her final stage: an elegant, flightless butterfly, subsisting without nourishment or effort as her one day's sun completes its circuit. Foraging, mating, procreating, are only memories now, perhaps dreams; it's increasingly hard to tell the difference. The piano helps since most of her history is captured in the heavily framed photographs that line the top. She goes there, now, and begins taking them off to allow the tuner to open the case.

First, of course, are those of Gloria, at seven under the Christmas tree at Rockefeller Center, at ten, with Pinto, and at fourteen, with Elliot.

Next, Lila picks up a wartime photograph of herself at 22, which used to be given to the servicemen who came to her shows. She wears what was then a daring one-piece swimsuit and stands leaning back just about to throw the beach ball, which she holds over her head. The top of the bathing suit has slipped down to show an inviting portion of the small, taut breasts and appears in danger of exposing them altogether. The legs below are long enough but a bit too sturdy for a real siren; they fit better with the open face and laughing eyes. The effort to be both naughty and nice doesn't work aesthetically, but she likes it, and the servicemen grabbed for it.

Men were always grabbing for her. Some of them are in the photographs she continues to remove from the piano. Willie, of course. Lila could always stop whatever he was doing, by slipping a shoulder strap or by raising her skirt a couple of inches to adjust a stocking. She would do it for fun at parties. He would stop in mid-sentence and stare at her. A moment later he would make his way across the room, and she would stand still until he caught her to him.

Others she allowed to catch her? There were more than she'd like to admit, although less than most people thought. Joe Prince, Gloria's father, was the first. He poses in his publicity photo in the style of Rudolph Valentino; black hair sleeked down, thin mustache trimmed, a little mascara in his eyebrows set above piercing eyes. A passionate man, one would think, dashing and dangerous. But it was all a performance.

•   •   •

Joe Prince (né Principato), was a first-rate performer. At 26, he played a suave villain in the 1939 Broadway musical in the chorus of which the now-named Lila Grand began her career. Off the stage, his hair rumpled, wearing faded sweatshirts and frayed khakis, Joe looked like what he truly was: a fellow Italian from Lila's own Brooklyn neighborhood, someone she could joke with, someone she could lean against, dozing, on the long subway ride home after the show. Whenever he could, he studied serious acting and took Lila to see Shakespeare and Ibsen and O'Neill.

After a while, Joe's protective arm began to linger around her shoulders, and his greeting kiss moved from her cheek to her lips. He was making his move, and Lila knew she had to make a decision.

Joe was handsome and entertaining, but she wasn't in love with him nor he with her. He was nice to her, but he was nice to everybody, even to his former girlfriends, two of whom, Sally and Meg, were in the chorus with her. What he cared about was his career. As Sally said, he'd push any of them under a subway in a second if it would get him a good part.

Besides, Lila didn't want love, not then. Love was something that made girls forget their lines, miss auditions and arrive late for performances. Lila didn't do those things; she might fail for lack of talent, but not for lack of effort.

Not that she had anything against men. Her father had been big and handsome with a commanding voice. He could fix any toy, answer any question, face down any neighborhood tough. She had been his adoring princess until she was seven when a thunderstorm swept him from a holiday fishing boat.

Lila's brother, John, six years older, had always been kind and protective. Slight of build, like their mother, he had driven himself to fill his father's place, working two and three part-time jobs while he was still in high school. Yet, he somehow found the energy to help Lila with her homework and to find an old radio in someone's trash and fix it in time for her birthday.

Nor had boys of her own age treated her badly. Her face attracted attention as far back as the fourth grade; by the ninth, her body drew crowds. Occasionally she liked one of the neighborhood boys who liked her and enjoyed eager kisses and fumbling caresses.

But she wasn't in high school anymore. Joe Prince was not going to be

3

satisfied with five-minute kisses and groping hands. Nor was she, she had to admit, after hearing her friends' vivid descriptions of the pleasures of sex. It might be years before she married. Was she supposed to live like a nun until then? Nobody did that anymore, at least nobody in the theater.

Sally and Meg made up her mind for her. Over coffee one day, Lila admitted that she was still a virgin, and they almost exploded with concern.

"You poor little thing," Meg gushed. "However can you bear it?"

Practical Sally had the solution. "Oh honey, you got to get Joe to do it for you. You want it done right, the first time, not messed up by some clumsy bozo who'll ruin it for years. Joe did it for me three years ago, and he was just wonderful about it."

Lila looked at Meg, who shook her head sadly. "No, luv. I wish he had."

The following Saturday night, Lila's mother was spending the weekend with her cousin in Massapequa. As usual, Lila and Joe took the same subway home. But this time, when the train neared Lila's stop, she took Joe's hand as she rose from her seat.

"What are you doing?" he blurted, struggling to his feet.

"Taking you home." She spoke too loudly, and an elderly man across the car lowered his newspaper and stared at them.

A block down the quiet street on which Lila lived. Joe halted, put his hand behind Lila's head and kissed her. His kiss was nothing like those of her high school boyfriends. There was no need to bob heads to get the noses right; he drew her mouth straight to his, fitting their lips together as though milled for that purpose. When he made a soft, questioning sound in his throat, Lila pressed her body against him and opened her mouth to his.

In Lila's bedroom, he sat on the bed and ceremoniously undressed her. As each portion of her body was revealed, he murmured effusive compliments: how firm and succulent her breasts, how silky her thighs. He knelt to pull her panties off, playfully kissed her navel, picked her up and laid her on the bed. It all happened so naturally that Lila felt no embarrassment. She stretched out in what she hoped was an inviting pose as her lover hastily stripped.

He took his wallet from his pants and fumbled through it. "Shit."

"What's the matter?" Lila sat up in alarm and pulled the sheet around herself.

"I don't have a goddamn rubber."

"Then we can't do it." Her first feeling was relief. She hadn't been so sure of her decision, and it wouldn't kill her to wait a while.

"It's OK. I'll just have to pull out at the end." Joe put his wallet on the dresser and came toward the bed.

"You can do that?" This was serious. A baby would be death to her acting career.

"Sure, I've done it lots of times."

"I don't know, Joe. I'm afraid."

His face became that of a little boy, and his penis shrank. "Trust me, Lila. Please. It'll be all right. I promise."

What could she do? Send him back to the subway after all that preparation? She could trust Joe. He knew a lot more about these things than she did. She smiled. He was on the bed next to her in a second, erect again. His hand moved over her breast then down between her legs. When Lila momentarily flinched, he stopped.

"It's OK," she murmured and reached down and guided his hand back to her. His fingers soon found a spot so sensitive that she moaned, and he rubbed the spot gently. The sensation was exquisite. After a while, he stopped, pushed her legs apart, and entered her. Lila wriggled a little to fit herself to him and marveled at how easily it was done.

Joe began to move up and down. She reached her hands to his shoulders to pull him down to her and raised her legs to grip his hips, and the pleasure intensified. God bless Sally and Meg. He began to thrust in and out rapidly, and Lila speeded to follow him.

"Yes!" he shouted, "Now!"

Lila gathered herself to make a final surge to meet his, then, suddenly, he was pulling out. Beyond thought, she dug her nails into his back, grappled him with her heels and thrust as hard as she could. A wave of pleasure and relief crested through her just as Joe released, and she shut her mind to everything but the sensations of her delighted body.

Afterward, they lay side by side, squeezed against each other in her narrow bed.

Joe kissed her hand. "That was wonderful. Who would believe that this little kid from Brooklyn turns out to be the most fabulous woman I've ever met? Are you OK?"

"Uh huh." She freed her hand and stroked his forehead. "You're all sweaty."

He laughed. "They say that's the best exercise for you. It's sure the most fun." He paused. "Don't worry about it. It's a hundred to one nothing will

5

happen. When I was a crazy kid, I never wore a rubber, and none of the girls ever got pregnant."

He was right, he had to be right. "It's OK, Joe." She put her hand over his mouth. "You don't need to tell me about all the other girls."

He put his arm under her and pulled her over, so her head was on his shoulder. "Lila, compared to you, there are no other girls."

•　　　　　•　　　　　•

Lila watches the piano tuner as he works, her head tilted a bit to the right, listening with her good ear. She nods with him when he gets it right, frowns with him when he misses, a fussy German immigrant she still calls Mr. Goetz after forty years, while he has called her by her stage name, since the day he learned that she had one. Ashamed or not, she had written "Lila Grand" on her first job application, not "Lina Granatelli."

"Ja, Miss Grand?" he asks now, gets up from the bench, brushes off the imaginary dirt left by his immaculate tan twill trousers and, with a courtly half-bow and wave of his hand, offers her the seat of honor, inviting her to try his work.

As always, she declines. "Later, I think, Mr. Goetz. It sounds lovely."

Modestly he pretends to misunderstand. "A good instrument, *ja*, very good." And he puts on his seersucker jacket, a new one every five years, closes his toolbox, shakes her hand and limps out. Mary, her personal maid, told her two years ago that he had started to leave a cane by the front door before being shown into the living room. Lila doesn't think this little deception has anything to do with business; it's male vanity. He's had his ideas about her, sneaked enough peeks over the years, schemed to get her on the bench with him. Always neat, shaved, after-shaved, showing off his sensitive fingertips as he adjusts a hammer here, tightens a string there, he can't break the habit of courting. And why should he? Maybe she'll offer him a little schnapps on his next visit. There was a time when she could have bent over the piano and given him something to peek at that was better than schnapps.

•　　　　　•　　　　　•

Over the next few weeks, they made love several times at Joe's apartment. Joe always produced the necessary equipment. Everybody knew the first time didn't count, so she wasn't too concerned when she missed her next period. But, when the one after that failed to materialize, she went to see a doctor and learned the truth. It had all been for nothing. The weary hours at part-time jobs, the denial of girlhood's treats and frills so that she could pay for the lessons, the alienation from her childhood friends, all the will, the concentration, the unrelenting effort. For nothing.

"You stupid bitch, you've ruined it all. How could you do it?" Over and over she cursed herself and beat on her knees with her fists. The alarmed doctor moved to stand between her and the office window.

"I'm not going to kill myself," she said, regaining control. "Or the baby." She was so self-possessed by the time she put her coat on that the doctor allowed himself to ask why all her anger had been self-directed; most women cursed the man responsible or God or both.

Lila looked at him as though he were stupid. "Because it was my own fault. I knew I shouldn't have let Joe do it that night, but I did. He didn't hold a gun to my head or anything; he was just doing what guys have been doing forever." And God, she said to herself, why should I curse Him? He's been doing this sort of thing forever, too.

The doctor's office was thirty blocks from Lila's home, but she decided to walk, to give herself time to think. It was still March, so she buttoned her coat. The snow from the last storm had long since been cleared out of midtown Manhattan, but here, in Brooklyn, there were still dirty piles. In places, she had to make her way between the deposits of the neighborhood dogs and to step over the pools of melting slush backed up from blocked sewer grates.

Despite what she had told the doctor, Lila had not yet excluded the possibility of abortion. The Church said that it was forbidden by God, but since He seemed to have turned away from her already, she had to make her own decision. As she walked, she looked for a sign. She saw beaming mothers kissing their children and harassed mothers screaming at theirs. That hardly seemed helpful to a decision about the tiny thing inside her. Was it an embryo yet or still just an egg?

She closed her eyes, trying to visualize it in its present state, and saw a tiny child, fully formed in miniature, with the face of a little boy holding a dog she had just passed during her walk. She shook her head, but the child was still there, now a girl who had been pushing a carriage with a doll in it. If she went ahead with an abortion, she would forever believe that she had killed one of those children, a block behind her. Or some other real child. Of course, she couldn't do that. At the realization, Lila was so relieved that she had to grab a lamppost to keep from falling. When she recovered, she saw she was just a block from home. With that decision made, she was ready to talk to her mother.

After her husband's death until Lila's brother was old enough to work, Serafina Granatelli had somehow raised her two children on a pittance of insurance and a little embroidery piece work. She had loved Lila's father so much that, eleven years after his death, she would not even consider taking a cup of coffee alone with any of the eligible widowers her family and friends urged upon her. And she had always been reasonable. She had disapproved of Lila trying for a stage career, but once Lila made up her mind, her mother stopped arguing and did everything she could to help.

Lila climbed the outside stairs of the two-family house they shared with her mother's older sister Julia, also a widow. In the kitchen, Lila's mother looked up from the chipped, white, enameled table, where she was sitting, telephone receiver cradled between her shoulder and her ear while she cut vegetables. The two sisters spoke on the telephone a dozen times a day but maintained privacy by entering each other's home only on special occasions.

Mrs. Granatelli smiled at Lila, but the smile quickly became a frown. *"Più tardi,"* she said into the receiver and put it in its cradle on the counter behind her. "Whatsa matter, baby?" She pushed the vegetables aside, put down the knife and wiped her hands on an old dish towel.

Lila bent to kiss her mother's cheek, sat at the table and took a deep breath. "I'm pregnant, Momma."

For a minute, Mrs. Granatelli sat motionlessly. Then she got up from the table and began to walk about the kitchen emitting sighs, imprecations, mumblings, and mutterings addressed in English and Italian to God, His saints and her dead husband, filling any moments of silence with extravagant gestures. A small, sharp-featured woman, she made Lila think of a sparrow in a birdbath. Finally, she took two cups from the shelf, brought the coffee pot from the stove, filled the cups, brought the sugar bowl and spoons, sat down across the table from Lila and spoke in a matter-of-fact tone.

"You're not thinking of doing something to it? No, you wouldn't have told me, then."

"That's right, Momma."

"Good. If you do that, God never forgives you, and you never forgive yourself. So you have the baby. What to do with it then? You don't want this man for a husband, right?"

"That's right, Momma."

"He's a bad man?"

"No, but he'd be a bad husband and father."

"He's only good for making the babies, is that it?"

Lila spooned sugar into her coffee. Her mother had a right to say that. Lila knew mothers who would have driven her from the house after her first sentence.

"You haven't even talked to him. Suppose he wants to marry you?"

"He won't, Momma. He'll run like a thief before he'll do that. He doesn't love me any more than I love him."

"So you don't love him, and he don't love you, but a baby's still coming. That's'a being modern, I suppose." Mrs. Granatelli got up and walked around the room again. This time she brought back a plate of chocolate chip cookies. "So, we got a baby, a mother, and no father. You want to have it and give it away? Lotsa nice people can't have their own, be happy to take it."

"I don't know, Momma."

"Like John and Catherine. I just get a letter; she's'a lose the baby."

"Oh, no. Not again. How is she?"

As soon as he completed high school, Lila's brother went into the machine shop their father and uncle had run. John worked for four years for wages, saying nothing while his uncle and cousin took out the profits. Every night, the light in his room showed under the door after midnight, while he pursued correspondence courses in aeronautics. Suddenly, one day, he was gone to an airplane factory in St. Louis, having answered an ad he'd shown to nobody. He sent his mother a money order every month, even after he married Catherine, a calm, quiet girl five years older than Lila. She and John adored each other and were dying to have children, but this was Catherine's second miscarriage.

"She's'a not too bad. The doctor say try again. So, what'a you want to do?"

"I don't know, Momma. It's mine. How can I let someone else take it?"

"You gotta do what you think is right."

"I feel like I want to keep it, but how will I take care of it? I can't stop working."

There was a pause as each ate a cookie and sipped her coffee. What was to be said now could not be said lightly, although, when Mrs. Granatelli finally spoke, she added no emphasis to her ordinary, practical tone. "All right, we got a baby and a mother. There's'a no father, but could be the old grandmother, she's'a help a little."

That settled it, and Lila could finally run to her mother, bury her head in the many folds of Mrs. Granatelli's skirt and cry. She cried for herself, her youth snatched from her, for the child within her who would never have a father, for her brother and sister-in-law who might never have a child, for her mother who had lost her love so young. That was everyone, so she stopped crying, got up and began to plan how to make the best of it.

First, she banished the idea of a husband from her mind. Maybe, someday, against all odds, she might find someone she could love as much as her mother had loved her father. It would have to be that or nothing. No pretty nice guys, who won't get anywhere and, when they realize it, become not so nice. No guys who will get somewhere but who aren't even pretty nice, to begin with. Better to work as a waitress than as a wife to one of those.

●   ●   ●

Lila didn't want to tell Joe about the baby. There was no point. They weren't going to marry. Joe wasn't suited to the lifetime role of a father, and Lila didn't want a father who would send occasional birthday cards and come to her door unannounced every few years to upset her child's life.

Mrs. Granatelli was horrified. "Not tell him he's going to be a father? You crazy. How you know he can't be a good one? A husband is all your business. Not a child's father. Did the baby say 'No, Momma, I don't want a Poppa?'"

At last, she succeeded in convincing Lila. The next night, after the show, Lila brought Joe back to her house. She led him into the kitchen and introduced him to her mother, who captured his outstretched hand and perused his face intently.

"E′ vero," she said to Lila and left the room.

Joe pulled out a chair and sat. "What's true?" he whispered urgently. "What have you told her?"

Lila could hear the nervousness in his voice. Good. Let him at least worry a few minutes. "Nothing," she replied innocently and opened the icebox.

"Oh, come on. You know. The way she looked me over? It was like a casting director making a final decision. You didn't give her the idea we were getting married, did you?"

Lila straightened up, a Coca-Cola in either hand and closed the icebox door with a twist of her hip. She set the bottles on the table and took an opener from the table drawer, opened the bottles and pushed one in front of Joe, then sat and took a swig from the other. "I guess she wanted to get an idea of what the baby will look like if it's a boy."

Joe turned toward her and looked into her eyes for a moment, then turned back to his Coke, lifted the bottle and took a gulp. "You're not kidding."

"No, Joe, I'm not kidding. And, so you don't have to ask me, I haven't been with anybody else—ever."

"Come on, Lila, I know that."

"Well?"

This was his cue. Against all reason, she began to count to herself ("one— two—three"). He had until ten to rush around the table and throw his arms around her ("four—five—six"), but what would she say if he did ("seven— eight—nine")?

He blew the line and remained in his chair like a propped-up dummy. She should be relieved; why were tears starting? She turned away to search for napkins. How stupid to imagine, even for a moment, that he might be the one.

Joe finished his Coke and began to roll the bottle between his hands. "What can I do to help? Do you want me to find a doctor? Do you need money?"

"I'm going to have the baby and keep it. The hospital and the doctor will cost about $500. If you can give me that, it would help a lot."

"Sure, Lila, I'd be happy to do that. I'll have it for you next week. After that, I'll be in Los Angeles. Keep it quiet, would you; my agent has gotten me a three-year studio contract. I guess I won't be around New York much for a while. Is that OK?"

Joe squirmed in his chair, but Lila found no satisfaction in it. She had known what kind of person he was. It wasn't his fault that he wasn't more. So she took his hand in both of hers and squeezed it. "It's OK, Joe. It'll all be OK. You go to California and knock 'em dead and forget about us. The baby and I will do just fine."

Joe slumped in relief. "Thanks, Lila. I know you will." He reached for his coat. "It's getting late, and there's a matinee tomorrow. I'd better go. Say good-bye to your mother."

At the door, he kissed Lila tenderly on the cheek. "I hope it looks like you, beautiful." Exit, stage right.

Joe avoided Lila for most of the next week, but came up to her before his last performance and handed her an envelope with the promised money. After the show, he disappeared without good-byes for anyone, and Lila never heard from him again.

•   •   •

There is a soft knock at the door and Mary, Lila's personal maid, enters. "Cook would like to know what you want for lunch. You'll be remembering that Mrs. Goodman is coming."

"I'll come to the kitchen in a few minutes," Lila snaps, "I haven't lost my memory yet."

"Yes, mum," says Mary flatly, and turns, obviously offended.

"I'm sorry," Lila says quickly. "I'm feeling old today and a little touchy about it. Like Mr. Goetz."

Mary turns back, a worried look on her normally placid face. "Don't go comparing yourself to that old mutt, now, Mum. You must be ten years younger than him and look twenty. All you need are some younger men around; that'd make you feel better soon enough." Having cheered herself, if not Lila, she departs.

Lila begins to put the photographs back on the piano. Younger men. There are some of them in the pictures from those terrible years of alcohol and adultery. In the photo of Willie's Saturday morning tennis game of the '60s, is a handsome young pro whom Willie paid to liven up the game. During the weeks when Willie was up in New York, Bruce sometimes came to hit the ball with her and more. The funny thing was that she enjoyed the tennis so much that she often wore herself out on the court and sent him off afterward in confusion. The same sort of thing also happened with the backgammon hustler; she would throw her dice like a springing leopard, and if her luck were on she'd play all night and go to bed at dawn alone.

Not with Willie, though. She was as eager for him as he was for her. If they could have stayed in bed all the time, they would have had the perfect marriage. And there were days, those first short years, when they did. They would often wake up late on a Sunday, shut off the telephone, turn on the radio and pile newspapers, magazines, cards, backgammon sets and trays of food and drinks all around their bed. They would doze and make love, eat, read, play and repeat the cycle until late at night when they would come back to the world and lay their clothes out for Monday morning.

•   •   •

The term of Lila's pregnancy was as bad as anticipated. She soon had to leave the show, and the promises of the producers to put her in another show some day couldn't dissuade her from the conviction that her career, its slight momentum lost, would now sink forever. She got a temporary job as a hostess in a local restaurant, and she and her mother saved what they could. Lila was always tired and uncomfortable. However much she tried, there was no joy in imagining her child in her arms, resentment at so much of her future as she could picture and fear of what she couldn't.

Then, to her surprise, her life became far better than she had expected. Gloria's delivery was easy, as though she couldn't wait to come into the world. She squalled appropriately during the post-partum procedure but stopped instantly when placed into Lila's arms. Like many babies, she was born with a little cap of black hair, but, unlike most, kept it giving her the look of an adorable doll. Sometimes Lila felt like a child at play, herself, as she washed or dressed or fed Gloria. She would take the little hands and feet and move them back and forth as though manipulating a puppet that smiled and gurgled happily.

For the first two months after Gloria's birth, Lila and her mother took a vacation from work. They enjoyed Gloria and laughed a lot with her and with each other. Mrs. Granatelli told Lila about her own childhood and just how each of the cousins was related and how she met Lila's father and what Lila and her brother were like as babies. Then, one morning, beyond all hope, the producers of Lila's first show called.

Two months later Lila was back on Broadway in the chorus of a barnyard review called <u>Chicks and Chucks</u>, with a bit in a specialty number with three other girls and a trained pig, which would oink on cue. Since she was the only one of the four who wasn't afraid of the pig, she got most of the action in the bit and showed a good sense of comic timing. It didn't hurt that her strategically torn costume fit her perfectly.

As a result, she became a minor celebrity and was pursued by men of various degrees of respectability. She kept them all at a distance until, at a party, she noticed a big man with curly red hair and a broad freckled face staring at her as he told a story to a small group. When he found Lila looking at him, he winked and returned his full attention to the story.

Lila didn't know about that. High school boys and smart-alecs winked. She retreated into the next room, picked a drink off a tray and joined two friends from the show who were discussing the rumored replacement of one of the leads. Feeling silly, she peered between them into the room from which she had come. The smart-alec had finished his story, and his audience was laughing and clapping him on the back, but he was ignoring them. He stood on tiptoes, his head swiveling as he cast his glance around the room. Was he looking for her? Lila raised her glass to hide her face, and his searching look swept past her.

When she looked again, the man was still in the other room, now talking to the hostess, his palms up in puzzlement, a worried frown on his face. The hostess shrugged and waved in the direction of the room Lila was in. Lila was only a step away from the hallway to the bathroom and ducked in. He was looking for her. Did she want to be found? She looked in the mirror, adjusted a few stray hairs and came out of the bathroom. Oops, there he was. Now what?

"Willie Burke, Miss Grand. Wonderful to meet you." He captured her hand in two great paws and bent over confidently, a grin spilling like honey over his freckled face. "You are the pearl of that show; it's truly terrible where they have cast you." Willie was proud of the cleverness of the metaphor, but truthfully, Lila didn't get it until someone explained it to her years later.

What she did get, was the intensity of the dark blue eyes, the excitement in the rich tenor voice and the irresistible claim of the pressing hands. She understood that she was not being asked a question or offered a choice. A condition existed over which neither she nor Willie had control, and so she led him to her coat and pocketbook and then to the elevator.

They kissed from the twelfth floor to the lobby. Throughout, they carried on a silent dialogue with their lips and their bodies. They swept through the lobby and into a taxi. As it rolled down Broadway to Canal Street, they studied each other's faces in the flickering lights of street lamps and passing cars. Lila traced Willie's face with her fingers and protested when he captured her hand and brought it to his lips.

"Wait, Willie, I have to recognize you in the dark, too."

Willie released her hand and whispered, "You'll have lots of chances for that, for sure."

Lila slapped him so hard that he fell off the back seat of the Checker and banged his head on one of the jump seats. Was it possible that he was just another stage door Johnny offering her an ingenious line? Awkwardly, he clambered back onto his seat rubbing his head.

Please, God, she prayed, make it all right, or I'll die.

Willie looked across the seat at her grim face and clenched fists and burst into a bellow of laughter. "In its own sweet time, Lila. I didn't say tonight."

She took a great gulp of air, and her taut muscles relaxed. She put her hand against Willie's cheek and rested her head on his shoulder. "Can you forgive me?"

He answered by pulling her closer, so she was fully supported by his hard-muscled arm, while he stroked her hair with his free hand. They were silent for a few moments, and Lila could feel the taxi bump over the rough pavement onto the Manhattan Bridge.

Willie took her chin and brought her face up to his. "Now, would you be wantin' a man who didn't think about being alone with you in the dark?"

She couldn't help imagining it and felt her body rousing in welcome. "No, Willie, I wouldn't, but I have to be careful."

He started to say something, but she put a finger over his lips and told him about Gloria. When she finished, he was silent for a while before replying, "All right, darling girl, we'll be careful."

They had come off the bridge and were heading up Flatbush Avenue. Lila brushed Willie's lips with hers and sat back against his shoulder. She took Willie's free hand and pulled it over her breast. It was still there when the taxi stopped in front of her house, and she awoke.

The next morning, Lila telephoned into the showgirl network and got a report on Willie Burke. He was 32 years old, Catholic and never married, but not for any shortage of willing women. He had played football at Fordham, was now in the family construction business and was "loaded." That was quite nice, but it didn't matter. Lila was bound to him, whoever he was.

She said nothing to her mother, yet. This was not the time to try to explain the situation. She needed to savor the unfamiliar taste of happiness, nibbling around the edges without distractions. But at the same time, she needed to tell someone who would rejoice with her. So, she bundled up Gloria, popped her into the carriage with Blinky, a black and white stuffed cat with long eyelashes and whiskers, and took her for a walk. When they got around the corner, Lila stopped and bent over the carriage.

"Now, Gloria, I have something very important to tell you, so pay careful attention."

Gloria stopped waving her arms and looked up into Lila's face.

"That's right, Now listen,Darling. Last night I met the man I'm going to marry. He's big and strong and could pick up the carriage with you and Blinky in it in one hand and me in the other, but he wouldn't do anything to hurt either of us."

Lila started the kissing game, quickly kissing Gloria in one corner of her face and then another while Gloria tried to catch her with her hands. This time Gloria was successful, and the chubby fingers grasped Lila's nose for a moment. They both laughed.

"OK, now, let's be serious. His name is Willie, and he has red hair and freckles. He's going to love you, and you're going to love him, and we'll all be very happy together. Won't that be nice?" But Gloria wanted to play the kissing game again and didn't answer.

Willie was to take Lila to an early dinner before the show and had insisted on picking her up although she was used to taking the subway. She sat at the window, scanning the street for the first glimpse of yellow among the trees to signal the arrival of the taxi and was surprised when a large gray car slid silently to the curb and Willie jumped out of the back seat. She grabbed her pocketbook and was out on the stoop before Willie made it up the steps.

He reached for her tentatively, but she hurled herself into his arms. Let her mother see her from the upstairs window; let the neighbors peer out between the slats of their blinds. She didn't care. One kiss, then Lila drew back to look at Willie.

"How do I look in daylight when you're sober?" he asked hesitantly.

"Awful, terrible, hideous." She ran down the steps to the car. The driver tipped his uniform cap and opened the door for her.

In the car and later at the restaurant they talked incessantly in a flurry of questions, as children, at Christmas, tear, and fling about the paper and ribbons to discover what's inside. It wasn't important that Willie still lived in the family home on Fifth Avenue with his parents and unmarried sister or that he liked dogs or that the car was a Bentley. But it filled in the outline, made him real and silenced the voice of self-doubt that had awakened her that morning whispering that it was all a dream. They became so engrossed that they lost track of time and had to rush to the theater.

•   •   •

They saw each other the next day and every day after that, even if for no more than a late ride to Brooklyn or a quick sandwich between the end of Willie's workday and the time Lila had to be at the theater. They seemed always to be laughing together. Willie would tell of Irish workmen just off the boat who, totally ignorant of the work, confidently presented themselves for skilled jobs because they had heard the Burkes would never turn them away. Or Lila would mimic the inordinately effeminate young assistant to the director of <u>Chicks and Chucks</u> who ran around backstage trying to keep both humans and animals ready for their cues.

As the days passed, they discovered that they were both perfectionists prepared to work hard at whatever they did. Lila backed out of a Sunday excursion to Philadelphia to spend the day working with a replacement pig when the original one suddenly refused to perform and was retired. Willie could be found at his desk at eight every morning, no matter how late they had been out the night before, and often went back to his office after their early dinners.

Willie's business fascinated Lila. She knew that Manhattan's skyscrapers had not just appeared at the snap of a magician's fingers, but found it difficult to comprehend how mere humans could carry out the countless steps necessary to raise tons of steel and stone and concrete, mixed with miles of conduit and wire, and football fields of glass to tower hundreds of feet above the earth. And they stood and remained standing, all while people worked and cooked and slept inside them as easily as in a single story house. She badgered Willie with questions, until, one night, as they were saying their goodnights on the porch outside her house, he ordered her to dress in old clothes and be ready to be picked up at 6:30 the next morning to come and see the office building the Burkes were building in lower Manhattan.

"Are you going to teach me the building business? Can I run one of those big cranes?"

Willie considered the question. "Bricks, I think. Yes, you should start by carrying a hod of bricks. That's what my father made me do. But seeing as you're just a slip of a girl, I'll tell the foreman to keep your loads down to fifty pounds."

"That's nothing. I can carry twice as much as that."

"Who are you kidding? You couldn't lift a hundred pounds, a wee thing like you."

"I can lift you, you big, fat tub." Lila grabbed him around the waist and gave an enormous heave, which did little to lift Willie's 210 pounds but did let her rub her body against his. As she did, she felt him harden against her.

She gave a little cry of triumph. "See, I can raise you easily."

She was surprised to hear herself speak so boldly. She could never have said that to another man, even to Joe. Sex was sinful, but talking about it was vulgar, which was worse. Lila didn't care. She and Willie could say anything they wanted to each other.

"Always, darling girl," Willie whispered and pulled her to him.

"6:30, Willie," she reminded him. He relaxed his grip and kissed her lightly in farewell.

•   •   •

The Bentley's horn sounded at 6:45 the next morning and Lila came down the stairs ready to chide Willie as a sleepyhead, although she, herself, had needed all of the extra fifteen minutes to get herself awake and ready.

Willie was not in the car. The chauffeur explained he had dropped "Mr. Burke and Mr. Willie" at the building site on the way to pick her up, which was why he was late. "I never knew such people for gettin' up in the *marnin'*," he said and gave a big yawn for Lila's benefit. So she was going to meet Willie's father. Willie had often spoken of his father, mixing themes of affection and resentment with powerful, unvarying respect. James Burke had come to New York at fifteen with a widowed mother and four younger siblings, had taken responsibility for the whole lot and made them rich and respected. In return, he demanded and received fealty from everyone born or married into or working for the family.

"He's proud, generous and loyal, opinionated, stubborn and insensitive. Just like me," Willie had told her. "Don't let him bully you and he'll love you."

It was a few minutes past seven when they pulled up to the building at the corner of Pearl and Hemlock Streets. She got out and looked around for Willie. An April wind sent ragged clouds scudding like newspapers above a scene of chaos. Workers swarmed over the ten stories already partially completed. Next to two huge cranes, trucks loaded with materials were backed into position, the drivers screaming at each other to get out of the way. One of the cranes was hoisting a steel beam guided by ropes tugged at by workmen like pre-historic hunters subduing a giant beast. A cage, loaded with men and materials, crept up one side of the structure, while, right next to it, a chute running up to the top dumped trash into the back of a truck. At the foot of Hemlock Street, a cement truck poured its contents into huge kettles; behind that truck, others stood in line, their pot-bellies rhythmically turning over and over. Everywhere were piles of materials and debris, from which dust and dirt rose to swirl in the wind among the din of cursing men, roaring engines and clanking machinery.

Lila finally spotted Willie and two other men, all in work clothes, standing by a truck loaded with slabs of marble. Willie was facing away from her but was unmistakable. He was the tallest, and his shock of red hair looked like a flag waving over a battle.

As she walked towards the group, Willie moved slightly unblocking Lila's view of the fourth member of the conference, a small, white-haired man, in a three-piece gray suit, fedora perched on his head. Spotting Lila, he tapped Willie on the shoulder and pointed past him to Lila. Willie turned, and his face lit up like a child's.

Lila stayed where she was and let Willie come to her. Would he kiss her in front of his father and all those people? She held out her hand to be shaken. He took it with his left hand and squeezed it as he stepped closer to plant a chaste but proprietary kiss on her left cheek.

"You made it. I didn't think anything short of a bomb could get you up this early."

Lila started to reply, but words deserted her as she saw the expression of joy on Willie's face. He does love me, she marveled. It's true. Oh yes, Willie, me too, and without a thought for the time or place, Lila flung her arms around him and drove her mouth against his.

By the time they pulled apart, the men in work clothes were walking away from the meeting, but the man in the suit remained. His eyebrows were drawn into a frown as he stared at her and Willie. She forced herself to stare back at him while Willie guided her over to him.

Father and son had the same red and white coloring, but the red was concentrated in the father's face into blotchy red islands, while someone had taken the trouble to sprinkle it evenly over Willie's face like paprika on potato salad. Willie's square jaw added character without dominating his broad face; his father's threatened like a bludgeon.

"Dad, I'd like you to meet Lila Grand."

"Lila, this is my father, James Burke, the best builder in New York. He's so good he can get the whole job done without getting a spot on his suit." Poor Willie, she thought, he doesn't know what to say to his own father.

"Is that so, Mr. Burke? This seems like such a titanic job. How do you keep all the different workmen from bumping into each other?"

"We schedule all the trades way before we start so we know who's goin' to be where every day. Surprises cause trouble." He tossed his head slightly and sniffed.

Willie stiffened.

Quickly, Lila said, "Excuse me, but I'm famished. Could I get a doughnut and some coffee from the wagon?"

A thin smile appeared on Mr. Burke's face. "Go on with you both. Brendan will take me back to the office."

She pulled at Willie's sleeve, and he came along with her to the wagon.

"I'm sorry, darling girl. He's usually not out and out rude. I didn't have a chance to tell him you were coming."

Lila selected a glazed doughnut and took a bite. She was hungry. "Ha,' you hol' him abou' me?"

Willie looked at her blankly for a moment before his face showed comprehension. "No. He stays out of my personal life. But I told my sister Kate that I met a terrific girl and she must have told my mother who might have told him. Why?"

Lila took a sip of coffee. "Oh, just curious." That was an understatement if there ever was one. What had Willie said about her and to whom?

They went up in one of the cages with a load of twisted steel rods.

"Who's this, Willie?" asked the foreman. "An inspector from the Building Department?"

"You got it," Willie shot back. "The City wants to find out if you put all the rebar in the cement like the Code says or if you're shorting us and selling some of it to someone else."

There was a shout of laughter from the men, including the foreman. "Not today, Willie. I heard that someone tried that on you a few years ago and got a rod bent around his neck."

The cage stopped, the men unloaded the rods, and the cage resumed its course up the side of the building. It lurched slightly as it stopped, and Willie put his arm around Lila's shoulders to steady her. On three sides, only a few pipes and some chicken wire stood between Lila and the empty air. She could easily see over the Fulton Fish Market to the shimmering East River and the buildings of downtown Brooklyn, silhouetted against the early morning sun.

"Hey, Willie. When you get higher, will you be able to see my house from the top?"

"Unless there are bigger houses in the way. I'll climb up on one of the beams and wave to you in the mornings."

"And put lanterns up at night if you're coming. 'One if by land and two if by sea.'"

"Oh, I'll be coming, all right. You won't need lanterns."

The cage began to descend. When it reached the bottom, Willie looked at his watch.

"What time is it, Willie?"

"A little after ten. Where the hell is Brendan?"

The tour was over. It was time for Lila to get back to Brooklyn and give Gloria her lunch. "Don't worry, I'll take the subway."

"What time shall I see you tomorrow? Want to go to a club after the evening show?"

"Would you mind if we just did supper between the shows?"

"Fine. What do you feel like doing Sunday?"

Here it goes, thought Lila, but kept her voice casual. "Didn't I tell you, my mother is going to make you an Italian dinner. I told her you're a big eater and she wouldn't miss the opportunity."

He grinned. "So I'd better eat light tomorrow. What time, Sunday?"

"One o'clock." A few minutes later she was on the subway planning the big dinner that her mother had no idea she was going to make. It wasn't that Lila's mother wasn't interested in meeting Willie; she was dying to meet him and was quite annoyed with Lila that Willie hadn't yet been brought into the house. The day before she had confronted Lila.

"Whatta you ashamed of, that he sees'a your house and your family? Or you ashamed of him? He don't look so bad from the window, a big, strong man who knows how to kiss."

"Momma? You're watching us?"

"Not me. Julia, she told me. It's a free country; you can put on a show and she can look out her own window. So which is it?"

"I'm not ashamed of anybody. I'll introduce you soon." She couldn't explain to her mother that when she and Willie were together, the happiness of the moment possessed her so completely that she couldn't think about anything else.

Willie arrived, on Sunday, loaded down with fat bottles of wine jacketed in straw, a jar of wrinkled olives and a big box of creamy cannoli. He bent to receive Lila's kiss.

"Where did you get all this stuff, you idiot?"

"Well, I didn't want to come empty-handed, so I stopped off on Mulberry

Street, and everything looked so good."

Lila giggled as she led him into the kitchen. "Momma, this is Willie, the delivery man. He was afraid we wouldn't have enough food." She cleared the counter and Willie set down the packages. "Willie, this is my momma." She put her arm around her mother's shoulders.

Willie reached under his raincoat, pulled out a bouquet of violets and bowed slightly. "These are for you, Mrs. Granatelli, in appreciation for inviting me into your home."

Lila's mother brought the flowers to her nose while her eyes inspected Willie from top to bottom. She put down the bouquet and reached out both her hands to capture one of his. "Thank you, Mr. Burke. You're very welcome here." She turned to Lila. "How you ever find a fella with manners these days? Take him into the parlor and give'a him some wine. Just'a ten minutes and dinner be ready."

As soon as they were out of sight of the kitchen door, Lila stopped Willie and gave him a long kiss. When she released him, she laughed. "I just can't help loving a fella with manners. Come, now you have to meet Gloria." She took his hand and drew him up the stairs.

They stood quietly next to the crib. Gloria lay sleeping on her stomach, her arms and legs curved, her fists clutching the sheet. Lila bent over and kissed the top of her head. "Isn't she adorable. Like a little frog getting ready to jump."

"Yes, she is," Willie whispered. "Let's not wake her." He backed out of the room.

"You could set off a bomb, and she wouldn't wake," replied Lila, following him.

It had been years since anyone other than relatives had come to dine, and they had always been served at the kitchen table. Lila had forgotten how nice the dining room looked with its gleaming mahogany furniture freed from the sheets that usually covered it and the table set with the linen placemats and napkins scalloped with lace by Lila's mother's mother for her own trousseau. In the center of the table were Willie's violets in the Venetian crystal vase Lila's parents had bought on their honeymoon just before taking the ship to America.

Lila felt awed by the unaccustomed formality, but Willie seemed at ease. He was lavish in his praise of the food and backed up his words by taking second helpings of both the gnocchi and the osso bucco. He kept Mrs.

Granatelli's wine glass filled and persuaded her to tell stories of her girlhood, matching each with an anecdote of his own family, until all three of them were laughing. As they were contemplating the remains of the main course, they heard a cry upstairs. When Lila brought Gloria down, Willie insisted on helping Mrs. Granatelli clear the table and bring out the cannoli and coffee while Lila gave Gloria her bottle and settled her on a blanket in a corner of the dining room from where she kept her eyes fixed on Willie.

"Why is she staring at me?" he asked.

"She's'a not used to men in the house," answered Mrs. Granatelli.

"Never seen one so big and ugly," added Lila. Her mother choked, while Willie grinned.

It was after four when they pushed their chairs back from the table. Willie put his coat on and lurched heavily to the door. Before he left, Lila's mother kissed him on both cheeks.

"You come back soon, Weelie, you hear me? Next time I make you something really special." She beamed at both of them and retired tactfully to the kitchen.

Lila was about to fling herself upon Willie when he raised his hand.

"No, don't come near my stomach. It'll burst if you touch it. Can you cook like that?"

"No," said Lila, forlornly.

"Thank God. If you could, you'd do me in before a year went by." He touched her lips lightly and left, clumping down the outside stairs as though carrying a piano.

•   •   •

After Willie's auspicious introduction to her household, Lila no longer felt it appropriate to be picked up and dropped off at her front door. Willie cheerfully exchange pleasantries with Mrs. Granatelli and, when he and Lila returned after the show, they found the front parlor a much more comfortable place than the back porch for their good night embraces. As the days passed, these grew longer and more intimate, although their pleasure was adulterated by frustration. The possibility that making love with Willie might be the way to lose him paralyzed her. And, though there may have been yes-yes in her eyes, Willie respected the no-no on her lips. So they settled for endless kisses and awkward groping. This situation seemed to last forever, although it was less than a month before they became exhausted, particularly Willie, who had to go to work every morning.

It was three o'clock on a Wednesday morning in the Granatelli parlor. The furniture, shrouded in its protective sheets, loomed menacingly in the dark. A taxi waited outside, the driver sleeping happily while the time on the meter mounted. Willie and Lila drew back from each other like matched gladiators fighting to the death. "We can't keep this up, for Christ's sake," groaned Willie through numbed lips.

"Shush. You'll wake my mother. She thought you left two hours ago." Lila's whisper was as dry as fingernails on the ancient fabric of the couch.

A long pause, then, faintly "Let's get—," the last word unintelligible.

"Let's what?"

"GET MARRIED," he roared hoarsely, awakening Lila's mother whose frightened scream was echoed by one from the baby. Lights came on, people rushed around the house and by the time Lila fully comprehended what had happened, Willie had left in the taxi.

What a mean-spirited joke some god must have played to make her miss the sweet moment between the question and the answer when all she wanted in the world was hers for a single word. When Willie telephoned the next morning, the moment had passed. But, they were engaged, and a time was appointed that very afternoon to meet at Tiffany's to pick out a ring. She must come to his family's house on Sunday to be formally introduced as his fiancée. Then they could discuss things and start making arrangements.

"What did they say when you told them?"

Willie's tone was guarded. "It's a little complicated. They were starting to wonder if I was ever going to get married, so that's good. Of course, they would rather I picked someone they knew. You know, from another rich, Irish family, not an Italian girl who's in the theater. It'll be fine when they get to know you."

"What about Gloria? What did they say about her?"

Willie paused before responding. "Don't worry. We'll work it all out. Remember, you're marrying me, not them. You still are, aren't you?"

There was only one possible answer to that question. Willie was it, was everything. That was enough. They would be together. She was happy when she hung up. Still, why did they have to discuss "things" and "make arrangements" and "work it out?"

Her mother reassured her. Did she think that weddings were held and households set up with a snap of the fingers? And the Burkes were wealthy;

the scale of it all must be far beyond Lila's family's experience. Then her mother grew worried. Would the Granatelli family disgrace Lila? Maybe they shouldn't come to the wedding. And soon Lila and Gloria would live in a big house in a fancy neighborhood, and she would never get to see them. Now it was Lila who did the reassuring and mother, and daughter cried together and hugged each other and then went to tell Gloria who laughed and waved her hands at their happy excitement.

At Tiffany's, Willie bought Lila a huge diamond, then she rushed off to look for a suitable dress for Sunday. After going to three other stores, she ended up back at Bonwit Teller going well over her budget for a navy blue, long-sleeved wool, with a high neckline and a skirt hanging a fashionable three inches below her knees. It was dignified, but fit closely enough to show her figure to advantage. Then it was too late to go back to Brooklyn before the evening show. She walked crosstown toward the theater, every so often holding up her hand to see the bright flashes of color as the afternoon sun refracted through the diamond.

●   ●   ●

Lila walks into the kitchen to discuss today's lunch with Cook. The discussion is short and succinct. Peggy Goodman is the widow of Gerry Goodman, Willie's lawyer. Cook has been preparing lunches for Lila and Peggy for over thirty years and knows Peggy's tastes as well as she knows Lila's. It's a choice between broiled chicken supremes or broiled pompano, in either case, brushed with a drop of olive oil and served with little boiled potatoes and steamed peas and carrots or string beans. All salt in the kitchen will be put into cupboards before cooking starts, lest even a grain should find its way into the food, but there will be no shortage of lemon wedges. For dessert, sherbet.

A certain ceremony is required, however. It must be remembered that Cook has successfully prepared six-course dinners for the elite of Palm Beach and cannot be dealt with as though she were behind the counter at McDonald's. First, Lila inquires as to the status of Cook's arthritis (a little better as the weather warms up). They discuss what supplies are needed. Cook observes that the last delivery of vegetables was not up to her standards, but assures Lila that she has properly reprimanded the grocer. Lila thanks her, pauses a moment, then says "Pompano? String beans? Raspberry?" Cook nods her assent to each, and the discussion is concluded.

After talking to Cook, Lila goes into her study to call her banker. The weekly discussions with Jack Schofield take a little longer than those with Cook, since they involve a great deal of money. She likes bonds: mostly U.S. Treasuries, occasionally tax-free municipals, which let her feel she is putting one over on the IRS.

"Good morning, Jack. It's Lila Burke."

"Mrs. Burke? I'm so happy it's you. How's the weather?"

Jack Schofield is a nice young man in his late twenties who has been Lila's account officer for three years. He is of limited intelligence but does everything she asks him. She is pretty sure Builders' Bank and Trust Company assigned him to her because he is unmarried and doesn't mind flying down from New York for a weekend every three or four months, so she won't start thinking she would get more personal attention from a Palm Beach bank.

"It's absolutely gorgeous. The sun has been out all week, but there's been a nice breeze. You have to come down before it gets too hot."

"I'd love to, Mrs. Burke, when would be best for you?"

"Shall we say the Memorial Day weekend? The colleges should be out, and maybe that pretty Harrington girl will be home. You liked her, didn't you?" Lila asks casually. She doesn't mention that the Harrington's housemaid told Lila's housemaid that Jack Schofield and Jennifer Harrington spent New Year's afternoon in Jen's bedroom screwing their ears off when they were supposed to be out water-skiing.

"Yes, she's very nice. Memorial Day will be fine. And, I'm glad you called, today, Mrs. Burke. Those Texas bonds are coming due next week, and we have to think about reinvestment."

"What should I get?" As though Jack knew enough to advise her. Lila knows, however, that more knowledgeable people at the Bank do and that Jack merely parrots what they tell him.

There is a pause, during which Lila can hear Jack shifting papers. "Well, there are some nice Denver water districts and a new Minnesota dormitory authority issue coming out Monday."

Chicken or fish?

"Which do you prefer, Jack?"

"I think I'd go with the Minnesota dormitories, Mrs. Burke."

Lila likes the idea of students studying for exams in buildings built with her money. "I agree." She then ends the conversation as she always does. "And what do you hear from your mother?" Jack's ailing mother is spending the last of her days in a nursing home near Seattle.

"Nothing direct since that card at Easter, but they called last week to report that she's holding her own."

"Well, I pray for her."

"Thank you, Mrs. Burke. I'm sure that helps."

A visit from her son might help more, Lila thinks but doesn't say it. If she did, the comfortable relationship she has with Jack would change, and she is too tired to change anything.

•   •   •

Lila devoted the next week to shopping for shoes, gloves and a purse to go with the dress and to a long session at the hairdresser. She almost cried to see so much of her long, tumbling, chestnut hair drop to the floor of the salon but had to admit that the neatly waved remainder was more suitable to the image she wanted to present to the Burkes. Her mother provided the jewelry: teardrop crystal earrings and an antique silver cross worn on occasions when there need be not the slightest doubt as to the piety of the wearer.

The Bentley came early Sunday, so that, Willie said, Lila would have time to meet the immediate family before the guests arrived.

"Guests?" asked Lila, in alarm.

"Not exactlyguests. It's just the aunts and uncles and cousins and a few close friends."

"How many altogether?"

"Oh, what does it matter? You know I really like that dress."

Lila grabbed his lapels. "How many?"

"No more than forty."

"I have to walk into that house for the first time with forty people staring at me, counting the *faux pas*, ready to be offended for life by my slightest mistake. How could you?" She let go of the lapels and gave him a push, which almost made him knock over a lamp.

"Dinna fash yourself, darlin' girl. They'll all love yez, as do I."

She threw her hands in the air. "You're crazy. They don't all love me in my own family."

Willie captured her hands and pressed them together. "Don't take me so literally, Lila. They will like you and accept you. You're lovely, charming and polite. And for everything else, you're Willie Burke's choice, and that better be enough for anyone. Trust me. It'll be easier meeting the crowd all at once than going through the whole boring list one at a time."

There wasn't any point in complaining further; she wasn't going to refuse to go, so she put on her sweetest, most charming, politest expression and got into the Bentley.

"Good day, Miss Grand."

"Good day, Brendan." The chauffeur liked her; that was something, at least. She rewarded him with her best smile.

The Burke home was not one of the grand New York mansions, but it was grand enough for Lila. Three stories of gray granite took up forty feet or so of Fifth Avenue frontage. On either side of the entrance stood fluted columns supporting a triangular pediment, in which two lions stood on their hind legs like sparring boxers. On the second and third floors, more lions supported small balconies, two to a floor and, at the top, the cornice rested on six more.

"I thought England used lions, not Ireland," Lila whispered, as she got out of the car.

"My father wasn't chauvinistic enough to spend the money to replace them when he bought the house." Willie took her arm and led her to the door and opened it with a flourish. "Welcome to Castle Burke, princess."

They stepped inside into a large entrance hall with open doors on either side and a staircase opposite the entrance. Uniformed men and women rushed through the hall carrying chairs and boxes and trays from one side to the other. As each passed the staircase, he would look up at a tall, gray-haired woman standing five or six steps up like a general reviewing troops.

"We're here, Mother," said Willie, weaving his way through the waiters.

The woman looked up with a frown. "You're early, William. I told you twelve-thirty, not noon. Take Miss Grand into the sitting room and see if you can find your father. Kate and I will join you when we can." She spoke like a reproving schoolteacher and, dressed in a severe black, long-sleeved dress, her hair in a bun and wire-rim glasses on her nose, looked like one as well.

"Where is Kate?"

"In the kitchen, but stay out, you'll just get in the way. That's how it always is: the caterer late and the guests early. Excuse me, Miss Grand. You, there." She called a waiter carrying a tray piled high with dishes. "Take those back to the kitchen. Tell my daughter that I don't want them brought out until dessert is served." She went back to her notebook.

Lila had not had a chance to open her mouth. Willie took her arm and led her into a hallway, past a large drawing room, and into a small sitting room. A table at one end was covered with a white cloth, on which were laid out bottles and glasses and a bowl of ice. A half-opened door showed a bathroom. Willie seated her on the sofa. "I'm going to find my father."

"Willie!" she protested. "You can't leave me here by myself."

Willie stopped at the door, turned around and came back to the sofa. "All right, we'll see the old man soon enough."

About ten minutes later, Mr. Burke arrived with Willie's sister, Kate. She was tall, like her mother, with a horse face and a docile manner. She shook hands politely with Lila, then excused herself to return to the preparations for the party. Willie's father went to the table and made himself a Scotch and soda. Lila and Willie stood awkwardly until he finished and turned to them and held out his hand to Lila.

"Miss Grand." His hand was cold from the ice in the glass but not as cold as his tone. She hadn't expected much from him, but the level of hostility surprised her. She was determined not to show any discomfort. "Call me Lila, Mr. Burke. How's the new building coming?"

"All right, I guess."

"When do you expect to be finished?"

"It'll be done when it's done."

Willie broke in. "Maybe four months for the first tenant. Right, Da?"

"Could be four, could be longer." Then, looking directly at Lila, "Willie always thinks everything'll work out just the way he wants it. His mother spoiled him."

Willie bridled. "That's because she knew you'd be working me like a dog as soon as you could. He started me the summer I was eleven. At fourteen I was doing a man's work."

Mr. Burke sniffed. "It didn't hurt you none, not so as to show, anyway."

The two men seemed to be edging up to each other. Lila sat on the sofa and patted the cushion next to her. "Tell me about Willie, Mr. Burke. What was he like as a boy?"

"You'd have to ask his mother or sisters. I was busy trying to make a living." He went back to the table and put another ice cube in his glass.

For all her resolve, her heart sank. He was obviously going to make it as hard for her as he could. Help me, Willie, she thought, and, the next moment Willie was pulling her to her feet.

"Come now, darlin' girl, you don't want to be hearin' *thim* old stories about how I read the newspaper when I was two and saved the Bishop from drownin' when I was four. I'll show you the house before the rest of the family gets here. His lordship can take a bit of a nap."

Willingly, Lila followed him from the room. His father glowered but said nothing.

In the hall, she grabbed Willie's jacket, pulled him down to her and whispered: "Is that what I can look forward to after we're married?"

"Ah, give him a little time to get used to you. He'll come around."

"I'm not used to being treated like dirt."

"Try to be patient. We don't want a scene now. Here's the rest of the family."

Down the hall came a small parade led by Mrs. Burke. Following her was a female version of Willie, broad-shouldered and freckled, with a baby in her arms. A girl of nine or ten came next, and a big dark-haired man towing a resisting eight-year-old boy brought up the rear. They came to a halt in front of Lila. Mrs. Burke stepped up to her and extended her hand.

"I am sorry I was unable to greet you properly when you arrived, Miss Grand. You are welcome in our house." Her tone was functionally formal. Her handshake was firm.

Lila tried her best to match her. "Thank you, Mrs. Burke. I'm happy to meet you. Please call me Lila."

"Lila, this is William's sister, Moira McConnell, and her husband Peter, my granddaughter Mary Louise, my grandson James and baby Michael."

Moira held their handshake while she examined Lila. "So you're the one who finally caught my brother. How did you do it? A lot of my friends tried but couldn't."

She didn't wait for an answer but moved on as the others came forward in turn.

Kate returned to announce that the drawing room was ready and Mrs. Burke marched them back down the hall and into a large room. The caterers had placed small tables, and chairs among the heavy oak furniture and one wall had been given over to a bar and a long table holding food. Mrs. Burke positioned Willie and Lila near the door and sent Kate back to fetch Willie's father to stand next to them. As though it were on cue, a bell rang.

"Our guests," she said and stepped into place next to her husband.

For the next two hours, that doorbell rang and rang, with never more than two minutes between rings. Willie's estimate of forty guests had some validity in that there were seldom more than forty in the drawing room at any one time. When that room became too crowded, Mrs. Burke would move a group into the sitting room or the den.

Through the endless string of mechanical introductions, Lila stood like a statue, the men appraising her legs, the women, her ring and her dress. The cross was often admired. Good.

A waiter came up to Mrs. Burke and called her to deal with an emergency in the kitchen. The second she was out the door of the drawing room, Willie's father headed for the bar. Lila looked imploringly at Willie who shrugged his shoulders. "All right, we'll go sit. She can't do anything worse than kill us." He took Lila to the food table and then to a sofa near the window and signaled a passing waiter for drinks. "What do you think of the clan?"

"I can't tell. They pop up, stick their hands out, say 'how d'ya do?', and *whoosh*, here's the next. At my family functions, they'll hug and kiss and try to remember the last time they met, and it can take forty-five minutes to go through a reception line. More if they brought the new baby."

"Oh, my mother wouldn't put up with such doin's. Step up, say your piece and step down. That's how Mary Burke runs this house."

"Your father too?"

"That's the way he wants it. 'The more talk, the less work,' is his favorite expression. She runs the house as well as he runs the business; why should he interfere?"

Some new guests came up to them, and Willie took over the introductions. "Lila, I want you to meet my Uncle Francis and Aunt Jean. Uncle Francis is my father's younger brother and my godfather. He taught me how to swim and ride a bike. And Aunt Jean makes the best pies you ever tasted."

After Willie's warm introduction, Lila was surprised at Aunt Jean's cool "We're pleased to meet you, Miss Grand." Uncle Francis's expression, as he grunted a confirmation, was as dour as James Burke's, which made the brothers' resemblance to each other remarkable. He did an about-face after the handshakes and marched away, his wife following close behind.

"What's the matter with them?"

Willie shook his head. "I'm sorry. My father must have said something to Francis. They're very close."

Lila looked down at the beef Bourguignon on her plate. Her head began to ache, and the thought of putting those brown lumps into her mouth sickened her. "Let me go. I have to go to the bathroom." She grabbed her purse, rushed from the room and back down the hall to the bathroom off the little sitting room, locked the door and emptied her stomach of everything she had ingested in that monstrous house. When she finished, she rinsed out her mouth at the sink and opened the window for air. Her head was throbbing so she closed the blinds, wet a towel in cold water, turned out the light and sat on the closed seat, the towel pressed to her forehead.

The throbbing in her head and the heaving in her stomach began to diminish. The fresh air coming through the blinds was clearing out both the room and her head. She heard familiar voices outside the window and went to peek between the slats. Willie's father and uncles Francis and Harry, Willie's mother's brother, had come around the corner of the house from Fifth Avenue and were standing, lighting cigars, a few feet away.

"It's your sister's doing," Willie's father was saying. "That doctor told her I shouldn't smoke so much, and now the woman climbs all over me if I light up in the house."

Harry laughed. "Don't blame me, Jimmy boy. I told you when you was courting her that she wasn't near so obliging as she made herself out to be."

"Jean's just as bad," Francis chipped in, "and didn't even wait for the doctor to say something. 'Get that smelly thing out of here,' she says, and if I put it down to pick up a newspaper, she'll throw it in the toilet quicker'n you can whistle."

"This is a damn good cigar, Jimmy. Where do you get them?" asked Harry.

"There's a fella down on Reade Street who still gets the best leaf in from Cuba and has a couple of old-timers rollin' *thim* for private stock. If you go in there, tell him who you are, and he'll take good care of you."

"I'll do that; this one first class. But then, the whole party is first class."

"It sure is," Francis seconded. "No one gives a better hoolie than Mary. And you, of course, Jimmy."

"Oh, she's the one that does it, all right. I put up the brass, that's all. I come damn near callin' it off, this mornin', though. Would have, too, but there wasn't time to call everyone. "

"You just found out this mornin'?" Harry was astonished.

"That's right. Francis's boy, Sean, was at a party with some theater people and mentioned her name and one of them even knew the father or, at least, the man who said he was. There was never any question of marriage; the baby doesn't even have his name."

"And Willie knew this? You're sayin', he knew this all along?"

"He admitted it to my face. If I'd a' been ten years younger, big as he is, I'd a' taken my belt to him till he wished he'd never seen the little tramp."

Lila dug her nails into the windowsill. No wonder there was so much hostility. They must think she had put Willie up to hiding the truth about Gloria.

Harry sounded puzzled. "But Mary told me Tuesday, when she called, that the girl already had a kid."

"We thought she'd been widowed. Willie swears he never said she had, but he damn well never said she hadn't." Willie's father hawked and spat. "I didn't care for it, even then."

"Quite right, Jimmy," Francis agreed. "You want your wife takin' care of your kids, not someone else's."

"And," said Harry, "maybe thinkin' about the man who gave it to her. No, leave the widows to the old men who can't afford to be choosy. They're not for a young buck like Willie. She's a good-lookin' piece, but there are a hundred Irish virgins in New York just as pretty."

Francis snickered. "A hundred, Harry? In this day and age?"

"Well, maybe fifty. So what are you going to do, Jimmy?"

"What can I do? I can't stop him from marrying her. He's got plenty of his own money; he's earned it. All I can do is say who can and who can't come into this house. The girl is in there now. I bit my tongue, and it didn't kill me. But she's not bringing her little bastard here, not while I'm alive and well enough to stand at the door. And I expect you both to back me."

Lila backed away from the window. She wouldn't bring Gloria to this house if that horrible man knelt before her and begged her. And his two cronies were just as bad. She would never again subject herself to the insults of the whole ghastly clan. And what was Willie trying to pull, making them think she was a widow?

She flushed the toilet to drown the sound of their voices, then filled the sink with cold water and held her face in it as long as she could. As she repaired her makeup, her rage cooled to hard anger. Her headache had gone, her stomach had settled, and she felt fine. In fact, she thought, as she exited the bathroom and walked through the sitting room, I'm the finest thing in this whole damn house, and she drew her shoulders up, straightened her back and paraded down the hall. She smiled, regally, as she passed the drawing room, as though to acknowledge the people who called her name, but didn't slow her pace until she reached the front door. The footman manning the door looked confused, but when Lila nodded to him and pointed to the door, he sprang to open it. As though by arrangement, the Bentley was parked out front, with the chauffeur standing next to it. Without hesitation, Lila went directly to the car, the chauffeur opened the door, Lila got in, the chauffeur closed the door, came around to the front and seated himself behind the wheel.

"My home, please, Brendan." As they moved off, she heard her name called. Willie was standing in the open door, arms apart, hands out, mouth open like Al Jolson, holding the last note of a big number.

The drive down Fifth Avenue calmed her. On one side was the lush May foliage of the park, on the other, fine buildings with their planters and window boxes bursting with flowers. It would be nice to live on Fifth Avenue, maybe down in the sixties, away from the Burkes. She could wheel Gloria's carriage right across the street and into the park. In a few years, they would walk together to the zoo. A nice apartment in one of the new buildings would be perfect. She hoped Willie wouldn't insist on a house; houses were so much work, and that would mean servants. In an apartment, maybe, it could be just the three of them with someone coming in to help during the day. Lila didn't mind doing housework. She would have to get her mother to teach her how to cook, though. She wasn't going to get a governess for Gloria. Even the word sounded terrible. What was the point of having children if you weren't going to have the fun of raising them? And Willie loved children. She hoped that their first one would be a boy. It would make him so happy, and a little Willie would be adorable. She could hardly wait.

Back in Brooklyn, a worried Mrs. Granatelli reported three telephone calls from Willie. What had Lila done to get the poor man so upset? Lila told her everything. When she finished, her mother waited a long time before speaking.

"It's'a hard to say this, Lina. You're my baby, and I love you. You're a good daughter and a good mother. I'm'a not judge you. That's'a for God, and I know he's gonna forgive your sin. But lots'a people think they're better than God. They can do anything as long as nobody knows. The sin is getting caught; thats'a what you did."

"I know, Momma."

"A man, oh, they maybe laugh at him, but a woman?" She shook her head. "Inna old country, you never find a husband now, unless some old'a man wants a housekeeper. Even here.

Waddya think happened to all those nice'a boys from school? They call'a you any more?"

"No, Momma. But, I don't care about that. What scares me is Willie." She went to the stove for a little more coffee.

"Yes, Weelie. I'd'a never even pray you find'a someone like Weelie or God get angry I ask'a too much. So he should'a told them everything right away. It wouldn't 'a made no difference, would it?"

"Probably not."

"He's'a love you and he's'a gonna marry you. That's'a all that matters. Forget everything else, you hear? There's'a not gonna be two Weelies inna you lifetime, so you keep'a this one."

Her mother's advice was sound but unnecessary. I'm not letting him go for anything, Lila, whispered as she went to her room to change her clothes. She stood for a moment in front of the mirror on her closet door. For all the stress of the day, she still looked sensational. If that girl isn't good enough for them, they're crazy. The thought cheered her. With great satisfaction, she took off the blue dress, made sure there were no stains and hung it in her closet. When the telephone rang, she ran to the kitchen in her slip.

"Hello."

"What happened, Lila? You stayed so long in the bathroom I was getting worried and was about to come after you when you came down the hall like a racehorse and were out in the car and away without a word. Are you all right? Brendan said you seemed OK."

"Hold on a minute." She covered the speaker with one hand. "Get my robe, Momma, would you, please? In the bathroom." She waited until her mother was gone. "How could you tell your family I was a widow?"

"I didn't exactly <u>tell</u> them that. Who said something, my father?"

"What <u>did</u> you tell them? Come on, Willie, I want the whole story."

"All right. I'm sorry, but everything happened so fast. Tuesday morning, my father went to the job early. I was grabbing a bite from the ice box when my mother walked into the kitchen, and, when I told her we were getting married, she got all excited. Were you Catholic, where were you from, how old were you, and so on. When I told her you had a child, she said 'Poor thing, to be widowed so young. She's lucky to find you.'"

Mrs. Granatelli returned with the robe and helped Lila struggle into it.

"Lila? Are you there?"

She shooed her mother out of the kitchen before answering.

"So why didn't you tell her right away that I'm not a widow?"

"Because the cook came in that moment and started crying when she got the news. And a couple of the other servants heard the ruckus and my sister came running, and there was a real Donnybrook a'goin' on what with one tellin' the next and the huggin' an' the kissin'. It wasn't the moment to clarify the situation."

"That was Tuesday. Today is Sunday."

"I know, darling girl, but I had to go to a meeting, then go to Tiffany's, then the job, then I picked you up and didn't get home until they had gone to bed. In the meantime, my mother told my father and by the time I tried to talk to him in the morning he had himself all worked up so he wouldn't listen to anything I said."

"What was he worked up about."

"Why hadn't I talked to him first? He'd have found me a nice Irish girl from a good family. Italian? A chorus girl? A widow? With a child, no less? He was at me from the minute I walked into the kitchen for coffee until Brendan dropped us off at the job. All week, I kept looking for a decent moment to tell him the truth, but there wasn't one. Or my mother and sister, either. Finally, I gave up. I thought that, after everybody met you and saw how great you are, he'd come around to where I could tell him."

Lila was so angry she could barely reply. "You... you mean like on our tenth wedding anniversary? I can't believe this. And you never said a word to me about it."

" I'm sorry. I was trying to clear things up. I was afraid that, if I told you I hadn't made things clear to my father, you'd pick up the telephone and call him yourself, and all hell would break loose."

"You're damn right. That's just what I would have done. Now, you've made me a liar, on top of everything else."

"No, no. I explained the whole thing to him this morning, the misunderstanding and everything. I told him you knew nothing about it."

"And he believed you?"

"Well, it's true, isn't it?"

"That's not the point, Willie." It was maddening how confidently he expected everybody to see things the way he saw them. "Let me tell you what happened."

She recounted the overheard conversation. Willie listened in silence.

"Willie? Say something."

"I don't know what to say." Willie's voice was subdued.

"Say that what they said was abominable."

"It was abominable."

"Tell me I will never have to go to that house again."

"You won't have to."

"Tell me I never have to see any of those horrible old men again."

There was a moment's pause, then, "You won't have to."

"Tell me that you love me and you're going to marry me as soon as possible."

Willie's exuberance returned. "Ah, that one's easy. I love you, and we'll get married as soon as possible. Let me check some things out, tomorrow, and we can discuss the arrangements tomorrow night. Good-bye, darling girl." And he was off the phone.

Running for cover, thought Lila, as she hung up. Well, his answers were the right ones. It was sad that she would never have a relationship with his family, but that was the way it was going to have to be. If only they could push a button and have it all happen instead of getting involved with "arrangements." She went in to give Gloria her bath, and her discomfort was driven out by the cuddling and splashing and laughing that accompanied Gloria's bath and the subsequent satisfaction of watching her gobble up her dinner.

•   •   •

The next evening, Lila met Willie at Stan's, an old-fashioned steakhouse in Chelsea. It was a cavernous place with a balcony running around a central hall, in which predominantly male diners were seated at long refectory tables planted in sawdust. They were led to the last two empty seats at one of the tables and gave the waiter their order.

"What are you grinning about?" Willie asked.

"They stared at me all the way back here," Lila spoke softly, so as not to be overheard by her neighbor at the table, a slim gentleman in his sixties. Her caution was unnecessary. The man's attention was totally taken up with tearing the meat from a giant rib of roast beef he was holding up in both dripping hands.

Willie nodded, smugly. "Do you think I'd be marrying a girl who didn't have them staring? That's a major test, and there have been a couple who failed it."

"Oh, you've been testing me, then. Was that what was going on yesterday? Was it all some kind of test?"

Willie winced. "No, it wasn't. I was just kidding about bringing you here, being one."

"That, I knew. But I don't know about yesterday."

He leaned over the table and grappled her with his eyes, his customary confident grin replaced by an almost childish expression of awe. "Lila, you are my love. You have been from the first, and you will be forever. I don't know how or why, but you're it. It's not a job you applied for. I didn't give you a test or interview you. It just happened, and you're stuck with it."

Willie's lumpy face, furrowed by intensity, was a Disney cartoon, but Lila was too happy to laugh. She held his look until she couldn't bear it any longer, then whispered, "Me too."

They were silent, and Lila began to examine the framed theatrical programs and posters that covered the walls of the restaurant. Would her name ever appear on these walls for anything other than two chorus turns in two easily forgettable shows? Since meeting Willie, she had given little thought to her career. Now, she realized it was coming to its end. Taking care of Willie and Gloria would fill her life. It would be like losing a part of her body. No matter; anesthetized by love, she would feel no pain.

Willie reached into a side jacket pocket and pulled out a scrap of paper, which he unfolded and smoothed flat in front of himself. He then unclipped a mechanical pencil from an inside pocket and worked the lead out to the proper length.

"This is all subject to your approval, darling girl, but I thought I'd work up a few suggestions. I had thought we'd have a nice big bash, with music, dancing, lots of booze, a good fight or two. But I guess we should forget that, now."

"I'm afraid, so, darling boy. Let's just get it done."

"All right." He looked at his list. "First, the date. How's three weeks from Saturday?"

"So long?" Willie looked worried. Lila laughed and squeezed his hand. "Fine."

"Would you like it at your parish church?"

"That's nice." As if she cared where.

"Is it all right if my mother and sisters come?"

Lila thought for a moment, then remembered what her mother had said. "And, Lina, don't ask'a him to choose between you and his family. Either way you gonna lose."

"Of course, Willie. If they want to."

"Joe will be my best man." That was good. Joe Malone was another Fordham football player. Joe had been so happy for Willie that he had almost broken Lila's ribs with his first hug. "And I guess that will be all from my side. Who would you like to have?"

Lila shook her head. Her old friends had been out of her life since her first show and neither they nor any of the girls from *"Chicks and Chucks"* would be a part of the life to come.

"My mother, my Aunt Julia, and my brother and his wife if they can make it East. I'll ask my sister-in-law to be my matron of honor."

Willie wrote on his list finishing with a big check mark just as their dinners arrived. With food in front of him, Willie behaved like every other man in the room and attacked his huge T-bone steak with a single-minded ferocity that precluded conversation.

The waiter cleared off the table and brought coffee and strawberry shortcake. Willie put his list back down on the table and began to discuss where they should live. This was a subject in which Lila had considerable interest.

As she herself had wanted, he suggested an apartment on Fifth Avenue. The Burkes owned interests in two such buildings. He accepted Lila's insistence upon the one further downtown. They agreed that a view of Central Park was important and that anything above the fourth floor would be high enough. There was one he had seen that might be perfect. It had twelve rooms plus bathrooms, kitchen, pantry and servants' rooms.

"That should be enough for a while, shouldn't it?" he said.

There was a little hitch in his voice as he asked the question and, although the apartment sounded enormous to her, she decided to explore the matter. "Well, what will we need?"

Willie looked at his list. "One, our bedroom, assuming we sleep together." He leered like Groucho Marx.

"Be serious, Willie."

"Two, a dressing room for you."

"Oh, goody."

"Three, a nursery, for babies. Four, a bedroom for a baby nurse. Five, a bedroom for an older child. Six, a playroom. Seven. A living room. Eight, a music room. Nine, a dining room. Ten, a den for me. Eleven, a sitting room or den for you. Twelve, a guest room."

Lila counted and thought. "I'm not sure about baby nurses, but with Gloria in number five when she's a little older, won't we fill up our bedrooms with our first baby?"

Willie took a big bite of strawberry shortcake and spent a long time chewing.

"What's wrong with your cake?" asked Lila. "Mine's good." She took another forkful.

Willie reached across the table for Lila's free hand. What was the matter with the man? He looked absolutely miserable.

"Lila, I don't know how to tell you this. Uh, I'm sorry. Uh. I'm afraid, uh, that Gloria—Gloria won't be living with us."

"What?" She couldn't have heard right.

He leaned forward; his narrowed eyes stared into Lila's as his grip on her hand tightened.

Realization smashed into her, detonating an explosion of breath. She heard her shout echo from the walls of the silenced room and saw the man next to them eject from his chair, bump against the table, and fall backward, showering Willie with beer. She tried to get away, but Willie's hand restrained her, so she struck as hard as she could with the fork. Willie cursed and snatched back his bleeding hand, and Lila grabbed her purse and ran down the aisle between the tables, through the door, and into a taxi.

●   ●   ●

Back in Brooklyn, Lila rushed to Gloria's room and grabbed her and kissed her over and over until the baby started crying. In a panic, Lila's mother telephoned Aunt Julia who made it up the stairs barely in time to keep her sister from calling the police. By insisting that there must have been some misunderstanding, they quieted Lila down so that, when Willie called from the hospital, she was calm, if shaky.

"Willie? Are you all right?"

"It takes more than a fork to do me in, though I lost a bit of blood, and they won't let me out of the hospital until the morning. Talk to me, darling girl. How are you?"

"Bad, Willie. I thought you said I'd have to give up Gloria. Please, Willie, you didn't mean that, did you?"

"No, no, you don't have to give her up. You can see her as much as you like. It's just that she can't live with us."

It wasn't a misunderstanding. "But she has to. Why shouldn't she?"

"Lila, we're going to have children together. I'm going to be the best father I possibly can to them, but I can't be a good father to someone else's child. It wouldn't be fair to Gloria. She'd feel inferior with brothers and sisters she could see were loved more than she."

"But you like Gloria already. Why couldn't you love her, too? It wouldn't keep you from loving your own children when they come."

"I thought about that, but I know I can't love her: she's not mine. She can live with your mother or any place else you want. I'll be happy to pay whatever it costs. And for doctors and schools and colleges. She'll not want for anything, I promise. And, of course, you can go see her. It's not like you're going to stop being her mother."

Every word pressed her deeper into despair, but she fought to stay afloat. "No, Willie. No. It's your father talking. Don't let him do this to us. He's a monster who's jealous because you're young and strong and generous, all the things he isn't. Don't let him ruin our lives."

She jumped up and began to circle the kitchen table, snapping the telephone cord over the tops of the chairs to keep it from catching.

Willie's voice was low. "It's not him, Lila, it's me. This bothered me long before yesterday. I thought that, maybe, meeting Gloria might make me feel differently. It didn't. She's a beautiful, sweet baby, for sure, but I can't love her, and I can't bring her up in my home. I'm sorry, darling girl, I wish I could, but I can't."

"No, Willie, no. You can't do this." She began to cry again. "Please, Willie, anything you want, but not this."

"Lila, you don't understand. It's not what I want." His measured voice lost its rhythm. "I can't help it. It just has to be this way."

She had to think of something that would change his mind, but nothing came to her. Her nose was running. She put down the receiver to open a box of napkins.

"Lila, darling. Lila?"

The receiver slid off the end of the table, clattered off a chair, bounced on the floor and sprung back. She watched it turn at the end of its cord while a faraway voice said, "Lila? Lila? Are you there?" Then nothing but a faint drone.

"Lina?"

Her mother's voice brought her back to an empty world that once could be filled by a moment's anticipation of their next meeting. She began to cry, but her grief could not be eased by any amount of tears, but only by the anger that succeeded them. She cursed Willie and all his family and friends and threw her engagement ring into the big garbage pail out back. Then anger ran its course and grief returned. It wasn't until two o'clock when, sedated with the bit of laudanum her mother kept for the baby's teething, that Lila fell asleep. In the morning she was calmer, determined. She carried Gloria around the house smothering her with hugs and kisses. She wouldn't leave her baby, not ever.

The telephone rang at eight. "Don't answer it," she hissed at her mother.

If Willie had changed his mind, he would have come pounding on the front door. She was going to have to say good-bye to him but wasn't ready yet. How long had she had? Three months? Not much for a lifetime. Her mother was right; there wouldn't be two Willies. Why did this one have to be so stupid? How could anyone not love Gloria? And the tears returned.

At nine, the telephone rang again, and, again, Lila waved off her mother. Mrs. Granatelli frowned but let it ring. Lila was still not quite ready. She went downstairs and out into the back yard where she wouldn't hear the telephone. For a minute she sat on the bench, her face to the sun, eyes closed, gathering her strength for the final effort. She ticked off Willie's faults. He was stupid, cruel, selfish, stubborn, insensitive. She and Gloria were better off without him and his whole family who thought they were so much better than she was. It was time to tell him so.

She labored back up the stairs and into the kitchen, shook her head at her mother and reached for the telephone, but something had wiped the number from her memory, and her fingers wouldn't work to turn the pages of the directory.

No one could say she gave in easily, though. First, her mother and Aunt Julia dug the ring out of the garbage and set to work. Mrs. Granatelli, after her initial joy at the news of the engagement, was just realizing that she was about to find herself in an empty house for the first time in her life. With a bit of help, Willie's money would pay for, she'd be only too happy to keep Gloria with her. And Lila could come to see them whenever she wanted. That was a lot better life than many immigrant families they had known whose children often ended up scattered over two continents, left with God knows whom or dumped out on the street like abandoned animals.

Next, they dragged her to Father Antonio, the parish priest, who had known Lila since her birth. He peered into the carriage at the sleeping Gloria and shook his head sadly. "Lina, Lina. Don't you realize what you are doing to yourself? You have committed a mortal sin and compounded it by fleeing from the Church instead of coming to me in repentance and asking God for forgiveness."

Not today, thought Lila. Today I have to save Gloria. God, let me do that, and I'll confess and repent and do anything You want.

"I'm sorry, Father. Please help me. Don't make me give up my baby."

"It's good that you love your child. But you've forgotten your love of God. You haven't been to Mass for over a year. And why haven't you had Gloria baptized?" He looked into the carriage again and grimaced as though it contained a small monster.

"I will, Father, I promise. But don't make me give her up."

"Nobody can make you do that. You're sure you want to marry this man?"

"Yes."

The priest paused, and Lila's mother spoke. "She's a' love him very much, Father, and he's 'a love her, too. He's a good man. It's just'a this terrible thing about the baby. Maybe you could'a talk to him?"

"He's Catholic?"

Lila nodded.

"Then he should talk to his own priest."

Mrs. Granatelli looked briefly at Lila and shook her head.

Father Antonio took Lila's hands in his. "I'm sorry, Lina. You'll have to make the choice and live with it. And who knows? The child may be better off with your mother. Many children without mothers have grown up to do great things." He thought for a moment. "Think of Moses."

"Moses?"

She couldn't keep the contempt from her voice, and Father Antonio stiffened.

"Even priests can't always see God's purpose. This may be the penance He has given you for your sins. I will pray for you and your child." He made the sign of the cross in blessing.

Afraid she would say something terrible, Lila turned away before he was finished and fled the church without waiting for her mother and aunt. It was insupportable that God had abandoned her to this stupid old man.

She regained control of herself by the time her mother and aunt returned to the house and resumed the battle. It was a terrible thing Willie was asking, but would Lila ever get such a chance again, the wealth, the position, his unquestioned love for her? Back and forth they swung until Lila's aunt came up with the clincher: once married, Lila would have the opportunity to work on Willie. Soften him, and, in a year or less, when Gloria would be walking and talking and looking like the beautiful child Lila had been, he would relent and they would all live happily together ever after.

It was a good script, but Lila held out for three more days, hoping for a miracle. Willie called hourly, but Lila wouldn't come to the phone, knowing it would end in her surrender. Mrs. Granatelli berated him for his inhuman demand but sounded too much like a mother scolding a spoiled boy who knows that if he's persistent he'll get his way.

Was it the twentieth call, the thirtieth? Lila had lost count. Supper had just ended. Lila's mother and aunt were bringing the dishes to the sink. The sisters had spent more time with each other during the past three days than during the three previous years. This time, the telephone's ring seemed to freeze them. They looked at each other. Aunt Julia shook her head once; Lila's mother nodded in agreement, and they continued to the sink. A second ring. The two stacked their dishes. Mrs. Granatelli turned on the water; Aunt Julia picked up a sponge. A third ring.

"Momma?" asked Lila.

"No, Lina. You gotta make up'a you mind." She began to soap a dish while Julia started to wipe the table as the telephone continued to ring.

Lila forced herself to her feet and picked up the receiver. It weighed a hundred pounds.

"Willie?" she asked dully.

"Yes, love, it's me."

"You're killing me."

"It'll be for the best, I promise." His voice was gentle but confident.

She choked and couldn't speak.

"Lila, say something."

Mute, she held the receiver out to her mother, collapsed into her chair, slumped over the table and, her hands over her eyes, nodded.

"All right, Weelie," said Mrs. Granatelli. "God'a help us all."

●   ●   ●

Once Lila came around, Willie was on his best behavior. Whatever Lila wanted, she got. The details of the wedding, the itinerary of the honeymoon, the furnishing of their big new apartment. An agency sent over a stream of women eager to come in to help Mrs. Granatelli, and, finally, Lila gave up finding imaginary faults and hired a widow with grown children. Mrs. Johansen was a big woman with a big smile, and both Gloria and Mrs. Granatelli took to her right away. Everybody seemed to be so happy with the situation, that Lila began to wonder if there was something wrong with her to have made such a fuss over it.

●   ●   ●

At noon of the day before the wedding, Lila met John and Catherine at Grand Central Station. It had been four years since Lila had seen her brother at his wedding, and when she saw him step down from the train, she ran to him as though she were still a child.

"Whoah, Lina," he said, his hands up to catch her in case she jumped into his arms as she had often done when she had been little.

But she stopped, and they hugged then stepped apart to look at each other for a moment. Small and neat, John still wore the thin mustache he had grown after their father's death.

"I hope you're ready, John. I told Willie that you'd get drunk tomorrow and sing Italian wedding songs." The idea was so ridiculous it evoked a rare smile. Of course, John was always serious. When had he ever had the time or the money for frivolity?

Lila turned to her sister-in-law. Catherine's black bangs framed skin like new snow with a calm smile posed between classic nose and chin. The perfection would have been chilling, but for her raccoon's eyes, which peered out inquiringly through oversized glasses.

"Teach me the words, and I'll sing them," she laughed, then blushed at her own boldness.

"Oh, Cath, I'm so glad you came." Lila plunged into the open arms.

It was Catherine who wrote the monthly letters. It was Catherine who enclosed photographs and remembered birthdays and, with quiet courage, reported the miscarriages that had thwarted their hopes. When she and John married four years ago, it had been Catherine who had insisted that Lila and her mother come to St. Louis and who had used the money intended for a new sofa to pay for their hotel.

All the way out to Brooklyn, Lila and Catherine chattered away about Lila's wedding dress, the old restaurant where the reception was being held, Catherine's department store job, John's likes and dislikes in food and Roosevelt's third term. John said nothing but, like a benevolent lighthouse, beamed his smile back and forth between the two women as they steered clear of the subject most painful to them both.

Of course, they couldn't avoid it indefinitely; not with Gloria living under the same roof. An hour later, Lila brought Gloria into the Granatelli kitchen. John and Catherine were seated at the table with Mrs. Granatelli.

"Well, everybody, meet the princess," said Lila in a hearty voice.

John, nearest to her jumped up from his chair. "Oh, Lina, she's beautiful. She looks just like you did when you were a baby."

Catherine came around the table to Lila, put her hand on John's shoulder and leaned over Gloria. Gloria reached for Catherine's glasses, but her hand missed and landed on Catherine's nose instead. For a moment, the little fingers closed, then let go, as Catherine straightened up and wiped her eyes. She pulled John's head to her, kissed his cheek and said, "We'll have one, too, Johnny. I promise you."

Lila could see the tension leave her brother. "Can I hold her?" he asked, and Lila happily handed her to him. "Come to your Uncle John," he said settling her in the crook of his arm, but Gloria started to fuss, so Lila took her and put her into her cradle while Mrs. Granatelli brought her warmed bottle from the stove. Gloria quieted and watched the strange faces thoughtfully as though considering whether to make a scene over her dinner or just eat it in the normal way.

Later that evening, John pulled Lila aside. "Come out on the porch and talk to me while I have a cigarette. Momma won't let me smoke in the house."

"All right, if you'll give me one, too." Why did she say that? She never smoked, didn't like the taste of tobacco. But she felt a little thrill as she took her first puff when they got outside. What was that all about? Then it came to her. She was a little girl, again, being naughty, but protected from harm by her big brother.

"Are you sure about this man, Lina?"

"I'm sure I love him and want to marry him."

"I know Momma likes him, but—Is he—?" John stumbled. "Uh. You think he's—uh, the right man to spend the rest of your life with?"

"John, that's corny. But OK, he is. He's the only one."

The light coming through the glass top of the door shone on John's face. He blew out a puff of smoke, then frowned and raised his lower lip before he spoke.

"This business with Gloria—."

Lila interrupted. "I can't help it."

"Maybe another man talking to him?"

She started coughing and flung the cigarette over the porch railing. "Goddamn things. Why did you let me have one? I'm going back inside. I told you I can't help it, so leave it alone, please. It'll all come right, somehow." He started to say something else, but she slipped past him into the house before he could get it out. It's not like fixing a broken toy, Johnny, she said to herself. I only wish it were that simple.

Willie insisted on sending a limousine to bring the Granatellis to the wedding, although St. Mary's was only five blocks from their house. Lila and Willie would spend the night at a hotel and embark the next morning on a three-week European cruise. Lila put her suitcases in the trunk of the limousine so she wouldn't have to come back for them later. Then she ran back upstairs to say goodbye to Gloria who was having her lunch with Mrs. Johansen.

When Gloria saw Lila, she squawked and spit out a mouthful of strained peas. Lila grabbed a napkin, but Mrs. Johansen stopped her. "Here, give that to me. You'll get it all over your dress. Hold still, Gloria." She expertly wiped off the worst of the damage.

She uses exactly the same tone with both of us, Lila thought and grinned. "I'm sorry to upset things Mrs. J. Let me have her for just a moment." Ignoring Mrs. Johansen's frown, Lila scooped Gloria from her highchair and held her up, so they were nose to nose. "Mama's going away for a little while, Gloria, but she'll be back soon. Gramma and Mrs. Johansen will take good care of you. Will you be a good girl and eat everything and grow like a good baby?"

Gloria wriggled and tried to reach Lila. "No, sweetheart, you'll get Mama's dress all gooey." Lila's calm began to crack. How could she do this? What if she brought Gloria to the wedding? Held her up to Willie, to Father Antonio, to Mary, herself, smiling serenely down from the great window above the altar? Who could say no to this adorable little face, a green spot on the chin somehow missed by Mrs. Johansen? Heedless of her dress, Lila pulled Gloria to her. It wasn't too late. She would tell Willie that he couldn't have her unless he took Gloria as well.

An impatient horn in the street brought Lila to herself. She had to forget the theatrics. Nobody could force Willie to do anything once he had set his mind against it. For now, this was how it would have to be. She gave Gloria a last kiss, put her back into the highchair and hurried down to the limousine, where Catherine hastily helped her repair the damage to her makeup as they drove to the church.

They arrived twenty minutes late at the side entrance to the vestry. Father Antonio, fully robed, looked at his watch and positioned them at the door to the main church. Then, he rapped on the door, paused a few seconds and opened it and went through accompanied by two altar boys and followed by Lila's mother, Aunt Julia, and Catherine. Through the open door, Lila could see Willie and Joe Malone scrambling into position before the altar. Then she was in motion, her hand resting lightly on her brother's rigid arm, and Willie saw her, and the joy in his face paid for everything.

As Father Antonio began the ceremony, Lila glanced at the Burke contingent in the front row. Mrs. Burke sat stiffly, Kate on one side of her and Moira on the other, the latter accompanied by her husband, Peter. Willie's father was not present, had not been expected. Next to Kate was petite Nancy Malone, wife of the best man. Several days before the wedding, Lila had received a note from Mrs. Burke thanking Lila for permitting her and her daughters to attend and apologizing "for all conduct on my part or on the part of any member of our family that may have given you offense." What that would mean in the long run, Lila couldn't tell, but when their eyes met, she nodded an acknowledgment.

Short as the ceremony was, it seemed an age before Father Antonio turned to Willie and began "Wilt thou, William..." What would become of them, she wondered. Suppose this was a terrible mistake? "...until death do you part?"

"I will." Willie's voice resounded in the empty church.

For him it was easy. All decisions came easy. He believed in himself; that was enough.

"Wilt thou,—Lila..." Father Antonio stumbled over her changed name.

She couldn't believe in herself that way. She couldn't be sure.

"...until death do you part?"

She had to believe in Willie; let that be enough for her, too.

"I will," and a moment later it was done.

•   •   •

A long table was laid in the back room of *La Luna Piena*, a block away from St Francis. As the families milled around, a waiter brought a tray of champagne glasses. Willie grabbed two, gave one to Lila and dragged her to where Lila's mother stood with John and Catherine.

"*Bellissima signora*." he greeted Mrs. Granatelli and bent down to kiss her cheek.

She smiled happily. "Weelie. Now you call'a me Momma. You my son, just like John."

Willie turned to John, hand outstretched. "I'm so glad you could come, John."

John paused a moment, and Lila's heart sank. Then his hand shot out to take Willie's and his voice was firm as he said, "Catherine and I are delighted to meet you, Willie, and we wish you every happiness." Then John opened his arms to Lila, and they pulled their mother to them and then Aunt Julia and, in a moment, they were all crying. Willie looked worried, but Catherine put her hand on his shoulder.

"Don't worry, Willie. They're crying because they're happy. The more, the better."

After a minute, Lila extricated herself and came back to Willie, a radiant smile on her face, blotting her tears with a napkin. "Do I look OK?"

"Gorgeous, darling girl, just gorgeous. Will you say hello to my family with me?"

"I'll come with you of, course. They're my guests, too." She resolutely led Willie to his mother, who was standing, sipping from a glass of champagne.

"Hello, Mrs. Burke. Thank you for coming."

Mrs. Burke smiled and put down her glass. "Please call me Mary, Lila. Thank you for having me. You look absolutely lovely."

"How about me, Ma?" Willie grabbed his mother in a bear hug.

"William, behave yourself." She wrestled free. "Lila, may I kiss my new daughter in-law?"

Lila presented her cheek to receive the brief pressure of Mrs. Burke's kiss, then the two women drew back and smiled at each other. Lila doubted they would ever become friends, but she knew she had Mary Burke's promise to treat her with the courtesy due her position. Next Kate then Moira came up to Lila and initiated a similar ceremony.

"I feel like the ambassador to the Holy Roman Emperor," she whispered to Willie.

"What's that, darling girl? You've won over my whole family. I said you would."

Lila bit off her response. She could explain later. "Let's sit down and get this over with and get out of here. Please, Willie, now." She signed to the head waiter, who nodded.

Willie banged a spoon against a glass for quiet. "Sit ye down and eat, folks." He and Lila squeezed together at one end of the table. Their mothers sat next to them, and the rest of the families trailed down the table, with Father Antonio on the Granatelli side. Waiters brought in dishes of antipasto, bottles of wine. A man in peasant costume began playing his accordion.

Course followed course; toast followed toast. It seemed unending, but, at last, the wedding cake was cut and passed around. Willie called over the accordion player and slipped him a folded bill. The accordionist struck a series of loud chords for silence, then launched into an impassioned "O Sole Mio." With the first note, Willie and Lila slid out of their chairs, hastened through the main dining room, out the door, and through the rain into the waiting limousine.

"Plaza Hotel," directed Willie, and they alternated kissing and laughing all the way there.

As soon as the bellboy left them alone in their hotel room, Lila tore off her dress and pulled Willie onto their bed with his shirt still half on and his trousers and shorts caught in his shoes. Freeing himself, he clambered over her. His weight rested on his knees and his elbows, while his hands gripped her shoulders. As he lowered himself, his eyes closed and his lips met hers. As comfortably as though she had done it a hundred times, Lila reached down and guided him into her. How good, how right. She put her arms around his broad back, locked her hands together, pulled him against her and held him, letting every part of her body relish the contact. As though a signal had been given, they began to move together. Her pleasure rose to a peak she hadn't known existed. But too soon, she felt herself going over. She fought to hold on, biting and clawing, but nothing she could do could keep her on the summit, and, shaking and shuddering beyond control, she fell.

As her climax abated, she tried to free herself, but Willie was now driving her into the bed, his thumbs buried in her shoulders. Each time he slammed down he cried out Lila's name, using all of his breath, refilling his lungs with a gasp when he raised back up. Her name. This tremendous force was for her. Her breath synchronized with his and she found herself crying his name as he cried hers. Once again she reached the peak, but this time Willie was there with her, and they came to earth together.

Afterward, Willie fell asleep on top of the covers, sprawled out like a powerful animal that didn't need to curl up and hide like lesser species. It was five o'clock. She went into the bathroom and started the tub. In Brooklyn, her mother would be starting Gloria's bath. When the tub was almost full, Lila turned it off and got in. If it had been Gloria's bath, she would have tested it with her finger before putting Gloria in. After bathing, she dried herself with the big hotel towel. Gloria loved her towel with Mickey and Minnie Mouse on it. Lila brushed her teeth, combed her hair, put on her nightgown, lay down next to Willie and pulled up the bedspread to cover them. They would be back from the honeymoon in twenty days.

•   •   •

When they returned, Lila wholeheartedly threw herself into her new life. Willie was strong and tender and considerate. Their lovemaking was better than her dreams, and he was as wonderingly grateful for it as she. They cared little for friends, preferring each other's company. When they went out, they liked to do things by themselves. Lila's skills as a dancer encouraged Willie to introduce her to sports, and he taught her to play tennis and took her to Forest Hills where she fell in love with the smooth grace of Don Budge.

When she wasn't with Willie, she had a million other things to keep her busy. She bought furniture and carpets, exchanged wedding presents, wrote thank-you notes. She had to hire servants and learn how to manage them, how to give orders to people twice her age to perform tasks with which they were infinitely more familiar.

Then there was her career. At first, she was a little awed by her new piano. White and gold, as though made for Versailles. This was only a <u>baby</u> grand? It was huge compared to the Granatelli's tiny spinet, usually so out of tune that a misstruck note might go unnoticed. She drove herself to practice and came to love the instrument, which made her feel so good when she got it right.

Then there was her career. She saw her singing teacher three times a week and her piano teacher twice. She felt as though she were married to the dressmaker and carrying on an affair with the arranger, and that was even before she started rehearsing for her first performance.

The Rye Shore Club was a small beach hotel on the shore of Long Island Sound, recently bought by a group including the Burkes. When they arrived on a Thursday evening in October, she was disheartened to see only a half-dozen tables still occupied by guests finishing dinner, notwithstanding the big sign by the door: "Thursday-Saturday Only, LILA GRAND, Sweetheart of Song, Evenings at Nine."

At 9:05, she peeked out from the kitchen as the hotel manager was finishing his introduction, and was relieved to find the room filled with tuxedos and evening gowns. She recognized many people; Willie must have gotten half of the Fordham class of 1930 to come. Well, a friendly audience always helps, she thought, and came through the door and walked to the piano with a big smile on her face to the sound of enthusiastic applause, led, of course, by Willie, who jumped up from his table right in front of the piano.

She had been terrified of the beginning, afraid that she'd start off key or forget the words or the accompaniment. It had gotten so bad that she had asked her singing teacher for help. His solution was to start her sophisticated program of Cole Porter, Gershwin and Harold Arlen with "Happy Days Are Here Again."

"The Democrats will be cheering and the Republicans booing," he chuckled, "and, if you make a mistake, nobody will notice."

So she sang it loud and fast, and they cheered and booed, and she didn't make any mistakes and wasn't frightened any more but sang her songs and told her jokes just the way she had rehearsed them. She was doing well; she could tell from the little smiles and nods. The audience wasn't overwhelmed, though. People drank their drinks and smoked their cigarettes, and the applause, though generous, was measured.

Except for Willie. After each number, he clapped so hard his palms were red, and he jumped up and down and poked Joe Malone in the chest and hugged Nancy Malone and made it clear to the whole room that he thought Lila was the greatest thing going. So when she finished her regular set and came back out to acknowledge the applause, her encore was "The Man I Love," and she blew a kiss to Willie at the end.

Friday and Saturday nights went much the same, as did her weekend at the Diamond Lounge in Westbury two weeks later. After that Saturday performance, she was introduced to an agent who was pleasant but noncommittal. He promised to look around and get back to her in a few weeks. As Lila went back to her dressing room, she started thinking about how to break Willie of the belief that she was going to set the world on fire. That was all right with her. "I just want to start," she sang to the mirror in her dressing room, "a flame in your heart." That, she knew she had. It was what she lived for, five days a week.

While Lila was on the Manhattan side of the East River, she didn't allow herself to think of Gloria. But each Monday and Thursday morning, she would shower Willie's sweat off her body, dress in her simplest clothes, fill her purse from the money drawer in Willie's desk and take the subway to Brooklyn. She would walk into the Granatelli house and be transformed. She was the devoted mother as easily and as she was the ardent wife, singing nonsense songs as she changed Gloria's diapers, whistling as she wiped up spilled food, tirelessly rewinding the yellow plush giraffe, which played the Brahms lullaby. In this world, an exciting trip went to Prospect Park, a fuss was made over a 50-cent toy, and Fifth Avenue was a thousand miles away.

Of course, the psychologists and psychiatrists have since told her that it was impossible, that, short of madness, you can't build a wall of denial with a door that lets you travel back and forth twice a week. But it stood up for over six months and might have stood up even longer if two terrible things hadn't happened. The first was World War II.

Willie's construction experience got him commissioned an officer in the Navy and sent to San Diego to build docks and storage facilities and anything else they could think of to hasten the delivery of men and materials to the Pacific theater. He found himself part of a permanent military community and was encouraged to bring out his young wife. Lila, as a good patriot, couldn't refuse; it would have been sabotage. Gloria was happy with Mrs. Granatelli, and everybody knew that the U.S. would finish off the war in six months, so off Lila went on the 20th Century Limited, with the piano, disassembled, crated and stenciled PRIORITY-MILITARY EQUIPMENT, riding in the baggage car.

•   •   •

Life was marvelous in San Diego. Although it was winter, she wore short-sleeved dresses and played tennis every day. It mattered less if Willie worked late since she had so much to do. She organized entertainment, practiced her own numbers, wrapped bandages and was cheerfully available whenever an extra hand was needed. Her exuberant helpfulness made her friends among the officers' wives; they forgave her beauty since she was obviously interested in no man other than Willie. His pride in her accomplishments helped to numb the pain she felt on a Monday or Thursday morning.

They had been in San Diego only three months when the second terrible thing occurred: her mother began to suffer abdominal pain. When she agreed to see a doctor, he told her she had a large growth blocking the intestinal tract. A risky operation was the only hope. Willie arranged a private room and nurses and wangled a few days leave to take Lila on the train east. John and Catherine were also coming from St. Louis. Lila took a taxi from the station directly to the hospital without even stopping to call. A doctor and a nurse were talking to John outside the door of the room. This morning he was not neat. His hair was uncombed, there was stubble on his chin and a coffee stain on the front of his shirt. He must have spent the night at the hospital.

John grabbed her arm. "Thank God you made it. They're about to take her down. The surgeon wouldn't delay any longer. You've only got a couple of minutes."

Lila couldn't recognize the tiny figure in the hospital gown, with a cap tied under her chin. It lay nested in tubes and wires and restraining bands of cloth, all enclosed by the raised bars of her bed. The head turned at Lila's approach, and it was her mother's face, which smiled up at her.

"Lina," she said softly. "You come'a all this way?"

Lila bent over to kiss her mother's cheek. It was as dry and fragile as millefiore. How could that be? Her mother's skin was soft and resilient. "I've come to take care of you, Momma. They'll fix you up, and you can take a little rest, and I'll do all the work."

"Maybe. It's enough that I see you again."

"Now, you're not supposed to talk, Mrs. Granatelli." The nurse took Lila's arm to pull her away, but Lila wouldn't let her.

"She won't talk. Just let me hold her hand for a minute." Lila curled her fingers around her mother's hand. The nurse frowned but said nothing. A few minutes later, two attendants pushed a gurney into the room, and Lila had to let go while they transferred her mother from her bed. As they began to wheel the gurney out, Lila stepped ahead of it, drawing John with her. All the way to the elevator, she kept the two of them where her mother could see them. When they got to the open door of the elevator, the doctor shook his head.

"We have to leave you here."

First John leaned over to kiss his mother; then it was Lila's turn. She tried to speak, but her mother pursed her lips and softly whispered "Shh." Lila straightened up, reached for John, and they clung to each other as the gurney rolled into the elevator and the door closed. When they separated, Lila realized, for the first time, that she was actually an inch taller than he.

They went downstairs to the telephones and called Brooklyn to talk to Catherine who had stayed to take care of Gloria while John had spent the night at the hospital. Although eager to see Gloria, Lila refused to leave the hospital until her mother came back from surgery. John also insisted on staying, and it was arranged that Catherine and Aunt Julia would come with a change of clothes for him when Mrs. Johansen arrived at nine o'clock.

They bought juice and toast and coffee at the cafeteria and brought it back up to their mother's room. They were too tired to talk and, after eating, while John dozed in the big chair, Lila climbed onto her mother's bed and turned her face into the pillow. When she had been little, Lila had loved to take her nap like this in her parents' bed, and the familiar smell made her feel safe again. After a while, she thought she heard Catherine and Aunt Julia, but maybe it was a dream. It wasn't until she felt John's hand on her shoulder and heard him say in a broken voice, "The doctor's here, Lina, it's all over," that she raised her head.

When Lila got to Brooklyn, she found Gloria much changed, talking a little, newly confident, not so ready to accept a mother she hadn't seen for so long, petulantly demanding her grandmother, taking comfort only from Mrs. Johansen. Lila popped Gloria into the stroller and fled the house leaving John and Catherine to deal with the funeral parlor. By the end of the afternoon, Gloria was starting to call Lila "Mama."

Later, while Catherine read a picture book to Gloria and Willie went out to bring back Chinese food, Lila went through her mother's address book and telephoned those few relatives and friends who hadn't already been called by Julia. Then she put Gloria to bed and picked at the food the other three had left. John and Catherine went out for a walk, and Lila tottered into the parlor and collapsed on the couch, with a cup of tea, her feet up on a pile of cushions in violation of all laws. Willie walked around the room for a few minutes, picking up a picture or a knick-knack and turning it over in his hands as though contemplating a purchase. At last, he lowered himself into the big easy chair and lit a cigar. "John and Catherine," he said.

"What about them?" Lila asked absently, taking a sip of tea.

"They're the right people for Gloria."

"What are you talking about, Willie? Can't it wait until tomorrow?" She was whining, she knew, and they both hated that, but she was exhausted and wanted only to sleep.

Willie was patient. "No, darling girl, it can't wait. We have to go back Wednesday, and the arrangements have to be made before we leave."

The word "arrangements" was an alarm signal. She put down the tea. "Oh God, all right. I'll try. What is it, Willie? Start from the beginning."

"Sweetheart, your mother is gone, and we have to find the best place for Gloria. John and Catherine want children but can't have them. With his job, John will stay exempt from the draft. They'll take good care of her. Will you talk to John, or do you want me to?"

She concentrated and hauled a thought up from the depths of her exhaustion. "How can they? They live in St. Louis, and she lives here."

"They'll take her back with them. This house will be sold. Julia has agreed. My lawyers will arrange it. Your brother can take your mother's half of the money and buy a bigger house."

That sounded reasonable to her. "But Willie, St. Louis is so far away."

Willie stubbed out his cigar and came and sat on the edge of the couch next to her. She leaned against his solid hip, and he took her hand in his. "We're in California, sweetheart, and nobody knows how long this war will go on. Believe me, this is the best solution."

He raised her hand to his lips and kissed her palm, and she couldn't think of anything else to say. She fell asleep and was only dimly aware of her brother's return and a conversation between him and Willie, and then Willie was helping her to a taxi, which took them home to their apartment where she slept twelve hours more.

The funeral service and the trip to the cemetery were a blur. She had said goodbye to her mother in the hospital; the rest was merely custom. By six o'clock, the few people who had come to the wake were gone. Lila busied herself with Gloria while the others cleaned up. When she returned to the kitchen, she found Willie, John, and Catherine, seated around the table.

"Sit down, darling girl," said Willie, pulling her into the fourth chair. "We have to talk."

"It's all right," she protested, "she can go to St. Louis, and I'll come and stay every few months. It'll be fine," and she looked at Willie, but he was looking at John.

"It'll be fine," Lila repeated. "Won't it, John?"

Her brother smoothed his mustache, glanced at Catherine's worried face, cleared his throat and spoke deliberately as though reading off unfamiliar instructions for installing an engine part. "Lina, I hope you can understand what I'm going to say. You're my sister, and I don't want to do anything to hurt you. But I'm not going to do something that will hurt Cath and me, either. Three times now, we thought we were going to have a child, and we lost it. Each time it hurt worse than the last." He half-turned to Catherine, who nodded agreement, her teeth clenched, her hands twisting and untwisting a napkin. He continued. "We'd give anything for a child like Gloria, but we can't take her home, learn to love her, and then give her back to you—when it's convenient." He stumbled over the last three words and looked down.

Lila waited for Willie's anger, but he was silent. "What are you saying, John?" she asked.

John looked again at Catherine who nodded encouragement. "We'll only take Gloria as our own child. You'd have to give her up. We'd be her parents. Not just for a year or so. For all time. If you can't do that, then we can't take her." He started to drop his head again, but caught himself and looked squarely at Lila.

Well, that was clear enough, Lila thought. It rated a nice clear answer, maybe just a dignified, "No, thank you." No, that would sound like he had offered her a drink. Or like sarcasm, and that would be wrong, too. She couldn't be angry with John; she knew what he and Cath had gone through. She tried not to show her satisfaction; now, Willie would have to accept Gloria. And he'd damn well better get his ass out to San Diego and get them a bigger apartment and a nursemaid. That wasn't going to be easy. He certainly was being cool about it, though; his whole attention was focused on that damn cigar. John and Catherine were looking very unhappy. Lila tried to think of a kind way to let them down but couldn't think of the right thing to say; obviously, they had gotten their hopes up. Well, that was just too bad. Willie shouldn't have let that happen. Let him fix it, the smooth bastard.

"Willie?" she asked and wondered why her voice was breaking. It must have been Catherine's sweet face, disappointed, downcast, knowing she would never have a child. What a joy to miss out on. It was so pathetic that Lila found herself crying and couldn't seem to stop. She wasn't up to this so soon after her mother's death. How her mother had loved Gloria. And to have only had her for such a short time. It wasn't fair; it was too cruel. Didn't they understand that? Now the tears were streaming down her face, and her body was shaking with the force of her sobs. Why were they all looking at her so strangely? Couldn't they see how sad it was that life could be so lousy? And the saddest part was how insensitive people were about it. Lila rocked back and forth now, keening with grief. She heard her brother and her husband make the arrangements that would take her baby away from her forever and was unable to say a word to stop them. Willie brought out a piece of paper and his fountain pen and put his arms around her to steady her as she signed it. She remembers that. But then came a gap of about a month before she woke up one morning in a San Diego hospital seeing the sun pouring in the open window and hearing the rustling of palm fronds in the warm breeze.

II

Awkward from sitting so long, Lila gets up from the piano bench, the last picture in her hand. It's in color and shows Willie and her in tennis clothes, standing proudly, rackets held aloft in triumph. She's ten years older than she was in the pinup, but the figure is still trim. Constant exposure to the sun has lightened and streaked her hair. She smiles remembering for how long those streaks camouflaged the gradual incursion of gray. But the years are beginning to show themselves in the crinkles around her eyes and the corners of her mouth. Not only the years, either. She suddenly decides to put this picture back into the storage closet.

The clock shows a quarter past eleven; she's been sitting there for forty-five minutes. That happens a lot, now. She remembers something and follows it into the past and then it all starts playing back like videotape. Longer and longer, too. Maybe one time she won't come back. Would that be good or bad? Is that what Willie did the last year?

At sixty-five, Willie had already sold most of his interest in Burke Construction and was a part-time executive. Like many big men, he had lost his agility and had already given up sports. The first stroke did little damage. He accepted the limp and successfully fought the slurring of his speech. They sold the Long Island house and stayed all year in Palm Beach except for July, August, and September, which they spent in New York.

The second stroke, four years later, was catastrophic. Willie was left with a little motion in his left hand and control only of his eyes and lids. Lila fought for his humanity for six months. One wing of the house became a hospital and doctors and therapists came daily. They taught Willie to blink in Morse code, and he blinked until his eyes teared. Often he was seized with frustration and would claw frantically at the sheet, and indescribable sounds would come from his throat. The doctors told Lila that the damage was irreversible, while they promised Willie recovery. Lila swore on Gloria's head that they were telling him the truth, but one morning, after the doctors had left, Lila came to Willie's bed, and the eyes blinked out "l-i-a-r" over and over, while the expression on his face remained frozen.

All of that day his eyes followed her around the room and, whenever he caught her watching, he blinked again "l-i-a-r." He wouldn't sleep and, after several hours she fled the room. A few minutes later, the nurse came running to her. Willie wanted her immediately. When she leaned over his bed, he blinked "f-o-r-g-i-v-e m-e."

"Of course I have, darling," she kissed his inert lip.

Again the lids closed and opened, closed and opened, very slowly, as though Willie wanted to make himself clear. "k-i-l-l m-e."

`Lila shook her head back and forth. "I won't, I won't. You can't make me do that, too." She grabbed Willie's hands and started to shake him, and then the nurse got to her and held Lila's arms to her body in a bear hug. Lila quieted and, like some giant four-armed insect, she and the nurse bent over together and lowered Willie's upper body back to the bed.

For another week Willie blinked the same message. Guilt, pity, the memory of love, all drew her back to his bed again and again. Each time he became aware of her presence the blinking would start, and Lila would flee before her rage again became uncontrollable. Each time, as she walked away from him, the sounds from his throat and the scrabbling of his fingers would start again. One time she turned back to the bed and whispered fiercely "Make the doctor do it," but Willie wouldn't ask either the doctor or the nurses, only Lila.

One morning, he stopped. He blinked no more messages. He made no more sounds. The eyes looked calmly straight ahead at Lila, without interest, and didn't follow her when she moved. The fingers of the left hand ceased their scrabbling, although they would still contract when the doctor drew a pin across the palm. Lila couldn't tell whether he was there or had gone to another time and place. She prayed that he had, every night for another year.

•   •   •

"Good morning, Mrs. Burke. It's going to be a beautiful day."

Lila sat up. Where? How? What? Bright sun blinded her as someone pulled up the shades. She shielded her eyes and looked around her. A hospital room. A nurse in a Navy uniform opening the window. It looked familiar. She must have been here for a while. Why?

"Why am I here, nurse? What's wrong with me?"

The nurse came over to Lila's bed and took her hand and located her pulse. "Shh," she said, concentrating on the count.

Lila tried to remember what had happened to her. A Navy hospital? She must be in San Diego. Had she fallen and hit her head? Hadn't she been somewhere else? Memories swam in and out of focus like fish in the great tank at the Coney Island Aquarium. A long train trip. She had gone to New York. Why? She shivered in the warm room. It had been something bad.

"Good, Mrs. Burke. Now your pills." The nurse handed Lila a cup with two pills in it.

"No pills," snapped Lila, annoyed at the distraction. Even if it was bad, she had to find out. What had happened to take her to New York?

"But the doctor says you have to take your pills. Please don't give me trouble, Mrs. Burke, I've been on my feet for twelve hours. I want to go home."

Home. Lila had gone back to her home in Brooklyn because—. Once again, she saw her mother's ravaged face disappear as they wheeled her into the hospital elevator. Lila began to cry.

"Oh, Christ," said the nurse. She came to the bed and put an arm around Lila. "Shh, Mrs. Burke, it's all right, you're all right."

Lila tried to answer her, but her throat was choked with grief. The nurse left Lila and went to the door and called for a doctor. That wasn't necessary, Lila thought. She would get hold of herself in a minute. Then, into focus came the scene at the Granatelli kitchen table: Catherine on one side, Willie on the other and John across, his hands steepled in front of him, his eyebrows lowered as if he were trying to shield his eyes from her. She tried to take the pills the nurse had given her, but her hand was shaking, and the pills fell to the floor. Her hand had been shaking that night when it held the gold fountain pen she had given Willie for his birthday, but she had managed to sign the piece of paper. She could remember that, now. Being able to remember must mean she wasn't sick anymore. She had lost her mother and her daughter, but she wasn't sick anymore. That was funny. She started to laugh and couldn't stop until the doctor came and gave her an injection.

This time, when Lila opened her eyes, she saw Willie standing over her, staring into her face. He bent over and kissed her softly. "Darling girl," he said, "Thank God you're back."

She put her arms around his neck and tried to pull herself up. Willie had been the rock she had moored herself to. Now he was all she had, and she must cling to him or drown. "What happened to me?"

"Here, you're breaking my neck." Lila let go, and he sat down on the bed next to her.

"How long have I been here? What day is it?"

"A week. Today is April 18. You got sick in New York, and I brought you out here when my leave ended."

She remembered an ambulance, then another long train ride. Telephone poles whizzing past so fast she kept losing count. Willie's voice murmuring and another voice. There had been a stranger in a white nurse's uniform with a high starched cap.

"What have I been doing, here?"

Willie looked away. "Mostly sleeping. Looking out the window, some. Let's not talk about it. Now, you're going to get well. That's what's important." He patted her hand.

She felt so much better with Willie there. She would get well, she was sure, but she needed to know something first. She captured both of his hands so he couldn't get away.

"Willie, look at me."

He bent over slightly, and their eyes met. "Lila—"

"Sshh. Do you love me?"

"More than anything in the world. I—"

"Sshh and listen. If you love me, you must tell me the truth. Did I do the right thing?"

His face was grave, his voice was steady. "Yes, Lila, you did the right thing."

She tightened her grip. "Swear, Willie. I must be sure."

He took a deep breath. "I swear by my love for you that you did the right thing. John and Catherine will love Gloria and take care of her all of their lives. You have made them happy; they will make her happy, and you and I will make each other and our children happy. I swear it on your mother's grave, may she rest in peace, who loved all of us." He held her look when he finished; his head was so steady she could have counted the freckles.

The weight lifted from her heart. The wound still pained, but in time it would heal. She could trust Willie. She would be happy; they would all be happy.

•   •   •

Lila soon recovered from the whatever-it-was they told their friends had hospitalized her. She resumed her duties and amusements, particularly tennis, which she played as often as possible. Soon there were no women at the base who could hold their own against her, and she began to play with Willie and his friends. Willie boasted about her to everybody. The first time she won a set from him, he bought her a tiny gold racket on a chain as a trophy.

They ganged around with the bachelors and their transient girlfriends and with the young marrieds, active, athletic people, always going somewhere to do something. There were lots of parties, with plenty of food and liquor cheaply bought at the PX. When the Burke's turn came they were generous; Willie never let a check sit long on the table. They drank with the crowd, but never got drunk. They were good sports, good fun and at the top of everybody's guest list.

They never spoke of Gloria, and Lila sometimes found that several hours had passed without thinking of her. Then anything, another child, a song, a utensil would trigger a memory, and Lila would see Gloria's little face frowning in concentration as she fitted the wooden shapes of her puzzle into their slots or exploding with glee as she splashed her bath water onto the floor. Pain would well up before Lila could reassure herself that Gloria was in a better place, well-cared for, loved and happy, something like her Momma, in heaven. The pain would subside to a dull ache that she wouldn't even notice if she kept busy enough.

One afternoon, about three months after their return from New York, Willie handed Lila a postcard from St.Louis. "We're all fine. Love, John & Cath & Gloria."

"That's wrong," she said and dropped the card in the wastebasket. Gloria wasn't anywhere that had postcards with riverboats on them.

Willie looked up from tying the laces of his tennis shoes. "What's wrong?" he asked.

Lila picked up her racket and went outside without answering. Damn Catherine for sending the card, and damn Willie for handing it to her. And for everything else, no matter how right he was and how happy they all would be. On the court, Lila played in a fury and won all three sets convincingly. That night, for the first time in her life, she got drunk.

It wasn't deliberate. She had recovered from the shock of the postcard; her anger had passed. But she felt a little down and, in the effort to get into the spirit of the party, she drank a little more Scotch a little faster than usually.

She felt something new: not out of control but beyond control. It was not just that no one could stop her from doing or saying what she wanted, but that no one but she had any right to decide what that should or shouldn't be.

Since there was nothing in particular that she wanted to do or say, she brought a drink with her to the ladies' room to savor this new sensation in solitude. She closed the door to a stall and sat on the lid of the toilet. Alone in her cubicle, she imagined herself as the pilot of a small airplane, free to fly wherever she wished. She started inland among the peaks of the high Sierras, then continued east, skimming just above the Great Salt Lake. She sipped from her drink and, deep in her throat, made the softest of engine noises as she sped along.

"Did you see that?" The door of the ladies' room banged open.

"Keep it down, Lizzie, you want the whole world to hear?" said a quieter voice.

"I don't care who hears. That skinny bitch puts her hand on his leg again, I'll break her fingers." The loud voice belonged to Liz Kleinhans, who seemed to be suffering again from the combination of alcohol and jealousy over her handsome husband.

"I didn't see anything, Lizzie." The calmer voice belonged to Jenny Gooden. It dropped to a whisper. "...in there."

"I don't care who hears." Someone rapped on the door of Lila's stall. "Who's in there, anyway?" Liz demanded.

Lila flushed, hid her glass behind the toilet and emerged.

Liz laughed. "Oh, it's you, Lila. Jenny was afraid you were the Admiral's wife."

"Hi, Lizzie, Jenny." She spoke slowly. If she wasn't careful, the other two might realize that she was drunk and it might get back to Willie who would be upset. She should say as little as possible. She busied herself with washing her hands and fixing her makeup until they left. The rest of the evening, she took care not to say or do anything that would call attention to herself.

Lila pretended to sleep in the car going home, then stalled in the bathroom. When she heard Willie snoring, she poured herself a drink, picked the postcard out of the wastebasket, went out onto the balcony of their apartment and took a swallow. The Scotch tasted terrible after the toothpaste, and she emptied her glass into the bushes. Then she looked at the postcard again.

John & Cath & Gloria. Gloria. Who was Gloria? Gloria Swanson? No.

Gloria Vanderbilt? No, not her either. Gloryoskey? No, no, silly, that's just an expression Little Orphan Annie uses. *Sic transit gloria mundi.* That must be it, Gloria Mundi. No dear, it's Gloria Granatelli, you know that. I know, I know. She's my niece. Is she a nice niece? Oh yes, a gloriously nice niece. How nice. Someday it would be nice to meet my niece nice. That's silly. I know. I'm a silly-billy. I'm just a silly-billy married to a silly-willie with a nice niece, and we'll all live happily ever after.

Careful. She must be careful, Lila reminded herself. She came in from the balcony, put the postcard back into the wastebasket and washed out the glass. Then she brushed her teeth again, went to the bedroom, hung her bathrobe on the silent valet and climbed into the bed next to Willie's warm bulk. Why am I so careful, she wondered. A Japanese invasion wouldn't rouse Willie. She giggled and wished that she could share the joke with him.

She continued to "go flying" but with great caution. She couldn't do it while alone with Willie or out with just another couple. He would be concerned if she showed anything beyond the mild buzz that was de rigueur for nights out. She began to accept more invitations for large parties and dances where she and Willie always steered separate courses collecting stories to tell each other on the way home. She experimented with different drinks and with the length of time she took to finish one. If her head felt dizzy or her stomach queasy, she would stop. When she got it right, she would tuck herself out of the way with a smile on her face, telling those who inquired that she was "just resting a minute," while she soared over jungles and glaciers and slipped between the towers of great cities. But never over St. Louis.

Willie continued kind, gentle and ardent. He worked hard, was promoted twice and received several letters of commendation. After the second promotion, his duties required him to inspect military construction in the South Pacific. Lila was frantic, at first, but Willie swore he'd never be near a Japanese airplane, and she allowed herself to believe him. Each time he went, Lila's social life doubled as their friends vied for the privilege of keeping her distracted. No one paid the slightest attention to her drinking, and she was able to fly at every party.

Lila didn't have an evening to herself during Willie's first couple of trips. On the third, however, she got the opportunity to try an experiment: flying at home by herself. It was not a success. Free from observation, she was careless, drank too much, got sick and had a terrible headache the next morning. She realized how easy it was to miscalculate; it could happen at a party. How shameful that would be. It wasn't worth the risk just for a half-hour's fantasy. And so she gave it up and resumed her previous two drink per night limit.

The months passed seamlessly. The blue sky, the palm trees, the beach, all changed little with the seasons. The uniforms, too, were always there, and though the names changed there was little difference in the mouths that grinned at her across the net, whistled up at her across the footlights or brushed her cheek as she left the party. She thought of Gloria less and less frequently and then only for a moment before her mind shut off the image. Occasionally, there was a postcard and, every Christmas, a letter with a picture. Willie would hand it to Lila, who would look at it for a moment, then pass it back without comment. The chubby toddler became a little elf with mischief in her eyes. At Christmas and Gloria's birthday, Willie bought expensive presents, and Lila signed the card "Aunt Lila" before he had them wrapped and shipped.

• • •

In time, the war ended, and the Burkes came back to New York. Willie's father was dying, and Willie had to take over the business with a half-dozen projects on the drawing board. Lila was busy reopening the apartment and organizing the flood of social invitations from Willie's friends and business associates. Willie wanted a weekend house as well as the apartment, so Lila went out to Long Island day after day looking at houses whose owners had died or grown old during the war. She found a nice big one in Westbury, not too far from Willie's golf club, had the tennis court resurfaced and the swimming pool relined and spent weeks with decorators filling up the house with furniture.

All those projects, however, were far less important than having a baby. Lila had learned how to manage the pain of losing Gloria, but the only thing that would truly heal the wound would be the love of the new children Willie had promised. Each night she reached for him eagerly. Each month, she tried not to show her disappointment at the postponement of her hopes.

They moved into the house in time for the summer. The commute made it a long day for Willie, so, one or two nights each week, Lila would come into New York to stay in the apartment. Lila liked those days the best. The house required live-in servants and Lila imagined they watched critically everything she did. She couldn't very well curse and swear if she dropped something in the kitchen—she wasn't even supposed to <u>be</u> in the kitchen. And how could she walk around on a hot day wearing only her panties?

On the days she stayed on Long Island, Lila learned to drive her new little Studebaker and went to the club for golf lessons or to hit with the tennis pro. She had no friends and was often bored, so she decided to find out how the house worked. She joined the local library and took out books on heating systems and swimming pools and lawn care. She learned what jobs were done by what servants, how long they should take doing them and what new equipment might help them do things more efficiently. Willie calculated the savings she had accomplished and deposited them monthly in a bank account in her name.

Since the house now ran smoothly, they started inviting guests. Willie searched out the best tennis players from the neighborhood for Saturday and Sunday morning men's doubles. Lila's serve and net game were not quite up to their standards, but Willie had a second court put in so that she could play singles with whoever was sitting out. Then Mike Stone brought his wife, Margo, and Lila, at last, found both a tennis partner and a friend.

Margo was then 39. In her early twenties, she had been invited several times to the National Championships at Forest Hills. Every ball she got to came back to Lila low and deep, but Margo smoked and drank too much and no longer liked to run. She preferred doubles to singles and taught Lila to volley and how to position herself. The Stones maintained a fine grass court and well-known players came out to play with Margo. Often, she invited Lila to join them.

When they played alone during the week, Margo would insist that Lila stay for lunch. They would find salads and sodas in the refrigerator beside the enclosed pool together with a big pitcher of sangria. Lila never had more than one glass of it, although it was delicious, but Margo downed it like Kool-Aid. They would shower and eat, then take their robes off, lie in the sun coming through the glass ceiling panels and dip in and out of the pool like dragonflies.

Lila felt uncomfortable lying around without any clothes on, the first time, when she noticed Margo staring at her.

"What's the matter, Margo."

"Let's see. Good face, classic features, lips could be fuller, but I know gals who would kill for that nose."

"What?"

"Hush. Let me finish. Athletic body in great condition, if a tad muscular for some. Skin blooming with health, as they say. Tits are small, but they stand up like troopers."

"Margo! Stop!"

Margo paid no attention. "You could bounce quarters off that ass, and I would call the legs perfect, although some like 'em a mite longer and skinnier."

A terrible thought struck Lila. Could Margo be viewing her as more than a friend?

Lila's face must have shown something, for Margo started laughing.

"If you could only see yourself. You look like Little Red Riding Hood. Don't worry, child, the men are enough for me. I was just checking the competition out, that's all."

Mike Stone was a reserved man in his fifties, whose importing business often took him to the Orient and seemed to occupy most of his attention the rest of the time. Lila once heard a woman at lunch at the club pause in conversation to ask whether Mike had been present on some recent occasion.

"Margo," the woman complained with mock annoyance, "The problem is that, sometimes, we can't tell when Mike's home and when he's away."

"Sorry, sweetie," Margo drawled, "I can't help you. I can't tell, myself, half the time. That's why our marriage is so successful."

Later, as they were leaving the club, Lila ran to catch Margo before she could get into her car. "How could you say such a terrible thing about Mike. He's the sweetest, gentlest man I think I've ever met and he treats you like a queen."

'Why child, he is all of that. I never said he wasn't."

"But then what did you mean?"

"I meant exactly what I said. I'm married to the sweetest, gentlest, dullest husband in Nassau County. All his originality and creativity go into his business. To show his success, he needs a beautiful wife like he needs a beautiful house. And of course, if you have beautiful things you must take good care of them. It's very Chinese. When I get too bored, I have a little discreet fling. Mike doesn't mind."

"Oh, Margo, I'm sorry."

Margo drew away, and her voice hardened. "Y'all think every husband and wife are as crazy about each other as you and Willie?" She cocked her head and arched her eyebrows.

I've hurt my best friend, Lila thought and grabbed Margo in a hug. "I'm sorry. I just want you to have the best because you're my friend and I love you."

Margo softened and put her arms up around Lila, then reached up to smooth her hair. "I love you, too, child, and I hope you two stay crazy about each other for fifty more years." She turned and stepped into her car in one fluid motion and was gone.

It would have been a wonderful summer, but frustration at Lila's delay in conception began to sour its pleasures. The first week in October, when she and Willie drained the pool and started to take down the screens and put up the storms, they went to see their doctors. They were given tonics and vitamins, books, charts and thermometers, and they learned the days they needn't and the days they must. There was nothing to worry about; they could make fun of the doctors and themselves, invent names for different positions, send each other alerting telegrams. It was a pretty good job, being ordered to do that which they most enjoyed.

Important as it was, baby-making could only take up so much of Lila's time. The rest of it dragged. She felt the lack of something to work at, but a performing career or any other long-term project was out of the question. Then, Nancy Malone mentioned to Lila that she and another woman Lila knew had started doing volunteer work at the diocesan nursing home and were finding it rewarding. It sounded good to Lila, but working the same place as her friends sounded too social, so she located a home in the far reaches of Queens and signed herself up for Mondays and Thursdays until "things changed" as she told the director.

She threw herself into the work. While other volunteers sat at the reception desk, wheeled carts of magazines around the home and gave classes in drawing, Lila went into the rooms of women too sick in body or spirit to join the communal activities. She listened to those who talked and spoke or read to those who didn't. Sometimes she would merely sit in silence while a wrinkled hand gripped hers so tightly that it hurt.

As fall turned into winter, the tension grew. Each page of the calendar became a log of failure, which was torn off and shredded at the end of the month. They began to bicker over trifles. Worst of all, making love, once so joyful, was becoming a chore that seldom brought Lila to climax. For present purposes, it was only Willie's that counted, and, as soon as that happened, they would pull apart, and he would roll away from her and go to the bathroom while she lay on her back to conserve the precious fluid. And still no success.

At Easter, they went to Miami for the first time, left their schedules at home, golfed, played tennis, fished and swam every day until they were exhausted and made love only when they felt like it. Their pleasure in each other returned, and they knew that this was it, at last. Sure enough, a few days after their return to New York, the magic day came and went, and, five days later, although Lila knew it was too soon and didn't dare say anything to Willie, she couldn't resist calling Margo to share her joy.

As she awoke the next morning, Willie already gone to work, Lila felt the familiar signals of her returning period. She refused to allow them, but lay still, tightening every muscle, closing every orifice, willing herself to go back to that wonderful yesterday when she could imagine new life within her. But her will was not enough, and all she accomplished was adding the embarrassment of dealing with the stained sheets to the pain of her loss.

She dragged herself out of bed, showered, dressed, stripped the bed, balled the sheets in the laundry basket and called Margo to tell her, in a leaden voice, that it had been a false alarm. Margo took the first train into town, bundled Lila into a taxi and dragged her through Bergdorf Goodman and Bonwit Teller and then to the Luau Room where she hid her among the vegetation and poured Mai Tais into her until Lila found herself flying for the first time since San Diego. But this time, there was something she wanted to say.

"It's all his fault, that son-of-a-bitch." She pronounced it loudly and clearly. Two elderly ladies in large-brimmed hats at a neighboring table turned in alarm. .

"Whose fault, Lila?"

"Willie. You remember him, Margo, my husband, Willie?"

"Hush yourself, Lila. People are looking at you. What are you talking about? Willie's not a son-of-a-bitch."

Infuriated, Lila shouted "He is so. Willie Burke is a son-of-a-bitch."

The room went silent. Lila clapped her hand to her mouth as the maitre d' hurried to their table. "Madame, this is impossible. You have to leave immediately."

Lila shook her head. "I'm sorry, Captain." She tried to get up, but her legs didn't seem to work, and she slumped back into the banquette. "It won't happen again."

"No, no, Madame. You must leave, now, or I'll be obliged to call the police."

"Excuse me, Captain. Could I have just a tiny, little word with you?" Margo purred, beckoning with her soft white hand cupped in invitation.

"I'm terribly sorry Madame," he responded firmly but took a step towards Margo's side of the table.

"Captain? Would you." She drew out the last word, her open lips quivering as the hand continued to beckon. He took another step, and she leaned forward to meet him.

"My sister has just learned that her broker in London has stolen a large sum of money from her. The shock has caused her to use language I am sure has never before passed her lips." Margo's hand dropped and fumbled with the clasp of her pocketbook. "If you could exercise the Christian charity of disregarding this unfortunate occurrence, I personally assure you that there will be no further disturbance."

The maitre d' took the last step as Margo's thumb and index finger rose above the level of the table. Lila could see something green between them for just a moment before the maitre d's hand swept smoothly over Margo's.

"Very well, Madame. On your assurance, we shall forget the matter." He bowed and left.

Margo turned to Lila. "Are you all right, Lila?"

Lila looked down at her glass. "No. But I won't make another scene."

Margo fished her cigarette case and lighter out of her pocketbook. "I hope not, sweetie. I don't have another fifty in here. Now, what was that all about? If you want to tell me, that is."

Lila had never told anyone the whole story. Things had seemed to work out for the best. Why talk about them? But now, if it turned out that she and Willie couldn't have children, she didn't know how she would feel. She reached over and took one of Margo's cigarettes and lit it. Maybe it would help her to tell Margo.

"What are you doing? You don't smoke."

"Just trying to calm myself. Yes, I do want to tell you." She stubbed out the cigarette. "I don't believe Willie, and I are going to have children. And it'll be because of Willie."

Lila went through the whole story, stopping sometimes to control waves of sadness and anger. At the end, they were both in tears and clung to each other on the banquette, surrounded by little paper parasols and uneaten rumaki, until their breathing returned to normal.

Margo lit a cigarette and offered one to Lila.

"No, thanks. I forgot how terrible they taste."

"I owe you an apology, darlin'. I've been thinking all along that you had everything your way: looks, brains, money, the perfect husband. I'd hate you if you weren't so damn nice. Have the doctors said anything?"

"Not yet, but I don't think it's going to happen."

"Now, don't be silly, child. It's just a year. These things sometimes take a while. There can't be anything wrong with Willie. Just look at the man."

"Margo? Can I ask you something?"

"Like, why don't I have children?"

"Uh huh." Lila looked down at the table.

"We don't talk about this, but Mike was married before in New Orleans and has a son named Victor who's close to thirty. Mike's wife was crazy but not enough to be put away, or Mike wouldn't go to court to do it. Whichever. She threw him out of the house, wouldn't hardly let Mike see Victor when he was growing up and turned him against Mike. When Mike wanted to marry me, the bitch wouldn't give him a divorce unless we both swore not to have children."

Lila put her hand on Margo's. "I can't believe God would hold you to such an oath."

Margo shook her head. "You're forgetting, Lila. Before God, Mike is still married to Annemarie. Anyway, I couldn't bring myself to push Mike, and, by now, it's too late."

"Oh, Margo," Lila reached for her friend, but Margo pushed her away.

"Now, don't get all mushy about it, it's long past, and I've never regretted marrying Mike in spite of it. Let's get out of here."

Lila went home, took two aspirins for her headache and lay down with a cold washcloth on her forehead. She had allowed the thought that children might not come, had done so mostly to ward off the bad luck that came to people who were too confident of the good. With fearsome clarity, she realized that much of her strength over the past five years had come from the promise of those future children. What would help her now, if Willie couldn't fulfill that promise?

Was that possible? Lila remembered last night. How vigorously he bounced through the door, picked her up and held her off the floor as he kissed her. How ferociously he attacked his dinner relishing every bite. How cheerfully he related the events of his day. How passionately he caressed her body. How much he loved her and how much she loved him. Margo was right. They just needed more time. Lila focused on that thought and, when Willie came home, met him with a cheerful smile even as she presented her cheek instead of her lips to his kiss, their signal of her body's change. Nothing in his face or voice showed Lila a reaction, but he was a trifle slow in hanging up his coat in the closet.

As far as Lila knew, only a handful of Willie's family knew of Gloria's existence. Most people assumed the continued flatness of Lila's belly to be the result of some deficiency in her plumbing, never dreaming that the handsome, athletic Willie, lover of many women before Lila, could have anything wrong with him. She had been given much unwanted advice, but she held her peace, until, the following weekend, an elderly cousin of Willie's mother suggested Lila undertake a pilgrimage to Lourdes to cure her barrenness. When Lila recounted this to Willie, she was astonished to discover that he was starting to think that something must have happened to her during Gloria's birth that was preventing a present conception. After all, didn't he prove his virility almost nightly?

That was too much. Lila demanded that they see specialists. Even then, it was not until Lila was pronounced U.S. Prime breeding stock, that Willie consented to submit his equipment for examination and testing.

The leading expert was in Boston, and they made a vacation out of it to lighten the pressure. They checked into the Parker House, spent their first day at the Museum of Fine Arts and had dinner at Locke Oeber. The next morning, Willie insisted on going alone to the doctor at 11. Lila sat on a bench in the Common trying to concentrate on a book.

When he hadn't come by 1, she knew it was all over. He would have run to her with good news. It came as no surprise; her heart had known the truth, but her mind had put off the final admission to give herself time to gather her strength.

Was this a punishment? Had Willie been wrong to push her to give up Gloria? Had she been wrong to give in to him? Was God angry with them all? Her mother and James Burke dead. She and Willie childless. Would something happen to John and Catherine? For one shameful moment, Lila tried to imagine some event short of death or terrible illness that would force them to give Gloria back to her. No. She must not think that way. Gloria was having a wonderful life, and she and Willie still might have one as well. Without children to share their love, they would just have to love each other more.

It was almost two when she got up to meet Willie coming toward her on the long path from Tremont Street. That was not the direction in which the doctor's office lay, and she was not surprised to smell whiskey when he kissed her.

"I'm sorry to keep you waiting, darling girl, but the son of a bitch wasn't even there at eleven o'clock. 'Tied up at the hospital,' they said. Cutting off some poor sod's nuts, most likely, and enjoying every minute."

"That's all right," Lila replied lightly. "I had my book." Let Willie tell it his own way; she wasn't going to question him.

"He sure seemed pleased with himself while he was just about cutting mine off."

Lila took his hand. "It's all right, Willie."

"Instead of coming right out with it like a man, he has to put on his glasses and read a bunch of numbers and fancy words from a report in that voice they have, you know, so you can tell that they don't care whether you live or die.

"'Low motility,' he says a couple of times, talking about—you know, my little things.

"'Did you say 'low mobility?' I ask him.

"'Motility, Mr. Burke,' he says then comes out with a long definition that must came from a medical dictionary."

Lila could see Willie was pushing himself. This was a story he didn't want to tell. He'd probably worked it out in the bar to break it to her gradually.

"'You mean they're not active enough, or something?' I say.

"The bastard grins at me. 'Precisely, Mr. Burke. You have enough sperm, but they're not active enough to penetrate the ovum.'"

Lila started to speak, but Willie held up his hand.

"I'd had about enough, but I had to get it right. 'Does that mean I can't be a father?'

"He studies the report for about thirty seconds, takes off his glasses, frowns, looks up at the ceiling, then back at me." Willie looked at Lila expectantly.

She had very little heart for the charade but managed "What did he say?"

Willie put his arm around Lila. " 'It's unlikely, Mr. Burke, but I wouldn't say impossible.' Do you hear that, darling girl? I was starting to think the jig was up, but we've still got a chance." He even managed a grin.

Remarkable, thought Lila. He's crushed by this, but nobody else would know it. She tried to match his grin but failed. "I don't know, Willie. I guess some hope is better than none."

"It'll happen, Lila. You'll see. Come on, let's go home. It's starting to rain." He took her arm and pulled her along toward the hotel. After a few steps, his pace began to slow, and he stopped and turned Lila toward him. His face was wet from the drizzle.

"It's my fault, Lila. I'm so sorry." His voice was broken.

She took his head in her hands. "It's not your fault, darling."

He shook his head free. "You thought I was a real man. "

Suddenly her pain was not important, her anger gone. Only her love for Willie mattered, and he was suffering, and she could help him. She took his head again and pulled him to her. "You're the best man I ever met, Willie Burke, and if there's a better one, I don't want to meet him. Come along, now."

Willie straightened up and smiled, but his arm was heavy on her shoulders as they returned slowly back to the hotel.

•　　　　　•　　　　　•

It's time for Lila's morning walk. In a small closet concealed by bookshelves, she keeps a collection of sun hats, sweaters, and footwear so she can go directly into the garden through the French doors without having to go upstairs to her room. It's warm enough, so she doesn't need a sweater, but she puts an old blue cardigan on anyway. She likes the heat; that's why she stays in Florida all year, now. But, she has to be careful of the sun. There have been several skin cancers already. Her mood is down, so she looks for a hat to cheer herself. She chooses a straw boater with a broad brim and red ribbons and, using the closet mirror, sets it at a jaunty angle.

In the garden, she puts her fingers to her mouth and whistles. A few seconds later a brown standard poodle trots around the corner up to Lila and sits down. Pumpernickel is fourteen, now, and has slowed down. A few years ago, he'd have come at a full run ending with a jump to kiss her. But he gets up and heels, without command, when she starts her walk. They work their way twice around the grounds.

After twenty minutes she stops and lies down on the chaise in the shade by the fountain. Pumpernickel takes a drink and stretches out, panting, next to her. In the summer, she comes here every afternoon; this is the coolest place on the property. She had to put in air-conditioning for Willie and to keep servants, but never runs it when she's alone in a room. The shade, the slight breeze and the splashing of the jets from the four bronze dolphins around the rim of the fountain, with the waking Aphrodite in the middle, provide all of Lila's cooling needs.

She would not have the fountain, but for Margo, who had come for a week that first ghastly winter Lila spent in the house. She had insisted that improving the grounds would improve Lila's spirits and dragged her south for miles along U.S. 1, looking at granite benches, bronze nymphs and antebellum Negro boys with grins on their faces and hitching rings in their outstretched hands. Even Margo was ready to give up until, at Hansen's Ornamental and Funeral, she spotted a plump bronze leg sticking out from under a pile of iron chairs. She prodded Mr. Hansen, as tired of the whole thing as Lila, into removing the chairs, disclosing a badly scratched, life-sized female nude, built to the standards of the Venus of Willendorf. She had originally been seated, leaning back on her hands, one leg extended, the other drawn halfway to her majestic bosoms. For the moment, she lay on her side, a jagged stump, the size of a small stack of poker chips, protruding from her divine *derrière*, showing where she had been cruelly torn from her place of repose.

Even Mr. Hansen was puzzled when Margo began negotiations to buy this piece of junk, although he recovered enough to get her up to twice her original bid. It might have been more, had he not been afraid that Lila would succeed in dragging Margo back into the car without her prize.

"You are a crazy person, Margo Stone," Lila said when they headed north again, the statue's head in the front seat, her leg sticking out of the rear window. " What on earth am I going to do with this thing?"

Margo looked at her watch. "Drive faster; we only have fifteen minutes."

Lila increased speed automatically, before complaining "Fifteen minutes for what, for Crissake? Are you nuts?"

Margo was patient, "Until it closes, darling, now drive until I tell you to stop." Ten minutes later, in a squeal of brakes, they pulled up at the junk shop, which had been their first stop. "Stay in the car," Margo commanded, "before you spoil the whole thing."

By then, Lila was too puzzled to say anything more. She waited patiently until two workmen emerged from the store carrying something heavy wrapped in a tarpaulin, which they managed to fit into the trunk by leaving it open and tieing it with a rope. When Lila got it back to the house and removed the tarpaulin, she found the matching base of the fountain, and it was a simple matter to weld the goddess into place. When it was first turned on, Margo walked around it smugly nodding her head. "Now we know how she always managed to wake revirginized. I name this statue 'The Divine Douche.'"

It is as ugly as anything Lila has ever seen, and she will adore it to her last day.

When her watch reads 11:40 she rises and returns to the French doors. She gives a biscuit from her pocket to Pumpernickel, sends him back to his water dish by the kitchen and steps back into the house.

•   •   •

In the following weeks, Willie fluctuated between self-berating despair and blind confidence in the remotely possible and brought these mood swings to their physical relationship. There were times when he was lustful almost to the point of mania and others when he would shrink from her as though there were something perverse in making love without the possibility of an issue. Lila lost sympathy. What was wrong with the man? Willie had met with serious problems before: the war, his father's death, building the business. He had dealt with them decisively and constructively. Bitterly, she recalled how forceful he had been with her about Gloria. What right did he have to go about whining like a spoilt child who won't accept that "no" is no and go on with his life? As she was doing now and as she had done before.

She thought of some of the terrible things that had happened to the old women she saw at the nursing home. All were sick or injured, one crippled by years of beatings, another blind from an acid attack fifty years ago, a third permanently scarred from the fire that had killed her two small children. Most were alone in the world, bereaved by death or abandonment. But almost all tried to make the best of it, welcoming Lila with smiles and kisses, absurdly grateful for a new comb or a handful of hard candy, clucking over the latest perils of their favorite soap opera characters. Willie's life was a party compared to theirs.

Summer came, but matters didn't improve. Willie behaved well in company but, alone with her, was stiff and polite at best, at other times, sulky and touchy. Nights together in New York were the worst; there wasn't enough room in the apartment for both of them. Lila discontinued her Thursday stint at the nursing home. On Mondays, Willie, grumbling at the inconvenience, dropped her off in Queens in the morning and picked her up on the way back to Long Island. One hot Tuesday, Willie stayed in town alone, and Lila went to a double feature in Great Neck with Margo. Later, she was surprised to find that she had no trouble sleeping alone. They did it again the next Tuesday, and it became routine. By the end of July, Lila wasn't coming to Manhattan at all; Willie would drive in Monday morning and come back Thursday night, and Lila did the easy drive to and from the nursing home in her own car. She found a Monday night series of lectures on art. Tuesday was Mike's poker night, and Margo and Lila went to the movies. Wednesday night she was alone.

Lila was uncomfortable the first Wednesday. She prowled the house making notes of things that needed work. When she stopped to check the liquor closet to see if they were running short of anything, she came out with a bottle of Canadian Club and brought it up to her bedroom, looking around her as though there were anyone there who cared. The Burkes kept a little refrigerator in their bedroom with sodas and juices and ice, and she poured herself a drink and found some music on the radio, and it wasn't so bad anymore, even if she didn't let herself go flying. The next week, though, she did, and it was fine. She didn't get sick, this time. Her stomach seemed to tolerate C.C. better than Scotch. As she had in San Diego, she kept her drinking secret, even from Margo, and took no more of the Sangria than she had been taking.

One Wednesday, after lunch, she decided, on the moment, to take the train to New York, spend the night in the apartment, pick up some special things for their weekend guests on Thursday and drive back with Willie. When she called Willie's office, she was told he was out at a job for the afternoon but would call in. She left word that she would meet him at the apartment at six. When she arrived, there was no sign of Willie. There was no answer on the office phone. He was not at his club or at his mother's. She called the Burke house. No, they hadn't heard from Mr. Burke. By seven-thirty, it was obvious he hadn't gotten her message and could be out with any one of a dozen cronies, so, cursing Willie, his temporary telephone operator, and her own impetuousness, Lila ordered up some food and waited for his return.

At midnight, she went to bed, but couldn't sleep and got up after twenty minutes. She poked around the apartment, then sat down and tried to read, but something strange nagged at her. She retraced her steps and, as she passed through the foyer, realized what it was. The Wednesday morning *New York Times* rolled up in a rubber band, lay on the little stand by the elevator. Willie always began his day by sitting on the toilet with the *Times*. Well, maybe they had delivered it late that morning. Hating what she was doing, but unable to stop herself, Lila went to the bathroom and opened the clothes hamper. One undershirt, one pair of shorts, one dress shirt and one pair of socks: all worn in from Long Island on Monday. The maid didn't do the laundry until Thursday. Unless Willie had forgotten to change this morning, he had not come home Tuesday night. An all-night card game, as in his younger days? That might explain Tuesday, but then he'd be exhausted and home early tonight.

The answer was obvious, but she couldn't think about it now. She needed time, and Willie might walk in at any moment. She got dressed, made the bed, threw the remains of her dinner down the incinerator and let herself out, taking anything that would show she had been in the apartment. She sat in an all-night cafeteria in Penn Station until the 5:45 A.M. to Westbury, picked up her car at the station and was home at seven. She slept until nine-thirty when Willie called to ask if she wanted him to bring anything out with him that evening. She thanked him for his consideration and gave him a small list. He said nothing about her message from the day before; if he had, she had a story made up about missing the train and then changing her mind. What if he had known but said nothing? The idea was too much like a Hitchcock movie.

She skipped breakfast and met with the cook and the housekeeper to discuss the logistics of the coming weekend. Then she made a few telephone calls, drove to the club, and hit golf balls on the driving range for an hour. In the locker room, she bumped into a new member who seemed nice, and they lunched together on the terrace overlooking the smaller children splashing in the wading pool.

It was not until she returned home, poured an iced tea and took it to the bench at the intersection of the stone boundary walls at the farthest corner of the property, that she allowed herself to focus on the problem. To her surprise, she didn't feel hurt, just furious that Willie could do something so stupid. He still loved her as much as ever; there was no question of that. Nor had he given her any reason to believe he was bored with her and in need of the excitement of a strange woman. He had had enough different women before they met.

It had to be the discovery of his sterility. He was trying to prove his manhood by getting another woman. It was so ridiculous. Willie, of all people, thinking he had to prove something. Competent, confident, forceful Willie, the exemplar of masculinity. And it was all a pose. Underneath, he was as insecure and unsure as anyone else. Well, he had fooled her along with the rest of the world. What should she do about it? The question stumped her, but she knew who to go to for advice. She returned to the house and called Margo who told her to come right over.

Margo let Lila speak without interruption, in itself a unique occurrence. Lila felt foolish describing her early morning departure from the apartment, but Margo clapped her hands and whistled approvingly. Lila finished and waited for a response.

"Well?" said Margo after a minute or so. "What are you going to do?"

Lila was nonplused. "I thought you could tell me."

Margo laughed kindly. "You've handled it so superbly so far I didn't think you needed any help. What do you want to do? Pack your things and leave him forever? If so, wait until after you've seen a good lawyer."

Could she lose Willie, too? The thought was insupportable. "I don't think I want that."

"Good. You're not going to do better. My God, who would think it? You know, of course, child, half the women on the North Shore have been trying to get Willie into their bedrooms, and no one has come close. I know two women who asked him explicitly; he could have had them separately or together."

"Who were they?" asked Lila, horrified.

"Secrets of the confessional, darling. You should be relieved to know that I may repeat gossip I hear second hand but never anything told to me directly."

"What if he wants to leave me?"

Margo waved that question aside. "Stop fishing for reassurance. The man adores you. You put your finger right on it. He expected to be a bigger stud than Man O'War, and now he's trying to prove it some other way. He'll find out soon enough that it only makes him feel worse."

"You mean I shouldn't do anything? Just ignore it?"

"I didn't say that. But don't be in a hurry to put him on trial. People will say and do anything when they're attacked. You want him to come to his senses and cut it out, not to stand in front of you lying and making up excuses he ends up believing."

Lila frowned. "I don't know. I want to do something."

"Well, for one," Margo said sweetly, "you might go into New York with him next week."

That was helpful, but Lila sensed that it wasn't enough, and, while driving home an idea came to her. She had the cook make up a chicken salad, gave her money and told her to take the rest of the staff out to dinner and the movies, not to return before eleven if they wanted to keep their jobs. When Willie arrived at seven, she gave him a perfunctory kiss, took his packages and ordered him to take a swim before dinner. She put the packages away then went to the pool and stopped around the corner of the cabana where Willie couldn't see her. Her idea didn't seem so good, now; she didn't have the right spirit for it, but she shed her clothes in the growing dark and slipped naked into the pool. Willie, unaware, was taking a breather holding on at the deep end when Lila surfaced and wrapped her arms and legs around him.

Willie's startled reaction almost drowned her. But he got her out of the pool onto one of the mats by the side and, after she spit out the water, he carried her up to their room and made love to her with a strange awkwardness, as though it were their first time. Afterward, he lay his head in her lap and wept while she stroked his hair. Lila made no accusation and Willie made no confession, but she knew she had him back. She supposed that was a good thing.

A few days later, Lila drove over to Margo's for tennis and found two men blasting the ball back and forth at each other. The elder of the two, Curt Baron, was Margo's old mixed doubles partner. He and Margo were starting to practice for the senior events at the grass court tournaments next summer when they would be forty. The younger man, Hank Hindman, about thirty, was a professional who would partner Lila against them.

They practiced for two hours. Lila was surprised at how serious Margo was, she who never stopped joking whether she won or lost, who never cared how well she played. Today, she yelled and cursed at every shot she missed. The session ended after she mis-hit an overhead, flung her racket against the wire fence and collapsed on the bench beside the court sobbing with frustration. Lila headed over to console her, but Curt waved her away. "What did I tell you?" he said to Hank as they toweled off, standing about ten feet from Margo. "She's still just a dumb Cajun who handles a racquet like a crawfish net and thinks that, because she has a nice ass, she doesn't have to work at the game."

The sobbing from the bench stopped abruptly. Curt turned to Lila. "You saw that time she let Hank's return go by without even waving at it and yelled at me. I always had to cover more than my share of the court, but fat as she's gotten now, it's ridiculous."

Margo sprang from the bench and flung herself upon Curt knocking him over on the grass and falling on top of him. Lila and Hank stood frozen in shock, and then Margo and Curt were hugging and kissing each other and laughing like children.

They helped each other up and stood hand in hand. "Isn't she great," Curt asked, "when you get her mad enough?"

"I was so afraid," Margo responded, "that you'd become a gentleman who'd try to make me feel good about playing lousy. Come on, drinks are on the house." As they went in, she whispered to Lila, "Did you hear that? He still likes my ass."

She went on until they were out of the shower and in the pool where Lila shut her up by pushing her head under. They splashed around for a minute, then heard a voice calling, "Margo, where are the suits?" It was Curt, wrapped in a towel, standing at the top of the stairs to the dressing room.

"Forget it," Margo called, "we don't use them." Curt waved an acknowledgment and came down the stairs, with Hank behind him.

"Margo," Lila whispered urgently. "What are you doing?"

"We don't have any suits for them. Do you expect me to bar them from the pool?"

"But we aren't wearing suits either."

"See, that just makes it even. Now don't go making a big thing out of it, sweetie. God knows, you've got nothing to be ashamed of, even if your tits are a mite small." She jiggled her own breasts in the water and made a face at Lila, who turned to hide her embarrassment and decided to swim a few laps to compose herself. Curt and Hank entered the water and swam over to Margo, and the three of them trod water and chatted casually.

When they got out of the pool, each of the men looked her over, briefly, but she thought, approvingly. To her surprise, that gave her pleasure, but she was quick to wrap a towel around herself before sitting down at the Sangria table. The men followed suit and even Margo, who had already taken her drink to a chaise, made a gesture towards modesty by pulling a towel across her lap and over one breast. They drank and talked tennis for an hour, took another swim and dressed and left. Driving home, Lila felt silly about her first reaction. It had all been quite innocent, even healthy, the four clean, athletic bodies casually displayed like Greek sculptures.

They practiced three times a week after that. The game was the strongest Lila had ever played in, and she enjoyed it greatly. She also enjoyed the postmortems, which were always lively, as the Sangria pitcher emptied. Criticisms would be presented and rebutted in vociferous argument, and suggestions on tactics demonstrated. Securing the pudicitous towels became of little concern.

One afternoon, Margo and Curt emerged from the pool, dried off and, without a word, walked up the stairs together to the dressing rooms each carrying two glasses of Sangria. Lila stared in distress at the retreating bare backsides, then looked at Hank, who shrugged his ignorance and buried his head in a newspaper.

A half-hour later, Margo, wrapped in a towel, reappeared and descended the stairs passing Hank who went up to change. She calmly lay down on the chaise next to Lila's.

Lila let her wait a bit. Then, "Take it off."

Margo was nonplused. "What?"

"The towel. Take off the towel, slut."

Margo stood up, took off the towel and tossed it into a chair, and sat down on the chaise, now facing Lila, her feet on the floor and the palms of her hands on the edge of the chaise ready to spring up, if attacked.

Lila inspected Margo. "No bites, no scratches. How considerate."

Margo squirmed. "Lila."

"Nothing shows; you're not even breathing hard."

"I'm sorry if you're upset."

"Upset? You have no idea how upset I am, Margo. What a terrible thing you've done. I don't know if I can still be your friend."

"But, you know I have affairs. Mike knows; everyone knows. What's so terrible?"

Lila got up and looked down sternly at the cringing Margo. "I'll tell you what's terrible, you tramp. While you were up in the dressing room, happily committing adultery, I had to sit down here bare-ass naked in front of Hank, while he pretended to read the paper. Besides, I had to pee and couldn't very well go upstairs where you were."

Margo's shoulders collapsed with relief. "Oh, you poor darling. I'm so sorry. Go now. They're in the men's room, and the women's is open."

"I don't have to, now, sweetie. I went in the pool." Margo whooped so loud that Hank stuck his head out the door. Lila waved him back inside with her racket.

When they calmed down, Margo addressed Lila seriously. "You know there's no good reason you couldn't have a little fun with Hank, yourself. He would obviously like to, and it doesn't have to be a big deal."

"Margo! I thought you liked Willie."

Margo got up and poured a drink before answering. "I adore Willie. But he hasn't done right by you, and it's not the same marriage as it was a year ago. Willie's had his affair. Sooner or later you're going to have one too, if only to balance the books. No, don't say it'll never happen. I've been around too long. It always does. But when it comes, you don't want to do something dumb like leaving Willie for a man who won't be half as good to you. You can go to bed with the Hanks of this world just as easily as you play tennis with them, if you want to."

"If I want to," Lila repeated and left it there. She was disappointed in Margo. Perhaps she had thought that enlisting Lila in the army of the unfaithful would validate her own infidelities. So, ignoring Margo's teasing, Lila brought a little backgammon set with her to their next practice session, and, afterward when Curt and Margo again went up to the dressing room, she had Hank give her a lesson. She didn't learn too much, but it passed the time. She didn't mind that he stared at her breasts while she was shaking the dice.

The next few sessions went the same way, but one Monday, Hank got a charley horse in his calf, and they had to stop early. After their swim, Margo and Curt retired from the pool area. While Lila set up the backgammon board, Hank sat back on a chaise massaging his leg.

"Does that bother you?" Lila asked.

"It's not too bad, but I'd like to work it out before I do much walking on it."

"Here, let me do it. I learned how in the theater." Hank rolled over onto his stomach, and Lila sat on the chaise next to him and began to knead the tightened muscles. Once or twice he winced, but she found out how hard she could press without causing pain.

"Hey, you're terrific," Hank said. "Do you do backs too?"

"Sure, why not?" Lila shifted to the middle of the chaise and leaned over and began to work on his shoulders. Hank's skin was supple over the bands of muscles that rolled like a cat's under her hands. He uttered little, contented grunts every time she pressed, and she felt the warmth where his hip touched the side of her leg. As she leaned further to reach his neck, her nipples brushed against his back, and his body vibrated like a plucked string.

Amazed at how easy it was, she climbed on top of him and molded herself into his back, pressing her lips into the crook of his neck. She could taste the salt of the new sweat on his skin and smell the chlorine in his hair. Hank reached for her hand and brought it to his lips. They lay like that for a bit, then she awkwardly climbed off and helped him to his feet and up the stairs to the men's dressing room where they lay down on the day bed.

Hank took a prophylactic from his wallet and knelt beside her and began to run his hands and lips over her body. As he moved his mouth between her legs, Lila realized the truth; she didn't want Hank or any man other than

Willie. She was too embarrassed, however, to say anything and made what she hoped were appropriate responses. Hank was not as easily fooled as Willie, however, and paused.

"Do you want me to stop?" he whispered. "It's OK."

His concern touched something in Lila, and she responded by pressing against him. Encouraged, Hank resumed, then after a few minutes, came up onto the bed on top of Lila.

"Whenever you're ready," she said softly, and he began to move,. Lila with him, accommodating herself to the body upon her. It was pleasant, but wanting the passion Willie could arouse, and she knew she would not have an orgasm. When Hank was finished, and they were squeezed together side by side on the narrow bed, trying to light a cigarette without getting burnt, he thanked her with a respectful gravity, and Lila responded in the same manner.

Once was enough, however. It wasn't that she felt guilty; Margo had been right about balancing the books. Continuing with Hank, however, wouldn't help Lila achieve a better life with Willie, which was all she wanted. So, when they emerged from the pool after the next practice session, and Hank pointed toward the stairs to the dressing rooms, Lila shook her head slightly, and they sat down at the table with their Sangria and backgammon set. And that was the end of it: as easy as the beginning. Margo was right again.

•   •   •

Lila and Willie moved back into the apartment a week after Labor Day and began a time of recuperation. Encouraged by business successes, Willie started to regain his self-confidence. His first cooperative apartment house sold out before it was finished, and several other projects looked promising. Without Lila's knowledge, he went to another fertility specialist who told him, flatly, he would never have a child.

He was calm when he told Lila. "That seems to be it, Lila. That first doctor was just trying to let me down easy. You knew it, didn't you?"

"Yes, Willie. But you had to find it out yourself. So there'll just be the two of us. If we love each other enough, then two will be enough."

"I'm so sorry, love, I—"

"Shush, Willie, you don't need to say anymore." She came up to him and put a finger to his lips.

He caught her wrist and kissed her hand before lowering it. "I'll love you always with all my heart, and I promise I'll make it up to you somehow."

There was no more talk of children. Willie quietly told family and friends, so that Lila would no longer be badgered. He drew even closer to Lila than before. They avoided parties and went to restaurants, theaters, concerts and sporting events by themselves. They bought a television set and spent quiet evenings at home, and much of their old passion returned.

In short, Willie was where he should be, even if a few months late getting there. In those few months, however, Lila had seen his weaknesses. No longer was he her god, all-wise, all-good, all-powerful, and, although she thought she still loved him, love's sweet flavor had soured with resentment over the past and apprehension over the future. She kept her changed feelings from Willie, didn't discuss them with Margo and tried not to think about them herself. What would be the point?

One morning, there was a letter from John. As always, she left it with Willie's mail on the table by the living room window with his after-work Scotch and soda. She was at the piano, that evening, fooling with a Billie Holliday number when he opened it and called out to her.

"Hey, listen for a minute. John's coming to New York for his company at the end of the November. What would you think of his bringing Catherine and Gloria along for Thanksgiving?"

Her hands came crashing down on the keys. "What?"

"Jesus, Lila. Don't break the damn thing. I just thought it might be a good thing if Cath and Gloria came with John."

The old pain struck her. "How can you - - -?"

Willie came over to the piano and put his hands on Lila's shoulders. "I'm sorry, darling. I just thought that maybe, after all these years - - -. Forget I said anything."

Lila sat in silent confusion. For years, she had forbidden herself any thought of seeing Gloria again. Lila had a niece in St. Louis about to have her eighth birthday but had never met her and never would. That subject was settled, and Willie had no business bringing it up now.

But of course, he got around to it again the next morning. He never gave up easily on anything he wanted; Lila couldn't fathom why he wanted this. He waited until the cereal bowls had been cleared and the second cups of coffee poured before he spoke.

"You know, Lila, it's possible that seeing that Gloria has become a healthy, happy child will settle any doubts you might have that you did the right thing."

She hadn't slept much, waves of memories had swept over her. As each receded, it left an aching void. Now, there would be no new babies to fill it. The yearning weakened her resolution. Maybe, just for a moment, even only as Aunt Lila... But the danger was so great.

"I don't know if I could stand it."

"Whatever you say, darling girl."

Why was he doing this? Did he want to see her suffer? "I'm only human, Willie."

"All right, then, we'll forget it." Willie took a last sip of coffee and closed his newspaper. He didn't get up but stared at Lila expectantly.

What else could she say? "Besides, John would never agree to it." But he did. Lila, immobilized between hope and fear, took no part in the negotiations and wouldn't even let Willie report on their progress, until one evening when he rushed into the living room from his study.

"John's on the phone. He's agreed to bring Catherine and Gloria, but he wants to talk to you first." He pulled Lila from the couch and dragged her to the study.

"Hello, John."

"How are you, Lina?"

"Fine. And you?"

"We're good. Uh. About this trip to New York. We've only talked to Willie. Do <u>you</u> want us all to come?"

"Yes," she said without pausing to think. Well, there it was.

"Forgive me, Lina, but I have to ask this. You know Gloria knows nothing. You'll be Aunt Lila, right?"

Lila kept her voice steady. "Of course, John. You can trust me."

"Ah, Lina. I'm sorry. I shouldn't have asked. It's just that she's our whole life, now, and I'm terrified at the thought of something bad happening. I worry when she's five minutes late coming down to breakfast. Catherine's better about it. Right away she said that we should come if you wanted us to and that you being a part of Gloria's life would only bring her good."

Sweet, loving, Catherine: were you thinking that when you tore her away from me? Lila swallowed the acid in her throat. "Thank you, John. And thank Cath."

So it was decided, good or bad. Lila went to the library and hunted through books and articles on eight-year-olds, their attitudes, and interests. She must be affectionate, she told herself, but not too emotional, not just to avoid alarming John but also not to discomfit Gloria. She rehearsed her role before her mirror and steeled herself for the inevitable bad moments by focusing upon the worst of her memories without changing expression.

Being prepared helped, but she was still racked by anxiety as she and Willie, and a porter stood on the platform when the train pulled in. She saw John step down three cars away and turn to offer his hand to a little girl in a red coat. Who was that, Lila wondered. Then it hit her; she had been expecting a year-old baby as though seven days and not seven years had passed.

Lila reached for a column to steady herself. Willie was hugging Gloria, while Catherine was handing suitcases from the train to John, and the porter was pulling his cart toward them. In a moment they would be turning to Lila; she needed time to pull herself together. She opened the clasp of her purse and let it slip from her hand. The contents spilled out onto the concrete, and she dropped to her knees and began to retrieve them along with her composure.

"Aunt Lila? What happened?"

Lila looked up from the last of the coins and found Gloria's face a foot away. Her eyes seemed enormous, the irises so dark a brown they were almost black.

"I dropped my purse, darling. Help me pick up everything."

"What's this for?" Gloria asked, picking up a perfume atomizer.

Lila retrieved the last items and stood up. "It's for putting on perfume. Can you give your Aunt Lila a kiss?"

She bent over and took Gloria's shoulders while Gloria jammed her lips against Lila's cheek. Lila wanted to hug her child and enfold her totally, but how could she do that to this unfamiliar body? She dropped her hands, and Gloria stepped back.

"You smell good. Can I try that thing with the perfume?"

"It's an atomizer. If it's all right with your mother. Cath, it's so good to see you." Catherine was a little plump, now, but her skin was still unwrinkled, her expression still calm. She was standing back, leaning slightly towards Lila, waiting for a signal. A surge of remembered love overrode the bitterness, and Lila opened her arms to meet her.

"Can I, Mommy?" Gloria demanded. How beautiful she was, with those killer eyes set wide apart, a generous mouth and a firm chin. Something in the face was specially familiar, and not from the photographs. Then Lila remembered. It was the nose: Joe's wonderful Valentino nose, in miniature, smooth and straight. Of course, Lila could never tell Gloria that, could tell her nothing. Fortunately, her dark brown hair was straight (again from her father), or she would look nothing like Catherine, who stepped back and smiled indulgently.

"A little, later, when you're dressed up for dinner."

John frowned. "Don't be in such a hurry to grow up, pussy."

Gloria stuck her tongue out at him, and he grinned. It was obviously a running joke between them.

"Just take your time and eat your vegetables and someday you'll be just as beautiful as your Aunt Lila." He froze at his tactlessness. She glanced at Willie; he was aghast. My God, she thought, they're all even more nervous than I am.

"Why thank you, John. When did you get to be so gallant?" She offered her cheek for a brotherly kiss. "Willie, let's get these people to the hotel so they can rest a little before dinner."

The porter took the suitcases out to the car, and they drove to the hotel. Willie went in to get the visitors settled, while Lila went on to their apartment. Roiled at once by joy and grief, she took off her dress, lay down on the big bed and pulled the afghan over herself. When she heard Willie come in the front door, she turned on her side facing away from the door and pretended to be asleep when he came into the room. His questions would have to wait.

"Lila. Wake up." She felt Willie's paw on her shoulder. "It's almost six."

She had actually slept for more than an hour but was even more exhausted than when she had lain down. Her mouth was dry, and she felt a subdued throbbing over her right eye as though someone in her head were plucking a bass in march tempo. She needed an aspirin; a shower might help, too, but she'd have to hurry. She swung her legs over the edge of the bed.

"Is it all right, darling girl?" Willie, in his underwear, sat next to her, put his arm around her shoulders and pulled her to him. He smelled of soap, and the curly hair above the scoop of his undershirt was still damp. Suddenly, she felt nauseous.

"Let me go." She pushed hard against his chest.

He took his arm away, stiffly.

"It's OK. I need a shower, too." She fled to the bathroom and stood over the toilet while the nausea subsided, then got in the shower. When she came out of the bathroom, it was late, and she told Willie she was too rushed to talk to him.

At five minutes past seven, Lila and Willie found the Granatellis waiting in the hotel lobby. Gloria was an adorable little lady in a midnight blue dress with a white collar. She greeted Lila and Willie demurely, but when Lila handed her the atomizer, she squealed with excitement.

"Thank you, Aunt Lila. Can I put it on now? How do you use it?"

"You squeeze the bulb, and it sprays a mist. Put it on your wrists and behind your ears. Careful, just a little."

Gloria followed Lila's instructions and smelled the result. "Mmm." She went to each of the adults and offered her hands. John was last, but instead of smelling her hands, he grabbed her and nuzzled an ear. It took a moment before Gloria started to squirm free.

"Delicious," he announced. "Smells just like roast beef."

"Daddy! Don't be mean. Isn't it nice?" she asked Lila. "I love it."

They went into the dining room, then. Gloria sat between Lila and Willie and chattered away about her school and her cat and her friend, Cindy, who would have to stop talking about her trip to Chicago now that she, Gloria, had been to New York. Lila sat attentively, grateful not to have to do anything more than nod and smile at this beautiful, charming, adorable child. And as she watched and listened, a strange excitement grew. The tilt of Gloria's head when someone was telling her something, the wave of her hand when she rejected string beans, the cascade of her laugh: Lila had known these seven years ago. This child was her baby, and she felt remembered love flow back into the empty place in her heart.

What would this revived love bring her? She didn't know. But she knew she mustn't alarm the others and pushed the question aside for the rest of the meal.

Gloria almost fell asleep over her ice cream, and Catherine took her up to their room, while John finished his dessert and coffee and Willie went to the men's room

Lila and John talked about relatives for a minute or two, then fell silent. John took a last sip of coffee, wiped his mouth, folded his napkin, put his hands together and looked squarely at Lila. This was a moment she had prepared for; there was only one thing she could say.

"You've done a good job, John."

He leaned across the table, took her hand and brought it to his lips. "Thank you, Lina. For everything."

They said no more; then Willie returned, and they parted for the evening.

It was still early when they got home, and Lila went to the piano. Willie draped his jacket and necktie on a chair and brought two snifters of brandy. Reluctantly, Lila closed the lid over the keys and took one of the balloon-shaped glasses. Putting Willie off again would only make the conversation more difficult tomorrow or the next day.

Willie raised his glass. "Here's to the finest lady in the land. You were just wonderful."

Lila touched glasses with him and took a sip.

He became cautious. "Is it all right that they came here?"

"Yes, Willie, it's all right."

"She's a nice little girl, isn't she?"

"Yes, she is." They might have been talking about a child at a neighboring table.

"Will we all have some fun this weekend?"

"Well, we can try."

Lila smiled brightly, and Willie jumped up.

"Great. Well, I want to watch the news at 10. Do you want to come in?"

As simple as that. "No, I think I'll practice for a while. Go ahead." A minute later Lila heard the television go on.

They got up early the next morning for the Macy's parade, went for a carriage ride in Central Park and had Thanksgiving dinner at Rumpelmayers, where Gloria met her first hot fudge sundae, covering it with whipped cream, chocolate sprinkles, and a maraschino cherry. On Friday, while John went to his business meeting and Willie to his office, Lila took Catherine and Gloria to Rockefeller Center, where they watched the giant Christmas tree go up, went ice skating and saw the holiday show at Radio City Music Hall. In the evening they went to Chinatown for dinner where Gloria became an expert with chopsticks and laughed when Catherine dropped her shrimp on the floor. Lila refused to think of the future, and there were no bad moments if Lila didn't count watching Gloria walk away from her into the hotel each night.

Saturday evening, Willie arranged for Gloria to sleep over at the Burkes' apartment, bribing John and Catherine with tickets to _Oklahoma_ and supper and dancing at the Rainbow Room. Gloria insisted on carrying her cardboard suitcase by herself into the guest room Lila had prepared for her. She stopped short as she looked at the bed and saw the stuffed Winnie-the-Pooh Willie had bought that afternoon.

"Is that for me, Aunt Lila?"

"We thought you might like to have a little company to sleep with."

"Ooh, thank you. It's Pooh, isn't it?" She put her suitcase on the bed and picked him up and hugged him. "Now, Pooh, I want you to meet someone. This is Blinky."

She took out of the suitcase the familiar black and white cat. The long lashes that went with the name were gone, and the fur was hatched by the scars of many mendings, but it was the same one. It had stayed with Gloria all these years.

"Aunt Lila? Aunt Lila?"

She felt a tugging at her arm.

"What should I do, Aunt Lila?"

"What, darling?" Lila tried to focus on the moment.

"Which of them should sleep with me?"

"Me, me-ow." Gloria approximated the high whine of a cat as she held Blinky up to Lila.

"I always sleep with her. It should be me, me-ow."

Gloria put Blinky down and snatched up Winnie-the-Pooh and held him up to Lila.

"Poo-poo," she said in a deeper voice appropriate to a bear. "Thith ith my houth and my bed and I should thleep with her."

"You want me to decide?" asked Lila.

"Yeth," said Pooh, shaking his head vigorously. "Tell that ratty old puthycat to get back into the suitcathe where he belongth."

Gloria picked up Blinky in her other hand. "How dare you call me ratty, you big fat slob? Reouwww. I'll scratch your eyes out."

"I'd like to thee you try."

The two of them began to pass back and forth, feinting an attack. "Do something, Aunt Lila?" Gloria implored.

"Hold on, you two. Don't start fighting. Sit down here on the bed, one on each pillow." Gloria, grinning happily, set each one down with a little pat on the head.

"Now, Blinky, tell me something. When you're home, are you always the only one who sleeps in the bed with Gloria?"

Gloria picked up Blinky who scratched his head with one paw as he tried to remember.

"Neowww. Not, always," he said reluctantly.

"Maybe you and Pooh could both sleep with Gloria while she's here."

"Me-meoww? Sleep with him?" Gloria held him up to look over at Pooh.

"Awwwl right, if you say so."

"Now, Pooh, did you hear that? Blinky is being nice. How about you?"

This time Gloria brought Pooh to look Blinky over, then set him back down.

"I gueth so, if he apologitheth for calling me a 'big fat thlob.'"

Blinky jumped up. "You insulted me first, called me 'ratty.'"

Lila clapped her hands. "That's enough, you two. There'll be no more fighting. It's settled. You'll both sleep with Gloria. Now kiss each other and make up."

The two approached each other cautiously, pulling back, then advancing, and finally touched noses and sat back on the pillows.

"You were very good, Aunt Lila," said Gloria. She reached up and gave Lila a hug, then began to take the other things out of the suitcase and put them in the dresser.

For the rest of the evening, Gloria tried to act womanly with Lila, trying on makeup and asking about boys. With Willie, she was more childish. She insisted that he tell her a bedtime story, which he did most willingly. Lila was able to keep her emotions in check, and the only bad moment came when, just before she went to bed, she ducked into Gloria's room and saw on the pillow the sleep-rumpled face, which was the miniature of her own.

The next morning, Lila felt exhausted and listless and allowed herself to be carried along on the ebullient wave of satisfaction that accompanied their farewells, replete with hugs and kisses and "remember when?" and "thank you so much" and promises to write and visit. By the time she got back to the apartment carrying Pooh, who had decided at the last moment to "thtay with Aunt Lila," she was coughing and shivering with the grippe and could gratefully lie in bed thinking of nothing for most of the next week. When she recovered, she found that remembering the past brought back the chills and the sweats and again pushed it out of her mind.

•   •   •

The front doorbell rings on the dot of noon. It's Peggy Goodman, the only person Lila knows who is as punctual as she is. Lila was aware that when the Burkes and the Goodmans saw a great deal of each other, Peggy never liked her, disapproved of much that she did and feared that she would make a pass at Gerry. She would have bet the only reason Peggy ever paid any attention to her was that Willie's company was Gerry's biggest client.

Gerry was different. He was polite to all women in an old-fashioned way, "courtly" Willie called it, but Lila knows Gerry genuinely liked her. He took her opinions seriously, answered her questions thoughtfully, hit a tennis ball to her as hard as to the men, but always had some little joke or playful story to make her smile. He could play anything on the piano by ear and loved the white baby grand. At parties, if Lila could be persuaded to sing, Gerry would accompany her, effortlessly transposing the newest pop tune to her best key. It was all totally innocent. Gerry didn't know there was another woman in the world besides Peggy, and Lila never considered Gerry except as lawyer and friend. On the rare occasions he would play from sheet music, she would turn pages for him and occasionally touch his shoulder with her breast, but only if Peggy was watching.

Gerry died a year after Willie, and Lila was sure that would be the last she saw of Peggy. The following November, though, Peggy called the day after she arrived at her little condominium in the Palm Beach Towers. She came to lunch, and they played two games of Scrabble. Well, once for old times sake, thought Lila. Two weeks later Peggy called again. Had Lila seen <u>The Remains of the Day?</u> Peggy bought the tickets and coffee and cake afterward. Since then they have seen each other every week or so each winter.

It's not like the friendship Lila had with Margo; she and Peggy are reserved with each other, considerate of each other's convenience. But Lila feels good that she has clearly won Peggy's respect and has found that Peggy, no longer blurred by the benevolent glow that always seemed to surround Gerry, is a stimulating companion and a fierce competitor at the board games they frequently play. They are kind to each other like survivors of the same catastrophe.

They eat their pompano and forego games to turn on Court TV for the O. J. Simpson trial. Lila watches for a few minutes every afternoon on the chance of catching a moment of live drama. She has seen little: only some of Fuhrman's cross-examination. The facts of the case are dramatic, but she can read them in the newspapers. What she would like to see is a moment when the process comes to climax, and the outcome of the case balances precariously as lawyers and witnesses strain to push it one way or the other. The wrangling of Clark and Cochran, children constantly squabbling before Judge Ito, an overly patient parent, brings her no satisfaction.

•   •   •

At Christmas, Lila and Willie went again to Florida, this time to Palm Beach. Lila liked it much better than the development boom of Miami. Roads and beaches were quiet; low, sprawling villas hid behind whitewashed walls and flowering trees, which lent the shaded streets exotic names like Via Jacaranda and Bougainvillea Row. In the late afternoons, while Willie played gin with a group of local real estate people, Lila would cycle up and down those streets stopping to peer through ornate iron gates or to follow wooden walkways to docks festooned with cabin cruisers. Willie said they could buy a house there if the big real estate project they were talking about at the gin game ever actually came to development.

Back in New York, one evening Willie came home from work, handed her a thick envelope with the name of Gerry Goodman's law firm in the upper left-hand corner and told her to read it and call him at his club when she was finished. In the meantime, he would play some gin or shoot a little pool.

The envelope contained a letter from Gerry to Willie clipped to a binder labeled "In the Matter of Gloria Granatelli." She picked up the letter first.

"Dear Willie:

As requested, we have undertaken a review of possible action to obtain the permanent return of Gloria to Lila and to permit you to adopt her as your child. As a first step, we found that Joseph Principato, Gloria's natural father, died in an automobile accident three years ago. A certified copy of his death certificate is enclosed herewith.

We then retained a St. Louis detective agency to investigate the status of Gloria's relationship with John and Catherine Granatelli and related matters and enclose herewith a copy of their report. We have prepared and enclose herewith a statement of certain facts that a court might deem relevant to the issue of Gloria's custody and a Memorandum of statutory and case law that would be applicable to litigation of that issue.

The portions of the Statement of Facts describing the circumstances under which the present custody arrangement was made have been derived solely from our interview with you and must be reviewed for accuracy and completeness by Lila as well as by you. Assuming that a court of applicable jurisdiction before whom the case were to be tried would find the facts to accord with those set forth therein, we believe it more likely than not that the Court would hold that (i) Lila remains Gloria's legal mother, (ii) as her legal mother, Lila has the right to Gloria's physical custody and (iii)since her natural father is deceased, with Lila's consent and subject to at least a pro forma investigation of your suitability, you may adopt Gloria and become her father.

I repeat my strong recommendation that you and Lila consider all implications of this matter before taking any steps to go forward or even discussing the possibility except with your professional advisers.

Sincerely,

Gerry"

By the time Lila got to the Roman numerals dressed in their cunning little parentheses, she was livid. What was wrong with Gerry? He always spoke so plainly and directly. This was gobbledygook. He can't possibly have meant she was going to get Gloria back.

She picked up the binder, turned to the colored tab "Statement of Facts," read a few lines and flung the binder against the wall so hard that it tore and loose pages spilled over the couch. What right did Willie have to tell Gerry and some leering snot-nosed junior and, of course, a stenographer, all those horrible details? And Gerry: she had thought he was her friend. How could he? Her hand shook as she dialed Gerry's home and the first time she got a wrong number. The second time, his wife, Peggy, answered.

"Where's Gerry?" Lila yelled.

"In the bathroom," Peggy hastily responded. Then, recovering some of her customary hauteur, "Who is this?"

"It's Lila. Get him."

"Lila. What on earth? Is it Willie?"

"No, no. He's not dead or anything. I have to talk to Gerry."

"Calm yourself, Lila. You almost gave me a heart attack. He'll call you right back."

At the top of the meter: "Fuck you, Peggy! Get him now!"

A minute later, Gerry was on, unruffled as always. "Ah, Lila. I assume you've been reading the documents I sent over."

With an enormous effort, Lila controlled her voice. "What are you doing to me?"

"Helping you get Gloria back."

"What?" A door was opening. Behind it was what she wanted most, yet a part of her was straining to hold it shut, telling her she mustn't admit hope, for its failure would destroy her.

"We're ready to begin proceedings so you can regain custody of Gloria."

Wait. There was one possibility. "Are John and Cath going to have their own baby?"

"Why no," Gerry paused. "I see. No, John and Catherine don't know about this yet."

Then it was impossible. They would never agree. It was just another device to torment her. And Willie was hiding under a pool table at the Club.

"Gerry, please." She could hear her voice wobbling like a top. She willed it to keep spinning. "Explain the whole thing."

"A few months ago Willie came to see me and told me that you couldn't have children together. I'm very—"

"Go on, Gerry."

"He said he didn't want to go through his life childless, and he couldn't stand being the cause of your not having a child. He asked me to look into the possibility of getting Gloria back. He didn't want to mention it to you if it couldn't be done. But it looks like it can."

Gerry's calm voice helped her control her emotions. "What about John and Cath? Why do you think they'll agree?"

"I'm afraid they won't. But they never took steps to adopt Gloria legally, and so their position is merely that of foster parents. The law, in Missouri as well as in New York, considers the rights of the natural mother paramount unless she is clearly unfit."

"But I signed the paper. Have you seen it?"

"I… I prepared it But, it doesn't matter what it said. You can't give or take away parenthood by agreement. You were under a lot of stress, at the time, with your mother's death and the War. The biggest problem will be the seven years. The investigators' reports show that John and Catherine have been devoted parents and have done an excellent job of raising Gloria."

"You put detectives on them? "

"Damn it, Lila. This is a serious business. You have to know everything you can before you start it. Whichever way it comes out, you won't have a brother anymore. If you get to court, you're going to have to relive the worst time of your life and bring up a lot of things that may be better left forgotten. If you lose, you'll have gotten your hopes up for nothing, and God knows what it will do to your marriage."

"But you think we'd win?" And as Lila spoke, something deep inside her moved. She reflexively put her hand against her flat belly.

"Yes, I think so. It's almost always the same. The judge writes an opinion confirming the governing principle that the best interests of the child must be protected, then he finds something in the facts to support a holding that the child is best off with the natural mother."

"We have something like that?"

"There are a couple of things. When they registered Gloria for school, they came in with a phony birth certificate showing them as the parents. A judge won't like that. Then, one time, John had a dispute with a neighbor over a lot line and went out one day when the neighbor was away and tore down and burnt the fence that had started the argument. That got him a conviction for trespass and malicious mischief."

"My brother went to jail?"

"Oh no, just got fined a few dollars. It doesn't have anything to do with his qualifications as a father, but it's on the record. And money may be a factor."

"Money. Don't they have enough money for the way they live? John has a good job, and Willie sends them something extra."

"John will soon be out of a job. His company is selling out to a bigger company, which will close the St. Louis operation. There are so many new developments in the aeronautical field that the companies want kids coming out of graduate schools. The investigators asked around. John won't find a new job at anything like the salary he's been getting."

Lila was shocked. "Why didn't he tell us?"

"Your brother is a proud man, Lila. There's a savings account in Gloria's name, and I think you'd find that every penny Willie sent went into that account and that there have been no withdrawals. But that's not the point. It's that Gloria is not going to get the benefits even the money John used to make could buy. I don't know how he's going to be able to pay a lawyer to fight. And once you start, you're surely not going to finance the opposition. So, if you decide to go through with it, there's a reasonable chance you'll win."

Again she felt the movement within. But there were two questions she had to ask Gerry. First, the easy one, "You don't think we should do it, do you?"

"You don't need my blessing, Lila."

"No, but I'd like to hear what you think."

"It's certain this will cause enormous pain to John and Catherine. It's uncertain whether it will bring happiness to you and Willie. It's certain that tearing Gloria from her mother and father, and that's what they have been to her for as long as she can remember, will do great harm to her for a considerable time. It's uncertain whether, in the long run, it will do her as much good. If I were the judge, I'd rule against you—and then be reversed on appeal."

"Thank you for being honest. Did you tell that to Willie?"

"He didn't ask."

"One last question, Gerry. Why didn't Willie talk to me about this, himself? Why did he make you do it?"

Gerry sounded uncomfortable. "I'd rather not go into that, you know, speculating on what's in someone's head. What difference does it make, anyway?"

"It makes a difference, Gerry. Let me help you. Is it because he realizes that this mess is all his fault? And he can't admit it to my face?"

"That could be."

"He never should have taken Gloria away from me in the first place, should he?"

No answer.

If he was going to be on her side, he had to say it. "Come on, Gerry, this is easy, it's over the phone. You don't even have to look at me when you answer."

"No, Lila, he shouldn't have." He halted, his last word hanging, unresolved, and Lila waited. "I... I should have said something when Willie came to see me then. But, I didn't, and you went back to San Diego the next day, and it was too late. I've always been sorry."

Sorry? Just sorry? But she would need Gerry, now. "That was a long time ago. I'll tell you what you can do now, though. Willie's been waiting at the club for quite a while. Call him, fill him in on our conversation and tell him to come home. Would you do that for me?"

"Of course, Lila, I'd be happy to," his voice sung with relief.

"But just one more thing. Tell him he'd better start by admitting how terribly wrong he was. Then we can talk. It's uncertain as to what we're going to do about Gloria, but it's certain that if he doesn't follow your advice he will not only be childless, he'll be wifeless, as well. Please apologize to Peggy for my rudeness." She hung up without waiting for a reply.

It was clear, now. She had a picture of them all at the time, Willie, her mother, John, Cath and Lila, herself, in position, poised like football players waiting for the snap of the ball to begin the play. She knew exactly who would block left, who would cut right, who would run how fast to get to where they would be when the play ended. If she had only seen it then.

She poured herself a drink and toasted her newly found clarity of vision. They had all manipulated her to gain their own ends; she wouldn't let that happen again. She would humble Willie, make him beg her forgiveness tonight and do whatever she wanted for the rest of his life to earn it. Then she would recapture her stolen child from John and Catherine.

The cost would be high. She didn't need Gerry to tell her how John and Catherine would suffer. How could she do such a thing? The answer was obvious, had always been obvious even though she had denied it for seven years. Her real brother could never have taken her child from her. John was a stranger, to whom she owed no more consideration than he had given her.

But, Gloria. What would happen to this beautiful, happy child? Lila reached for the photograph of Gloria that Catherine had sent at Christmas. That laughing face would be twisted by pain and confusion. How could Gloria understand, at her age, what was happening to her? No, it was unthinkable.

With the realization that she couldn't do this to her child, pain grasped Lila. But it was a familiar pain, one she had borne for years. And look how happy Gloria was. Lila could subsist on what bits of love were left over from John and Catherine's feast, couldn't she? There would be more visits to New York, and she could go to St. Louis. Thanksgiving had been bittersweet, but still sweet. Wouldn't that be enough?

Then she remembered that, at Thanksgiving, she had believed that anything more was impossible. She had survived the weeks of yearning since then because she had no choice. Now, she did. She looked again at the photograph. She had the means to see this face every morning, to hug this body to her, to make up for all the years of deprivation. Her baby would be hers again; could she give her up a second time, knowing that they shouldn't have made her give her up the first time?

Never! It would be hard on Gloria for a while, but Lila would give her so much love, so much kindness, that she would soon recover. Children were resilient. Lila had already drawn Gloria to her, as though something in Gloria recognized the connection. Lila would do anything necessary to complete that connection so that someday Gloria would love Lila as her mother and forgive her for everything.

She went into the kitchen and sent Mrs. Thompson home. Mary was off so nobody would overhear what would be said. Back in the living room, Lila closed the cover over the keys of the piano and spread out Gerry's papers. This time, she knew where all the players would go and what would happen to them when Willie's key in the lock would start the next play.

An hour after her conversation with Gerry, Willie stormed into the apartment roaring, "LILA! WHAT THE FUCK'S THE MATTER WITH YOU?" That was an act, she thought. Willie never yelled.

She didn't answer but made a pencil note on the page she had ostensibly been reading and turned to the next one.

He took off his jacket and tie and flung them into a chair, then took a couple of steps toward her and stopped with his hands on his hips. "Damn it, Lila, will you please stop that bullshit and answer me." That sounded a little more like him but still calculated.

She made another note and turned another page.

He stood unmoving for a minute, then walked rapidly over to the piano and stood behind Lila for two beats and put his hand on her shoulders. "Come on, honey, talk to me," he rumbled.

Without taking her eyes off the page, Lila shrugged off his hands.

"Lila!" he cried, and, this time, the hurt and anger were genuine. For a moment she could feel his urge to strike her, then he rushed past her into the bathroom and slammed the door.

She felt her resolution drain as the minutes passed. What good would an apology do? Now, after so long? The bathroom door clicked, and Willie shuffled into the living room.

"Lila?"

"Yes, Willie."

"What you said to Gerry. You know. You didn't really mean all that, did you? You wouldn't leave me, you couldn't do that, could you?"

"Yes, Willie, I could." Her voice felt weak, but Willie's response was desperate.

"Lila, no, please. I wouldn't know what to do without you. Don't you know how much I love you?"

Even now, she yearned to relieve him and let him lock his arms around her. She didn't dare to speak again and began to assemble the papers.

"Things just happened so fast. You know. I mean, I never got a chance to prepare my family. Christ, my father just went crazy and everyone else and then there was that terrible party and everything and then the War and your mother dying. Please, Lila."

"What are you trying to say, Willie?"

"I'm really sorry, you know, uh about what happened with Gloria. But we'll get her back now, and I'll make it up to both of you, I promise. She'll be my daughter, too, and I'll love her as much as any father for the rest of my life. OK, Lila?"

"Wait a minute. You mean taking Gloria away from me wasn't right?"

"I don't know. I guess it wasn't. But I really felt that—You know. Like I said. Uh. I believed that I couldn't love Gloria and she'd be happier with John and Catherine. I really thought it was for the best. Everyone, not just my father, tried to make me not marry you at all, but I couldn't not marry you, I loved you so much. I still do."

"Then how could you do such a thing to me? You almost killed me."

He reached for Lila, but she recoiled. "I was sure it would be all right, that we loved each other so much that we would be happy just the two of us. And of course we'd have our own children soon enough, and you'd forget—"

"Forget? Are you crazy, Willie?"

"I didn't mean *forget* altogether, I meant that it wouldn't be so bad after a while—"

"It hurt so much I had to convince myself that it never happened, that I never had a child I sacrificed for you. That's insanity, isn't it?"

He put his hands over his face and began to cry. "I'm so sorry. I had no idea. I thought it would just be a little while and it wouldn't be so bad. And after a while you seemed OK I never wanted to hurt you at all, but this—How ...?" He couldn't finish the question.

She took a deep breath. Let him know the worst. "I loved you so much that I believed you had to be right and that it was for the best no matter what it did to me."

Willie turned away from her and took two stumbling steps to the back of an easy chair, put both hands on it and bent over.

"No more, Lila, please, no more. I can't stand anymore. I'm sorry, forgive me, please, forgive me, I'll do anything you want, or if you can't forgive me, just don't leave me, please stay, let me make it up to you, I mean, let me try, I know I can't, but whatever you want. We'll get Gloria back, and I'll be so good to her, anything, but please say you'll stay—"

It was a total victory, but it brought Lila little satisfaction.

"All right, Willie, that's enough. I don't know if I'll ever forgive you, but I'll stay."

Then she endured his gratitude and his promises for another five minutes until she sent him around the corner to the delicatessen. She had won. Why did she feel so empty?

The answer was easy. She had destroyed the Willie she had loved, the one for whom she had sacrificed everything. By taking Gloria from her, Willie had taken a part of Lila's womanhood from her. Now, she had taken what was left of Willie's manhood from him. She no longer had a man for a husband, and could, therefore, no longer truly be a wife. Her only hope of filling the emptiness of the rest of her life was to become a mother again.

In the morning, she called Gerry and told him to start the case.

•   •   •

Gerry retained St. Louis attorneys who prepared papers and served them on John and Catherine. Lila refused to change their telephone numbers, as Gerry had suggested, but tried not to answer herself. Three or four times John called leaving increasingly urgent messages with the staff. At three o'clock one morning, Lila, half-asleep, picked up the ringing telephone.

"What are you doing, Lina, for God's sake?"

Willie sat up and turned on the reading lamp. Lila put her hand over the receiver.

"It's John," she whispered.

"I'm sorry, John. I'm taking Gloria back."

"No!" John shouted, and Lila flinched. He lowered his voice "You have to stop it. You can't have her. She's ours. We're her parents, you have no right…"

"I'm sorry, I have to do this."

"But you can't do that. She's our child. You gave her up, forever. I've got the paper."

"She's my child, and I never should have let you take her. "

"But you did, and it was for always. You can't just change your mind. Do you think you're still that spoiled brat who got our parents to buy you whatever you wanted?"

That was ridiculous, but Lila couldn't stop her answer. "She's my child, and you're talking about toys? She was my baby, and you stole her."

"Steal her? You had already given her up to Momma." His voice rose. "So you could get a rich husband. God knows what you might have done after Momma died if Cath and I hadn't taken her. You'll have to get Willie to buy you some other child. We'll never give Gloria up."

"I'm sorry, John. The lawyers say you'll have to."

"Never. I don't care who says what. I'm not letting anyone take Gloria, not you, not some judge, not the President."

"I'm sorry."

Now he was shouting, "You hear me? No one takes her. Ever. I'll see you dead, first."

When she reported the call to Gerry, he asked her to write down everything she could remember of the conversation to be used in case of a trial. Then he had the St. Louis detectives follow John constantly for fear he might come to New York.

After its stormy beginning, the case proceeded. John's lawyer made several motions, all denied by the court. Gerry thought that was a good sign. Lila read John's affidavit in support of the first one and was horrified at what he said about her.

"In spite of our mother's objections, plaintiff worked from the age of eighteen as a scantily clad chorus girl. When the plaintiff became pregnant, Mr. Pricipato refused to marry her because he knew he was only one of several possible fathers.

"After Gloria was born, plaintiff returned to the stage, while she sought to find a wealthy husband such as Mr. Burke. While engaging in this conduct, she forced our ailing mother to take full-time care of Gloria and do all the cooking, cleaning and other work in their house. Then, when she married Mr. Burke, she was able to move out of the house and desert Gloria altogether.

"After our mother's death, plaintiff was ready to do anything not to have the burden of a child and willingly consented that my wife and I raise Gloria as our own child. For the past seven years, she showed no interest in Gloria; all our communications during that time were with Mr. Burke. We believe that it is only at his insistence that she is attempting to tear Gloria from us."

It was terrible that she and John were at war. He had always been kind and protective. Now he was the enemy. She tried not to think about Catherine; how could Cath be her enemy?

As had always been her custom, she began to learn everything she needed for her performance in court. Gerry and a trial lawyer from his office explained that she had to amalgamate two roles into one believable character.

Most important would be showing herself to be a devoted, loving mother, ready to do whatever was necessary for the welfare of her child. At her first preparatory session, Mr. Cutler, the trial lawyer, a thin, hollow-faced young man with unruly hair, was pleased to find that Lila had already investigated schools and pediatricians and was reading extensively on child care and child psychology. He was troubled, however, that the Burkes were interviewing for a governess.

"What's wrong with that?" asked Lila. "Hiring someone with experience to help us?"

"The lawyer on the other side will draw pictures of you out gallivanting around while some German governess locks Gloria in the closet. You have to show that there's nothing in the world you want more than to spend every minute taking care of your child, crazy as any mother would have to be to feel that way."

Suddenly he snapped, "Now, Mrs. Burke, tell us the real reason you want Gloria." Again and again, he threw that question into her face. Sometimes it came by itself, sometimes at the end of a long discussion, sometimes even in the middle of her answer to a totally different question. She would think about the question; it wasn't all that simple, after all. She would come out with a fair and reasoned response, and Cutler would launch himself at it like a hawk taking a songbird. She begged him for the right answer, but he refused to give it to her. "Can't have counsel putting words into our mouth, can we?"

Badgered beyond toleration, she said "Because she's my daughter and I love her, and that's all."

Cutler put down his yellow pad and applauded. "That was perfect, Mrs. B. If you can only do that again at the trial, it'll be fine."

The second role was the confused young girl who had signed away her baby forever.

"I can't fully remember what happened. There was the train ride, the hospital, my poor mother—." Lila stopped and, with both hands, gripped the edge of the table in the little conference room she had learned to hate. She had to keep under control. "My mother and I were very close. I had been arranging the funeral and spending every possible minute with Gloria. It's like trying to recall a nightmare that's so horrible your mind refuses to go through it again."

Cutler got up from the table and examined one of the prints on the wall: a red-robed, white-wigged judge with a large, bulbous nose. When he turned back to her, he was frowning.

"That's just not enough, Mrs. Burke. So you didn't know exactly what you signed that night. You thought it was something your brother could show to the authorities to prove he wasn't kidnapping Gloria while they took care of her for a while. Your husband knew what it said; he had it prepared by a lawyer. When did you first find out that it purported to surrender all parental rights? It can't have taken seven years. Six months? A year? Two?"

Lila said nothing.

"All right, it was wartime, everything was crazy. And it just seemed to go on and on. You knew Gloria was safe and sound. That's all you thought about the situation. Strange, but possible. The war ends. You want to thank your brother and sister-in-law and take back your child. You find out that you have been tricked by your brother and your husband. Do you confront them, demand your child back, see a lawyer to find out if it was legal?"

Lila said nothing.

"You do nothing, improbable as it seems. That means you have consented to the situation in 1945 when you are four years older. Three years later you change your mind and start this action. Why? What's different now? Could it be the discovery that you and Mr. Burke couldn't have children together? The judge may think that you didn't care about Gloria until it became clear she was going to be the only child you would ever have."

The words kept falling on Lila, all those confusing words that they always heaped upon her, each one light as an autumn leaf, but gradually smothering her. She gestured to sweep them aside. "That was Willie, not me. He changed his mind. Don't you understand? Didn't Gerry tell you? I had to give her up. Willie kept saying there was no other choice. And then afterward, how right it was, how it was best for everybody. Over and over. For seven years. If I believed it one day, I had to keep believing it every day of those seven years. Can't you see that?" Lila's voice rose, and she shook her fists in frustration. "Now you say 'That's not quite right, Mrs. Burke. You had another choice, whether you knew it or not, but it expired on VJ Day.' Who am I supposed to believe? What do you all want of me?"

Cutler captured her hands and put them together on the table between them. "It's all right, believe me. The judge will give you back your child. He'll understand. Your mother was dead; your brother would only help in one way; you had to rely on your husband. To keep Gloria, you would have had to leave your husband with no money and a year-old baby. Gerry did tell me. Mr. Burke was wrong to put you to such a terrible choice, but for you, the choice you made was the only right one for Gloria. You were being a good mother. Soon, you'll be one again."

She wondered what Cutler or Gerry or the judge would say if she told them the fear of single parenthood had played no part in her decision. Lots of young women alone with babies during the war got by somehow. She would have, too. Truthfully, she hadn't been certain Willie would have left her if she had refused him. Now, knowing Willie's weakness, she doubted it. All she had known was that he had commanded her to surrender her child for him as God had commanded Abraham to sacrifice Isaac, except that Willie, a failed god, had not stayed her hand.

●   ●   ●

The trial came up the last week in July. St. Louis was steaming, but Willie was able to get them one of the few hotel suites with air-conditioning, and, when the court adjourned each afternoon, they fled back to the suite and showered and shivered in the strange delight of the chilled air. They kept to their unspoken agreement not to discuss the case with each other and could almost have been on vacation as they chattered over room service food and liquor and listened to the unfamiliar country music on the radio.

They dressed for the first day of the trial following the directions of Cutler and their St. Louis lawyer. Lila wore a blue pleated skirt long enough so that only an inch or two of her nylons showed above comfortable, low-heeled shoes. The collar of a plain white blouse was unbuttoned and pulled over the neck of her matching jacket, making white wings upon the navy blue lapels. On her head, she wore a small navy and white pillbox hat with a bit of an openwork veil. She kept the hat on and the veil down at all times, although she removed her white gloves when she entered the courtroom and took her seat. She left off her engagement ring, with the big diamond, and wore only her plain, gold wedding band. Her face bore a touch of powder and lipstick. Lila normally wore none, but Margo insisted that, outside New York, no self-respecting woman would be seen in public without make-up on her face.

Willie was dressed to contrast and emphasize Lila's modest, middle-class image. His suit, shirt, tie, and shoes were new and obviously expensive. That was not unusual; Willie liked good clothes. But the pinstripe was wider and bolder, and the pattern of the tie more aggressive than anything Willie would ever choose for himself. When he rested his hands on the table, the polished gold of his chunky cufflinks, heavy Rolex and broad wedding ring heliographed messages of wealth around the room and the diamond in his father's pinkie ring, worn by Willie for the first time, winked smugly.

Cutler had explained it to Lila. "We want your husband to be a typical strong, overbearing, member of the *nouveau riche*, impressed with his own money and insensitive to people's feelings. That will make it easier for the judge to understand how he bullied you."

That wasn't Willie, ever, but Lila knew enough not to say it. "But if the judge thinks that Willie is a bully, won't he be afraid to put Gloria into the same house with him?"

"No, your husband has realized what a terrible thing he did and will do anything to make amends. He wasn't her father so his sin can be forgiven where yours if you weren't acting under duress, couldn't be." Cutler smiled at his own cleverness.

"I see," she replied gratefully, happy to allow him his self-satisfaction. The strategem was a good one. Men were expected to dominate and women to submit. Willie would be forgiven and then she would have to be forgiven, too. But then, if the judge were to forgive Willie, wouldn't she have to forgive him too? Could she? She didn't know, but she had to appear to, so when they first entered the courtroom, she stumbled, clutched Willie's arm for support and then continued to hold on. He looked down at her with concern, but she smiled and gave his arm a little squeeze.

They sat, with their two lawyers, at a battered oak table at one side of the courtroom. A similar table, at the left, was still unoccupied as was the judge's chair behind a huge desk, which loomed above them on a raised platform at the front of the room. Next to it, the clerk sat at a table piled with folders. Mr. Purnell, Lila's St. Louis lawyer, sauntered over and engaged this man in conversation. A minute later, a fat man with a briefcase bustled into the courtroom and joined Purnell, and the clerk and a serious discussion ensued. The clerk shook his head disapprovingly, got up from his chair and retreated through a door behind the platform. Purnell rejoined the Burkes and Cutler, while the fat man sat down at the other table.

Purnell leaned over and whispered, "The Granatellis aren't here, and their lawyer doesn't know where they are. He's trying to adjourn the case until this afternoon. Judge Fogarty will be furious. He wants to stop early before it gets too hot." Air-conditioning had apparently not yet reached the courthouse, and it was, even now, more than hot enough, although the windows were wide open and the overhead fans stirred the soupy air. Just then, Lila heard the door behind her shut, and she turned to see John and Catherine hurrying down the aisle between the benches.

But, this man couldn't be John. A weedy beard spilled from the ends of his mustache over the corners of his mouth and down his chin. He was thin, and his old suit was too big for him. When he saw Lila, he glared at her, and his lips moved, but he took his seat in silence.

There were changes in Catherine, too. The gray in her hair could be seen from across the room as could frown lines around her eyes, marring her smooth, calm face. Every few seconds she would glance apprehensively at John. She was dressed much the same way as Lila, but the brightly colored artificial flowers on her hat showed a gaiety not otherwise present in the courtroom. It was Cath's best hat, Lila knew, having helped her pick it out at Thanksgiving.

The Clerk came back through the door, banged on it three times with his hand and shouted. "All rise, this Court is now in session, Honorable Joseph Fogarty, presiding."

As the last word reverberated through the all but empty courtroom, the judge in his black robe swept through the door up two steps and planted himself firmly in his chair. Judge Fogarty had a large head covered with white hair and a grim mouth beneath a luxurious white mustache, like pictures of Mark Twain. After a nod from the judge, Purnell began his opening statement.

Lila felt a frisson of fear. The lawyers had all said that she had the stronger case, but that it would ultimately be up to Judge Fogarty. This stern, forbidding personage, looking down at them, was preparing to judge her, as, someday, God would judge her.

Someday, after she had forgiven the sins He had committed against her, she would turn back to Him and confess her sins, and He would forgive her. But now, when He had taken her father and mother and Gloria and the Willie she had loved, all too soon to be just, how could she come to Him with love and beg His forgiveness? She couldn't and, judged in such a state, must be condemned and lose her child forever. Lila looked down so she would not have to see His face as He pronounced judgment.

But when she looked up again, there was only an old man wiping the perspiration from his face with the sleeve of his robe and looking at his watch. Purnell must have noticed that gesture too, for he smoothly skipped a few minutes of material and finished up a minute later. Lila thought Judge Fogarty's "Thank you, Mr. Purnell," expressed some real gratitude. "Mr. Hassler, you may proceed." The fat lawyer rose in his turn.

As expected, he attacked her with indignation for most of his fifteen minutes, ending with "A child is not a piece of furniture to be left in your brother's attic for seven years until you redecorate and want it back. Any woman who does that with her child is not fit to be a mother."

What was the judge's reaction? There was no hint in his face as he thanked Hassler and declared a recess. John, however, had shaken his head vigorously in assent throughout the statement and clapped Hassler on the back when the red-faced lawyer returned to his chair.

"Are you all right, darling?" asked Willie solicitously. Incredible. Could he think that she would be upset by anything Hassler might say? She felt constantly lashed by the irony of Willie's present dedication to the pursuit of her cause and the protection of her feelings. But all she did was smile and put a finger to her lips.

Purnell began her case with documentary evidence, certified copies of Gloria's birth certificate and Joe Principato's death certificate. Next, with Hassler's consent, he read depositions from witnesses to Lila's character, the Burke parish priest, Willie's commanding officer from San Diego and the U.S.O. official who ran the shows in which Lila performed and the director of the nursing home at which Lila worked.

Lila, examined by Cutler, took the witness stand the morning of the second day. They had been through it together several times, Cutler varying the order of his questions to make Lila pause and think before answering. The real thing went just as the practice sessions had. He finished just in time for the noon lunch break, allowing Lila time to rest a little before cross-examination.

As soon as Judge Fogarty began the afternoon session with, "You may inquire, Mr. Hassler," the fat man attacked.

"Which of them told you what to say, this morning, Mr. Purnell or Mr. Cutler?"

"Nobody told me what to say."

"Are you trying to tell us you never rehearsed your testimony?"

"Mr. Cutler asked me questions, and I answered them."

"Oh, so it was Mr. Cutler. Did he tell you why you should give the answer you gave when he asked you why you signed the paper?"

Cutler rose. "Objection, your honor."

"Sustained."

"What did he tell you to answer when he asked you why you signed the paper?"

"He didn't tell me what to answer."

"He never told you how to answer any question? Do you expect us to believe that?"

Cutler again, "Objection. That's two questions, not one."

"Sustained."

"All right, I withdraw the second. Answer the first. Stenographer, please read it."

" ' He never told you how to answer any question?' "

"He told me to think before I answer, tell the truth and only answer what I was asked. I shouldn't volunteer, and I shouldn't try to explain things."

Judge Fogarty then made Hassler move on. This pattern was repeated several times, Hassler hammering away at Lila, repeating questions, making speeches, getting angrier and angrier. He made her read out loud the paper she had signed releasing Gloria, then grilled her about it until the judge stopped him. He asked her nothing that Cutler hadn't prepared her for and her answers were those she had given before.

After an hour or so, Hassler seemed to run out of questions. He obtained the permission of the judge to confer with his clients and returned to the table, mopping his face with an enormous handkerchief. John leaned over and whispered to him, and they argued for a minute. At one point, the fat man shook his head and started to get up, but John grabbed his sleeve and pulled him back down and continued his argument.

"Are you ready, counselor?" Judge Fogarty asked impatiently.

Hassler shrugged in resignation and John let go of him. Hassler walked over to the reporter. "May I have Petitioner's Exhibit One, please?" The reporter handed him Gloria's birth certificate, and Hassler returned to the position he had maintained throughout the cross-examination, as close to Lila as the judge had allowed him. Hassler peered into the railed witness box. What new torment had he devised with which to bait her?

"Just a few more questions, Mrs. Burke. What was Gloria's date of birth?"

Why did he ask her that? It was on the certificate.

"October 15, 1940."

Hassler perused the certificate as if looking for further information. "And what date was she conceived."

Cutler jumped up. "Objection. That's completely irrelevant to the issues in this case."

Hassler was ready and replied, ponderously, "With all due respect to my learned opponent, I'm afraid he is in error. If the Court is going to tear this poor child from my clients who have loved and cared for her for seven years, I am sure that the Court will want to be very certain that Petitioner is a suitable person to be entrusted with her. Now, yesterday, seeking to show Petitioner's suitability, counsel presented this Court with affidavits from prominent citizens including, if I recall correctly, a priest, a nun and an Admiral in the U.S. Navy. Now, it seems relevant and proper to allow a few simple questions of Petitioner, herself, on the subject, since none of those prominent citizens are present in this courtroom and I am unable to make inquiry of them as to whether they were aware of Petitioner's sexual activities."

At this, Cutler slipped his leash and sprang at Hassler. "That is reprehensible. You stipulated to the admission of those depositions. Your honor, Mr. Hassler's statements are scurrilous innuendo, and I move to strike them from the record."

Judge Fogarty banged his gavel. "Enough, Gentlemen. Mr. Cutler, there's no jury here, and the Court knows the difference between innuendo and evidence without the necessity of your instruction. Mr. Hassler, I'll give you a little more rope, but be careful what you do with it. Objection overruled. Mrs. Burke, you have to answer the question. Reporter, please."

" 'And what date was she conceived?'"

The debate had given Lila time to think. "It must have been the middle of January."

"Do you remember the exact date?"

"No, I don't."

"Were you married to Mr. Pricipato at that time?"

"No."

"Was Mr. Principato the father?"

"Yes, of course."

"And how many times did you and Mr. Pricipato have relations."

Sullenly, she dug in her heels. "I don't remember."

"As many as that, eh?"

"Objection."

"Withdrawn. But at least often enough during January of 1940 that you couldn't be certain which time produced Gloria. More than two?"

"Yes. Probably five or six," Lila answered wearily. She didn't want to look at Cutler. She wasn't supposed to talk about probabilities.

"Well, enough so that it was probably Mr. Principato's, even if there was someone else."

"Objection, your honor, this—"

"Sustained and strike that, reporter. Mr. Hassler, you're about out of rope."

"I'm sorry, your honor. I'm almost finished. How about Richard Gagliano? Didn't you have relations with him?"

Was he crazy? Richie Gagliano, from next door, who walked to school with her from kindergarten through High School. "No." Richie was in love with Jenny Moretti from the ninth grade on. They had four children, already.

"How about Jeffrey Pons?"

Another neighborhood boy. At least they had gone out a few times in high school. "No, not him either." John must have given Hassler the names of every boy she had known whom he could remember.

"How many men did you have relations with before Mr. Principato?"

Cutler was on his feet, but she was exasperated. "None, he was the first."

"And after that, how many men, besides Mr. Burke?" She barely heard Cutler's useless objection. Enraged at this growling, sweating, bulldog of a man, she was about to shout "None" when she remembered Hank. They would all see it if she lied. She was going to lose Gloria, now forever, for a few minutes of meaningless play. And Willie? She looked at him in despair, but he was watching Hassler who was turning and walking back to the table. Only then, did she realize that Cutler's objection had been sustained; she didn't have to answer.

The next day, Hassler put on his case. There were witnesses to testify what good parents John and Catherine had been, but that had never been questioned. John and Catherine were terrible witnesses. John, totally beyond Hassler's control, launched into lengthy explanations where simple answers were all that was required, and constantly broke into angry tirades against Lila and Willie. Catherine stumbled over the few simple questions Hassler asked her, and he soon gave it up. Cutler looked at Lila. She forced herself to shut off the part of her that wanted to run across the room and hug poor Cath and cry with her, then nodded slightly.

Cutler walked over to Catherine. "Mrs. Granatelli, could I ask you just one thing?"

Catherine raised her head with an effort. "Go ahead. I'll try."

"When you visited the Burkes in New York at Thanksgiving, how did your sister-in-law behave toward Gloria?"

Cutler hadn't wanted to ask this question. The wrong answer would be damaging, but Lila had insisted; she knew what Catherine would say and was determined that everyone hear it.

"Lila was very sweet and gentle with Gloria. She still loved her. She always loved her; that's what made it so terrible."

After that, there was nothing more to be said.

•   •   •

How was Gloria's return to be accomplished? Lila had given no thought to it, having focused single-mindedly on the trial. It was not until a week later when Cutler called to read the decision to her, that she dared to think of herself as a mother again.

Judge Fogarty had awarded her temporary custody of Gloria, to begin in time for the start of school in September. Custody will become permanent in one year unless a guardian from the St. Louis Juvenile Bureau found Gloria's care unsatisfactory. The guardian, a Mrs. Warren, was to take one trip to New York in October and another in May. Gloria must be brought to St. Louis for Christmas and for four weeks in the summer. She keeps the name Granatelli, but John and Catherine are enjoined from claiming she is their daughter.

Lila hung up the phone. Three weeks. That was all. First, the decorator, so that Gloria's rooms in New York and Long Island could be ready for her. Next Lila made an appointment at St. Agnes Girls School. After that, she had Mark Cross send Cutler their most expensive briefcase. As she started to make a list, she realized it was time for lunch. On a impulse, she put pencil and a clean notebook into her handbag, walked the two blocks to Central Park, found a hot dog vendor next to the playground and established herself on a bench.

God, they were cute. In the swing nearest to her, a little boy not much more than a year old was being pushed by his father while his mother stood in front of him. Occasionally one of them would catch the swing and bend down to kiss the boy while he squealed with excitement. A little black-haired girl came running to her mother at a neighboring bench and climbed onto her lap. The girl was crying, and Lila watched the mother stroke and soothe her child. In a minute the girl ran back to the other children. She looked just like the pictures of Gloria at that age. For just a moment, Lila allowed herself to feel the loss of the years, then went to work on her list.

Mrs. Warren called three days later. "Mrs. Burke? This is Alicia Warren, Gloria's guardian in St. Louis. We need to talk seriously."

"What's the matter?"

"Well, I went to see the Granatellis this morning and, there may be some trouble."

"What do you mean?"

"Well, naturally, we want to give Gloria a little time to hear what's going to happen and to get used to the idea. I've been through these custody changes quite a few times, and it's generally helpful when I go into the home and explain it to the child. So I drove out this morning. Your brother wouldn't let me in the house. He said we'd have to take Gloria by force."

"Oh, my God. Is Gloria all right?"

"Well, I didn't get to see her, but shortly after I got back to my office, Mrs. Granatelli called me and told me her husband had calmed down. He wants Judge Fogarty to see Gloria. He thinks that will persuade the judge to change his mind."

"No, no, he can't do that. He—"

"Wait a minute, Mrs. Burke. Let me finish before you get too worked up. She said he promised her that if the judge didn't change his mind, he would give up and let Gloria go. I was able to see Judge Fogarty for a minute, and he agreed to do it next Friday."

Lila was frantic. "The trial took two days, and it's not over. How can that be?"

"Mrs. Burke, listen. The trial is over. Judge Fogarty has decided. This is a hearing to assist in implementing the decision; that's all. Reconsideration can only happen if I find you're not taking proper care of Gloria after she comes to you."

"Oh, I see." Fear subsided again. Lila felt like a swimmer in the surf trying to reach the shore. She had survived one wave after another, but each time she thought she was safe, the undertow pulled her back. She couldn't take much more. "What can I do?"

"Could you and Mr. Burke come out here for the hearing?"

"I suppose so. But I thought you said the judge didn't want to hear anything more."

"Oh no, not to testify. But I think, and the judge agreed, it would be better if you could be there. He may decide it's best that you take Gloria on the spot. If they're not going to use the three weeks constructively, it could make matters more difficult rather than less."

Lila heard disapproval in Mrs. Warren's voice, but let it pass. As long as she gives me back my baby, Lila told herself, she can think what she wants. So she thanked Mrs. Warren, took down her telephone number, then called Cutler and Willie to reassemble her team.

She was ready when they arrived at Mrs. Warren's office the following Friday. Mrs. Warren was a plump, graying woman in her fifties. Over her dress, she wore a paint-spotted smock whose pockets bulged with crayons, yo-yos, and little animals. She frowned when the four of them crowded into her tiny office, with its lone guest chair wedged between her desk and a file cabinet. "Lawyers, Mrs. Burke? Why did you bring lawyers? Judge Fogarty will have a conniption if I bring lawyers into his chambers." Cutler started to protest, but she raised her hand authoritatively. "No, don't start with me. If Mrs. Burke doesn't want to attend without a lawyer, then we'll just have to cancel the hearing, and she can come back in three weeks and find out then what the Granatellis are going to do."

Cutler turned to Purnell who was trying to hold back a smile. Lila was frozen. How could she go before the judge, alone, without her clever knight? But she couldn't afford to antagonize Mrs. Warren, whose findings would be crucial to Lila's obtaining permanent custody.

"No, no, Mrs. Warren," Lila said. "I appreciate the trouble you and the judge have gone through to set this up. Where should we meet the gentlemen afterwards?"

Mrs. Warren addressed Purnell. "Why don't you give your colleague a planter's punch at Marcy's." Then to Cutler. "That'll cheer you up counselor. I don't want you to think badly of our hospitality." She arose from her chair. "All right, let's get it over with."

In the Judge's conference room, John and Catherine and Gloria were already seated at one side of a rectangular table. Gloria jumped up, before Catherine could stop her, and ran to Lila and Willie, while John, who had knocked over his chair in getting up, stood, open-mouthed, as though paralyzed by the decision whether to pick it up or to speak.

"Aunt Lila! Nobody told me you were coming. Will you take me to the zoo? There's a baby elephant, and he's so cute." Without waiting for an answer, she turned to Willie's hug.

John found his voice. "What's going on?" he demanded of Mrs. Warren. "Why are they here?" Then, to Catherine, "Get Gloria out of here. Quick."

Gloria broke away from Willie, stepped back and looked from face to face, her nose wrinkling as though catching a threatening scent. How quick she is, thought Lila. Catherine took Gloria's hand and started to pull her towards the door.

"Hold on, Mrs. Granatelli," said Mrs. Warren. "Remember, you asked for this hearing."

"But, not with them," said John, and Lila winced at the bitterness in his voice.

"Well, this is the way the Judge wants it."

John frowned. "But, then Gloria can't be here." He gestured to Catherine who started toward the door with Gloria again.

"Mr. Granatelli," Mrs. Warren said firmly. "I said this is the way Judge Fogarty wants it. Anything you don't like you can take up with him when he comes in."

John looked at Catherine, and, when she turned away from the door back toward the table, he shrugged his shoulders and nodded assent.

Mrs. Warren held out her hand to Gloria. "My name is Mrs. Warren. We're all here to talk to the Judge. Come, sit back down," and she took her back to her seat. The four adults also sat down as Mrs. Warren continued. "Do you know what a judge is, Gloria?"

Gloria answered in a schoolroom voice, "A judge says whether someone has to go to jail or not if they do something bad."

"Very good, Gloria. But it's more than that. Judges decide who's right in all kinds of arguments, not just about bad people going to jail. Like, if two people each say something belongs to him, then a judge can decide."

Gloria turned to Catherine. "I don't want to see the Judge, Mommy. Can I go to the zoo with Aunt Lila and Uncle Willie?"

Catherine caught her hand. "Just sit down, kitten," she said, "it'll just be a few minutes."

At that moment, Judge Fogarty, in his black robes, came in and sat at one end of the table, while Mrs. Warren sat at the other. This Judge Fogarty was very different from the one at the trial. He greeted everyone at the table by name, smiling benevolently; Mark Twain had become Santa Claus. He saved Gloria for last. "I don't believe I know this lovely young lady. What's your name, my dear?"

Gloria was not fooled. She looked back and forth at John and Catherine and, finding no reassurance seemed to shrink down into her chair. After a moment, Mrs. Warren intervened. "This is Gloria Granatelli, your honor. You've heard me talk about her."

"So you have." The judge nodded formally. "I hear you are a very nice little girl, Gloria. I'm delighted to meet you. You're almost the same age as my granddaughter. She's nine. How old are you?"

Catherine leaned over and whispered something to Gloria, who squirmed uncomfortably but managed a tremulous "Eight."

The judge beamed. "I thought so. All right, Mrs. Warren, why don't you proceed? It's too nice a day to spend too much time in this stuffy courthouse." And he clasped his hands in front of him on the table like a pupil dutifully awaiting the teacher.

"Wait, your Honor," John's voice was controlled, but Lila could see the strain as his hands clenched and opened spasmodically. "Why are my sister and brother-in-law here? We thought this was just going to give you a chance to talk to Gloria."

The smile disappeared from Judge Fogarty's face. He leaned forward. "Have you told Gloria about this case and my decision?"

"No, your Honor. If you'd just talk to Gloria for a little, I'm sure you'll see that the way things are now is the best for her and you'll change the decision. Please, Judge, just talk to her a little. We'll go out of the room if you want, so we can't tell her what to say."

"Daddy," Gloria started to cry. "I don't want to talk to the Judge. I want to go home."

Judge Fogarty shook his head." I'm sorry, Mr. Granatelli, but this is the way it has to be." His voice was gentle. He's speaking to Gloria, Lila thought.

"But, you can't, Judge." John started to get up.

"That's enough. Sit down, Mr. Granatelli. I'm the one who decides what I can and can't do. Mrs. Warren, please tell Gloria what this is all about. And no interruptions, Mr. Granatelli." The gentleness was gone.

Mrs. Warren began. "Gloria, you know that the United States had to fight in World War II just a few years ago." Gloria made no response. "It was a terrible time. Men were sent away to battle or to do other things to help those doing the fighting. Women, too, were sent away, sometimes, and had to leave their children behind."

Mrs. Warren frowned and hesitated for a moment before continuing.

"Well, your Aunt Lila had a baby girl when the war started. And she had to go away and couldn't take her baby with her. She thought very hard about who could do the best to take care of the baby while she was gone. And she found two wonderful people who would take care of that baby just as well as if she were their own. Now, do you know who those people were?"

Gloria didn't answer but began to move her head back and forth, her eyes fixed on Mrs. Warren. Catherine, one arm around Gloria's shoulder, extended the other and took John's hand.

Lila put her hands below the table and gripped her knees. It's all right, my baby, my precious. Just a minute and it will be all over, and we'll be together again, and I'll do everything to make you happy. You'll see. It'll be so good.

"Well, those wonderful people were Lila's brother and sister-in-law, and they have taken care of Lila's baby just as well and loved her just as much as if she were their own."

"NO!" shouted Gloria. "They didn't. It's not true. Daddy, tell them. Mommy!" Her face was contorted as she turned from one to the other. John, eyes shut, shook his head convulsively, while Catherine, mouth open, lips quivering struggled helplessly with speech.

Mrs. Warren's voice was firm. "It's true, Gloria, you were that baby, and Lila is your real mother." With her last words, she pointed her finger at Lila.

"No, no," Gloria moaned.

Lila dug her nails into her knees, but try as she could to feel that pain, it was nothing. "It's all right, baby. Mama's here."

Gloria whirled. "NO! You're not my mama. Go away." She tore herself loose from Catherine's arm and ran for the door. Mrs. Warren, with astonishing agility, stepped in front of her. Gloria punched wildly at the dumpy woman who managed to capture the flailing arms.

"Let me go! Let me go! I want to go home." Suddenly Gloria collapsed and began sobbing, and the room erupted. Lila, John, and Catherine all converged on Gloria.

"You can't take her," shouted John and he grabbed Lila and flung her aside. Her shoulder struck the conference table and pain shot down her arm as she fell to the floor. Willie sprang at John, who grappled with him evenly although outweighed by sixty pounds. Even Catherine clawed to get past them, while Mrs. Warren pulled Gloria away from the melee.

"STOP IT," a voice thundered with such authority that all motion ceased. Judge Fogarty stood at the end of the table quivering with rage. "Get back to your seats. Now." Meekly, they picked themselves up and went back to their places at the table, except that Mrs. Warren stood behind Gloria's chair, stroking the hair of the sobbing child.

Lila fought back the pain in her shoulder. She couldn't let people notice. The judge might stop the hearing.

The judge was furious. "If anything like this happens again, the guards will come and handcuff you to your chairs. Mr. Granatelli, I'm holding you in contempt."

Lila looked at her brother. His head was down contemplating his hands spread flat on the table. As the judge spoke, she expected defiance, but there was no response except for the growing moisture under his eyes. Lila spoke without thinking. "Please, your honor, don't do anything more to him. It's not his fault."

Was the expression on Cath's face gratitude? It didn't matter. There was so much pain in the room, it didn't matter who was at fault.

Judge Fogarty nodded gravely. "Thank you, Mrs. Burke. I'll consider what you said. That's the proper spirit in which to conduct these proceedings. Now, has anyone anything to say that would be helpful?" His eyes swept the room thoughtfully. There was silence. They were all beaten. Even Gloria had stopped her sobbing and was slumped in her chair like some captured animal that no longer cared what happened to it.

"Mrs. Warren, what do you recommend?"

"I don't think there's anything to be gained by putting off the transfer, your honor. The best thing would be for Mr. and Mrs. Burke to take Gloria back to their hotel. I can go with the Granatellis, and we can pack up a few things in a suitcase, and I'll bring them over later. The rest can be shipped railway express."

Lila held her breath as Judge Fogarty looked over at John. "Mr. Granatelli?"

John didn't answer, but, after a moment, Catherine said, woodenly, "Yes, your Honor."

The judge continued. "All right, Mrs. Warren, you do that. Gloria. Listen to me, child." Gloria raised her head and stared at him. "Mrs. Burke is your mother. She had to give you up, but she has come for you, now, and you're going to go with her and be her daughter from now on. But you'll be coming back here to spend Christmas and Easter and again next summer. You'll always have two families to love you and take care of you. I know it seems bad right now, but it will get much better soon. When you're older, I hope you'll understand everything and realize that this was the best for you." He got up from his chair. "This hearing is closed."

Lila looked at the three dead faces across the table, and a forlorn voice inside her asked how could this be the best. But as she walked around the table to claim her own, she stilled the voice and said, as much to herself as to Gloria, " I'll make it the best, my darling. You'll see."

The pain in Lila's right arm had become insistent, so when she drew Gloria to her feet, she gripped Gloria's right hand with her left hand. Willie moved to Gloria's left side, and the three of them followed Mrs. Warren from the room to the back door of the courthouse and across the street to the bar where Purnell and Cutler were waiting. Purnell called for a doctor to meet them at a hospital. Willie wanted to take Gloria back to the hotel, but Lila would not permit Gloria to be parted from her, and so all five went to the hospital. Lila was given codeine and her separated shoulder strapped. Then they returned to the hotel where Willie ordered up lunch. He had to guess what to order for Gloria, who wouldn't speak, but sat, staring in front of her. She would get up, sit, eat, go to the bathroom, as she was told, but showed no other reaction, not even when Mrs. Warren appeared after lunch with one suitcase filled with Gloria's clothes and another with her toys.

Lila and Willie pulled Mrs. Warren aside. "Do you think she's all right?" Willie asked.

"All right, Mr. Burke? Her whole world was turned upside down today," she snapped and shook her head, before continuing in her normal voice. "No, she's not all right. She's gone into hiding. It's a common way of coping. She'll come out of it when she's ready. That could be a few days or even longer. What yoy have to worry about is what she's going to do then. Keep your eyes open, particularly with Mrs. Burke being injured."

Lila was puzzled. "What do you mean?"

"Gloria may try to run away, she may try to break things. She may refuse to do anything you ask her to. Sometimes they think that if they're very good, they'll be allowed to go back; sometimes, unfortunately, it's just the opposite."

"What should we do?"

"The most important thing is to be patient. Give her time, and she'll come around."

When Mrs. Warren left, Cutler and Purnell did, too. Willie tried to interest Gloria in a game, with no success and they sat together like statues. Remembering Gloria's first greeting that morning, Lila decided to take her to the zoo to see the baby elephant, and nothing Willie could say would dissuade her.

They stood in front of the enclosure. Lila gripped the bars with her left hand to keep from falling down, while Gloria stood motionless, not a flicker crossing her face as the baby elephant happily bumbled about.

Lila tried her best. "Look, darling, what's he going to do now? Oop's. Isn't that funny? Gloria, darling, say something." Nothing worked.

Willie hovered, ready to grab either one as the action might demand, but they got back to the hotel without incident. Lila was not up to the hotel dining room, and it was room service again for dinner. At bedtime, they put Gloria into one of the two beds in the bedroom, and a cot was set up for Willie in the living room. Gloria docilely allowed herself to be changed into her pajamas and washed her face and brushed her teeth. She got into bed but seemed agitated.

"Do you want something?" Lila asked, sitting on the bed. "Tell mama, do you need anything? Water? Is there too much light?"

Gloria seemed to be struggling to speak; her head rolled back and forth, her fingers clenched the covers.

"What is it darling?"

The little mouth opened and croaked one word. "Blinky." Lila almost cried with relief. She went to Gloria's suitcase and pulled Blinky out, brought him to the bed, and was rewarded by the softening in Gloria's face as she clutched the animal to her and fell asleep. A few minutes later, Lila climbed into the other bed.

The next morning, Lila was drained of strength and was grateful for Willie's logistical skills that transported them smoothly from the hotel to the train and made porters appear magically with food and ice and pillows. Although ashamed of the feeling, she was grateful, too, that Gloria woke up in the same trance-like state in which she had gone to bed the night before. Lila doubted she could have coped with a normal child and certainly not with the hysterical one Mrs. Warren had warned them Gloria might become.

As the ride wore on, Lila's shoulder began to throb in rhythm with the jerking of the train. Over Willie's protests, she took more codeine and slid into an exhausted stupor. She was conscious of their arrival at Grand Central and of the ride to their building, but fell asleep in the elevator and retained no memory of the return of her child to her home.

III

Most afternoons, Lila falls asleep. Today, Peggy's visit has stimulated her, and her mind is unwilling to shut down. That doesn't bother Lila. The blinds are drawn, and the staff knows not to disturb her. The clean sheets feel cool and refreshing and, for the moment, no part of her body is complaining. In a way, this state is more restful than sleep, since she can control her thoughts and direct them away from anything that might disturb her peace. It's not too different from the days when the right amount of alcohol took her flying.

She smiles at that recollection, but the thought of alcohol leads to the memory of the terrible things that happened in the years when she drank not to fly but to crash, deliberately plunging from the clean skies into the muck. Once she awakened in this very bed with a terrible hangover, remembering that Willie was in New York but unable to recall the identity of the man snoring next to her or how he got there.

Point taken, Lila thinks. But her peace has been disturbed, and she is not unhappy to hear the distant sound of the front doorbell. She gets out of bed, pulls on her bathrobe and goes from her room to the head of the stairs, just in time to hear Mary say to someone "And God bless you, too," followed by the sound of the closing door.

"Who was that, Mary, and where's Jeffrey?" Lila calls.

Mary comes to the foot of the stairs. "He's fetching the newspaper, Mum. It was them Witnesses, again. I said you couldn't be disturbed. Do you want this?" She holds up a leaflet.

After the first visits from the Jehovah's Witnesses forty plus years ago, Lila has not looked at the reading material they always leave. Today, on a whim, she asks Mary to bring the leaflet up to her. She takes it into her room, opens the blinds and sits down with it.

The cover shows a familiar peaceable kingdom of people of all ages smiling in a sunny landscape complete with friendly animals. There is one difference from those covers she remembers: now all races are represented. She is pleased that God has decided to admit His black and brown and yellow children to the Kingdom. Lila turns a few pages. The sentiments are exemplary, extolling kindness, decency, love, and prayer. Those who live as the leaflet tells them are promised the rewards of happiness during life and Heaven afterward.

That's the problem, she thinks. Those promises. They're not God's own; they've been put into His mouth by men for their own purposes. She has seen too many blameless people rewarded with suffering to believe in promises of happiness during lifetime, so how can she believe those who preach it when they promise Heaven as well?

Father Antonio encouraged her to give up Gloria because he knew that Lila's mother would keep Gloria in the Church. What suffering that had brought. How could a loving God have let Lila do that when she had prayed herself hoarse begging for His help? And, years later, when she had come back to the Church in a desperate effort to pull herself out of a life of sin and had confessed every sordid detail and sincerely repented and been absolved, it was less than a week before God let her plunge back in. It was only when the catastrophic stroke hit Willie that she decided they had both been punished enough and changed her life herself.

Oh, there is a God, all right. Lila believes that firmly. But she no longer believes He has ever promised her anything or expected anything from her. He will do whatever He wants with her in this life and in the next if He has any interest in her at all. Which she doubts. And if a peaceable kingdom can ever exist, it won't be on the Earth she knows too well.

She tosses the leaflet into the wastebasket, dresses and goes downstairs. She picks up a book, takes it out into the garden and settles next to the fountain.

•   •   •

At two the next afternoon, Lila awakened, disoriented by the confusion of dream and memory, until the pain in her shoulder brought recollection. Mary, her new maid, was standing in the doorway, carrying a tray with orange juice and coffee. Lila gingerly climbed out of bed, took up her robe from the back of a chair and the juice from Mary's tray and walked stiffly out of her bedroom to the guest room next door where Gloria was to stay until her room was completed. There was no Gloria, but Blinky and Pooh peaceably shared the head of the neatly made bed. Lila turned to Mary who had followed her.

"Mr. Burke took the little girl to Mass and then to the Park," Mary said.

There was something unsettled in the tone that caused Lila to snap back "Gloria's my daughter, and she's going to live here from now on. Do you understand?"

"I know, Mum. You explained that before."

"So, what's the matter?"

Mary stood silent, the tray still in her hands; she offered it, awkwardly. Lila realized that she was still holding the glass of orange juice. She drank it, then put it back on the tray. Mary offered the tray again, the coffee, this time, but Lila shook her head. "What's bothering you, Mary?"

Mary looked at the coffee cup as she answered. "It's just that the poor little thing won't say a word, Mum. I helped her get dressed and brought her into the kitchen to have her breakfast with me while Mr. Burke was reading his paper, and I asked her what she liked, and she wouldn't answer. Well, I gave her some juice, and she drank it down and then I asked Mrs. Thompson to make her a poached egg on toast. Children seem to like that. And she ate it all right and drank a glass of milk and all the time I was trying to talk to her, but she made no answer at all. Is there something wrong with her voice, then?"

"No, Mary. Gloria's fine. It's just that everything is strange. I'm sure she'll be all right soon. Thank you for being so nice to her." Lila put her hand over the girl's for a moment. "Now, help me get dressed."

With Mary's help, Lila dressed and got into her sling and took her cup of coffee to her workroom. She set it down on the big, square table in the middle of the room, where it sat, cooling, while Lila stared blankly at the bright red cover of the notebook she had started to fill with lists and memos in preparation for Gloria's arrival.

Lila had expected grief and anger, of course, but not this total withdrawal. After all, Gloria was in a safe, familiar place surrounded by people she knew. What was it Mrs. Warren had said? Hiding. Gloria was in hiding somewhere that Lila couldn't reach. Lila knew what that was like. She had been there, too, escaping a world that was too painful to bear, building walls against the unendurable reality.

The way to bring Gloria out of hiding was to show her that her new life would be filled with love and joy, would be a life she would come to welcome. Lila knew she could do that. She just needed time. Hadn't Mrs. Warren said that? All in good time. She took a sip of her coffee and opened her notebook. At the top of the master list, Margo had written "FIRST THING: CALL ME" in big red letters. A few minutes later, they arranged for Margo to take the train in from Long Island the next morning to go shopping with Lila and Gloria.

Lila concentrated on her work, oblivious to household noises. At one point she realized that Mary must have come back since the cup had been refilled with hot coffee. Lila smiled and went back to work. Another hour passed before Willie's key sounded in the front door. She froze and listened for the little running feet, the little searching voice. Nothing.

Finally, Willie. "Liiiii-lah. Where are you?"

The tone told the whole story. Tired, frustrated, apologetic. The little feet would not be running. The little voice would still be silent. Lila closed the notebook, set her back straight, printed a smile on her face and came out to welcome her family. Willie was flushed and sweating; grass stains marred his slacks. Gloria was unmarked. Her curls, as fine as moss, were undisturbed; her sable eyes looked straight ahead without curiosity, and no hint of emotion disturbed the smooth line of her lips. On a finger, a glittering ring from a Crackerjack box winked in vain for attention, and she held the string of a bright yellow balloon with the bored air of a coatroom attendant.

"Sweetheart!" cried Lila, and ran to give Gloria a one-armed hug, which was neither welcomed nor rejected. "You and Willie must have had a great time."

She turned with an outstretched arm to Willie. In mid-gesture, seeing his face dripping and his shirt dark with perspiration, she switched her hug to a pat on the cheek. "My goodness, Gloria, what have you done to Willie? Did you push him in the lake?" Silence. "Look at the poor man; he's almost drowned."

Willie took his cue. "We bought a kite, and I had to do a lot of running to get it up."

Lila clapped her hands. "That sounds so exciting, I wish I had been there. How long did it stay up, sweetheart?" she asked Gloria.

Silence. "Not long," said Willie. "There wasn't much wind, and if you didn't keep running the kite would come right down." Lila looked at Gloria, dry and cool. Willie continued, "The third time, the kite got caught in a tree."

"And then?"

"We had hot dogs, Cokes, and Crackerjacks and walked around the Reservoir. Then I pushed her in a swing, and we came home."

"Oh, Willie. Gloria, sweetheart, didn't you tell him you're too old for Crackerjack rings and balloons and swings? She's a big girl, now, Willie. You can't treat her like a baby."

Willie's red face flushed even redder. "She liked the swing. At least, I think she did. How the hell am I supposed to—uh, uh, sorry? Uh, I need a shower." He bolted from the room.

Lila shook her head. "That's what men are like, sweetheart. Sometimes they behave as though they have no idea whatsoever what a woman wants. Come, let's see if Mrs.Thompson has made any lemonade." She took Gloria's hand, without resistance, and led her to the kitchen.

The rest of the day, Willie hid in the den, claiming work. He had done yeoman duty already, and Lila sincerely apologized for having been critical. It wasn't his fault that he had gotten no reaction from Gloria. Gloria didn't react to any of the toys, games or other activities Lila came up with either, didn't answer anything Lila said to her and continued through the entire day like a beautifully carved figurine.

The next morning was Monday. Lila got Gloria settled at breakfast then called St Louis twice before Mrs. Warren got to her office, reaching her on the third try. Lila began a detailed account. Mrs. Warren announced she was busy, asked two or three questions, told Lila to keep up the good work and hung up. Lila didn't dare call again; the woman might change her mind about how well Lila was doing.

The next call was to the nursing home. Lila hated to make it, but there was no question of her spending a day away from Gloria under present conditions. Things had changed, she told the director, and she didn't know when she might be able to come back.

She returned to the dining room. Gloria was watching the last of her Cornflakes bobbing in the milk in her bowl as she made waves with her spoon. The doorbell rang. Margo was here.

"Gloria, darling, it's your Aunt Margo. Come."

Lila couldn't believe it. Gloria's head didn't even turn. She had met Margo on her visit to New York and had been enchanted by Margo's dramatic personality. Lila had felt pangs of jealousy as the two of them had whispered secrets and giggled every time their eyes met across the table in the restaurant. Now, no reaction at all. Lila went to the front door, and Margo came stumbling in carrying the most enormous stuffed panda Lila had ever seen.

"Where's Princess Gloria?" Margo demanded loudly. "I bring her a special gift from her devoted admirer, the Emperor of China. Where are you, Your Royal Highness?"

Lila shook her head and pointed to the dining room. Margo paraded in, singing the march from "Aida" and holding the panda in front of her, making its arms move back and forth to the music. All around the table she marched. Gloria's head turned slightly so she could follow the progress, and Lila felt a thrill of hope. Margo came to a halt next to Gloria and set the panda on the floor. His head came up higher than Gloria's, as she sat in her chair, and she reached up to feel one furry ear. Her face began to shiver like the surface of a glass of water tapped on the side.

"Isn't he wonderful? Thank Aunt—," Lila stopped, but it was too late. Gloria's face froze, and her hand fell back into her lap. Lila wanted to scream, to tear her own hair out or Margo's, to pull Gloria from her chair and slap her face until she spoke or cried or fought back. But she couldn't do any of these things, so she counted silently to ten and said, "Put the panda in your room, darling. We're going shopping with Aunt Margo."

Gloria got off the chair, put her arms around the panda and solemnly left the dining room. As soon as she was gone, Lila sat down and held her head in her hands. Margo came around the table to her and put her arm around Lila's shoulders.

"You poor things. It could break a person's heart to see you both like this." She hugged Lila tightly.

Lila drew herself together. "I'm all right." She removed Margo's arm. "Give me a handkerchief, will you." She took it and wiped her face. "We'll both be all right. I'm just so stupid, I can't figure out what to do, yet. You have to help me. You always seem to know how to get to people. How can I get to her?"

"I don't know, sweetie. I haven't got a whole lot of experience with children."

"I know, but you still always do it right. Look how close you just came. Help me."

"I'll try to. Hush now and let's think about the rest of today."

Lila hushed and they pulled themselves together and made their plans for the day and got Gloria from her room and went out. They went to Best's and Saks and Bonwit Teller, and they bought Gloria clothes and shoes and a makeup set.

They went for lunch to Reuben's where they ran into Willie and his partners. Willie had them make up a special Gloria sandwich, mixed chopped turkey and ham on toast with Russian dressing and a slice of tomato cut in the shape of a heart pinned to the top with a toothpick. They went to

Bloomingdales and bought Gloria a radio-phonograph and records, a bookcase and books and a dressing table to put the makeup set on. They went to Schraffts for hot fudge sundaes and came back to the apartment where Lila and Margo collapsed in the living room, and Gloria disappeared into her room.

Lila was calm and cheerful. Margo was Margo. It didn't matter. Gloria said nothing. She tried on the clothes they gave her, but showed no preference for one dress over another, for black shoes over brown or for maple furniture over white lacquer. She ate the Gloria sandwich without reaction, to the great chagrin of Willie and Arnold Reuben. The only sign of any like or dislike she gave them was leaving the chopped walnuts uneaten in her sundae dish.

•　　　　•　　　　•

Gloria's withdrawal continued. She spent most of each day in her room with the door closed. If Lila turned the radio on, Gloria would leave it on. If Lila handed her a book and told her to read, she would sit reading, or appearing to read, until Lila told her to stop. Lila had to postpone Gloria's interview at St. Agnes. School would not start for another three weeks, and Willie's connections had her place assured, if only—. Lila could not complete the thought.

A second call to Mrs. Warren, Thursday morning, was even more disturbing than the first. Although she was still optimistic, Mrs. Warren seemed less confident than before. She asked Lila several questions and seemed to continue to approve of what Lila was doing but "You never know, with children." She ended by suggesting that the first telephone call between Gloria and John and Cath be made earlier than the second week as originally planned.

When Willie came home from work, Lila took him into the den and reported her conversation with Mrs. Warren. Willie objected to calling St. Louis.

"She's our child, and we have to deal with her. You think the judge ended the war? That we've won it for all time? Wrong, darling girl. Gloria, herself, has to tell us. If we run to John and Cath now, they'll know they still have a chance, and we'll be right back where we were. Worst of all, Gloria will know she's winning, and we're losing."

"What are you saying, Willie? I'm at war with Gloria? My own daughter? That's crazy."

Willie took time to pour himself a drink before he answered. "I'd have thought it crazy, too, a week ago. Now, I'm not so sure. This may be like a cowboy breaking in a wild horse. You know. Not roughly. Gently, with love. But firmly. So she knows she has to accept it."

Lila was furious. "You want to treat Gloria like a horse? You are crazy, Willie. She just needs time to realize that I love her and she loves me. It's love, Willie, not war. If you can accept that, you and she will come to love each other as well. If not—"

Willie put his hands up. "Hey, calm down. We're on the same side, here. I didn't mean that the way you took it. I just think that Gloria has to understand that this is not a good way to behave and she doesn't seem to be getting that from the way we've been reacting. Will calling your brother tonight help? Go ahead, if you think so."

Lila waited until Gloria had finished her supper and was getting out of her chair.

"Gloria."

Gloria stopped and waited, her napkin still in her hand.

"Would you like to speak to John and Catherine on the telephone, tonight, sweetheart?" Lila had kept her voice steady, but her heartbeat grew faster. She had no idea what Gloria's reaction would be. Out of the corner of her eye, she saw Willie tense up, too.

Gloria said nothing.

"Did you hear me, darling? We can telephone out to St Louis, and you can talk with them now. Would you like that?"

Gloria said nothing, just put her napkin on the table and walked from the room.

Willie became very busy pouring himself another cup of coffee from the carafe left on the table, adding precisely the right amount of cream and a level teaspoon of sugar. "He'd better not say anything," Lila thought, but her anger turned into despair. Would nothing work? She tried unsuccessfully to run through the possibilities; her brain seemed disabled by the palpable tension in the apartment. Maybe things would be better out at the house.

Willie and Lila had organized their households so that weekends in Long Island could be arranged on short notice. One of the maids and a houseboy lived at the house from Spring to Fall, and there was a full supply of linens and dishes and a stock of canned goods. Lila and Willie both had clothes in the closets; the tennis courts and pool were always ready for use.

This time, however, Gloria had to be considered. Country clothing was packed along with sets of sheets and towels and a selection of toys, books, and games. Then there was the food for the weekend, ordered by Mrs. Thompson. Jackson, the chauffeur, carried suitcases and boxes down to the Lincoln until the trunk and most of the back seat were full. At last, the passengers, including the panda, were crammed into the wagon for the hour-long trip.

When they got to the house, Lila gave the staff a few orders and took Gloria's hand and led her out to the back where the huge lawn sloped down to the woods. One of the gardeners, on a tractor, was mowing and the sweet smell of cut grass and clover blossoms came drifting up to them. They walked down the hill together, and for once Lila, too, was silent. As they passed through the mown area, Lila kicked with each step, and little clouds of grass flew into the air. At the edge of the woods, she turned right, still holding Gloria's hand. They continued until the corner of the lawn, where an old stone wall ran perpendicularly back up the hill.

A few yards up, the wall had been dislodged by the roots of a large oak tree. The grass among the roots was uncut, and a little cluster of dandelions found shelter from the blades. Lila sat down, her back against the tree and drew Gloria down next to her. They sat still for a couple of minutes watching the tractor swing back and forth as it worked its way up the lawn. The heavy air muted the sound of the mowing machine to the buzz of a giant insect. Lila plucked a dandelion, tied its stem into a knot with a loop and put the dandelion on her finger, the bloom on top like the jewel of a ring. Gloria seemed interested, and Lila picked a second dandelion and handed it to her. Gloria tried to follow what Lila had done, but her knot came untied, and the dandelion fell off. Lila picked it up, put it back into Gloria's hand, and guided her fingers to make a proper knot. Gloria held out her hand, and the dandelion stayed in place.

Lila could hardly breathe from joy and tension. She was afraid to speak; that would surely break the spell. She could think of nothing to do except to sit, motionless, hoping to prolong it. A figure emerged from the house and started down the hill toward them. "Not yet," she thought. "Just a few minutes more." But, too soon, Ellen reached them.

"Missus Thompson says to tell you she has lunch ready, Missus. What shall I tell her?"

"Thank you, Ellen. Tell her we'll be up in a few minutes. And Ellen, this is my daughter, Gloria, who's come home to live with us from now on."

Ellen dipped slightly in some vestigial remnant of a curtsy. "What a beautiful child, Mum. I'm pleased to meet you, Miss Gloria. I'm sure you'll be very happy here." She spun around and headed back up the hill.

"You will be happy," Lila wanted to tell her child and hug her close but stopped herself. Soon, now, though. Instead, she said pleasantly "Time for lunch, darling," and got up and took Gloria's hand and pulled her up. As she did, Gloria's dandelion ring fell from her finger to the ground. Gloria made no effort to pick it up.

After lunch, Lila and Mary took Gloria to the upstairs guest room. New furniture had not yet been obtained, and the adult bed was just the right size for the panda who lay on his back, paws in the air, Blinky stretched out across his tummy. Lila grinned at Mary, who giggled. Gloria smiled. It wasn't a big smile, and it only lasted a second, but it was a smile.

"Take a little nap," Lila blurted and fled the room to keep from shouting in triumph. It was working. She had been right. It wasn't over yet, oh no, but it was working. In time. She just had to be patient. There was a soft knock on her door.

"Come in."

It was Mary. "She's gone to sleep. What do you want me to do?"

"When she wakes up, take her to the kitchen for something to drink and then out on the back patio. I'm going into the village for a few minutes. Keep an eye on her, Mary."

"Yes, Mum," she turned.

"Mary?"

"Yes, Mum."

" Did—did you see her smile?"

"Oh yes, Mum. Wasn't it lovely?"

Lila couldn't help running to Mary and giving her a hug. She had to hug someone, she was so happy. "Oh thank you, Mary. Yes, it was lovely."

An hour later, Lila returned from the village. Coming around the corner of the house, she saw Gloria and Mary sitting in the shade of a big umbrella on the patio. Mary was talking animatedly and Gloria listening. Occasionally, Mary would stop talking, but when Gloria made no response, would continue her discourse. She fell silent when she saw Lila approach.

"What were you two talking about," Lila asked gaily.

"I was telling Miss Gloria about my family in Ireland. My youngest sister is eight years old now, just about the same age, isn't she?"

"That's right. You must miss your family a lot."

"Sometimes, I do, Mum. But it's hard over there. We were seven children and no money. Work's not easy to come by, in Ireland. And it's nice here and having Miss Gloria around will be a little like having my sister here. If that's all right to say, Mum."

"That's a very nice thing to say, Mary. Gloria would be lucky to have a sister as nice as you. And I think you should just call her Gloria; forget about the "Miss." She's not used to it. Tell the others to do the same. It doesn't sound right for an eight-year-old. I'm going to take Gloria on a tour of the place and won't need you until five. Go see if Ellen needs any help."

They walked the same way as before but, at the bottom of the hill, turned left to the tennis court, shaded by a rectangle of blue spruces. Lila led them between the trees, through a gate in a high fence and out onto the red clay court. It was rolled and brushed smooth.

"Willie and I love tennis," Lila said, "and Aunt Margo is a very good player. If you like, you can take lessons and become a good player, too." She walked to the net and picked up a ball lying there. "Catch." She tossed it underhand. Gloria put up her hands and caught the ball cleanly, then let it drop.

They went on to the flower garden and the vegetable garden and a pen with a half-dozen chickens. Gloria remained docile but showed no interest. The same for the greenhouse, although one of the gardeners took them through, pointing out species of flowers and showing them how the misting machine worked. Next to the greenhouse was a big red barn and the gardener showed them the tractors and the mowers and the gardening equipment.

Movement in the back of the barn caught Lila's attention. "What's that, Harry?" she asked the gardener.

He laughed. "That's Molly and her pups. She had four this week. You can go look at them but don't get too close." He threw a switch, and a light went on in the back of the barn. Lila and Gloria tiptoed back and saw a beagle, lying in a pile of rags with four puppies, like fat, fuzzy mice with big ears. Three of them were asleep, but the fourth, a little smaller than the others, was pawing at a piece of fabric a couple of feet from its mother.

Suddenly Lila heard a thin voice say "Oohhh, look." Gloria was standing on her toes, both hands pointing at the puppy, her face transfigured. She took a step toward it, and the mother raised her head and growled. Gloria stepped back, her hands still held out. In a few seconds, the mother lowered her head but kept her eyes on Gloria. The puppy caught a paw in the fabric and fell, but got up immediately and scrambled back to the mother. Again Lila heard "Oohh," sounding so natural, so much what she almost said herself, so obviously what an eight-year-old would say, that it still took a minute for her to realize that her daughter had just spoken for the first time since that terrible melee in St. Louis.

The gardener grinned. "Do you have a dog of your own, Miss?"

Gloria shook her head.

"Well, then, would you like to have this one, if your mother says it's all right?" They both looked at Lila, and she realized what she had to say. Nothing. She willed her mouth to stay closed, her face to stay expressionless, her eyes to stay fixed staring into Gloria's. Five minutes ago she would have given anything to hear Gloria speak at all, but now she knew it was not enough. Gloria must speak to her, must acknowledge her. Terrible as it sounded when he said it, Willie was right. Lila was engaged in a conflict. Not with Gloria, her own loved and loving daughter, but with some demon that had taken possession of Gloria at the moment that a roomful of people committed to her protection had all turned their attention away from her to hatred and anger. Sooner or later the conflict must come to a head, and Lila might never find a better battleground.

"Come on, darling," she willed. "Ask me."

Gloria inhaled deeply, then exhaled, her face straining as she expelled her breath. "C-c-can I?" she asked Lila.

Lila spoke as if it were nothing. "Of course, sweetheart. You'd better leave him with his mother for a while, though. Harry, how long do you think we should leave him?"

"I'm not sure, Miz Burke. Two weeks, anyway. Maybe a month. We'll have to see. He's not going anywhere, though, and you can come see him whenever you're out."

"That sounds fine, Harry. All right sweetheart?"

Gloria nodded.

They walked back to the house without speaking. Now that the silence had been broken, Lila did not need to continue her previous parody of conversation. When they got to the house, she asked Gloria if she wanted to go for a swim. Gloria said yes. They went upstairs, and Lila took Gloria's new bathing suits out and asked her which she wanted to wear. Gloria said she wanted the blue one. They went to the pool. Gloria swam sedately near the shallow end, then floated in an inner tube. After the swim, she said she was thirsty, and Lila got them Cokes.

They sipped their drinks as they dried in the sun. The pump chugged away cheerfully; occasionally a bird chirped. How comfortable and companionable it was to be sitting quietly together. There was nothing Lila felt like saying; there was nothing she needed to hear. She realized she almost never did this. When she and Willie were together now, they were either busy doing something or else talking about doing something. If neither spoke, it was because one or both of them were thinking things that should not be spoken. This, however, was a good silence. She was sure Gloria was thinking nice thoughts, too.

As if on cue, Gloria said, "Could we—?" She looked in the direction of the barn.

"You want to go back and see what he's doing?" Gloria nodded. "OK, let's get out of these wet suits and go take a look."

The puppies were feeding. Gloria stared, fascinated, as they tugged on their mother's teats, slipping off and scrabbling frantically over each other to get back. Finishing they went to sleep, collapsing against each other in a heap among the rags. The one Gloria had chosen was the last. He dug himself into the pile and joined his siblings in sleep.

Lila said, "We have to ask Harry who the father is so we can get an idea what he'll look like. What are you going to name him?"

Gloria hesitated. "Is it a boy?"

"I don't know, actually. Let's go find Harry."

They located Harry who came back with them. Molly allowed him to pick up the puppy and examine it briefly but was quite relieved when he put it back. "It's a girl," he said. "The daddy must be that black Labrador mix at the Jamisons who comes through the woods now and then. See, some of their coats are almost all black already. This one's got more beagle in her, though. Looks like she'll be spotted like a pinto pony. What are you going to call her?"

"She hasn't decided yet," Lila said, but Gloria interrupted.

"Yes, I have. Pinto."

Lila was to tell that story many times, over the years. As she would say, it didn't take Gloria long to make up her mind or a lot of words to speak it.

The rest of the weekend passed pleasantly. Friends came over for tennis and lunch on Saturday and, although Lila was unable to play because of her shoulder, she was happy to be able to relax in the company of adults for a while. Mary trotted around with Gloria who seemed content as long as she could visit with Pinto every hour or so.

Early Monday morning, Willie drove in with Mrs. Thompson and Mary, and Lila had a quiet day alone with Gloria. She was disappointed to discover that conversation would be limited to practical matters requiring present attention. Was Gloria hungry or thirsty, what would she like to eat or drink, had she brushed her teeth, did she know where Mary was. Occasionally, Gloria would initiate the exchange on her own. She wanted to visit Pinto, she needed the bathroom, which towel should she take at the pool. Physical contact had its own rules. Lila was allowed to take Gloria's hand when they were walking someplace, but not while they were sitting or standing in one place. Lila might hold Gloria up to pick an apple off a tree or to help her out of the pool, but anything intended as a hug or other form of affection was rejected or, worse, ignored.

•   •   •

Back in New York, Tuesday was the pediatrician and Wednesday, the dentist. Both found Gloria in perfect health. When she reported this to Willie, he asked when she was going to be examined by a veterinarian. Lila let that pass, considering that he had brought home a book on raising a dog and read a few pages with Gloria after dinner.

Lila had listened at the door while Gloria was reading.

"Dogs need a lot of attention. They are soc—."

"That's 'sociable,' Gloria."

"What does that mean?"

"They like being with other dogs or with people."

"They are sociable animals. Dogs, like their cousins the wolves, used to hunt in packs before they became do—do-mest—What's this word?"

"Domesticated. That means coming in from the wild and being owned by humans. Like cows and horses. There are still some wild dogs in Africa, I think, but not in America."

Lila tiptoed away. Bedtime could wait.

Wednesday evening had been scheduled as the time for the first regular telephone call to John and Catherine. With Mrs. Warren's concurrence, Lila had not repeated the attempt of last week to make an earlier call and was very glad that the call had not been made. She had even asked for a deferral, hoping that Gloria's progress might continue, but Mrs. Warren had insisted. She had said she would warn Catherine not to expect too much.

As soon as dinner was over, Lila led Gloria into the den. Willie, coached by Mrs. Warren, had already placed the call and was waiting with Catherine on the line. "Don't ask her first, just get her on with them as quickly as possible," Mrs. Warren had told her. Willie nodded, and Lila led Gloria to the phone. "Someone wants to talk to you, Darling," she said, and Willie shoved the phone up to Gloria's ear. She took it from him, almost to keep it from falling to the floor, and Lila could hear Catherine's voice saying "Hello, Gloria."

Panic flashed across Gloria's face. She dropped the telephone and would have jumped up, had Lila not still been holding her. The telephone clattered on the desk and fell to the carpet. "Gloria? Gloria?" said Catherine faintly. Willie grabbed Gloria's free hand in his and bent down and picked up the telephone with his other hand.

"Sorry, Catherine," he said, "we dropped the phone." He smoothly put it back in Gloria's hand. "Here, Gloria, now talk to Catherine."

Gloria put the telephone to her mouth "Hello," she said without inflection. There was a pause while Catherine spoke, then, "Yes." Another pause. Again, "Yes A few more yes's, a couple of no's. Then Lila heard John's faint voice, speak, then stop, then speak again more loudly, "Give the phone to my sister!"

Gloria handed the telephone to Lila who released Gloria's wrist. Willie bent over Gloria to say something, but she was past him and out of the room before he could get it out. He started to follow, but Lila raised her hand to stop him.

"Hello, John," she said.

"What have you done to her?" he screamed.

"Didn't Mrs. Warren tell you?"

"I don't care what she says. You must have drugged her. I'm going to—"

Lila hung up, shaking. Willie put his arms around her, and they stood together until the telephone rang. Willie picked up the receiver. "Yes?" he said in a challenging tone. Then, softly, "Oh, Catherine." Pause. "I'm sorry, too." Lila nodded at him. "Here's Lila."

Lila took the phone, "Hello, Cath." She motioned Willie to the door and mouthed "Gloria" to him, and he left.

"How is she, really? Tell me everything, Lila. Please."

For a half-hour, Lila went through the past two weeks of Gloria's life, hour by hour. Catherine never interrupted her, except for involuntary expressions of concern and relief. When Lila finished, she waited while Catherine composed herself.

"Thank you, Lila. I know it's all the truth. You owe me that much, you know."

"I'll never lie to you, Cath. I promise."

"Never again, you mean. If I hadn't believed you and persuaded John to bring Gloria to New York..." Her voice broke. "Good-bye, Lila." She hung up.

Exhausted, Lila put down the telephone. She couldn't go through this every two weeks. She had to hope that subsequent calls would be less painful—perhaps when Gloria was ready to carry on a conversation.

In the hall, she heard Willie's voice, the deep, rolling one with the Irish accent he used for jokes and stories. She peeked from the edge of the door. Gloria was sitting at the head of her bed, her back up against a stack of pillows, the dog book open in front of her. Willie was in the big quilted easy chair, pulled up next to her. Gloria followed his dramatic gestures as he talked.

"Oh they're *divils*, all right. They'll eat anything you leave unprotected, 'specially when they're still young. I remember this big, red setter named Seamus my Uncle Francis had. You've seen them, they call them Irish setters?"

"Uh-huh."

"Well, Uncle Francis had a party, once, in his backyard. I was maybe eleven or twelve. And Seamus was having the best time running from one to another and getting patted and fed little bits of crackers and things. He was such a handsome creature and the friendliest thing you ever saw. You couldn't hardly say no to him when he'd put his big paw on your knee and his head up close to yours. So, as you can well imagine, he'd been eating more than he should and of some of what he begged he shouldn't have eaten at all.

"Anyway, one of the guests was drinking a martini. You know what that is, darling girl?"

"No. What?"

"It's mostly gin with a few drops of vermouth, that's another kind of booze, with an olive floating in it. There's no soda or anything mixed with it, so you have to be real careful; you can get drunk on two or three of them. So this fella had one, and he takes just a sip and puts it down on the table next to him and starts arguing with someone about something.

"Along comes Seamus and puts his paw up on the fella who's too busy arguing to pay attention to the beast and just shoves him away. Then Seamus spots the glass on the table and stands on his hind legs and puts his front paws on the table around the glass. In about three seconds he lapped up the whole thing, olive and all."

Gloria's mouth was hanging open. "Was he punished?"

"No, everyone was laughing too hard. In a few minutes, he started staggering around, bumping into things. Then he wobbled over to the bushes and threw up and went under the porch to sleep it off. He was fine in a few hours, but he never stole another drink."

Gloria clapped her hands, and Lila said, "You may think that's a good story, now, Gloria, but wait until you've heard it as many times as I have."

Willie started to protest, but Lila shut him up with a big kiss on the cheek. "Go along, now, and think up a new one. Gloria and I have to get ready for bed."

Gloria changed into her pajamas, washed her face, brushed her teeth and dutifully went to bed. After turning out the light, Lila sank into the easy chair, waiting for Gloria to fall asleep. As she waited, she reviewed the ghastly telephone call. She didn't know what she would have done if Willie hadn't been there to help. Willie was as helpful as he could and patient and gentle with Gloria. Why couldn't he have accepted her from the beginning? Damn him and all his smug, intolerant family. How happy the three of them could have been.

Stop it, she told herself. That page had been turned, and they were on a new one. Willie was trying to do the right things, now. If only Gloria became the daughter she wanted, Lila would be content to live out her days as Willie's wife.

• • •

Gloria began to answer, regularly, when addressed. She spoke first on several occasions and would even carry on a conversation, but only on the subject of Pinto, who was scheduled to come to New York with the family right after Labor Day. Lila never tired of the sound of Gloria's voice, even when raised impatiently in argument. Lila discovered that, once Gloria had formed an opinion, she would assert it vigorously.

"She has to sleep with me."

"But darling, she needs to be near her water bowl and food dish in the kitchen."

"You can leave them in my room."

"But dogs are messy eaters. She'll ruin your beautiful new rug."

"I don't care about the dumb rug."

"That dumb rug cost six hundred dollars."

"She'll be lonesome in the kitchen. Dogs are sociable animals. Ask Willie, he'll tell you."

Coming under Gloria's scornful tongue was a small price to pay for the pleasure of seeing her face animated and her arms waving, of hearing her voice raised as she made her point. There were still moments of withdrawal, and she still kept Lila and Willie at an emotional distance, but Gloria had clearly returned from that eerie world of silent solitude.

Emboldened, Lila brought Gloria for her school interview, which could be postponed no longer. It came off reasonably well. The Sister in charge of admissions was more pleased than not by the shy, quiet, respectful child. Who wouldn't be apprehensive at a strange school in a new city? Sister assured Lila that Gloria's third-grade teacher was kind and patient and, she said laughingly, would not whack her over the knuckles with a ruler every time she made a mistake.

•   •   •

The big weekend arrived. Gloria was so excited that she couldn't sleep Thursday night and came into Lila and Willie's room three times. She was after Lila as soon as she was out of bed and had to be sent out to the market to carry packages for Mrs. Thompson so Lila could have her breakfast in peace. At last, they got on the road. The station wagon had barely stopped rolling in front of the house before Gloria, clutching a collar and leash ran ahead to the barn.

Pinto was thrilled to see Gloria and shook her whole backside wagging her tail. The collar went on easily enough, but when the puppy felt the restraint of the leash she pulled and bucked in growing discomfort. Gloria tried to calm her, with no effect. Harder and harder Pinto tugged, yipping hysterically, while Gloria held fast to the leash, digging her feet into the soft ground. For a moment the two were balanced and motionless, straining against each other like a masterpiece of Renaissance sculpture. Then, with a gigantic effort, Pinto popped free from the loose collar and fled into the barn.

Lila was amazed at the sounds that came out of the delicate mouth. How could such a fragile body feel so much despair and still live? For it did live and turn its head in search of succor and was in motion toward her. Lila instantly opened her arms to her stricken child. Gloria shook and sobbed and said things that Lila could no more understand than if they had both been under water, while she, herself, uttered little sounds of sympathy in the elemental language of mothers comforting their young. It lasted a long time, long enough for Lila to realize just how happy she was at that moment and to feel guilty that her happiness resulted from her daughter's unhappiness.

"It's all right, darling. She just got a little scared. It was because it was the first time. Next time will be easier. No, she doesn't hate you. No, darling, you didn't hurt her. She's fine. You're just not used to each other yet. I don't know why; did you do it just like the book said? You're sure? Why don't we go look and see? That's right. I'm sure you'll be able to do it, and she'll get used to it just like all the puppies do."

They went back to the house and up to Gloria's room and got out the dog book. Lila turned on the bedside lamp and sat down on the bed, Gloria pressed up against her.

"Let's see where it says about collars and leashes. Here we are. 'Put the collar on particularly gently the first few times.'"

"I was gentle, really gentle."

"You were, sweetheart, you couldn't have been any more gentle. I could see that. 'Next, leave the collar on him for a long time so he can get used to it. Don't attach the leash until he seems comfortable with the collar.'"

"Oh, I forgot that part."

"That was the trouble, you put the leash on too quickly. OK, Next time you won't."

"But now, maybe she won't let me even put the collar on." And there were more tears.

"She will, darling, I know she will."

"Can we try now?"

"I don't think so, sweetheart. Let her calm down a little. We'll go back after lunch. I'm sure she'll be fine by then. Why don't we read the rest of this part, so we don't make another mistake? Here, 'When you clip on the leash for the first time, try to let him walk around a little just dragging it with him. When you do hold it, keep it slack.'"

"What's slack?"

"That means loose. 'If he feels it pulling him, his natural instinct will make him pull against it to try to get away.' That's just what happened, darling. 'If you can, let him pull you around at first.' You can do that out on the lawn. There's lots of room."

"Can I take her there after lunch?"

"Let's try it with just the collar, first, this afternoon. See how it goes. Maybe tomorrow she can drag the leash around a little, and you can try holding it Sunday."

"OK. I want to tell Mary and Mrs. Thompson." Gloria jumped off the bed and ran from the room. How quickly they recover, thought Lila. She was still shaking and lay down for a minute with her head in Gloria's pillow until her heart, and her brain slowed to their normal pace. The pillowcase smelled of laundry soap and sun with just a wisp of a scent of something else. Lila snuffled at it, then pulled back the pillowcase to sniff the pillow. It was Gloria's smell. That was just how she had smelled a few minutes ago, sobbing in Lila's arms, but Lila wasn't thinking about smells at the time. And that had been the first time Lila had been that close to Gloria since—since she had been a baby.

And she hadn't smelled like that as a baby. Lila could remember that well. Bland, milky, unassertive, overwhelmed by soaps and powders. Lila mustn't do that; such memories could cause terrible damage. But she could no longer control the memories. She was awash in sights, sounds, smells, and best of all, touches. The feel of the fat little bottom nestling in her hands, the tug of the hungry mouth upon her nipple. She gripped the sides of the mattress in anticipation of the pain, but miraculously, it didn't come. How could that be? Maybe she had won back the rights to those memories when she had won back Gloria. Lila ran down the stairs and into the kitchen where she shouted like a five-year-old "What's for lunch," startling Mrs. Thompson and bringing a disapproving frown to Gloria's face.

The whole household held its collective breath over the long weekend as Gloria made progress with Pinto, assisted by Lila and, after he joined them, Willie, who contributed the brilliant idea of dipping a slice of white bread in chicken gravy to reward Pinto for allowing the leash to be clipped to her collar. By the time they packed up to return to New York on Tuesday, Pinto had accepted collar and leash as a part of her life.

•   •   •

Wednesday was Gloria's first day at school. It would be a strange school in a strange city. Lila would bring her and pick her up; fortunately, this was not unusual for third-graders, although many were picked up and delivered by the school's bus service. Next year Gloria might do that or take the Madison

Avenue bus. Next year, she would be used to the school uniform, a long-sleeved white shirt with a Peter Pan collar worn with a maroon skirt, white socks and black shoes and a matching maroon blazer with the school insignia over the heart. Next year, she would know almost all of her classmates; some would be friends. Next year she would know the teachers, the location of the rooms, the expressions the other girls used. Next year, she would be eager to go.

Gloria protested until bedtime, Tuesday night. When Lila and Willie, together, rejected her final appeal, she stiffened as though a switch had been pulled and turned away from them in her bed. The next morning, she was subdued and withdrawn. She made no resistance, put on the uniform and got her book bag as instructed, preceded Lila into the car downstairs and out of the car at the school without speaking. Lila got directions to the proper room, led Gloria to it and saw Gloria docilely seated with a half-dozen other early pupils.

Lila tried to speak with Gloria's teacher, but Sister Mary Francis, a breezy, robust woman in her mid-thirties, seated Gloria, then ushered Lila out the door before she could finish the first sentence. How could Gloria relate to these self-assured, sophisticated Sisters, so different from the simple, parochial nuns of Lila's childhood.

And the children. They didn't run, they didn't shout. They carried leather bags with Vuitton labels and called each other by fantastic nicknames, speaking in the accents of English actresses. They compared tans and smelled each other's perfume.

Gloria was used to a local public school in a middle-class section of St. Louis. She sat among familiar neighborhood children who played in backyards and playgrounds. Their mothers gave them haircuts, and their fathers taught them to ride bikes. They wore the clothes of older siblings, and putting on their mothers' makeup was a game played once in a while on a rainy day. Gloria wasn't used to competition with so many precocious children. She would fall short of St. Agnes's standards and, before the first day was done, the other children would gather around her in a circle laughing, and Lila would have to come and take her home.

All day, Lila sat, dressed and ready to run when the call for help came. But the telephone didn't ring all morning. The minutes crawled by until, grateful to be allowed to move, Lila left the apartment and Jackson drove her up to St. Agnes, arriving twenty minutes before the end of school, where she waited, alone except for the dozing driver of the yellow school bus. Soon, mothers and governesses began to arrive on foot and in cars they double-parked along the street.

A bell rang inside the school. The bus driver woke up, stretched, put his cap on and opened the front door of the bus. A minute later, a nun opened the double doors and hooked them back, and a great red and white caterpillar came through the doors and humped down the steps. First, came the smallest with their teachers who led them holding hands. The next in size also came out with their teachers but walked freely down the steps. Gloria was among the last of this group and stood for a moment at the top of the stairs with Sister Mary Francis as the next group, older girls without any teachers, flowed around them.

Sister spotted Lila and pointed her out to Gloria who came down the stairs to her. Her face was as expressionless as when Lila had last seen her taking a seat in the classroom. Just before she reached Lila, a voice called out "Bye, Gloria." A little, redheaded girl getting on the bus was waving to them. Gloria smiled and waved back, and Lila breathed a prayer of thanks.

Gloria said little on the way home, responding to Lila's flood of questions with monosyllabic answers and shrugs. Lila was learning to interpret this language and was able to determine that the day had been bearable, Sister Mary Francis was OK, the food at lunch was terrible, and the other children had left her alone except for Julia, the little redhead, who was very nice. From then on, Gloria went to school regularly with no major problems reported.

•   •   •

With Gloria safely in school on weekdays and romping with Pinto at the house on the weekends, Lila's life improved considerably. Even the Wednesday night telephone calls became less painful. On the third call, when Lila, handed over the receiver, Gloria pointed to the door of the room. Lila shook her head. Gloria put her hand over the mouthpiece and said, "Go."

"But darling," Lila replied, "I have to know what you're telling them because if you get something wrong, they'd get very upset."

Lila heard Catherine saying "Hello, hello," her voice rising in both pitch and volume.

Gloria hung up the receiver. Lila began to argue with her, but the telephone rang. It had to be Catherine calling back, and Lila just didn't have the strength to fight the battle that was sure to come. She marched out of the room, slamming the door as she heard Gloria pick up the receiver and say "Hello," in a smug tone that was new to Lila.

Lila was angry with Gloria for refusing to do what she was told, for the manner in which she announced her refusal but, mostly, for what sounded like pleasure at Lila's discomfiture. But the anger made Lila feel guilty; none of this was poor Gloria's fault. There must have been something Lila could have said. Of course, that was Willie's reaction, too, although he had no good ideas as to just what that "something" was. So she was angry with him, as well. The following Wednesday, Lila didn't even wait for Catherine to answer the telephone, but handed the receiver to Gloria after the first ring and quietly left the room. She admitted to Willie that she was relieved to be spared further exposure to either John's hostility or Cath's quiet misery.

Later, Lila realized that this period had been like the early rounds of a match between two boxers fighting each other for the first time. They sparred at long range, appraising strengths, testing for weaknesses. Gloria's early docility gave way to an opinionated determination that Lila suspected might, at the last, be a match for her own. But all daughters struggled against their mothers' authority; all the books said so. So Lila kept calm and patient during the month before Mrs. Warren's follow-up visit to New York, fairly confident that the social worker would find no cause to recommend that Judge Fogarty change his order.

•   •   •

Mrs. Warren bustled off the train like an overloaded bumblebee. She had switched from her smock to a denim jumper teeming with pockets, and, had apparently transferred all of the contents of the former to the latter. There was no other way to explain the blackboard eraser that poked out of one pocket or the crayons overflowing another. To Lila's surprise, Gloria had asked to come and took charge of one of the four shopping bags Mrs. Warren brought off the train. "Thank you, Gloria. Here, carry it by both handles. I apologize, Mrs. Burke; I look like a hobo with this stuff. We couldn't find the key to our good suitcase, and my husband keeps his World War I uniforms in mothballs in the other. He looked so miserable when I suggested moving his things, I hadn't the heart to make him do it."

Mrs. Warren counted to eight for her paper bags, pocketbook, umbrella, hat and a big red folder with "ST. LOUIS JUVENILE COURT" printed across it, then allowed Lila to carry two of the bags and swept up the rest herself. Lila had invited Mrs. Warren to stay with them the two nights she was to be in New York.

"It's real kind of you, Mrs. Burke," Mrs. Warren had replied, "but the Department wouldn't like it, this being a business visit, so to speak." Since Willie had agreed to pay for the trip, Lila had thought that this answer was a bit nervy and had vetoed the Plaza.

"The 'Department' might think we were trying to bribe her."

Instead, Lila reserved at the Dolly Madison, a modest hotel on Lexington Avenue. The "Department" seemed to permit meals together, and Mrs. Warren joined the family for dinner. For a while she made all the conversation, telling stories of her childhood on a farm just before the automobile displaced the horse. Then Willie joined in with a reminiscence of the Burke family carriage and the two old bays that were brought out of retirement every year on his grandmother's birthday to draw her in splendor around Central Park.

Gloria ate quietly. She listened to Mrs. Warren's stories and laughed on several occasions. If addressed, she responded politely. When Pinto came into the dining room and started to jump on Mrs. Warren's legs, it took only a look from Lila for Gloria to get up and take the puppy back to her room. Mrs. Warren nodded her approval..

After dinner, Mrs. Warren asked to talk to Gloria in private, and the two went into Gloria's room. They came out almost an hour later, smiling like conspirators. Mrs. Warren said she was tired and Willie took her back to her hotel. As soon as they had left, Lila went into Gloria's room, but Gloria was either asleep or pretending to be.

Willie gave no more information when he returned. "She didn't say anything the whole trip. She just yawned. And when we got to the hotel, she said 'Please thank Mrs. Burke for the lovely dinner.' And she popped out of the cab and into the hotel."

"Oh, Will—ie!" Lila cried in frustration. "Why didn't you ask her something?"

"And what? And maybe say the wrong thing? You'd kill me if I did. Don't fash yourself, darling girl. You know it went well. Gloria was a little angel."

"It seemed to. But what were they talking about in there for so long? What was all that grinning at each other when they came out?" Willie had no more idea than Lila, not then, and not when Lila, sleepless, woke him at two in the morning to ask again.

The next morning, Mrs. Warren went sightseeing. Lila picked her up at the hotel after lunch and brought her to St. Agnes School to meet Gloria's teacher. Mrs. Warren came smiling out of that room, too. They stopped by the Headmistress's office to thank her for the school's cooperation, then went outside to wait the fifteen minutes until dismissal. They were going home and then Mrs. Warren was to take Gloria and Pinto to the Park.

It was a gorgeous fall day and quite mild, even though most of the leaves were off the trees. Jackson came around to open the car door, but Lila waved him off. She stood in front of it, as though barring Mrs. Warren from entering. Mrs. Warren stopped and smiled. Lila wanted to scream. She had rehearsed several opening questions, but found that she had forgotten them all, and stood speechless and gawky as though she were the eight-year-old in the strange school in the upside down world.

Mrs. Warren reached for Lila's hand and held it in between her own. "It's all right, Mrs. Burke. You're doing fine. Please don't worry. I'm delighted with what I've found, and the Judge will be too when he sees my report."

Lila felt tears of relief start and tried to pull away, but Mrs.Warren tightened her grip. "Be a little easier on yourself. Gloria looks good, but you look tuckered out. Lost some weight?"

"I guess I have."

"You're going to be on this job for a long time; you can't afford to wear yourself out."

"Well, I was afraid that—"

"Don't be afraid. Just keep doing what you've been doing. You can see for yourself, can't you, how far she's come in the last two months? She expresses herself, functions at school, has made a friend, smiles, and laughs. It's wonderful."

Lila looked at Mrs. Warren. Suddenly she saw the older woman's smile as genuine. "Thank you." She gave Mrs. Warren's hand an answering squeeze, and they dropped their hands and smiled together. But there was one thing that still bothered Lila. "I don't want to ask you anything I shouldn't, but why has Gloria taken to you so much? You know, the bedtime story, this walk in the park, the way she smiles at you? I don't mean you're not very nice, but—"

"Oh, that's easy. I'm the representative of the Judge, who's the supreme authority in her life. She's trying to make me her friend, her ally."

"But why? "

"So that I'll help her get the Judge to let her go back to your brother and sister-in-law."

Lila gasped. "But you said it was going so well."

"I did, Mrs. Burke, and it is. You've been doing a fine job in helping Gloria recover from the trauma of what's happened to her."

"Then why is she trying—- to do what you just said?"

"I'm sorry, Mrs. Burke. You're forgetting that there are two different problems. One is to bring Gloria back to a condition of good mental and emotional health. The second is to get her to develop the feelings for you a healthy child might have for her mother. Didn't we go over this in St Louis? You're not starting to think they are one and the same, are you?"

"But of course they are, Mrs. Warren." Lila was aghast at herself. How could she get into an argument with this woman? But she couldn't stop. "It's my love calling to hers, buried deep down, that's making her well. When Gloria comes fully to herself, she will love me as her mother, just as I love her as my child."

A disapproving frown furrowed Mrs. Warren's placid face. "Mrs. Burke, when she comes to herself she will be emotionally capable of loving you. I can't promise you more than that."

The three o'clock bell rang as they talked and the doors opened, and the girls started leaving. Lila pointed to Gloria coming out the door. "See her, Mrs. Warren? Someday she'll come out of that door and run and throw her arms around me."

"I hope you're right, dear," said Mrs. Warren, and they raised their hands in unison to wave until Gloria saw them.

•   •   •

When Lila got home from seeing Mrs. Warren off, she weighed herself. Mrs. Warren was right; she had lost five or six pounds since she had brought Gloria home. And she wasn't sleeping well. She lay awake most nights for an hour or more, her mind turning over and over like a generator that never shuts down. She needed something to think about other than Gloria.

Considering all her options, Lila decided upon the piano. She could easily play at times when Gloria was absent. She had enjoyed playing years ago and had thought that some day she might try to go beyond accompanying her own voice. So she had the white baby grand tuned, pulled out her old sheet music and barred the staff from the living room between 11 and noon.

It didn't take long for Lila to regain her former level, but she wanted more. She should take lessons, but was she up to the drudgery of practicing exercises for hours to meet the demands of some elderly emigré with bad breath who had once played before Paderewski?

Willie applauded her renewed interest and suggested that she consult Gerry, who occasionally did legal work for jazz musicians. Lila was dubious about getting stuck with some cool cat strung out on reefer, who wouldn't show up for appointments, but she called Gerry.

"You want Elliott Zinn," he said.

He told her very little about Elliott. "See him, tell him what you think you want to do, play a little for him, then ask him to play a little for you and see what happens."

That was all. It sounded strange, but Gerry usually knew what he was doing, so she made an appointment for the next afternoon at Mr. Zinn's apartment, which turned out to be a third-floor walk-up in a dingy building on West Fifty-Second Street.

The door was opened by a boy (?) young man (?) with a blond crew cut and wire-rimmed glasses wearing a white shirt, a knitted blue wool sleeveless sweater, freshly pressed khaki pants, and spotless white bucks.

"I'm Lila Burke. I have an appointment with Mr. Zinn," Lila told this advertisement for college clothing.

"I'm Elliott," the college boy replied and stared at Lila. "You're Mrs. Burke?"

As this registered with Lila, she realized that Gerry hadn't told Elliott any more about her than he had told her about Elliott, who was probably expecting a stereotypical middle-aged matron. "It's nice to meet you," she said, extending her hand; Elliott came out of his daze and shook it. Very funny, Gerry, she thought, a little annoyed.

Elliott ushered her into a big room, crowded with a piano, a couch, an *armoire*, a dresser and a heavy antique hexagonal oak table surrounded by folding chairs. One wall held a sink and combination range and refrigerator with cabinets above; the others were covered by floor to ceiling shelves, filled with books, stacks of sheet music and labeled file boxes. A saxophone and a guitar hung from pegs in the door of the *armoire*. Lila seated herself on one of the folding chairs, and Elliott sat across the table. They inspected each other for a while, then Lila spoke.

"Whose deal is it?"

Elliott grinned. "Are you a poker player, Mrs. Burke?"

"No. But my husband is. He has a table like this, but not as nice." She ran a finger over the smooth join between two of the wedges that spread from the center to the edges. "Where did you get it?"

"Actually, I won it in a game. This cat whose house we played at had been getting creamed for weeks, and one night, after he got cleaned out of cash again, he announced he was quitting permanently and put the table in the pot. The rest of us put in ten bucks each for a hand of showdowns. I won the table, and he took the fifty."

"Fifty dollars? It must be worth ten times that."

"It was three in the morning, and he wanted it out of his house right away."

"You had to take it with you? How did you do that? It wouldn't fit into a taxi."

"The five of us agreed before the hand that the losers would help the winner carry it home and the winner would host the game after that. It wasn't such a great deal, though. Jack's losing streak came with the table, and it took me a couple of months to break it."

"But you didn't quit?"

"Nope. I'm stubborn, Mrs. Burke."

Lila made a face. "Would you call me 'Lila' or is there a rule against it in the piano teacher's manual?"

"No, it's cool, Lila." Elliott grinned again. He looked no older than a high school sophomore. How experienced could he be?

"Have you been teaching a long time, Elliott?" Lila asked casually while examining the inlay work on the table.

"I've been teaching at Juilliard for three years since I graduated. I don't give a lot of private lessons anymore, but I lived off them while I was there. What are you interested in?"

Lila rummaged in her pocketbook. Juilliard. Now he was too good for her. "I had some piano lessons when I was a child and liked it. Then I sang a bit at the piano, mostly at USO shows during the war. I dropped it about three years ago. Now I'd like to learn how to play better, by itself, not as an accompaniment."

"In public?"

"Oh no, just for myself, but I'm a little stubborn, too. I like to do things as well as I can."

Elliott stood up. "Let's hear where you are, first. Play something."

Lila went to the piano and began "Smoke Gets in Your Eyes," her favorite among the handful of songs she could play from memory. It sounded different, here, than it did in her living room, and, for a moment she thought it might be the piano. Plunk – plink-plunk-plink-plink- pliiiink. It wasn't the piano; it was her playing. It was lifeless; there was no music in it. She forced herself to continue, but at "laughing friends deride," pulled her hands from the keys.

"What's the matter?"

"It's dead, that's what's the matter. I'm sorry. This was a bad idea." She started to get up, but Elliott stepped behind her and pressed her shoulders back down.

"Wait a minute. What are you giving up for? You're supposed to be stubborn."

"It was dead. You heard it. I must have been kidding myself."

"Hold up. That's an arrangement to accompany yourself when you sing, right?"

"It was, but I don't sing when I play it now."

"You're sure you don't sing a little, softly, or, maybe, hum as you play?"

"I might hum a little."

"Please, play it again and sing it." Lila shook her head. "All right, hum it."

Lila felt ridiculous, but he was the teacher. To her astonishment, this time it sounded acceptable. She was even emboldened to sing the last verse.

Elliott grinned. "There you go. Somebody arranged that accompaniment for you, for your voice and your singing style. You played it the same way both times. By itself, it's only one part of a duet. Of course, it was missing something: the other instrument."

"Do I have to sing to play that song?"

"Just use a different arrangement. Get up a minute."

Lila rose, and Elliott opened the seat of the bench and fished out some sheet music, put it up on the rack and played the song from the sheet. It was more difficult than her arrangement but very much alive. Just for fun, she sang the last verse, but she had to sing it faster than she was accustomed and ended a moment behind Elliott.

"You can sing with that arrangement, but it's a different song. The singer is tougher, ready to go on. Your version is more plaintive."

Lila laughed. "I used to do it late in the show, as though I were a little drunk from the glasses of ginger ale they brought out from time to time. My hair would be messy, and I'd let a strap on my dress slip down. I looked like a pushover. It was always a big hit with the sailors."

"Crazy. That's the idea. A lot of music can be played different ways to convey different moods or meanings. How does this sound?" Elliott sat for a moment, bobbing his head, then began with a series of simple chords, which stated the melody, then broke apart into off-beat excursions up and down the keyboard. The ending came as an abrupt resolution into the original dominant chord, that he held for several seconds, followed by a single short high note. He looked up at Lila for a reaction, and she felt it was some kind of test.

"I haven't listened to a lot of jazz, but it sounds like someone searching for something." And what's happening at the end? I think he finds it, but doesn't realize it, and starts off again."

Elliott applauded her. "That's it exactly. If you can dig all that then you can get a lot more out of music than most people. I'd be happy to work with you, if you'd like."

They scheduled Monday and Thursday at 2, made their financial arrangements and Lila raced off to Schirmer's with a list of exercises and beginner's pieces. The next morning, as soon as she got back from taking Gloria to school, she set to work. The first three weeks were all exercises as Elliott focused on the most basic aspects, how she sat, how she held her hands, how her fingers struck the keys. Practicing the exercises was drudgery, but she mindd it less and less as she felt herself losing the bad habits and acquiring good ones.

The lessons were more fun. It would take only a few minutes for Lila to demonstrate her exercises. With no pieces to critique, the rest of the time Elliott would talk about the piano, frequently playing a few bars to demonstrate a point or putting a record on the phonograph. He sprinkled his lectures with anecdotes about clubs he had played and musicians he knew.

"They call me Eli, you know."

"Is that a nickname for Elliott?"

"Nope. It's because of the way I look and dress. Dizzy Gillespie's piano player was in a taxi accident one night, and someone told his manager to call me as a replacement. When Dizzy saw me, he was disgusted. He said, 'What are you doing here, man? I didn't ask them to send me Eli Yale.' But he let me play, and I was OK, and the word got around. It was good. People remembered Eli where they would have forgotten Elliott."

This gave Lila the opening to ask, "You don't look like a jazz musician. How come?"

"You don't like how I look?" His eyebrows narrowed, and his lip twitched.

"You look fine, don't worry, just not what someone might expect."

"I know. This is how my friends and I dressed in high school. They were nice, middle-class Jewish boys from Long Island who wanted to go to Yale and wanted to look like they were there already. I figured that looking like this would help persuade my parents that going to Juilliard was respectable."

"It must have worked."

Elliott grimaced. "The war started during our senior year in high school. My older brother enlisted in the Navy and was killed within months. My parents were so relieved that my eyesight made me 4-F that they would have let me study anything, anywhere."

He turned from Lila and studied the clock behind him. Something impelled Lila to get up from the bench and put her hand on his shoulder. "It couldn't have been your fault." He nodded but didn't turn back, so she gathered up her music. "Got to run. See you next time."

As Lila had hoped, this new activity made her feel better. Each practice session left her tired but with her mind at rest. She found herself more patient with Gloria and Willie. Her own ears told her that her hard work was bringing the reward of perceptible improvement. If only her hard work with Gloria could bring the same reward.

• • •

Thanksgiving came. After the death of Willie's father, Lila had been obliged to sit through several heavy Thanksgiving dinners with Willie's family. Although they tried to be pleasant to Lila, she was always the outsider, standing in the doorways of overheated kitchens, listening to the women chatter about the price of chops and the births and deaths of strangers.

With her child returned to her home, she could now feel she had her own family, and politely declined this year's invitation from Willie's sister Kate. Instead, the Burkes went out to the Long Island house and invited Mike and Margo Stone to a belly-bursting Thanksgiving feast.

There was something else Lila wanted to accomplish over the

Thanksgiving weekend. She had not yet told Gloria anything about Joe, nor had Gloria shown the slightest interest in finding out anything about her natural father. When Lila had mentioned this to Mrs. Warren, the cheerful face had reacted with a frown.

"That's a result of denial."

"What do you mean?"

"Well, part of Gloria must still cling to the belief that your brother and sister-in-law are her parents, so there is no other father to be curious about."

"But she seems to admit that I'm her mother."

"Has she said so?"

Lila thought for a moment. "No, not in so many words. You mean she may think everyone has lied to her, even John and Catherine?"

"Not exactly. People can know in their heads that's something is true, but deny it in their hearts and act in many ways as though it's not true. Getting Gloria to take an interest in her natural father is a good way to help her accept reality, but you should understand that she isn't going to like the idea at first."

Lila had kept a publicity photo of Joe and brought it with her to the house. The Saturday after Thanksgiving was cold and rainy, and Gloria was forced to occupy herself with indoor activities. Boredom sent her in and out of Lila's study for pencils, paper, cards and suggestions for amusement. On one such visit, Lila gave Gloria the photo.

"Who's he?" asked Gloria casually.

"Joe Principato. He was your father, but he died four years ago."

Gloria put the picture down on Lila's desk without giving it another look. "Do you have any scotch tape? I made a drawing of Pinto, and I want to put it up in my room."

Lila thought furiously as she started looking through the desk drawers. Forcing the subject wasn't going to help, she concluded, so she gave Gloria the tape without further comment. Time, she reminded herself. There's lots of time.

•   •   •

Lila had been putting off planning for Christmas and Gloria's return to St. Louis, but could not continue to do so after Thanksgiving. Mrs. Warren had put Lila on her guard that Gloria still harbored hopes that her return might be permanent. Was it possible that John might try to keep her there? In a panic, she called Mrs. Warren, who reported a recent conversation in which John had assured her that he would cause no more trouble.

That left logistics, which was Willie's department. He arranged for Mary to take Gloria to St. Louis by train and come back to New York. Willie and Lila would travel by airplane to Palm Beach and look for a winter home. With airline service improving they hoped they'd be able to spend a reasonable amount of time there. And maybe, thought Lila, someday Gloria will want to spend Christmas with us. On January 2, they would fly to St. Louis and bring Gloria home.

Three weeks proved barely enough time, but on the appointed day, after seeing Mary and Gloria off at Grand Central, Lila came home, flung her coat over a chair in the living room, kicked off her boots and poured herself a drink. Three days to herself in New York, then a week in Palm Beach sounded just fine.

By the time Pinto came wandering into the living room looking for her mistress, Lila was no longer reveling in her freedom but was wishing the two weeks were over and Gloria safely back. She swept up the startled puppy, hugged her to her shoulder and was rewarded with a swipe of a warm tongue across her ear. Ellen, dressed to go out, came into the living room with Pinto's leash, but Lila stopped her and got dressed again and took the dog herself.

That night, Lila and Willie went to a Broadway show. The next night, it was a jazz club where Elliott was playing, and the following night, they stuffed themselves at *Le Pavillon*. Lila tried to enjoy herself but couldn't keep from speculating on what was going on in St. Louis.

Her first airplane ride was exciting and, fortunately, smooth. It was like a dream to walk out to the plane in boots wet from the snow in the street in front of the airport and get off a few hours later under a tropical sun. Whether it was the ride or the change in venue, something in Lila loosened, and she began thinking about the next ten days rather than what would happen after the holiday season was over.

Palm Beach was as she remembered it, green and peaceful and quietly elegant. Willie's friends were delighted that they were thinking of buying a house and provided Lila with a list and a broker and she set out to look.

There were eleven houses on the list, but none of them seemed just right to Lila. In desperation, the broker took her to see *Beauséjour*, a two-story limestone villa running south from Via Amalfi, along the shore of Lake Worth, with wings extending at right angles to the east. She trudged listlessly behind him, paying little attention to his cheerful patter. The interior was dark and smelled of mold and had not been lived in for years. Between the wings was an overgrown garden with rusty benches, broken trellises and paths choked with weeds. The plumbing would largely have to be replaced and new wiring installed. Walls needed to come down or at least be opened to the light and the orange tile roof needed to be replaced. It was too much work for a vacation home, and she couldn't possibly do it from New York with Gloria occupying all of her time and energy.

She brought Willie out to see the two best of the houses on the list. The newer one was too close to its neighbors, he said, and the older one had no views and was too far from the beach. Lila didn't disagree. Instead, she took him to *Beauséjour*. As they walked through one or the other would say "What if you knocked out the living room wall and installed French doors to the garden?" or "We could put in a dock and keep our own boat on the Lake."

So they bought it.

Lila called St. Louis Christmas Day. It took a while for Catherine to get Gloria on the line and the subsequent conversation was brief. A lengthy greeting from Lila was answered with a sullen "Merry Christmas." Willie got much of the same. On her New Year's Day call, Lila didn't even try to get Gloria on the phone.

"How is she?" she asked Catherine.

"She's fine," Catherine replied in a dull voice.

"And you and John?"

"All right."

"What have you been doing?"

"We try to keep Gloria busy."

"Doing what?"

"You really want to know, Lila?"

What did that mean? "Of course I do."

Lila could hear Catherine take a deep breath before continuing. "Movies, shopping, walking, cooking. Anything that will distract her from begging us to let her stay—"

"My God!"

"—because then when we say she can't she starts crying again."

"No, no, Cath, that can't be. She's doing so much better here. Everybody in the house loves her, and she seems to like school and—"

"Lila, stop it. I can't hate you for what you've done to John and me. Maybe it's a punishment for what we did to you. But for how you've destroyed Gloria – I can't even say it. You'll have her back tomorrow." The line went dead.

Lila put the telephone down. That had been the worst possible news, told in a quiet, implacable, hopeless voice. Gerry had warned her before she started that this might happen. She had wreaked destruction upon Gloria, as well as upon John and Catherine. She must turn back, let Gloria stay in St. Louis and try to live out the rest of her empty life hoping that the damage she had caused Gloria was not irreparable. She must give up her child again.

How calm she felt, once she had made the decision. No shouting, no weeping, no loss of consciousness or memory or sensation. She looked around the hotel room, noticing the suitcases taken out of the closet so she could begin packing, Willie's pajamas folded on his pillow, the morning newspaper sticking out of the wastebasket. There was pressure in her bladder. She would go to the bathroom, then call Catherine. She would tell Willie when he returned in an hour, and he would make the arrangements to ship Gloria's things to St. Louis. It would be easy.

She urinated and flushed the toilet but didn't get up right away. Something was wrong. How could it all be so easy? The answer was inescapable.

She didn't mean it. She wasn't going to give Gloria up again, ever. She couldn't deny that events had made Gloria suffer, but the suffering was only temporary; already the recovery was proceeding. No force less than death could take Gloria from her now or in the future. She went into the bedroom to begin packing.

Willie's arrangements continued to work. The change of planes in Atlanta went smoothly, and they were settled in their hotel suite in St. Louis when Mrs. Warren arrived holding fast to a tearful Gloria. Mrs. Warren's usually calm, confident face showed substantial stress, but she put a finger to her lips before Lila could ask her what had happened.

"Happy New Year, Mr. and Mrs. Burke. Take off your coat, Gloria."

"No," said Gloria and crossed her arms. Ignoring this, Mrs. Warren started to unbutton the coat. Gloria didn't resist. Lila moved to help, then froze as Gloria clenched her fists. Mrs. Warren shook her head at Lila and finished taking off the coat and put it over the back of a chair.

"Now your boots."

"Please, no, Mrs. Warren." Gloria began to sob. Mrs. Warren guided her to a chair and took off her boots.

"They'll have her bags up in a few minutes. Come, dear, crying when you say goodbye is all right. But you've done that. Now it's hello and you're going to your own home with your own room and your dog and your school and your friends and your mother. It's your own life, Gloria and it's a good one, and you shouldn't cry about it."

Gloria shook her head at each word and continued sobbing. Lila couldn't keep still and rushed to comfort Gloria despite Mrs. Warren's signals. She had barely bent to Gloria's face before Gloria exploded in a flurry of kicks and blows. Lila stumbled back. Gloria tried to pursue her, but Mrs. Warren held her and then Willie grabbed her firmly. She continued to struggle for a few moments then, abruptly, slumped and gave, not a cry, but a strange, soundless, exhalation of breath and spirit that went on and on as though she were expelling life itself. At the end, her body betrayed her, her lungs drew in a deep breath, and she began to cry again. Willie picked her up and, crooning unintelligibly, carried her into the next room and shut the door.

Lila's hands were shaking, and her cheek stung from one of Gloria's blows.

"I'm sorry, Mrs. Warren, I couldn't just sit there and watch her cry."

Mrs. Warren sighed. "Well, you love her, all right. There's no question of that. But that's not enough, yet. Coming to St. Louis and having to go back to New York is very upsetting. It's unfortunate, but it can't be helped."

"What if—"

Mrs. Warren held up her hand. "Forget it. The visitation rights are not going to be changed. It won't be so bad in the future; she probably persuaded herself that something would happen so that she could stay here. Look, you're all trying to adjust as well as you can to a very difficult situation. And doing pretty well. Showing grief and anger is healthy. Would you rather she reacted like the last time you came for her?"

"No, you're right, of course. But she only shows me grief and anger. When will she show me, love?" There was a knock on the door.

"I can't tell, you. Right now, she sees you as the person who devastated her life."

Is that what everybody thinks? My poor baby. Lila began to cry, and Mrs. Warren had to open the door for the bellboy with Gloria's luggage.

Back in New York, Gloria was sullen with Lila and reserved with everyone else except Mary and Julia and the man who ran the service elevator in their apartment house and gave Pinto puppy biscuits when she came back from her walks. There were no more attacks.

•   •   •

Lila hadn't touched a piano over the holiday period and had only gotten in one practice session on her return. When she got to Elliott's apartment for her first lesson of the new year, she ran clumsily through her exercises, put her hands in her lap and waited.

"I don't know what you've been doing over the last three weeks, Lila, but it sure wasn't practicing the piano." He sounded hurt, as though she had personally insulted him.

"I'm sorry, Elliott. My attention was taken up by other things I couldn't put aside."

"Ozzer sings? More important *zan ze* piano? Impossible." He frowned to go with the fake German accent. "*Vot ozzer* sings?" Now he smiled encouragingly.

"Mostly Gloria."

"Your daughter? What happened?"

His voice was so sympathetic that Lila couldn't stop herself from pouring out the history as she had never done before. Yes, she had given bowdlerized versions to doctors and school teachers, but that was so they could make their little notes in their buff-jacketed files and, if Lila was lucky, prepare themselves properly to deal with Gloria in the performance of their professional functions. Even with Margo, she had not been the one to tell the story first. By the time they met, Willie had already told a version to Mike who had repeated it to Margo.

It only took a few minutes. Elliott asked no questions, made no comments but often nodded his understanding. When Lila finished, he sat down on the bench next to her, took her hands in his, pressed them for a moment and moved them back to the keyboard.

"Back to work," he said, opened one of the sheets of music in the rack and struck the first chords of a simple four-hands piece they were learning. Lila raised her hands and came in on the fifth bar. Elliott nodded. They played about half of it, stopped for correction, picked it up again and worked on it for the rest of the hour.

Lila felt good waiting for the cross-town bus. Telling her story to Elliott had lifted some of the tension from her, and his wordless sympathy had been just the right reaction. Then playing the piece with Elliott had given a big boost to her confidence. There was something special about knowing she had played correctly by the way her part blended with Elliott's. It was like good tennis doubles. She recalled one point against Margo and Curt during which she and Hank had switched three times to cover each other before she had extended herself full-length to cut off Curt's passing shot and flick it into a corner for a winner. Her body still remembered the feel of that lunge, that flick. Then, unbidden, came the memory of the coupling with Hank and his hard body. Elliott wouldn't have such a hard body; he never exercised.

Lila crimsoned with embarrassment as though the woman standing next to her could read her thoughts. Oh my God, not with Elliott. Not with Hank again, either. Not with anybody, except Willie, but particularly not with Elliott, her teacher, her friend and now her confidant.

·　　　·　　　·

At the end of January, Gloria came down with the grippe and had to stay home from school. Lila canceled everything to stay home to nurse her, offering glasses of orange juice, cups of chicken broth and comic books that were usually rejected. For the first two days, Gloria ran a fever, and Lila skipped piano practice for fear of disturbing her, but on the third morning, with the thermometer almost at normal, Lila sat down for her regular eleven o'clock practice.

She had been playing for twenty minutes when, upon finishing an exercise, she felt, more than heard, someone behind her and to her right. She turned to find Gloria, in her pajamas, hands behind her back, head cocked to the right, staring at the keyboard.

"Did I disturb you, darling?" Lila asked.

Gloria ignored the question. "What are you playing?" she asked.

"That was an exercise. It helps me learn."

"But you know how to play already."

"I want to play better, so I'm taking lessons and practicing. I practice at least an hour every morning while you're in school."

"You're taking piano lessons? Janet takes piano lessons. I didn't know grown-ups did."

"It doesn't matter how old you are. If you want to learn something, you need someone to teach you. Would you like to learn how to play the piano?"

There was no answer. Gloria had slipped away as suddenly as she had come.

The next day was Thursday. Lila had canceled Monday's lesson. She didn't want to miss Thursday's, as well, but it was Mary's day off, and Gloria was becoming more demanding as she felt better. With some trepidation at changing a routine that was working so well, Lila called Elliott on Thursday morning and asked if he would mind coming to the Burke's apartment for the lesson. He agreed, and Lila asked Gloria not to disturb them during the hour.

While Lila was hanging up Elliott's coat, she took a long look at him. His face was even more boyish than usual as he took in the crystal chandelier and the oriental rug in the foyer. She felt like hugging him, not taking him to bed, and smiled broadly with relief.

Elliott returned the smile. "I must have passed."

"Passed?"

"Inspection. You were inspecting me to see if I met the minimum standards for admission. From that smile, I guess I did. Frankly, I was worried. The shoes aren't as white as they could be and you must have missed the moth hole in my sweater."

Lila took his hand. "I didn't miss it at all. But I don't care. I'm just glad to see you. You're my friend, aren't you? Not just my teacher?"

Elliott squeezed her hand. "We're more than friends; we're buddies. You'll be my good buddy and I'll be yours."

Lila let go his hand and led the way into the living room.

"Here's my piano. Try it."

Elliott ran some scales and played a few bars of one of his own compositions that Lila had heard before. It was atonal, not at all to her taste; she suspected he had chosen it to tease her.

"It's terrific," he said. "Take good care of it, and you'll never need another." They switched places and began the lesson. As it ended, Gloria came into the room and up to Elliott.

"Are you the piano teacher?"

Elliott snapped to attention. "Yes, sir. Elliott Zinn is my name and teaching piano is my game. Please to tell me who are you and what fadiddle do you do?"

Gloria's eyebrows crinkled. She looked at Elliott, then at Lila, then back at Elliott. "I'm Gloria. What's fadiddle?"

"It's what you do most of the time. You probably do school-fadiddle. Right?"

"I guess so."

"Do you like it?"

"No."

"Oh, that's a shame. I used to like it a lot, but you have to find something else when you grow up. I do piano-fadiddle, now. I like that a lot, too. Would you play something for me?"

"She can't play, Elliott," said Lila. "I thought I told you that."

She was astonished to hear Gloria protest loudly, "I can, too. I just don't want to."

Lila smiled tolerantly. "Of course, darling. If you don't want to play, you don't have to." Halfway through the sentence, she could hear the sarcasm, but it was too late. Gloria smiled and spoke to Elliott.

"I'll play for you."

Lila didn't wait for Elliott's answer. "I'll get us some cocoa," she chirped as she went to the kitchen.

What was Gloria talking about? John and Catherine had no piano nor had Gloria been given any lessons elsewhere. Lila knew that children might sit at a piano and pick out the notes of a tune, but she had never heard Gloria even do that. She placed an order for cocoa and cookies with Mrs. Thompson, then tiptoed back through the pantry to the closed door to the living room.

At first, she was puzzled at what she heard. There were dissonant chords, some in the bass, some in the treble and occasionally the crash of hands striking the keys in both. Between the chords, single notes jumped around the keyboard in march tempo. Remarkably, it wasn't a total muddle. A few times chords actually worked, and one combination of four single notes recurred in several places as a recognizable theme.

It took a little more than a minute. When Gloria stopped, Elliott applauded. Lila retreated to the kitchen, where she queried Mrs. Thompson. Yes, Gloria often played when Mrs. Burke was out of the house. Mary had told them that it was after being a surprise for Mrs. Burke and they shouldn't mention it. She hoped that wasn't wrong. It hardly seemed likely that the little thing could harm that great, big *pianner*. Lila agreed.

A few minutes later, Lila, carrying the tray, returned to the living room door, behind which she could hear the unusually animated voice of Gloria. Overcoming her annoyance at having to request permission to enter her own living room, Lila knocked. Elliott opened the door, and Lila brought the tray to the coffee table. Gloria stopped talking and watched Lila intently.

"That was very nice, darling. You never told me you did that." Lila kept her voice casual. She handed out the cocoa and held the plate of cookies, first for Elliott, then Gloria and took one, herself, set the plate on a little table and sank into an easy chair near the piano.

"I can play it?"

"You may play it, darling, whenever you like if Willie and I aren't using the living room. Just wash your hands first, if they're icky, and don't put anything to eat or drink on it. Elliott, do you know the Khachaturian concerto? Someone was raving about it the other night."

Gloria was squirming, but Lila pretended not to notice. Come on, Elliott, she thought. Follow my lead. She's my daughter.

"I don't like it that much. It's too consciously ethnic. But Kapell gives it a great ride. It's worth hearing. You know he was finishing at Juilliard the year I started."

"Lila," Gloria piped.

"Why don't you go back to your room, Darling? Mr. Zinn will be leaving soon, and I'll come and play a game of backgammon with you." Lila turned back to Elliott. "What's he like? They said he's becoming the greatest American pianist."

"Could be. He's got a big talent, and he used to work his *tukhas* off at Juilliard; still does, I hear. Nobody could keep up with him."

"Lila. Can I take lessons?" This was a different voice from the ones Lila was accustomed to hearing: the scornful voice of rejection, the angry voice of conflict, the grudging voice of temporary surrender, the condescending voice of acceptance of meals, clothing, books, movies, dolls, games, jewelry and treats of any kind. Lila was not used to this hopeful but uncertain voice, had only, in fact, heard it once before when Gloria had asked for Pinto.

"Can I? Please?" Lila's heart ached as she felt her child's wanting, but she frowned and pretended to consider the matter. If Lila put off the discussion until after Elliott left, she might be able to obtain concessions. But that worried face.

"Of course you can, darling."

The face broke into a big smile and Gloria jumped to her feet and rushed into Lila's arms. But as Lila ecstatically hugged her child, she felt Gloria stiffen. Lila loosened her grip, and Gloria stepped free, whirled and ran from the room. Unable to speak, her eyes tearing, Lila held out her hands, palms upward in despair. With one quick step, Elliott came to her, put his arms around her and pulled her to his shoulder. After a few seconds, they parted.

"Thank you, good buddy." Lila took a napkin from the cocoa tray and blew her nose. "Now you see what I have to fight against. But I got closer, that time. I'll wear her down, yet."

"You will, you will. Just stick with it."

After Elliott left, Lila went to Gloria's room. She found the door left open, something Gloria never did. Gloria was lying on top of the covers reading her geography book. Pinto lay across the foot of the bed. At the sound of Lila's step, Gloria put down the book, and Pinto jumped down from the bed and came up to Lila. Lila bent down to her.

"Do you want to go out?" Lila asked, and Pinto wagged her tail and jumped up on Lila.

"Can I come, too?" Gloria pleaded. "I haven't coughed all afternoon."

"One more day, darling. If it's nice tomorrow, you can go out for a little while."

"OK, Lila." The voice was cheerfully complaisant. What a change. What a pleasure. "When can I start?"

"Start?"

"You know, the lessons."

"Well, you'll have missed this whole week of school, so, next week, you'll have to work hard to catch up. Maybe the week after that. Mr. Zinn gave me the name of a very good teacher. I'll call her when I get back with Pinto."

"What teacher? Mr. Zinn is going to be my teacher."

"But Gloria. Mr. Zinn doesn't teach children. He only teaches grown-ups who know how to play already."

" I know how to play already, too. You heard me."

"Gloria, sweetheart, that wasn't really playing. Playing the piano isn't just hitting notes that sometimes sound nice. You have to learn how to read music and the scales for the different keys and a lot of other things. You'll be very good someday after you've learned all those things. But you need to go to a teacher who teaches them. Elliott, I mean Mr. Zinn, doesn't."

"I don't care. I want him." The voice was no longer either complaisant or cheerful.

"I'm sorry, darling, but it's not possible."

"You're just afraid that if he teaches me, I'll play better than you."

"I hope you will play better than me. I'd be proud of you if you did. Don't cry, darling. I'm sure you'll like this other teacher, or, if not, we'll find one you do."

"No!" Gloria shouted.

"I'm sorry, darling. Then you won't have lessons. Think about it. Maybe you'll change your mind. Come on, Pinto." The dog, who had been looking back and forth between them, her ears flattened in distress, ran out of the room. As Lila passed through the doorway into the hall, the geography book hit the back of her leg. She didn't stop, having no better response.

A few seconds later a loud bang told her that Gloria's door was once again shut against her.

What Lila had told Gloria was merely what Elliott had told her. He didn't teach beginners, didn't know how to do it, didn't want to start doing it and had a full schedule already. It wasn't her fault, though she had not been altogether unhappy to hear Elliott say what he had. Their relationship had become one of the nicer things in her life; there was no telling what lessons for Gloria would do to that relationship. What could she do now? Maybe if she pleaded with Elliott? At least, maybe, he could talk to Gloria so she wouldn't blame it all on Lila.

As Lila got off the elevator after the walk, she heard Gloria screaming, "Let me go! Let me go!" and the muffled sound of a voice responding. Lila fumbled at the front door.

When the door opened she heard Mary say, "No, Gloria, you can't do that."

"I will! Let me go!"

Lila rushed into the living room and found Mary grappling with Gloria next to the piano. Mary had a tight grip on Gloria's right hand, which held a pair of scissors. Mrs. Thompson was trying to capture Gloria's legs as she kicked and squirmed screaming, "Let me go! It's not fair!"

"Gloria!" shouted Lila, and the action stopped; Gloria dropped the scissors and began to cry. Mary switched from restrainer to comforter and scooped the unresisting body into her arms. Lila nodded once, and Mary turned and carried Gloria to her room. Mrs. Thompson remained frozen, staring at the piano. Lila followed her eyes and saw several huge scars in the white lacquer. She went over to look more closely. Two of the white keys were chipped where Gloria had tried to pry them loose, and the fabric on the bench was shredded.

"She was just climbing up to go inside when I come in to get the tray," Mrs. Thompson recounted, breathlessly. "Clumsy like I am, I was afraid of hurting the child, so I yelled for Mary, who ran in and grabbed her like you saw. I'm sorry I didn't get there earlier, Missus."

"That's all right, as long as nobody was hurt. You did the right thing."

What to do now? Lila had never punished Gloria; there had been no cause. Was that possible in, how many, five months? It was true. At school, too, her conduct had been exemplary. In fact, she had been a remarkably well-behaved child. There had been no outbreaks of violence such as this except for her attack on Lila in the hotel room in St. Louis. Lila remembered Mrs. Warren's warning: Gloria might behave badly trying to get sent back to her old home. If that's what Gloria was about, she had to learn that the tactic wouldn't work. Lila picked up the scissors and went to Gloria's room.

Gloria was lying on her bed, her head in Mary's lap. She stopped snuffling as Lila marched in and sat down in the easy chair.

"Thank you very much, Mary. That was very good of you. And brave, too. Gloria might have cut you with the scissors."

"Oh, no, Mum. She—" Lila raised her hand, and Mary stopped.

"Gloria?" Gloria shook her head vigorously and clutched Mary around the waist.

"Or Mrs. Thompson?" Gloria shook her head again.

"I don't think you would have on purpose, but you might have done so by accident. People can be very badly hurt by scissors. The point could put out somebody's eye. Can you imagine doing that to Mary?"

Gloria started crying again. Mary started to say something, but Lila stopped her again.

"And didn't I see you hit Mary in the face with your left hand?" The crying increased. "And you kicked Mrs. Thompson in the knee. Mrs. Thompson, who came back early from her day off on Monday so she could make you brownies because you were sick."

Sobbing uncontrollably, Gloria burrowed into Mary.

Lila sat patiently for almost a minute as the sobbing died down, then got up and went to Gloria's dresser. "I'm putting the scissors back on the dresser, darling. This is your home. That's your beautiful piano. If you're foolish enough to want to ruin it or to destroy anything else in the apartment, then go ahead. Mary, tell everyone that if she does they're not to stop her. Get up, darling, go find Pinto and give her supper. The poor thing is off hiding from all the commotion."

Gloria looked at Lila, then looked down. "Okay," she said in a small voice.

Lila expected Willie to have a fit when he saw the piano. After all, he had picked it out personally for Lila and had lovingly supervised its shipment back and forth across the country. But he said nothing as he sat down with his evening cocktail until Lila was seated next to him on the living room couch. "Well?" He pointed to the damage, just eight feet away. It took Lila all of their first cocktail and half of an unusual second one to tell the whole story. When she finished, he raised his glass in a toast. "You're terrific. I wouldn't have thought to react that way; very few people would have. Of course, there's a chance she might want to test your sincerity. Should we put the good paintings in storage for a while? And some of your jewelry?"

"That would be backing away. She belongs to me, to us, to our homes. We can't hedge on that position, ever, or we'll never have a chance."

He lifted his glass again. When Lila talked about having the piano repaired, it was Willie's thoughtful idea to hold off. "Let her be reminded for a while that her acts have consequences. We're not just going to sweep it under the rug." But on one issue they disagreed. Lila had been inclined to try to persuade Elliott to take Gloria as a pupil. The attack on the piano didn't change her mind. Willie, on the other hand, argued strongly that getting Elliott as Gloria's teacher, now, would appear to reward Gloria for conduct was unacceptable.

"You shouldn't have told her no the first time. Then we'd not have this tizzy at all."

"I just repeated what Elliott told me. How was I supposed to know she had to have him and no one else?"

"Well, to hear you tell it, the fella's the greatest thing since sliced bread. Why shouldn't Gloria want him, too? Ever since you started, all I hear around here is 'Elliott this' and 'Elliott that.' It's a good thing I'm not a jealous man."

"Oh, Willie, please."

"Well, you never know. Although they say, the ones you have to watch out for are the ones the women don't talk about."

Some devil made Lila say "If they don't talk about them how do you know about them?"

Willie put his finger to the side of his nose. "You don't. That's why you have to watch out. I'll just be after checking the closets." He folded his paper and headed for the bathroom.

There was no further discussion of pianos over the weekend. Gloria seemed completely recovered from the grippe and Lila detailed Willie to spend a couple of hours with her at a movie on Saturday and at the Museum of Natural History on Sunday. While they were gone, Lila spent the whole time practicing. Nothing Gloria had done affected the way the piano played, although Lila had to put a towel over the bench.

On Monday, Gloria went back to school. Shortly before her bedtime, Lila asked whether she had thought any more about taking lessons from a "regular" teacher, maybe the one her friend Janet studied with.

Gloria looked incredulous. "Lessons? I don't want any lessons. Janet says she hates them.

Her parents make her practice all the time." She made a sour face and turned away. As the week passed, she seemed to have put the subject of pianos completely out of her mind. The scars from the scissors were the only remaining evidence, and Gloria walked past them a dozen times a day without a glance.

Lila returned to Elliott's apartment for her lessons. When he asked if a teacher for Gloria had been arranged, Lila told him that Gloria had changed her mind. Elliott, puzzled, asked why and Lila brusquely changed the subject.

Two weeks later he raised the subject again and, this time was not put off by Lila's answer. "Hey, Lila, what happened? She was totally into the idea. What changed her mind?"

Lila started hunting among her sheet music so she wouldn't have to look at him. "I don't know. Kids change their minds. Everybody does."

"Don't blow that noise at me, Lila. What happened?"

Pressed, she told him the story. He winced as she described the scars left by Gloria's attacks. "Why didn't you call me right away?"

"What were you going to tell her? She wanted you, not your friend or some other competent children's teacher."

"Well, I suppose it wouldn't kill me to take her on for a while."

"But you were barely able to squeeze me in, and you've got an extra class this semester."

"I guess I can spare an hour a week. And if she'll stick it out, it may be worth doing. She seems to have a feel for it. You heard her. You shouldn't discourage what might prove to be a real talent. If she still wants me to teach her, I'll try it." He smiled, generously.

Lila felt like shaking the smug expression from Elliott's face. Why didn't he say that originally. Now, Gloria would believe that Lila had lied to keep her from getting Elliott and would conclude she got Lila to change her mind by throwing a fit. Willie would criticize her lack of resolution, and Elliott obviously viewed her as an uncaring mother. It wasn't fair.

Strangely, Gloria received the news of the change in plan with little enthusiasm and totally refused to have her weekly lesson at home. Neither Lila nor Elliott could figure out why she was making such a fuss about the venue and Gloria refused to explain. When Lila went to Willie with the problem, he laughed and called Gloria into the room.

"I hear you want to go to Mr. Zinn's place for your lessons, darling."

Gloria set her face and nodded.

"Is his apartment so special, then?"

Gloria didn't answer, and Willie turned to Lila who shrugged. What was Willie up to?

"Is there something there you particularly want to see?" Gloria looked blank at this.

Willie frowned in thought. "Maybe, his piano?" Gloria nodded. "He has a fine piano you'd like to learn on?"

"Yes, please, Willie."

Willie walked over to the piano and ran his hand over it. "I thought this was a fine piano, too, Gloria."

Gloria looked down.

Willie went on. "It needs a little repair work, though, doesn't it?"

Gloria nodded in agreement.

"Do you think that if we got it fixed, it would be all right to have your lesson here?"

Gloria brightened. "Yes, Willie."

Elliott threw himself into his new role and was enthusiastic about Gloria's potential and her attitude. He spent as much time talking to Lila about Gloria's playing as he did about Lila's. Although Lila was delighted to hear of Gloria's progress, she couldn't help feeling that Elliott was short-changing her and told him so.

"I have to admit that I'm a little jealous." She laughed to show how ridiculous that was.

"Lila, sugar," this time he adopted a Southern accent, "don't be jealous. Y'all are the only one for me." He bent down to the piano bench and before she could react, kissed her lightly on the lips, then pulled away, stood up and started hunting something in the bookshelves.

How could he do something so stupid? Did he want to spoil everything? Look at him, fumbling among the books, his shoulders hunched as though he expected her to hit him with a whip. She had to be careful; he was so sensitive.

Lightly, lightly. "Why thank you for that compliment, General Lee. You Southerners are such gentlemen."

On the cross-town bus, she replayed the scene in her mind. The kiss had felt comfortable, even familiar. She thought for a while before the answer came to her. It was like the first kiss of those shy boys of fourteen or fifteen, so ready to flee rejection, so unprepared for acceptance. How much fun there had been in those safe approaches. But after-school jobs and dance and acting classes had left no time for boys, and soon she was a woman and had met Joe and Willie. Elliott had come too late. It was a shame. He was so sweet.

•   •   •

In the middle of March, Gloria's teacher summoned Lila to a conference. Lila was worried. Gloria had done very well in the first and second grades in St. Louis, and Lila had hoped she would also be able to do well at St. Agnes, but she hadn't. Both homework and the weekly arithmetic quizzes had recently been coming back with numerous mistakes pointed out.

The conference was held in the classroom while Gloria's class was at gym. The desks were cluttered with books and papers, and blazers dangled from the backs of chairs. Gloria's new sweater had fallen to the floor, and Lila could not resist detouring to pick it up on her way to the chair beside the teacher's desk. The smile on Sister Mary Francis's round face broadened.

"Somehow we don't seem to have the time to be as tidy as we'd like to be."

"I can believe that, Sister. I find one is a lot to handle and you've got, what, twenty?"

"Twenty-six, actually, Mrs. Burke. But sometimes it's easier with the lot of them than with one child by herself."

"Is Gloria giving you trouble, Sister?"

"Not at all, Mrs. Burke. No trouble. She's a quiet, obedient child, follows our rules, does whatever I ask her to."

"How does she get along with the other girls?"

Sister Mary Francis turned her hand over and back equivocally. "She had other things on her mind when she joined the class." Lila nodded, and the teacher smiled and continued. "She was standoffish with the other girls, so they generally decided to leave her alone. I think she'd like to change that, now, and become part of the group, but that's not easy. Julia is the only friend she has. It may be better in the fall if Gloria comes back to St. Agnes."

"Why wouldn't she come back?" Lila's voice raised.

"She's still having difficulty keeping up with the class in arithmetic." Sister raised her hand to keep Lila from speaking. "She seems to understand things when we take them up in class but gets them wrong in her homework. I asked her, and she says you don't look at it. It's all right to do that, you know, and, in Gloria's case it would be a very good idea."

"I'd love to do that, Sister, but she won't let me near it."

"Oh." There was silence while the one word seemed to echo around the empty classroom. The teacher looked down at her hands. "I'm sorry. I assumed that she was accepting you now."

"Not completely, Sister. But are you telling me that you're going to fail Gloria?"

"I hope that it won't end up that way, but we have a real problem. Gloria started slowly. It didn't come as a surprise under the circumstances. I gave her extra attention, and she seemed to be doing better, so I didn't pressure either of you. That was a mistake."

"Why?"

"Because she got herself up to a point and leveled off, and the point wasn't quite high enough in arithmetic. She has to think about how to do easy steps that the other children do automatically. She has the same problem in grammar, but it's not as serious. It wouldn't be fair to Gloria to send her on to the fourth grade at St. Agnes with that kind of a handicap."

"So you'd leave her back?"

There was a pause while Sister Mary Francis picked up a pencil and tested the sharpness of the point upon her finger. "We don't like to do that unless a girl has missed a lot of the year through illness. It tends to stigmatize. We prefer to help the parents find a good, but less demanding school, where we feel she can keep up with their students in her regular grade."

"Excuse me." Lila tried to stifle her flaring anger. Now? Two-thirds of the school year gone and she's first telling me now? She got up and walked to the wall with the cork-board and pretended to examine the pictures and the papers and the chart of assignments. Gloria was on "chalk" that week. Lila took as much time as she felt she could before returning to her seat. "Sister. There must be some way we can bring her up. There are three months left in the school year. We could do a lot in three months."

"It's possible, yes. But she would have to do extra work to keep up with the new material while reviewing the old. I don't know if she's up to it. We set our work to challenge the brightest girls in the city. And someone has to work with her. If she won't work with you, I don't know who. I can't give her any extra time, now. My schedule is filled with parent conferences."

"We have to try, though, don't we?"

Sister Mary Francis pushed back her chair and stood. "That's all we can do, Mrs. Burke. I'll pray for you both tonight." She smoothly ushered Lila to the door.

Lila thought the walk home and her activities for the rest of the day would cool her anger, but when she told Willie about the conference she found that she was still furious.

"That smug, self-satisfied idiot didn't want to 'pressure' me, did nothing and now is going to pass Gloria off to some school for the retarded and make it up by praying for us."

"Having a fit isn't going to help the child. Maybe another school would be better."

"Come on, Willie. She's smart enough to keep up with them. It's the goddamn third grade, not Harvard Medical School."

"Well, what do you want to do?"

"I don't think I could help her with the arithmetic even if she let me. We either find her a tutor, or you'll have to do it. Numbers are easy for you."

"Sure. I can figure out how much I'll owe the bank if I stop construction at 330 Park Avenue because I'm too busy tutoring Gloria. Try to find someone."

Lila called Gloria into the living room and sat her on the couch. Since she and Willie had drinks, she poured Gloria a ginger ale in one of the big bar glasses with the gold horse heads.

"You know I saw Sister Mary Francis today."

"Uh-huh."

"She said you're having trouble with arithmetic and grammar."

"A little."

"Why haven't you let me help you with your homework, sweetheart? She said I should."

No response. Gloria appeared to be fascinated by her swizzle stick.

"She said they might not let you come back in the fall if you don't do better."

Gloria looked up suddenly. "That's not so. Sister likes me."

"Don't take my word for it. Ask her yourself, tomorrow. You can go to the public school on York Avenue. I hear it's very nice. I went to public school."

Lila spoke casually, but she had overheard Julia and Gloria agreeing that going to public school was the ultimate humiliation.

"That would save us some money, too," added Willie.

"Can you do something, Lila?" Now the little voice became soft and sweet.

"I don't know. Maybe, if you're willing to work hard for the rest of the term. You talk to Sister, and Willie and I will think about it, and we'll meet before dinner tomorrow and decide what to do."

It turned out that Elliott had a friend whose wife was an elementary schoolteacher taking a year off from teaching to be with her new baby. Mrs. Elkan was happy to come to the Burkes every school evening to help with the homework while her husband stayed with the baby.

There was an immediate gratifying result; all of the next week, homework was handed in complete and correct and was returned by Sister Mary Francis with big check marks and little drawings of smiling faces. The Burke family, drawn together by concern, spent the weekend in Long Island in anxious anticipation of the results of Friday's arithmetic quiz. Gloria thought she had done a little better, this time, but wasn't sure.

When Lila saw Gloria straggling at the end of the line of her classmates at dismissal on Monday, it was obvious the news was not good. Lila waited in the car; she could at least give her daughter privacy. Finally, the crowd around the entrance dissipated and Gloria made her way to the curb, opened the door of the Lincoln and climbed in next to Lila. She said nothing; just opened her bookbag, took out two sheets of paper, shoved them at Lila, turned her face to the window and began to cry. Without even looking at the quiz, Lila scootched herself over on the seat and kept her arm around Gloria, without resistance, while Jackson drove them home.

Lila stayed in the room as Mrs. Elkan went over the quiz with Gloria that evening. Half the problems had red x's next to them with little red circles around the mistakes.

"Look, Gloria, you didn't carry the one here. You know how to do that."

"I guess so, but I forget sometimes."

"But here, you got the fractions right just like we did together last week."

It was as Sister Mary Francis had told Lila: the old material was not firmly enough embedded. Lila left the room as they turned to the next day's homework. After the session, she intercepted Mrs. Elkan and, without consulting either Gloria or Willie, made arrangements for sessions over the weekends to review all of the work for the entire school year. So as the buds of April became the blooms of May, Lila, Gloria, and Pinto saw them in Central Park and not in Long Island. Willie stayed with them the first two weekends but weakened the third. He drove out early Saturday morning and back right after lunch Sunday, bringing back baskets of flowers and vegetables from the garden to atone for his disloyalty.

It was not until the Monday of the last week of the school year that the mail brought the envelope with the St.Agnes crest. Lila took it into her sewing room and closed the door before she opened it. They were pleased to accept Gloria Granatelli into the fourth grade.

•   •   •

There was little time to relax. Gloria's month in St. Louis was to begin in a week, arranged by Lila to give Gloria as much time as possible after her return to recover before the resumption of school. Jackson drove Gloria and Mary to the airport with Lila along for support that proved necessary, when Mary was overcome by fear. Lila and Jackson had to frog-march her to the gate, from which point Gloria tugged her by the hand while a stewardess pushed until she was safely loaded on the airplane.

Again, Lila flew to St. Louis to pick up Gloria. This time, John and Catherine brought Gloria to Lila's hotel room, themselves. When Lila opened the door to their knock, John's gaunt face glared at her like the Benton painting of John Brown. Gloria stood in front of him, looking down, expressionless. His hands were on her shoulders, his fingers stained with nicotine. Catherine stood next to him, her right hand pressing down on his left. She, too, had aged; marks of worry ringed her eyes, and her beautiful long black hair was now streaked with gray.

Suddenly, John pulled back his hands, knocking Catherine's away, spun around and strode down the hall. Deprived of support, Gloria stumbled backwards, but Catherine caught her and held her for a long moment before letting go. Gloria came through the door, past Lila, and into the bedroom, closing that door behind her. Catherine turned and, wordlessly, followed after John.

Gloria relapsed into silence on the trip home and showed little interest in anything for several days thereafter. She wouldn't even touch the piano, and her next lesson with Elliott had to be canceled. Soon, however, as before, she gradually came out of the spell.

•   •   •

They moved out to Long Island. Willie commuted to the office three days each week; Lila and Gloria came in on Tuesdays for their piano lessons. Julia visited for a week. On a couple of weekends, Elliott stayed with his parents, who lived not far from the Burke's and came over for Sunday lunch. They saw a lot of Margo. It wasn't an exciting summer, but Lila was grateful for some peace after the struggles of the preceding months.

•   •   •

School began again. This fall, Gloria was more interested in the preparations. She grumbled at having to dress in the school uniform and fussed over the fitting of the maroon blazers. Her out-of-school clothing was dictated by fourth-grade fashion about which she had endless telephone conversations with Julia and a new friend named Amanda. They impatiently rejected all of Lila's suggestions, and Gloria's drawers were soon filled with shirts and her closet with blue jeans. Hairstyle, also, became an important subject, and Lila silently suffered to see that delicate, elfin face squared off with bangs. As a result of all of this, Gloria became almost indistinguishable from the other girls in her class, and Lila had difficulty, the first afternoon, picking her out in the line of girls squeezing out of the school door like striped toothpaste. Then Gloria announced at dinner that picking up was for babies and that, henceforth, she would be coming home on the Madison Avenue bus with Amanda, who lived near the Burkes.

Right after dessert, Gloria excused herself and went off to do her homework. An hour later, she came into Willie's den where Lila and Willie were playing backgammon.

"Hi, darling," said Lila. "What's up?"

"Can I watch for a minute?"

"Sure,' said Willie. "Come blow on my dice and bring me luck. Lila's killing me."

Gloria came around to his side of the board and blew into the cup and Willie rolled double 5's. Gloria clapped her hands and Willie reached out a big arm, hauled her to him and gave her a big smacking kiss.

"No fair," exclaimed Lila. "Now, you have to blow on mine."

"I can't, Lila. Not this game. That was a no-take-back jinx. You roll, now."

Lila took the dice, blew on them herself, then rolled a 2-1, opening a spot that Willie promptly hit with his next roll. Two minutes later, Willie had won, and he and Gloria were chortling while Lila was complaining bitterly. Willie got up to get another cup of coffee. Gloria remained standing by the table, something obviously on her mind.

Lila pushed a stack of pieces across the board. "Help me set up, darling. Do you want to play one quick one?"

Gloria sat down and began to place the pieces. "Uh-uh." She paused. "Lila, could you look at this thing I wrote for school?"

"Why of course, darling. Where is it?"

"Could you come to my room?"

Lila followed Gloria to her room, sat in the big chair and read a page of Gloria's big, round writing. It was about getting Pinto used to the collar and leash, and Gloria had clearly worked hard on it; there were many words struck and replaced. Out of the corner of her eye, Lila could see Gloria fidget as she worked at the desk on her arithmetic.

"This is very good, darling. It describes what happened very clearly and the sentences are good, and there are very few mistakes."

"Could you help me fix the mistakes?"

"Sure. Come over here, and I'll show you." Gloria came over and perched on the arm of the chair and leaned over the page, her arm on Lila's shoulder for balance. "Here, where you wrote "She pulled out of collar,' you forgot to put in an article. ' What collar?'"

"The?"

"That's right. And you don't spell 'leash' 'l-e-e-s-h.' It's 'l-e-a-s-h.' And here, you ended a sentence and started a new one and forgot something, didn't you?"

"Oh, right. A period then a capital 'T.' I'm so dumb."

"No, you're not, at all. Three little mistakes; that's nothing." Lila dared a quick hug and got away with it. "Now fix them, before you forget. Is your arithmetic finished? It's getting late."

"Only one more problem. Could you look at them, too, when I finish?"

"Even better, I'll get Willie to do it. He owes you for getting him off the hook, tonight."

"Thank you Lila." Lila's cheek felt the lightest of touches; then Gloria was off the chair and over to the desk. Wordlessly, Lila got up and left the room.

For days she tried to recapture the moment. Had it been her imagination? Or maybe the breeze from the wide-open window? Her hopes had been trampled so often in the past year; she couldn't allow them to take over her judgment again. So she told no one, not Willie or even Margo, of her child's first kiss.

•   •   •

Lila hears the crackle of the gravel in the driveway as a car comes around the house and pulls up in front of the garage. It must be Jeffrey, returning with the New York edition of the *New York Times*. She could have the national edition delivered in the morning and wouldn't care about missing the Metro section and the movie schedules, but the obituary page of the national edition only contains articles about famous people. Lila is less interested in learning of the death of actors and politicians than of people she once knew. To learn of these, she follows the notices in the New York edition, the daily collection of twenty or thirty paid announcements inserted by the families of the newly deceased and the various organizations they had supported in life.

So every day at this time, after Plunkett's Magazine Center makes its pickup at the airport, Jeffrey makes a special trip to get Lila's copy. This is strictly his idea. Lila could easily wait until the evening or the next day, for that matter. She gets her national news from morning television. But Jeffrey has been captured by the illusion of immediacy and likes to be there watching as Plunkett's station wagon pulls in, the driver unloads the package of newspapers and Mr. Plunkett cuts the yellow twine and hands him the very first copy.

She waits for the slam of the car door. As always, it comes a full minute after she hears the car stop. It's one of life's great mysteries what Jeffrey does during that minute. Say a prayer of thanks for surviving traffic? Zip up his fly? Lila should talk; she's not moving so fast these days, either. Another minute and he has brought the newspaper to her. She finds nothing of great significance on the front page and continues to the table of contents where she locates the obituary page. She turns to it and peruses the daily list, the "snatch" portion of what Margo calls the "Hatch, Match and Snatch" section listing births, marriages, and deaths.

"Adams, Candace" sounds familiar, so she looks for the announcement below and finds a surviving daughter named "Alison" whom Lila vaguely remembers as a classmate of Gloria's.

Lila goes back to the list, using a finger to help her eyes follow the small print. She finds an old card-playing crony of Willie's, whom she would have bet had died twenty years ago. She remembers him well, a handsome man, with slick black hair; they called him "Duke." As she stirs her memory, it comes back to her that he dropped out of Willie's game for some unpleasant reason. Had he made a pass at her or something like that?

She has no feeling for these people, as is often the case when she reads of the deaths of casual acquaintances. Her most common reaction is a momentary regret, as she remembers something appealing about the deceased. Why, then, is it so important to her to read this page every day? For it is important, no question. Once, a few years back, Jeffrey had a minor automobile accident on his way to Plunkett's and never picked up the *Times*. Although Lila wouldn't have admitted it to anybody, she found herself more upset at missing the newspaper than at the damage to the car.

Mary has asked her why she reads that depressing page. The answer, that she needs to know so that she can attend the funeral or send condolences, is no longer valid. There is almost no one left whose passing will impel her to send condolences, and she hasn't been to a funeral since Willie's. But she can't explain to Mary how important it is to her diminishing control over her life to know who among the host of people who have played some part in it are still alive and who have gone from it forever.

"McCarthy, Elizabeth." Oh, God, not Betsey.

But it is. Devoted wife of the late Charles, loving mother of Francis, William, Matthew and Elaine, grandmother of a long list. It's Willie's cousin, Betsey, the only member of the Burke family to welcome Lila at that terrible engagement party. Lila had hoped that Betsey might become a close friend, but it never happened. Betsey was locked into her house as effectively as though with a key. Lila visited her a few times and sat in the kitchen drinking coffee while Betsey came in and out responding to demands of her children and her husband, who seemed to be perpetually "between jobs." Sometimes, as Lila would leave, Betsey would grip her hand as though trying to pull herself up off the floor, but they never again hugged as they had done at that first meeting. Willie had said that Betsey had been slim and beautiful just a few years before Lila met her. Lila hadn't believed him until, years later, she happened to pick up a book on Botticelli and found a reproduction of a pale Madonna. It was Betsey, divinely beautiful, free of the cover of fat behind which she had hidden all the years Lila knew her.

• • •

Gloria, as much as Lila, had been alarmed by the academic crisis of the previous Spring, so, as a precaution, weekly tutorials with Mrs. Elkan were continued. The first round of quizzes brought satisfactory results, and the tension dropped. Even Gloria's social life improved. Her new friend, Amanda, was popular with the other girls, and Gloria found herself included in parties and other group activities more often than previously. Lila encouraged her to return invitations and cheerfully made herself available as a guide and chaperone, and both their apartment and the Long Island house often swarmed with children.

At Christmas, Gloria insisted on flying to and from St. Louis by herself, a decision gratefully accepted by Lila, who returned to Palm Beach to oversee the finishing touches on the house. As in the past, Gloria returned subdued and withdrawn, but only for two or three days. Lila hastened the recovery period by suggesting that Gloria invite Amanda to come with them to Palm Beach for the Easter vacation. In time, there was an evening with Amanda's parents, a somewhat pushy couple who seemed impressed by the Burke's wealth and willingly agreed to entrust them with their daughter.

Easter vacation was successful. With unfinished work on the house to supervise and Willie busy in his West Palm Beach office most of the days, Lila was grateful that Gloria had a friend with her to occupy her time, although Amanda was not whom she would consider the ideal friend. As long as she got her own way, she was charming. Since she usually did, she usually was. If she wanted to go to the beach and Gloria to swim in the pool, they would go to the beach, and all would be well. But one morning, Amanda wanted to go shopping on Worth Avenue, and Lila wasn't free to take them, and a different Amanda emerged. She scornfully rejected all other suggested activities and marched from the breakfast table up to her room and refused Gloria admission for over an hour. Gloria was reduced to tears, and Lila felt obliged to cut short her tour of inspection with the decorator to belatedly accompany the girls. But there were no other unpleasant incidents, and Amanda was effusive with her thanks when her parents picked her up upon their return to LaGuardia Airport at the end of the week.

•   •   •

Lila and Gloria were by themselves a great deal that summer. Amanda was away at riding camp in Maine for eight weeks. Although Gloria had wanted to go also, it would then have been impossible for her to spend the obligatory month in St. Louis. Two other girls from her class came out for one weekend, only, and Elliott, "tied up with projects," didn't come at all.

So Gloria had to look principally to Lila and Willie for her entertainment. They hit hundreds of tennis balls to her, and Gloria and Lila practiced the piano in between their weekly trips to New York for their lessons,.Willie taught Gloria how to chip and putt on the green behind the house. And if they were ever in too much danger of getting bored, Margo would blow in like a hurricane and snatch them off to go to a sale of old costumes or a dog show or for lunch at a restaurant in the shape of a giant duck, and they would come home exhausted from laughing.

Lila had never realized what a big laugh Gloria had. It took possession of her, scrunching her face and shaking her whole body. Margo could get her going almost instantly; Willie's complicated stories brought her more slowly through smiles and nods of recognition to guffaws at the climax. And to her surprise, Lila found that she could also sometimes evoke the magic response, by mimicking a pompous waiter or a prissy tour guide. Lila and Gloria were laughing over some silliness loading the car to go to Jones Beach with Margo on a scorching August morning when Lila was called back into the house.

"It's Mrs. Granatelli, mum, on the telephone" Mary informed her.

"Hello, Cath. I hope it's not as hot out there as it is here." There was no response. "Cath, are you there?"

"I'm sorry. John died last night. A heart attack." Catherine's voice broke. "I'm sorry; I have to call back." She hung up.

Lila felt numb. She tried to visualize John but was unable to summon any memory of him except that of an angry, haggard face staring at her at from the doorway of her hotel room.

"What's wrong, Lila? You look terrible." Gloria's voice brought Lila out of her paralysis.

"John is sick." The lie came automatically. The truth was unthinkable.

"Daddy? What is it? Let me talk to him." She grabbed the telephone, put down the receiver and started to dial.

"No, you can't now. He's in the hospital, resting." Lila reached for the telephone, and they wrestled for it. "He had a heart attack."

Gloria let go of the telephone. "Is he going to die?" she choked.

"I don't know, darling. Catherine will call us later."

Gloria reached for the telephone again. "I want to talk to Mommy."

Again, Lila stopped her. "Catherine's at the hospital, I don't know which one. When she calls back, we'll get you right away." She tried to put her arm around Gloria to comfort her, but Gloria jumped up and ran upstairs.

Lila couldn't decide what to do. Was it be better or worse for Gloria to hear the truth in two stages rather than all at once? Should she hear it from Lila or from Catherine? And the funeral. Lila had to go to the funeral. What about Gloria? It would be terrible for her. Maybe Lila should stay home with Gloria. But it might be worse for Gloria not to go, not to be able to say good-bye. Lila rolled her head back and forth with the effort to think. Then the telephone rang again. Lila picked it up. "Cath?"

"It's Margo. What's the matter?"

"Hello?" Gloria's voice broke in on the upstairs extension.

"It's Margo, darling. Hang up please." There was a click. "Gloria?" No answer. "Oh, Margo. My brother is dead."

"That's terrible. Does Gloria know yet?"

"No, Catherine broke down on the phone, and I just told Gloria he was very sick. I don't know whether to tell her everything or wait until Catherine calls back. What should I do?"

"I think you have to do it. It's part of the job."

Margo was right. It was a part of a mother's job. Would she ever get the good parts?

"You're right. I'll do it right away. I should have told her, but—oh, shit. Let me go before Catherine calls back."

"I'll be over in ten minutes. You poor sweeties."

Lila hung up. She sat for a moment thinking about what to say, but got nowhere and dragged her reluctant body up the stairs. She opened Gloria's door without knocking. Gloria was sitting quietly on her bed, her back against the headboard, clutching the panda Margo had given her. She looked up at Lila and her face shattered into shards of pain.

"Daddy." It was only one word, but it seemed to go on forever. When it ended, Gloria flung herself onto her side facing away from Lila and pressed her face into the panda's chest muffling her sobs. Lila rushed to the bed beside her and put her arms around her from behind, but Gloria pulled loose, sat up and pushed her away, using the panda as a shield.

Down the hall, the telephone began to ring. Lila stepped back, and Gloria dropped the panda, got off the bed and went to answer it. Lila picked the panda off the floor and put him back on Gloria's bed. Was it barely ten minutes ago that she and Gloria were laughing together? In the hall, she paused, uncertain where to go. Gloria had closed Lila's bedroom door to speak to Catherine in privacy. Entry was unthinkable, but Lila wanted access to Gloria as soon as the telephone call ended. She went into the guest room across from her bedroom and moved an easy chair to a position from which she could observe her bedroom door, but far enough away that it was clear she was not trying to eavesdrop. She looked around, found a book of prints of birds and sat down in the chair, a blue heron glaring up at her.

After a few minutes, the door opened, and Gloria came out. She stopped and looked about her. Her movements were mechanical.

"I'm in here, darling. Come and talk to me."

Gloria turned toward Lila, "She wants you," she said, pointing to Lila's bedroom, then turned down the hall back to her room.

Lila went in and picked up the telephone. "What happened? What can I do? Should we bring Gloria out? She's so young; to go to the funeral—?"

"Lila, listen."

"Yes, Cath."

"I want you to do something. Will you, please?"

"Of course."

"Put Gloria on the morning plane tomorrow. By herself. It's what John would want. Can you do that?"

"Yes." It was hard to speak, but she forced herself to say "Tomorrow morning," before hanging up.

So she would not get to say good-bye. With that realization, the image of John, the stranger, faded and memories of childhood returned. She saw the frown on his acne-ravaged face as he bent over her arithmetic problems, teasing her that he couldn't possibly solve them either, then, just before her tears started, grinning as he showed her how. She remembered his hands, bruised and scarred by hammer and saw, gently gluing together her broken dolls.

"Johnneee." she cried soundlessly, a little girl, calling her ever-patient big brother. But it was too late. Her love for John had been the first casualty of the terrible war for Gloria. Mourning him today would be a self-indulgence she couldn't afford. She wiped her face and telephoned Willie.

"How can you not go to your brother's funeral?" he asked. "I'll come too, of course."

"Leave it alone, will you?" she responded wearily. "Going, not going. Neither one will change anything."

•   •   •

A week later, Lila stood at the gate waiting for Gloria to come through the door from her return flight. It was not until the very end of the parade of passengers that Gloria appeared, engrossed in conversation with one of the stewardesses. She seemed changed from the child who had left just a few days before, and Lila watched her closely as she approached. For one thing, she was gesturing vigorously as she spoke, for another, her steps were strong and measured, as though she were marching. And, yes, her face was different, stronger, heavier.

"Can we get something to eat? I'm starved." She surrendered her overnight case to Lila.

"Sure, darling. Didn't they give you lunch on the plane?"

"That was hours ago, and it wasn't very good. Some kind of fish."

They picked up Gloria's suitcase and went to the coffee shop, and Gloria ordered a hamburger with extra cooked onions, french fries, and a chocolate malt, which soon disappeared. While Gloria ate, Lila related the odds and ends of news about the Burke households for the week of her absence, Gloria occasionally grunting a question. In the car going home, Gloria refused to answer any of the questions. Instead, she recounted the complicated family saga she had just heard from the stewardess. Lila might have been picking her up at the Club after a half-hour tennis lesson.

When they got back to the house, Gloria went straight to the telephone, leaving Lila to unpack alone. When Lila finished, she found Gloria in the kitchen, watching Mrs. Thompson mixing cake batter.

"How's Amanda?"

"She's at her grandmother's and won't be home until late."

Mrs. Thompson turned away from the table to light the stove, and Gloria grabbed the mixing spoon and scooped a big spoonful of batter into her mouth.

"Gloria! That's for tonight's cake."

Mrs. Thompson grinned when she saw what had happened, "Oh, there's more than enough, Missus."

"Well, she should ask, first. And don't take any more. Mike and Margo are coming for supper, and Willie is going to barbecue spareribs the way you like them. You'll spoil your appetite." The words came out without thinking, and Lila cringed. Gloria didn't like being told what to do under the best of circumstances.

But the reply was merely a casual "I won't."

At dinner, Gloria politely responded to Mike's awkward attempts at conversation, vociferously rallied with Margo over who had the bigger crush on the assistant tennis pro and lavishly complimented Willie on his barbecuing skills. She tore into the spareribs, smeared the rich red sauce all over her face and dripped it down onto the giant lobster bibs that Willie had thoughtfully provided for all. Lila was surprised; Gloria had always been a picky eater, extremely fastidious in her habits. But tonight she attacked one corncob after another, gleefully licking the melted butter off her fingers and crunched her way through two portions of coleslaw. She finished with a huge slab of strawberry shortcake, then said goodnight and went to her room.

Lila waited ten minutes before following and knocking at the door of Gloria's room. There was no answer. Could Gloria be asleep already? There was no light under the door of her bathroom. Lila entered quietly and started as Pinto jumped up on her.

"What is it?" said a cranky voice. The bit of light from outside the window showed Gloria, in her pajamas, lying on her back on top of the covers.

"I just wanted to find out if you're all right."

"I'm all right." It sounded as though she were confirming that she had enough blankets.

"I mean, you've had a terrible thing happen to you, darling, and we haven't had a chance to talk about it. I want to know if there is anything I can say or do to make it not so bad."

"I'm tired. Let me go to sleep." She pushed down the covers, thrust her feet under them and, as Lila leaned over the bed, raised her arm to guard her face.

That much hasn't changed, Lila said to herself, bitterly, and finished her motion by patting Gloria's shoulder. "Good night, darling."

There was no further response.

Later, Lila asked Willie whether he had noticed anything different about Gloria.

He paused in taking off a slipper. "She seemed fine to me; better than I expected."

"How about the way she ate?"

"She tied into it, didn't she? Well, everything was delicious. I trimmed the fat off the ribs, this time, and they weren't greasy at all. It just takes a little more basting."

"Yes, Willie. They were wonderful. Still, have you ever seen her stuff herself like that?"

Willie set the slipper under his side of the bed and put its mate next to it. "Catherine probably wasn't up to cooking." He plunged happily into bed, ending the conversation.

Lila was doubtful. That didn't sound like Catherine. If anything, Gloria had gained weight in the week she had been away. Weight and something else, self-assurance, maybe. She seemed much less concerned with how she looked and sounded. As Lila went back over the evening, there were several occasions when Gloria had interrupted others in the conversation, where she would formerly have been silent. Of course, Mike and Margo were long accepted friends, but still, it was unusual behavior. Was this just Gloria's reaction to John's death? Or was the beautiful, sensitive, fragile little girl Lila had brought home two years ago gone forever? If so, what would life be like with a sturdy young woman with a dirty face and a loud voice?

With the school only a week away, there was a lot to be done. Lila called a planning conference with Gloria the next morning right after Willie left for New York. Gloria's first priority, however, was connecting with Amanda, and the conference was adjourned while Gloria went into the den to telephone to invite her to the house for the Labor Day weekend. A few minutes later she stamped back into the dining room and sat down so hard the chair shook.

"She can't come out for the weekend. She's going riding with a girl she met at camp who has a house someplace, and they're going shopping together tomorrow and to a play on Wednesday and the only time she can see me is Thursday afternoon." A few months ago she'd have been helplessly in tears, thought Lila.

"What about your piano lesson?"

"We can change that." It wasn't a question.

"You know how busy Elliott's schedule is, darling."

"I can go instead of you on Tuesday."

"Then I'd only have one this week? Can't you wait to see Amanda until next week? You'll be seeing her every day in school."

"No, I can't wait. Why do you have to have two lessons every week, anyway?"

And so it was arranged. Elliott had already refused payment for Gloria's canceled lesson of the previous week, so Lila insisted on taking a 'double' lesson on Thursday. Since Amanda was coming to the Burke's apartment, Lila went to Elliott's apartment. After the first hour, they took a coffee break, and Lila asked Elliott how he had found Gloria on Tuesday.

"She's become one tough little chick. I told her I was sorry and she just shrugged me off. Then she played badly, which you'd expect since her practicing was interrupted, but it didn't bother her at all. She usually flips when she makes even one mistake."

So it wasn't just at home. It looked like the new Gloria was here to stay. Just as Lila seemed to be making some progress with the old one.

The Burke apartment was surprisingly quiet when Lila returned at five, but Mary explained that Gloria had asked Jackson to drive her and Amanda to the riding academy across the Park. Lila was not pleased by this. For one thing, she felt Gloria's excursions should still be first submitted to her for approval, and, for another, Gloria had no business ordering the use of Jackson and the car, a prerogative reserved to Willie.

"And how are they getting home?" she asked sharply.

"Jackson, will stay with them, Mum, and drop off the other little girl on the way to pick up Mr. Burke at the Club. She's after giving him a bit of a surprise. Is that all right, Mum?"

Lila modulated her tone. "Yes, Mary. But next time, either Mr. Burke or I should approve that kind of trip, particularly with the car.

"Yes, Mum. I'll remember that."

Willie and Gloria didn't return until after seven. Gloria had never been to the Club before, and Willie had given her a tour. They were in the best of spirits when they sat down to dinner, Willie was teasing Gloria about almost walking through the wrong door into the swimming pool where the men didn't wear bathing suits.

"That's not fair, Willie, you should have warned me."

"I never had the chance. I can't believe it, Lila. Eleven years old and after the men already. She had that door half-open before I could stop her."

"Don't pay any attention to him, darling. He did the same thing to me on my first visit and let me get the door all the way open. I think it's an official Club ritual."

They joked their way through dinner, Gloria at her most charming. Lila was emboldened to ask about the date with Amanda.

"It was OK" She obviously had more to say but paused to look at Willie who nodded.

"Lila, can I take riding lessons? Horses are so beautiful, and riding looks like so much fun. Amanda loved riding camp and she and her friend Jane are going to go all fall at the Armory, and I could go with them. Willie thinks it's a good idea. Can I, please?"

Willie suddenly concentrated his attention and began to closely inspect his T-bone. So there had been an ulterior motive to Gloria's surprise visit to Willie. Another new trait had appeared. Gloria had never been devious before. If she wanted something, she would come straight to Lila to ask for it. She must have sensed that Lila would be negative this time and decided to get Willie on her side from the beginning.

Not that there was anything terrible about riding. But Gloria's motivation was obvious: to hold on to her friendship with Amanda, who was not Lila's favorite child. Besides, Gloria had enough to do with school, the piano, Pinto, weekends in Long Island and trips to St. Louis.

"You think it's a good idea?" she asked Willie, challenging him to persuade her.

He squirmed in his chair. "Uh, I don't know. I haven't thought about it much. If Gloria, really wants, then—What do you think?"

Gloria's shoulders drooped; her ally had turned tail on her. The movement caught at Lila and weakened her.

"Let's find out a little more about it, anyway, then we can see. All right, darling?"

"Oh yes, Lila. Thank you." She turned in her chair just slightly away from Willie and towards Lila and ate the rest of her meal that way.

Lila signed Gloria up for the Wednesday afternoon riding group in which Amanda and her friend were enrolled. Over Gloria's protest, Lila insisted on watching the first class.

There were problems from the beginning. Gloria and two other children who had never ridden before, both younger than Gloria, were pulled out of the group and seated at one end of the bleachers. An instructor led up a horse and began to teach them the names for the parts of its body and for the saddle and bridle. Lila could see that Gloria was furious. Meanwhile, other instructors brought horses to the other group who began to ride around the ring in the center of the huge building. Amanda and Jane seemed to be the best riders.

After about half an hour, Gloria's instructor began to show her group how to mount and dismount. Gloria's turn was last. As Gloria approached the horse, the other group, with Jane at the head followed by Amanda, came around. The two waved to Gloria. She waved back and, in one motion, grabbed the instructor's outstretched hand, thrust her foot into the stirrup and made a violent vault up onto the saddle. For a moment it appeared a gloriously successful maneuver, but her momentum carried her past the perpendicular, and her foot came out of the stirrup. She leaned forward, her hands scrabbling at the pommel before sliding off the far side of the horse and falling to the ground. There was a collective gasp, as she fell, followed by a burst of laughter. Lila, her heart pounding, was down the bleachers in a second, but Gloria was already sitting up on the dirt floor. They both looked to see who was laughing; it was Amanda and Jane.

Gloria did not appear to have suffered any serious injury, but she allowed Lila to take her to the pediatrician who agreed. The next morning, she complained of generalized pain, and the pediatrician, when called, allowed her Thursday off from school. She improved enough to suffer, with the aid of a pillow, through her afternoon piano lesson and, limping sporadically, through Pinto's walk. The next morning, Lila was adamant that she return to school but felt guilty, as well as concerned, when the school office called her at twelve-fifteen to come and bring Gloria home, although the secretary assured Lila that Gloria was not sick.

She didn't look sick when Lila arrived in the school office. She looked angry and disheveled; her blouse was stained and a sleeve, missing a button, hung open. She was sitting on a bench under a picture of the Sacred Heart, an open book on her lap. When she saw Lila, she closed the book with a clap that brought up the heads of both of the school secretaries.

"Let's go." She stood up and put the book into her bookbag.

"What's the matter, darling? Are you all right?"

"Yes, not that anybody cares." This was said in the direction of the closed door to the Headmistress's office.

"Mrs. Burke." One of the secretaries called her over. "Sister Josephine said to send you in as soon as you arrived."

"What happened?" asked Lila.

"She'll tell you all about it."

Gloria walked over to them. "Can't we just go, Lila?"

"Just a minute, darling. I have to talk to Sister Josephine for a minute."

The headmistress was businesslike. "Why don't you sit for a moment, Mrs. Burke, and I'll tell you what's happened." She pointed to a chair pulled up to the front of her desk.

"Apparently Gloria is very angry at Amanda Morrison over something, but she won't tell us what. Do you know?"

"They were at a horseback riding class, and Gloria fell off. Amanda and her friend Jane were nearby and laughed. That must be it."

The headmistress frowned. "That may not have been very nice of them, but it hardly justifies violence. Fortunately, Amanda wasn't hurt, but she could have been."

I don't want to hear this, thought Lila, but she had to ask, "What happened?"

"When Gloria came into class this morning she went straight up to Amanda and said something in a very angry tone. Sister Mercy didn't hear exactly what. Amanda replied 'I didn't,' and Gloria shouted 'You did too, and so did Jane,' and then Sister Mercy stopped them. She felt that the class had been overly interrupted already and let the matter go. These little storms usually blow over."

"But this one didn't?"

"No, it didn't. Nothing further happened in the classroom, but a hurricane hit the dining room at lunch. Amanda took her tray first and sat down with it; Gloria then sat down next to her. There were other empty seats. Gloria started arguing with Amanda again; several children confirm that. The argument grew louder, then Gloria jumped up, dumped her tray on Amanda's head, yanked her chair over backwards and started hitting her until two of the teachers pulled her off. As they led her away, she pointed back at poor Amanda and started laughing."

"Oh, my God. Uh, I'm sorry, Sister." Lila crossed herself penitently. "I'll make sure that Gloria understands that she has to control herself so that nothing like this happens again. It's a very bad time, for her now, though."

"I know, Mrs. Burke. Sister Mercy told me of your brother's death. I'm sorry for both you and Gloria. And her conduct here has always been excellent, so I've decided not to suspend her on conditions that she comes in Monday and reads an apology to Amanda and the class. Unless she's changed her attitude in the last twenty minutes, that's an angry girl out there who doesn't feel the least bit repentant."

"Thank you, Sister." Lila was out of her chair before the headmistress could change her mind, but as she reached the door she heard behind her, "And she writes the apology herself."

Gloria said nothing until they had left the building, then asked Lila what the headmistress had said. Lila decided to let her worry for a while. "Tonight, when Willie gets home. We'll have to have a very serious discussion."

"Did she suspend me?"

Lila didn't answer.

"She did. For how long?"

No answer.

"She didn't expel me? She couldn't do that."

Lila looked as grim as she could. "Tonight," she said again in a lugubrious tone and wouldn't budge.

Gloria turned away. "I don't care, I hate that school anyway." She sulked all the way home, dragged Pinto outside for her walk, then disappeared into her room with no further questions. That evening, she finally agreed to the conditions, but only after Lila followed Willie's suggestion and told Gloria, she would be expelled if she didn't.

Miraculously, the Monday penance was accomplished, but the problem didn't go away.

The friendship with Amanda had turned into bitter enmity on both sides. And Amanda had allies. Her group of friends now turned against Gloria, even though she had been a member of the same group last year. The next weeks brought a spate of offenses and insults. Gloria's increasing weight became a favorite target of gibes. Her pencils disappeared, and her new raincoat was trampled on and left on the floor of the coatroom. Fear of expulsion kept her from retaliating, and the bravado with which she had first confronted Amanda melted into a sullen silence.

Lila tried everything. She went to Sister Mercy, who dealt with the problem by reading the class selected texts on forgiveness. The headmistress was even less helpful, suggesting that if one girl was having trouble with four or five other girls, maybe the one was to blame. In desperation, Lila went to Amanda's mother and begged her to get her daughter to call off the persecution. Mrs. Morrison said Gloria must be imagining things and presented Lila with a bill for a school outfit to replace the one with food stains that the cleaners couldn't get out.

The effort to survive each day's social stresses sapped Gloria's energy, and her schoolwork suffered. Mrs. Elkan had returned to full-time teaching, and Lila and Willie were Gloria's sole resource. They might have been enough, however, if Gloria had wanted to work as she had the year before, but she no longer seemed to care about schoolwork, or anything else.

One Friday afternoon, Gloria delivered a letter from the headmistress and led Pinto out without a word. The letter informed Lila that Gloria's work "fails to meet required standards," her conduct "lacks the spirit of cheerful obedience taught by Our Lord" and that, "Unless Gloria's work and general attitude show substantial improvement by the end of the fall term, we will regretfully be obliged to ask her to leave St. Agnes."

That sanctimonious bitch. If she had done her job and stopped Amanda and her friends, Gloria would be fine. No, that would be too much like work, and apparently "Our Lord" didn't require that. It was easier to sacrifice one girl than to restrain four or five. But Lila's indignation wouldn't help Gloria; Lila had no good idea what might.

On Gloria's return, she followed Pinto to the kitchen to give the dog her customary biscuit. Lila went after them. Gloria was cutting a big wedge out of a freshly baked chocolate cake. She looked up with a grim face. Lila took a plate from the cupboard, picked up the cake knife and cut herself half of Gloria's piece.

"Do you know what was in the letter, sweetheart."

"Uh huh."

"How do you know?"

"Sister Josephine."

"What did she say?"

"I don't remember. She tried to make me cry, but I wouldn't."

Lila hadn't seen Gloria cry since she had returned from John's funeral. "You poor darling." Lila started to reach for her child, but a warning look stopped her.

"I don't care what she says."

"Good. It will be all right. We'll find another tutor, and maybe those terrible girls will get tired of bothering you. They weren't so bad, this week, you said."

Gloria shook her head.

"What happened today?"

"Nothing."

"Well, something must have. Tell me, sweetheart."

Gloria shook her head again.

"I have to know."

"They all waited by the bus stop and yelled together "Gloria's on probation" three times and then "Hooray.""

"Did any teacher hear them?"

"No. It wasn't at the school; it was at Madison Avenue."

"Well, I'm going to have a talk with Sister Josephine. Don't do that, darling."

Gloria had finished her cake and was sticking the fork into the table-cloth. She put the fork down and gathered the crumbs on her plate into a ball that she rolled between her fingers.

"I'll come in with you Monday, and we'll go straight to her office."

"No."

"What do you mean, no?"

"I'm not going back there, ever."

"But they didn't expel you. You're just on probation."

"I don't care. I won't go back, and, if you try to make me, I'll call Mrs. Warren."

When Lila had called Mrs. Warren a year ago to report Gloria's successful beginning of the fourth grade, Mrs. Warren had told her that the file had been closed and that there would be no further supervision. But this was not the time to discuss that with Gloria.

"I don't want to make you do anything. But you have to go to school, sweetheart. The law makes you do that."

Gloria tossed the ball of cake crumbs into the air and tried to catch it in her mouth. She missed, and the ball fell on the floor and rolled under the stove.

"I don't care," she said and got up and left the kitchen.

"Gloria, pick that up," Lila called after her, but there was no response.

Lila retrieved the ball and threw it in the garbage pail, then rinsed their plates and forks and set them on the drainboard. She was sick and tired of cleaning up after Gloria, who left food everywhere, even on the piano where it was strictly forbidden, and scattered clothes and balls of Kleenex on the floors of every room of the apartment. It would have been too embarrassing to leave them for the servants to pick up. Gloria was turning into a spoiled brat who did nothing for herself, and it was high time that Lila did something about it.

She poured herself a cup of coffee and sat back down at the kitchen table. If only her Momma were still here to advise her. Was it ten years already? After her mother's death, Lila, trying to hold on to something, had occasionally called their old telephone number. Even that imagined connection was soon broken when a new holder of the number answered.

Thinking of her mother, calmed Lila, as talking to her had always done. The problem was Gloria's education, not a little messiness. Continuing at St. Agnes might still work, even after Gloria's absolute refusal, if something could be done to convert Sister Josephine to an ally instead of an enemy. In desperation, Lila reached for the telephone and called Willie to get the Bishop, or someone, to talk to her.

Willie objected violently. "That's how we got her into St. Agnes in the first place. He'll be angry with me for having him make them take an unsuitable child, to begin with and be embarrassed to call them now."

"He's met Gloria and knows she's not unsuitable."

"For Christ's sake, Lila. That was for what, two minutes, at my mother's party? He doesn't know anything about Gloria, and, if I call him, he'll know that she's gotten into trouble and that Jimmy Burke's son can't deal with it himself. It's out of the question."

That evening, Lila, using Willie's own tactic of persistency, asked him again and, the next morning forbade him to leave the house without calling the Bishop. He was at his most charming self when he made the call. An hour later he picked up the ringing telephone.

"Hello? Oh, Father Gower. How are you? ... Yes.... Yes....I understand....Of course....Please express my thanks to His Grace and thank you, too, Father."

Although Willie's voice had betrayed nothing to the person at the other end of the line, the expression on his face told Lila they had failed.

"I knew when it was his secretary who called. 'His Grace has spoken to Sister Josephine who has assured him that the child's well-being will be given every possible consideration consistent with the interests of the other pupils and the school.' That means she's dropped her plan to have Gloria flogged on stage during assembly. I'm sorry."

Lila kissed him for trying, sent him off to his squash game and sat down to reconsider. It made no sense to fight a huge battle with Gloria to try to get her to go back to St. Agnes Monday morning. The situation was not going to improve, and there would likely be another incident triggering her expulsion before the end of the term, when she would surely be asked to leave.

There was no difficulty finding Gloria; her radio was playing some obnoxious pop song at a deafening volume. She was lying on her bed teasing Pinto with a squeaky rubber mouse.

"Sweetheart, are you still against going back to St. Agnes?"

"I told you, I'm not going back, ever."

She threw the toy across the room; Pinto jumped off the bed after it.

"All right, then you won't. Have you heard about any other school you might like?"

"I don't care, as long as I don't have to go back there."

Pinto jumped back onto the bed; Gloria snatched the mouse from her and, ignoring Lila, began the game again.

Monday morning, Lila called Sister Josephine and, keeping herself well in restraint, told her Gloria was being withdrawn.

Sister Josephine's voice was icy. "That's a wise decision, Mrs. Burke, and I'm sure the Bishop will agree. Good-bye."

She hung up before Lila could say anything further, not that there was anything more to say. Over the next few days, Lila assembled information on private schools, both Catholic and secular and called several, pleading for expedited consideration. "The work at St. Agnes is just a little too difficult for her," she told them.

Initial reactions from the schools seemed favorable. Two interviews were scheduled; other admissions personnel cordially promised to set them up. Then something happened. The two interviews were perfunctory, and, within a day or two, Lila was told that Gloria had been rejected. The other schools apologetically reported that, after checking with the teachers, there was no place open for Gloria. It was obvious to Lila that calls had been made to St. Agnes and that Gloria was *persona non grata*.

Gloria showed little interest in the news and seemed prepared to abandon her schooling altogether, which did not surprise Lila. Willie's reaction did.

"Maybe we should look into boarding schools. Some of them are a lot more tolerant of kids who have had problems elsewhere."

Lila exploded. "Never! Gloria stays with me! Do you understand?"

Willie seemed to shrink in size. "OK OK, I was just mentioning it as a possible last resort. You know, if we can't find anything here."

"Not as any resort. I'd sooner see her back with Catherine than turn her over to people who don't give a damn about her. "

"OK, OK, calm down. Forget boarding school. But what are you going to do?"

"She'll just have to go to the public school. Maybe we can find a good private school that will take her next fall."

Gloria put up no resistance to going to the public school. The next morning, she docilely accompanied Lila and allowed herself to be led from the principal's office to a fourth-grade classroom, her lunchbox filled with the most tempting treats Mrs. Thompson could think of. Lila went home and sat still all morning, but the telephone didn't ring until two o'clock when she had finally relaxed enough to eat some lunch. Gloria had not returned to her classroom from the lunchroom and could not be found anywhere in the school building.

Frantically Lila dialed Willie's private number known only to her.

"Willie?"

"Yes, darling girl. What's the matter?"

"Gloria has disappeared. You have to find her. She must have tried to come home from school and—she's gone."

"When did they see her last?"

"At noon, someone took her to the lunch room. That's all they know."

"Have you called the police?"

"Oh, my God. You think she's been kidnapped?"

"No, no, she probably didn't like the school and just went to the Park or something, because she thought if she came home you'd take her right back."

"You must be right. I'll go to the playground, now."

"No, darling, you stay by the telephone. You can send Mary out to look. I'll call the police. They know what to do."

"What if she's been hit by a taxi? Willie?"

"The police will check the hospitals. It'll be all right. Let me go. I'll come right home after I've called them. Keep the telephone free." He hung up.

Lila took a deep breath, then another, and regained control. She went to the kitchen and sent Mary and Jackson out to the Park. Mrs. Thompson was too upset to be of any use, and Lila was occupied for the next five minutes calming her. Then, she began her vigil by the telephone.

Alternating with images of the terrible things that might have happened to Gloria, came the terrible questions. What should Lila have done differently so that this wouldn't have happened? Was the public school a bad idea? Could Lila have prevented the disaster at St. Agnes? Should she have sent Gloria to the public school right away, since it was what she had been accustomed to in St. Louis?

In St. Louis, yes. Lila had almost forgotten that Gloria had lived in St. Louis. Lila never saw her there, had only the evanescent contact of a handful of snapshots of a beautiful, happy child. Was that child, her child, now dead, or crippled or in the hands of some monster because Lila had taken her from her little house and two people she loved and a neighborhood school she wouldn't dream of running away from?

The telephone rang.

"Mrs. Burke? This is Sergeant Hennessy from the Harmon police department. We have your daughter."

Relief almost choked her. "Uh, is… is she all right?"

"Oh, she's just fine. Eating my ham sandwich, actually. She went to Grand Central and got on a train for St. Louis. When the conductor came around, she tried to talk him into letting her ride all the way out there without a ticket. Said she lost it. He said she was real persuasive, but he put her off here. We're the first stop, you know."

"Thank God. Yes, Sergeant, I know. Can we drive up now and get her?"

"Yes, Ma'am. It should take you a little more than an hour. We'll be here."

A few minutes later, Willie arrived, and they set off for Harmon. After the first rush of relief, Lila's brain began to work feverishly. Gloria had now proved herself mobile. She could walk away from school, or the apartment, for that matter, at almost any time and, in a few minutes, buses, subways or even trains could take her God knows where. And the school problem was even worse, now. Obviously, the public school was not going to work. Was Willie's suggestion of a boarding school, one used to taking all kinds of girls whose parents could afford to pay, in some isolated New England village the only thing left?

And then the solution came to her.

"It's all right, Willie," she said, patting his knee. "It's all going to work out just fine."

It wasn't easy, but once Lila had made up her mind, she could not be dissuaded. Ten days of chaotic activity ensued as the Burke household split in two like the halves of an island wrenched apart by an earthquake. Early one morning, at almost the exact moment Willie left their New York apartment for his office, Lila and Gloria sat down to eat their breakfast in a hurry so that Gloria would not be late for her first day at The Palm Beach Day School.

IV

Lila has put off her appointment with the decorator three times. The last time was two weeks ago, and she let him get as far as the front door before she threw a tantrum and refused to see him. She made Mary tell him that the doctor had just left and that she was forbidden visitors, but Mary is a terrible liar, and Lila knows he didn't believe a word of it. When she called to reschedule he was "out on a job," the first time, "with a client," the second and "on a conference call," the third. She knew better than to expect him to call her back: she was no longer a good enough client for him to grant absolution before her penance was complete, but she seemed to be getting closer. Sure enough, on her next call, she was allowed to apologize profusely, after seven minutes on hold, and he condescended to reschedule for 4:00 this afternoon. Not surprisingly, he arrived twenty minutes late, declined the offer of iced tea and stood in the foyer tapping his notebook impatiently with a pencil while Lila explained the purpose of the visit.

She used to enjoy working with decorators. Good architects and decorators, she found, welcomed a knowledgeable client. She most loved the design phase. When all things were possible. When crumpled sketches filled the wastebasket, and hard minds chipped the rock from unworkable ideas to find the gems within. With Willie's help, she learned about wiring and plumbing, insulation and sound-proofing, heating and air-conditioning and more than once caught out a careless engineer or contractor. But that was a long time ago when Willie had been there to appreciate what she did and proudly show her work off to the guests who thronged their residences. It's no fun anymore. All she now has is the Palm Beach house, and she doesn't care what it looks like these days.

The present project is all her doctor's idea. He doesn't want her climbing stairs and has ordered her to move down to the first floor. Alternatively, she can install an elevator. That's the choice. She has no serious intention of doing either, but she might as well see what Mr. Harris, who supervised the alterations to the north wing, has to say.

Mr. Harris runs to fat and Panama hats. He has adopted a short beard since Lila has last seen him, which makes him look like Burl Ives in <u>Cat on a Hot Tin Roof</u>. When Lila speaks of her heart condition, he stops tapping his notebook, his drawl thickens, and he becomes a courtly southern gentleman, offering her his arm as they ascend the offending staircase.

Lila first takes Mr. Harris to her quarters in the upstairs portion of the north wing. The master suite was originally built for less intimate marriages, each spouse having his or her own bedroom, bathroom, and dressing room, When the Burkes bought the house, they knocked out the wall between the two bedrooms creating one huge one. Lila asks about running an elevator up to what was Willie's dressing room. Mr. Harris takes measurements.

Off the hallway, between the master suite and the staircase, are several guestrooms, musty with years of disuse. Mr. Harris suggests work. Lila demurs. They negotiate with each other and settle on painting and replacement of faded curtains.

On the other side of the staircase is Gloria's suite: bedroom, guest room, bathroom, and soundproofed playroom. The walls are hung with posters of Elvis and Fats Domino and banners from the 1954 Orange Bowl. There is a radio-phonograph and shelves stacked with records and magazines. In one corner is a large papier maché alligator with a cigar in its mouth, a souvenir of a <u>Pogo</u> party. The rooms are well kept up, and Mr. Harris makes no suggestions. Beyond these rooms is the south wing containing the servants' rooms, so they turn and descend the staircase.

On the ground floor, the south wing contains the kitchen, pantries, and storerooms. Underneath Gloria's suite are the formal dining room, a smaller family dining room, and several large closets. On the other side of the staircase are the office, the music room, now used as Lila's living room, and Willie's den and card room, also soundproofed, in which Lila and Peggy play their backgammon games. Mr. Harris has ideas for this room that Lila rejects colorfully. Mr. Harris takes it in good spirit; their old relationship seems to have been reestablished.

Most of the north wing, under the master suite, consists of one big room. The floor is tiled, and there are numerous electrical outlets and connections for water and even oxygen so that Willie's bed could be moved around allowing him to look out of different windows. T.V. brackets and lights depend from tracks in the false ceiling. On the side facing the garden, a large door has been installed, with a ramp, so that the bed could be easily wheeled outside. Lila gave the bed, specially designed for Willie, to St. Mary's Hospital. Near the door is an extra-large bathroom including hydrotherapy equipment. A nurses' suite, bedroom with twin beds, sitting room with T.V. and bathroom completes the wing. Mr. Harris has brought a copy of his plan with him and doesn't need to take measurements.

They return to the living room and Mr. Harris, now, is pleased to accept the offered iced tea. His shirt-front and collar are damp, and he loosens his tie, increasing his resemblance to Big Daddy. He is the only sloppy-looking decorator Lila has ever seen, and she wonders how he is able to sell himself to new clients.

"Well, now, Miz Burke, there wouldn't be any problem in putting you downstairs; there's plenty of room and all."

" 'And all' is right, Mr. Harris. It's all ready and waiting for me to have my stroke. Maybe St. Mary's will loan me back the bed."

"I didn't mean it that, way. We can do anything you want down there. Of course, we'd put down new flooring, maybe parquet, and some nice orientals. You can easily make two rooms out of that big one; you'll want the dressing-sitting room over by the bathroom. Close off some of those windows so you'll feel more private and rip off that false ceiling and there you are."

"And the nurses' suite?" Lila inquired with interest.

"Well, you could just leave it like it is, in case you ever did need a nurse for a few days. Or, we could find something to do with it."

"Oh, I'm sure we could, Mr. Harris, as long as I'm paying for it. Let's see. That sounds like about one-twenty-five plus the orientals and new furniture; my old stuff upstairs will look too shabby. Say two hundred thousand or so in all if I've got the energy to haggle. That's to make it like it was before we altered it and that cost two seventy-five if I remember correctly."

"Oh, you do, Miz Burke. I looked it up this morning."

"That's a half a million dollars with no net change. Don't you find that depressing?"

Mr. Harris walks over to the piano and plays "Moon River" with one finger. "This piano still sounds terrific. Y'all ever want to sell it, call me first. I'm in a service business, Miz Burke. My job is to give my clients what they ask me for. And I do it well, and they come back to me, like you have, and they recommend me to their friends like you recommended Mrs. Goodman. I'm not an artist creating work for the ages. If they like the way it looks and works for five years, I know I've done a good job. No, I'm not depressed. But if you are, then let's forget it. Does your doctor realize how much it would upset you to move? That could be worse than stairs."

"That's exactly what I said to him, and he mumbled something about how up or down shouldn't make any difference. Well, what about an elevator?"

"The problem is that you don't have a basement and you don't have an attic. Where's the machinery going to go? If we dig down, we'll hit too much water too soon. To go up means a tower on the roof and the Landmark Committee won't allow it. In either case, it'll cost plenty. I'll have to do some homework. Maybe, what we should do, is put one of those gizmos on a track on the staircase that'll let you ride up and down."

Lila shudders. "Those are the ugliest things. I'd rather be cut into pieces and sent up in the dumbwaiter."

"There you go," says Mr. Harris, cheerfully, and makes a note in his little notebook.

●   ●   ●

Lila ran to meet Gloria at the front door. "Guess what, darling," she panted.

"What now?" Gloria whined, dropping her book bag on the bench beside the door, from which it immediately slid to the ground. "God, that bus is hot. Why didn't they get the new ones air-conditioned?" She pulled off her Palm Beach High School sweater, balled it up and flung it on top of the book bag.

"Why didn't you take off your sweater on the bus?"

"Why don't you mind your own business." Gloria headed for the kitchen. She was always cranky when she got home from school, and Lila generally stayed away from her until after she had taken a snack up to her room, turned her radio to its maximum volume and "chilled out" for at least an hour. But this couldn't wait.

"Elliott's coming down spring vacation. For a week."

"What?" Gloria stopped dead. "You're kidding."

"No, he's coming. Here's his letter. A song he wrote is being introduced by a singer named Garrity at a concert in Miami—"

Gloria screamed. "Tom Garrity! Elliott wrote a song for Tom Garrrity?" She grabbed the letter from Lila. "Oh my God, he did!"

"I've never heard of Tom Garrity, he's not like Sinatra or Como, is he?"

"What am I going to do with you, Lila? You are so square. Tom Garrity is like Elvis Presley. You know who he is?"

"Yes, Gloria, I've heard of Elvis Presley. Not that I like the way he sings. It's -—"

"Oh, please, Lila. I get enough lectures in school. Tom Garrity sings like Elvis, but he's gorgeous and not at all greasy. And Elliott knows him? Wrote a song for him? It's crazy. I have to tell Sally." She ran off clutching the letter.

One of Lila's few regrets in moving to Florida was the diminished role Elliott now played in her life and Gloria's. Three months of lessons when they came north in the summer and one visit each winter: that was all. Neither of them had found a replacement in Palm Beach, but by periodically prodding each other into a few weeks of practice, they maintained the fiction that they were working on their own.

They had maintained other fictions during the past five years. Gloria was doing fabulously in school and had a host of friends. Lila was constantly busy working on fascinating projects in a stimulating, socially conscious community. Mother and daughter were building a deep, mutually supportive relationship to which Willie, even though only present every third or fourth week, added the stabilizing leg of the family tripod.

Truth, Lila had found, was a luxury that could be afforded only by the lucky few with fully satisfactory lives. She and Gloria and Willie lived on lowered expectations and fictional successes. They were easy on each other. Lila didn't nag Gloria about her appearance or her grades that were barely good enough to get her promoted each year. In return, Gloria allowed Lila the occasional caress in front of others. Willie never complained of their desertion and was welcomed once a month by Gloria's smiling face and Lila's compliant body. If Lila felt the truth threatening to come to the surface, she would wait until Gloria was asleep, open the little bar and the refrigerator in the master bedroom and pour herself a drink, two at the most, still Canadian Club and ginger ale. The urge would recede, and she could climb into her bed, close her eyes and feel herself float away, the truth left far behind.

Only the occasional visits from Margo or Elliott brought excitement. This one was going to be a lulu. Of course, Gloria was going to insist on going to the concert. Should they do it in one day, a three hour drive each way, or stay overnight in a hotel in Miami? Willie was going to have a fit. She laughed as she went into the study to begin her lists. She gave Gloria ten minutes.

It was only five or six. "Lila. Where are you?"

"In the study."

A moment later, Gloria appeared, a sandwich in one hand a glass of milk in the other.

"No plate, darling? Oh, here." Lila put a legal pad on the corner of the desk, and Gloria took a big bite from the sandwich and put the rest on the pad.

"Ca sa—ee—." Gloria stopped, raised a finger, chewed, swallowed and took some milk. "Can Sally come with us to the concert? She's just dying to. Can we meet Tom Garrity? Elliott will do that, won't he?" Waves of milk threatened to overflow her glass.

"Who said anything about anybody going to the concert besides Elliott?"

"Lila!" Gloria's mouth stayed open. "We have to go."

Lila hadn't seen Gloria so agitated at any time in the past five years. "All right, darling. I can try to arrange it, assuming there are still tickets available. But don't promise Sally anything until we find out more." Gloria sprung to her feet and grabbed the sandwich. "And don't say anything to anybody else." It was useless; Gloria was already on her way to the telephone in her room. By noon of the next day, Lila had received phone calls from three parents of classmates of Gloria who had asked their parents for permission to go to the concert "with the Burkes."

After numerous telephone conferences over the next weeks, matters were resolved. Elliott would drive Gloria and up to eight friends to the concert and back, and they would be admitted backstage beforehand to meet Tom Garrity. The limit of eight was based upon the capacity of the station wagon, after Willie and Lila yielded their places, Willie, happily, Lila, regretfully. Gloria was to pick the lucky guests during the week before the concert.

A new piano tuner was found, a recent immigrant from Germany. His English was incomprehensible, but he coaxed the piano to sound better than it had since it had come down with them from New York. Both Lila and Gloria practiced furiously in the hope Elliott would not be disappointed in them.

As the day of Elliott's arrival approached, a new Gloria appeared. This Gloria came to meals on time, put away her clothing and magazines and responded promptly and cheerfully to anything Lila asked her. Lila's surprise at this became astonishment when Gloria asked that Lila take her to the hairdresser and help her pick out new clothes for the occasion, functions from which Lila had previously been totally barred.

"You'll help me, won't you, Lila? I don't want to look like a total slob, and you always manage to look so nice."

"You 'd look beautiful if you just paid a little more attention to your appearance."

Uh, oh. Lila knew she had gone too far and braced herself for the response, but Gloria only grimaced. On Friday, Lila picked her up at school, sat by her side at the hairdresser and tactfully suggested that she leave her hair halfway to her shoulders rather than have it shorn close as usual. Gloria's smile when she looked in the mirror was thanks enough, and when she cheerfully approved Lila's selection of skirts and blouses at the department store, Lila was in heaven. She had to caution herself that this was for now and didn't signal a permanent change.

Gloria wore one of her new outfits when she accompanied Lila to the airport to pick up Elliott. She looked quite grown up as she stood waiting at the gate, but became a little girl again when he came through.

"Elliott!" She rushed to him, almost knocking him down with the force of her welcome. Lila, herself, was close behind, and they hugged and kissed him together.

Elliott was still slim, neat and boyish. "Nice outfit," he said to Gloria, who blushed with pleasure and immediately began to tell him all of her plans for the week. He listened attentively to Gloria as they walked to the car, but sneaked glances at Lila's legs. So he still had an eye for her after all his girlfriends. She was glad she had worn high heels.

Lila had agreed to Gloria's request that some of her friends be allowed to come to the house to meet Elliott. It had seemed harmless, and Lila was not prepared for the army of Huns who descended upon her. Every day they came on bikes and in boats or piled into broken-down cars driven by the occasional boy old enough to have a license. The staff was put to work producing hamburgers, chilling cokes, dishing ice cream, and hastily rushing it all to the pool to keep the hungry hordes from storming the kitchen. They played soccer on the tennis court and hit softballs through the roof of the greenhouse. They left towels on the bushes, cigarette butts in the pool, forbidden beer cans in the tool shed and muddy footprints in a semi-circle around the piano in the drawing room where they gathered whenever they could persuade Elliott to play for them.

Lila shrugged off the damage to the property and the disruption of the staff. Finally, she had become the successful mother, who could sit on a bench at the playground and watch her child playing happily with the other children. Naturally, Lila was not included in their play; it was enough that she was still needed to provide food, bandage scrapes, and replace broken toys.

Lila had never seen Gloria so happy. On the few occasions in the past when Gloria's classmates had come to the house, she had been less than a full participant in the festivities. When they huddled to decide the next action, Gloria had stood on the outskirts, listening. When they chose up sides, she had been the last one picked. The boys hadn't thrown her into the pool; the girls hadn't run to her with their secrets.

This week, Gloria's control of the invitations to the concert put her in the center of everything, listened to, flattered, sought after. She posed and smirked and flirted and thoroughly enjoyed herself as she put off the formal invitations until "my folks tell me how many guys I can bring" and "we find out whose parents will let them come." It was not until Friday afternoon that the lucky eight were chosen.

Meanwhile, Lila tackled the project of provisioning the trip. They would have to leave at three to make sure of getting through the traffic early enough to get to the Orange Bowl in time to go backstage. That meant supper for ten big appetites plus late night snacks on the way home. At two-thirty, Saturday afternoon, George, the butler, loaded two huge coolers filled with fried chicken, potato salad, coleslaw, rolls, tomatoes, fruit, cake, sodas and juices and a box with condiments, napkins and utensils, ponchos and sweatshirts onto the top of the station wagon and covered them with a tarpaulin, while Lila ticked off items on a giant list and drilled Elliott on his directions and what to do in case of trouble of any kind.

Lila had only gone through half her list when Gloria came out of the house. When she saw the loaded station wagon, a look of revulsion came onto her face, and she climbed into the front passenger seat, slammed the door and turned on the radio to full volume.

"Gloria!" cried Lila, but her voice was lost in a blast of music.

Elliott stepped over to the station wagon, leaned over and brought his finger to his lips. Gloria smiled and lowered the volume, but when Elliott turned back to Lila, the smile vanished, and the car window was raised.

Lila gave up. "Oh, just go, Elliott. Nobody's going to eat this food, anyway. You'd rather have hot dogs and whatever junk they're selling."

"Who, me?"

"Especially you. Now, go get your buddies before Gloria has a fit." Lila kissed him maternally, and he ran around to the driver's seat, started the car and spun the wheels in the gravel of the drive before pulling out into the street.

Lila waved as they disappeared around the corner. When she turned back to the house, Willie was lounging in the doorway, shaking his head and grinning.

"What's funny?"

"Maybe you overdid it a bit. They're just going to Miami, not invading Normandy."

"Is that so?"

Willie put his hands up. "It was very nice of you to go through all the work. And I'm sure they'll enjoy the spread. I know I would."

Lila scanned that for sarcasm; luckily for Willie, it passed. As she started to go into the house, he caught her wrist. "Are you sorry you didn't go with them?"

"Oh, Willie, this is the fifties. Kids don't go to pop concerts with their mothers." She pulled her hand loose. "You go to the pool. I need to practice. I'll come out in a while. Maybe I'll feel less grouchy after."

Inside, Lila stared at the keys but couldn't focus. She was still sticky with perspiration from loading the station wagon and, at mid-afternoon, the room was hot. The pool would be more comfortable, but going there would show Willie weakness.

She started to play scales, mindlessly. She knew she shouldn't even do that. Playing without concentrating was the worst sin in Elliott's bible. Even scales, it didn't matter what. She couldn't believe that he actually wanted to go to this concert. How could such a sophisticated musician sit through hours of this new rock and roll music with its endless repetitious beat and its incomprehensible screaming vocals? "You ain't nothin' but a hound dawg—." She played a verse and sounded so bad that she couldn't even laugh at herself.

What was wrong with her? Why couldn't she relate to this music? Why couldn't she relate to these kids? And it wasn't just Gloria. Lila was uncomfortable with all of them. Why should that be? It wasn't her age. She was only thirty-five; Margo, nearing fifty, could walk into a room full of teenagers and in five minutes would have the boys flirting with her while the girls begged make-up tips and traded gossip. True, Margo was still half-kid herself.

So what about me, Lila asked herself. She got up from the piano, took a Coke and ice from the bar and sank into the easy chair in the corner. Can't I be a kid, too? She tried to recall being childlike with Gloria over the past eight years, but could only remember elaborate costume parties, carefully researched presents, and well-planned surprises. When Gloria was a baby in her carriage, oh yes, then Lila could wiggle her fingers and make strange noises and echo the little laugh with a bellow of joy. But that was when she and Gloria trusted each other. Then Willie and John took away their trust, and Judge Fogarty and Mrs. Warren could give them nothing better than caution in return, and what's sadder than a cautious child?

She stopped herself abruptly. Where was Gloria now? Why on her way to a concert to spend three hours jumping up and down screaming ecstatically with fifty thousand other kids. Perfectly normal. And Lila was working herself into a state because—because she wasn't one of them. Willie was right. Lila was jealous of the whole bunch of them; they played tennis and swam and went to concerts. When she was their age, she had to work after school and on weekends. How could she relate to a bunch of spoiled, lazy brats who should be working in the garden or doing the dishes? That was all it was.

Lila jumped to her feet and strode to the pool, changed into her bathing suit and, without a word to Willie (how dare he be right), plunged in and swam back and forth as fast as she could until her arms and legs were ready to fall off. She took him up on his offer of a night out, ate a good dinner, was diverted by a movie and felt pleasantly tired when they returned at 11. To be caught "waiting up" for Gloria would have dire consequences, Willie reminded Lila, so she went to bed, expecting to lie awake for several hours.

In fact, she was asleep in minutes. The slamming of car doors heard through her open window, brought her to a drowsy consciousness at 2:30. Reassured, she went back to sleep but was awakened again by voices coming from the swimming pool in the back. Elliott and Gloria must be cooling off with a swim before going to bed.

Lila got up and went to the window. Although the pool area was completely shielded from the house by the hedge, she could see firefly-like glimmers from the pool lights. There were more voices. One was of a classmate of Gloria's. Elliott must have brought the whole crew back. That wasn't reasonable, not this late. The racket was increasing. They could wake the neighbors, not to mention the servants. And some of the other parents might well be up and starting to worry. Elliott should know better. Although Gloria was going to be angry with her, Lila left the bed and the undisturbed Willie, put on a tennis dress, combed her hair and came down the stairs and out through French windows, trying to think of a tactful way to break up the party.

As she neared the hedge, there was a moment of silence, followed by a big splash and a cheer. Then the voices, "It's Sally's turn," "Yeah, Sally, c'mon," "You gotta go, SalGal." Lila turned the corner to the pool deck and stopped short.

On the edge of the pool, by the diving board, Sally Johnson stood, hesitantly, wearing only her panties, water dripping from her long blonde hair. The rest of the kids, treading water in a semi-circle around the end of the board, shouted encouragement. In a quick movement, Sally shed her panties and jumped up on the board. She was a gymnast, and Lila, shocked as she was, had to acknowledge the beauty of the toned young body poised for a second in the flickering light before the girl took three quick steps and dove into the cheering of her friends.

Lila came out of her spell, shouting "Hey!" her tactful lines forgotten. The cheering stopped. Two of the kids disappeared underwater. Sally came to the surface with a whoop of triumph, saw Lila, swallowed a mouthful of water, coughed and flailed her arms.

"Hi, Lila." Gloria spoke from the pool. "It's your turn." She pressed down with her arms, raising her body so that her bare breasts cleared the water. "It's fun," she continued, then porpoised, the lower part of her body coming out of the water as the upper part went under.

She can't wait to show me that she's stark naked, thought Lila. "OK, everyone out of the pool." She tried to keep her voice down. The last thing she wanted was for the staff to see this spectacle. She could drown Gloria. And Elliott. Where was Elliott? As the kids started to climb out of the pool and fumble for their clothing, she confirmed that, at least, he hadn't been in the middle of it. A New York musician conducting an orgy with nine naked sixteen-year-olds. The Palm Beach papers would love that.

And the kids were naked, all right. There seemed to be only one boy and one girl with as much as a pair of underpants on. But it was hardly an orgy. She couldn't help but notice how the kids had avoided touching each other in the water. As they climbed out, they were now self-conscious, the boys using their free hands to cover their genitals, the girls hysterically anxious to get to their clothing, all except Gloria who walked leisurely to get a towel and stood, legs apart, drying every part of her body.

Lila was amazed by this. Gloria had always been more than ordinarily modest and extremely self-conscious of her weight problem. While no longer seriously overweight, she was still stocky, and it was usually next to impossible even to get her into a bathing suit. Lila walked over to her. "Get your clothes on. And where the hell is Elliott?"

Gloria stretched the towel behind her to dry the small of her back, thrusting her chest at Lila. "Oh, he's in the men's changing room, probably peering out the window and drooling. He wouldn't take off his clothes, and when we all did, he said he couldn't stay."

"Gloria, get your clothes on, now. How could Elliott have let you do this? It's crazy. You're not two-year-olds."

"It was all perfectly innocent, and you know it. You're just jealous because you're afraid Elliott won't want your old body after seeing nice young ones like ours."

Lila's hand moved by itself. She didn't want to do this, she thought as it raised from her side. This would end her hopes, she told herself, as her palm exploded against Gloria's cheek.

Gloria's head snapped to her right, then swung back. She put her hand to her cheek, then tossed the towel to at Lila's feet. "I'd better get dressed, now. Shouldn't I, Mother?" She turned and walked to her pile of clothes and drew on her panties without a further glance at Lila.

Lila stood frozen. Only one blow, but it was enough to destroy the work of eight years.

"Lila, what are you doing?" It was Elliott, in his bathing suit, coming toward them from the changing room. "Gloria," he went on, "are you all right, baby?"

"Oh, Elliott," Gloria cried and ran into his arms. "Did you see that?" She buried her face in his neck and sobbed uncontrollably. He patted her back comfortingly, then stopped and stiffened. Apparently, it had gotten through to him that the body pressed against his was almost naked. He tried to loosen her hands from around his neck, but they were locked.

"Let go, baby, come on, it's all right. It's over; it's cool, now. Lila didn't mean it. It was a kind of accident, right Lila? Just let go now and get dressed." Gradually, Gloria allowed her hands to be loosened and Elliott to step back. Suddenly, as though first discovering her nearly nude state, Gloria snatched up the rest of her clothes and fled to the women's changing room.

"Lila," Elliott started, in a reproving tone. As he turned to speak to her, Lila could see an unmistakable bulge in his bathing suit.

"You son of a bitch," she yelled and again her right hand connected, fisted this time, and Elliott staggered back, stunned, and fell over the edge of the pool. A great whoosh of breath came simultaneously from the kids, followed by the splash of Elliott's entry and then by a moment of silence before everyone rushed to peer into the pool. Elliott surfaced and splashed to the edge where he hung on with one hand and felt his jaw with the other.

"Let's go, kids. To the car. Hop it." They sheepishly followed Lila to the station wagon, and she distributed them to their homes. When she got back at four, both Gloria's and Elliott's windows were dark. Just as well. Whatever more had to be said could wait until morning.

She changed into a nightgown, went into her bathroom, filled the sink with cold water and repeatedly plunged her head in. Toweling off, she looked at herself in the mirror. Her face was drawn tight, her jaws clenched, her mouth narrowed. The whites of her eyes were webbed in red, the skin underneath, puffed. A few faint lines ran from the corners to the tanned skin of her cheeks.

Abruptly, she faced the full-length mirror on the door and let her nightgown fall. She moved an arm, lifted a leg, bent forward and then back. Each time, her body responded as it always had, easily, gracefully. It was still lean and smooth. Naturally, the breasts were a trifle heavier, the tummy and the buttocks looser than when she had been a high school girl. But all in all, she needn't be ashamed of her body. She was a grown woman, after all, not an adolescent like Sally Johnson. Even so, she still looked better than some of the girls.

Oh, Jesus. Was that what was going on? Lila pulled up her nightgown and turned back to the mirror. "Did you get into a catfight with your own daughter over a man neither of you can have?" she whispered, and the face in the mirror nodded. "You've ruined everything, haven't you?" Again the face nodded. Gripping the sides of the sink, Lila cursed the face and was cursed by it, for every mistake she had ever made in her life until, exhausted, she crumpled to a sitting position on the floor and rested her cheek on the cool rim of the bathtub.

•   •   •

She must have fallen asleep, for, when she looked at her watch, it was just after six. She was cold. Her jaw ached where it had rested on the bathtub; her mouth was dry and foul. She got up painfully, rinsed her mouth, washed her face, stripped off her nightgown tiptoed into the bedroom, silently put on a sweatsuit and sneakers and came down and out the front door.

The morning was clear and cool. Not a soul observed Lila walking up the street, across South Ocean Drive and down to where a tame ocean affectionately licked the beach. She began to run south on the damp sand, jumping over small puddles and swerving to avoid larger ones. Sandpipers scurried out of her way and a pelican, perched on the end of a dock, swiveled his head to watch her. Otherwise, she was alone.

An hour, maybe a little more, before Willie would get up. Her time, nobody else's. She was free to savor the spring of her feet bouncing from the sand and the sting of sweat in her eyes. No decisions to make except where her next stride should land. She was tireless, could run forever, if time would only stand still, but the orange sun on her left was rising and changing color through copper to brass. Ahead, the beach narrowed to end at an inlet with a marsh on the other side: the half-hour mark, the turnaround, unless she went up to the road and past the marsh to the next beach. If she did that, she could run on for eight or ten or a dozen miles to the end of the island where she could swim to the mainland and then continue down the coast past Boca Raton and Fort Lauderdale and Miami and out along the Keys and across the water to Cuba. She halted at the inlet and stared across it for a minute, then began to jog back.

Not even one hour, Lila thought, her mind following the direction of her feet. All right, what's happened? She rewound her memory to the point when she had awakened and replayed the whole film as she went from gaffe to mistake to disaster. Then she ran an edited version, changing all the lines. Instead of slapping Gloria, Lila cracked a joke, and they laughed together, and the hostility vanished, and Elliott came over and laughed with them. How easy life was when you could order unlimited retakes for all the bad scenes.

Lila couldn't help but be impressed with the actress playing her daughter. How self-possessed she had been. Yes, Gloria had somehow recognized that Lila's emotions were not under their usual control and had deliberately driven her to the point of striking. And what had Gloria said right afterward? "I'd better get dressed now. Shouldn't I, Mother?"

"Mother." Gloria had called her "Mother" for the first time. During eight years of devoted kindness and attention from Lila, Gloria had never called her "Mother." Last night she had. What had caused that? It must have been Lila's anger. Lila had always suppressed her anger, maintaining an affectionate cheerfulness no matter what Gloria had said or done. Gloria must want a mother who was complete, who loved her child enough to express her emotions honestly, even anger. She had goaded Lila to test her, and Lila had passed. The realization invigorated Lila, and she jumped up and ran strongly the rest of the way home.

Before going upstairs, Lila went to look at the pool area and was pleased to find the assistant gardener already at work with a big trash bag picking up yesterday's debris. The pool looked fine except for a couple of sunken towels: no dead bodies or forgotten underwear. The changing rooms were a mess but no worse than every other morning for the past week. As Lila left, she spoke briefly to Sarah, the second maid, who was coming to clean them and told her to try to get the laundry done that afternoon. There wasn't a clean towel left in the house. Sarah grimaced. Lila wouldn't be the only one happy to see the kids go back to school on Monday and Willie and Elliott to New York.

Elliott. In her hysteria over Gloria, Lila had forgotten Elliott. She clenched her fist reflexively and winced. Yes, she had certainly hit someone with it. And he had deserved it. Then Lila remembered the wounded look he had given her from the pool, like a punished puppy who didn't understand why. She allowed herself to smile and her anger dissipated. So long as she still had Gloria, she could forgive Elliott. And Elliott would forgive her; that's what good buddies did. It was time to get rid of that little crush of his, though. It was flattering and fun, but not worth having Gloria or anyone else get the wrong idea.

Lila came up the stairs, the house still quiet and cool. Cool, that's how she would be. How was the concert, guys? Later in the week, when she and Gloria were alone, and the mood seemed conducive, she might explore the situation, maybe bring a maturing Gloria closer to her than Gloria, the child, would permit.

As Lila reached the top of the stairs and headed toward the master bedroom, she heard a click behind her. She turned and saw the door of the guest room open. Gloria, in her nightgown, slipped out, quietly closed the door behind her, stepped across to her room and equally quietly entered and closed her door.

You didn't see that, an inner voice told her. You thought you heard a sound and then your imagination just came up with the worst thing it could think of to explain it. Gloria's just a baby. Go back to your room and run a hot bath. Elliott wouldn't dream of it. You hallucinated. IT DIDN'T HAPPEN. See, there's nobody in the hallway. IT DIDN'T HAPPEN. You can go into Gloria's room and see how soundly she's sleeping. IT DIDN'T HAPPEN. Just open the door softly, tiptoe through the playroom to her bedroom and see her sweet little face with the cap of black hair on the pillow next to Blinky.

"I thought you promised to knock first." Gloria stood in the doorway of her bathroom.

"Gloria, darling." Lila took a step forward.

Gloria stood still. "Do you want to hit me again?"

"No, no, I never wanted to, it just—happened."

Gloria went into the bathroom and put toothpaste on her toothbrush. "So you want to apologize?" She began brushing.

Lila came to the bathroom door. "Gloria, I just saw you come out of Elliott's room. What were you doing?"

Gloria spat into the sink. "None of your business." She poured mouthwash into a glass and began to rinse.

"Everything you do is my business. I'm your mother, even if you don't want to admit it." This time she would remain calm no matter what Gloria said.

Gloria spat out the mouthwash. "I admit that you're my mother. I've seen the birth certificate and Judge Fogarty's order. OK, Lila? Now please get out of my room."

Lila took a deep breath. "Being your mother isn't just a biological fact or a judge's order. It means that I have to do whatever I can to protect you and make you happy. To do that I have to know everything about you, like what you were doing in Elliott's room."

Gloria turned the water in the sink back on, took washcloth and soap and bent over the sink to wash her face. Lila stood patiently until she finished, straightened up and dried herself.

"Is that what being a mother means? Then you haven't done your job very well, Mother. For half my life you didn't do it at all, Mother. I think I'll just do it myself from now on, Mother." She yawned. "I'd better get some sleep, now, Mother."

Each repetition of the word was a blow. Lila stepped back as if she could avoid them, and Gloria brushed past her to go to her bedroom. She turned just before closing the connecting door and said one more thing. "And if you must know, Elliott and I made love. It was wonderful."

Lila barely made it down the hall to her own room, where she collapsed upon the empty bed. The toilet flushed in the bathroom and Willie came out yawning.

"Been for a run, have you? If you'd gotten me up, I'd've gone with you." He opened the blinds. "Gorgeous morning. Maybe I'll go myself. Hey, what's the matter? "

He came over to the bed, next to Lila, and tried to turn her over, but she dug her hands into the sheets and shook her head. She had to be careful. Willie had come to love Gloria. If angry enough, with his strength, he was capable of seriously injuring Elliott.

"What is it Lila? Darling, say something."

She held up her hand. "Wait," was all she could say. Willie waited, stroking her back until she sat up. She took his hands firmly in hers so he couldn't get away from her and told him everything that had happened while he was asleep but omitting Gloria's last announcement. "That stupid son-of-a-bitch. Get him out of here. He must be crazy letting a sixteen-year-old girl into his room? Not that I think he did anything to Gloria." He looked at Lila. "Of course, he didn't. No, he wants the mother, not the daughter." He put up his hand. "Come on, any idiot could see that. I've put up with it because you handle him well and have been getting so much out of the music that I didn't want to make a fuss. This is too much, though. And that insanity at the pool? Just get rid of him. And, for Christ's sake, keep your eye on Gloria. She's not a little girl anymore. You should never have let her get to you like that. She's just a screwy teenager and doesn't know what she's saying or doing. Just be careful, and this will all blow over."

Oh God, let him be right, Lila prayed. Let it have been something Gloria made up to hurt me. She's not ready for men, still so childish, much more so than I was at her age. But what if ...? No, it couldn't be, she couldn't even consider the possibility. Willie had to be right this time.

They showered and went down to breakfast, where they divided up the Sunday paper and ate in silence. Midway through the meal, Willie left the table for a couple of minutes. He returned with a scrap of paper on which he had listed the Sunday schedule of flights back to New York. Lila nodded her agreement. The sooner Elliott was gone, the better.

Breakfast was finished, but they lingered in the dining room, sipping from cold cups of coffee and crumbling crusts of toast, calling each other's attention to news items in which neither of them had the slightest interest. At 9:15, they heard footsteps on the stairs, but it was just the maid coming down from cleaning their room. Ten minutes later, however, Elliott poked his head into the dining room, a timid expression on his face.

"Is it safe, Lila? Or are the punches still flying?" He stepped into the room and started toward Lila. "Hey, I'm sorry I let things get out of hand. I didn't know how to stop it. They weren't listening to me and—"

"Sit down," interrupted Willie, "you've got some questions to answer."

Elliott shrugged and obeyed. Lila nodded to Willie. Let him be the inquisitor.

"What was Gloria doing in your room this morning?"

Elliott shook his head. "Talking, Willie, just talking, that's all. She came in a few minutes after I went to bed and talked until after four. I don't know exactly. I fell asleep. She was hysterical. Lila, what did you have to hit her for? In front of all her friends?"

"Elliott," Willie said firmly. "Lila is Gloria's mother. She doesn't have to answer to you. You have to answer to her. Go on."

"Well, she read me the story of her life. I'm hip to most of it, but I didn't say anything."

Willie put his hand up. "How do you know so much?"

"Come on, Willie," said Lila, "It's old news. Everybody knows, and nobody cares anymore. Let Elliott finish."

"The general idea was to convince me that she's the daughter of a monster. I won't repeat the details. I don't believe most of them. I know how much you care for her, Lila, and how hard you've worked at the mother thing. I tried to tell her that, but it just got her more upset."

"Is that all?" asked Willie. Elliott was silent, and Willie's voice rose. "Was it, Elliott?"

"No. She said—Oh, man, I hate to repeat this. She said she was in love with me and asked me to take her back to New York to live with me. I told her she was a great little chick but too young to think of anything like that. Then she offered to prove she was old enough by—by doing it, you know, right there. I said if she didn't cool it I would go and wake you guys up, and I got up out of bed. That stopped her, and she made me promise not to tell, but she wouldn't go back to her room. She wrapped herself in the bedspread and lay down, and we talked some more, and I zonked out. When I woke up a few minutes ago, she was gone."

"Did you touch her? " Willie leaned forward his eyes fixed on Elliott. Lila watched him, too, but had already decided. Gloria had been lying. Everything Elliott had said sounded true.

"I put my arm around her to calm her down when she first came in. I held her hand for a while. That's it. Come on, Willie. I've known Gloria for years. She's like a kid sister. I wouldn't touch any chick that young. Gloria? I couldn't imagine it."

Willie looked at Lila who nodded agreement. "OK, Willie. That's enough."

Willie turned back to Elliott. "I believe you, but you had no business letting her stay there. And the mess down at the pool: how could you let that happen? We've got to live here, even if you don't, and we'll be lucky if nothing worse comes from this than having two or three couples stop talking to us. I'm sorry to be a bad host, but you've been a bad guest. Finish your breakfast and pack. George will drive you to the 11:30 flight. We don't want you here when Gloria gets up." He rang the bell and ordered breakfast for Elliott, then got up and left the room.

George brought in fresh coffee and filled Elliott's cup, then cleared away Willie's dishes. Lila could see that Elliott was bursting to say something, but had to wait until they were alone. When the door to the kitchen closed, he exploded. "What's the matter with you, Lila? You can't think for a second that I might have done something to Gloria. That's ridiculous."

"Shut up, Elliott. She said you did."

"What? She's nuts!"

"Keep your voice down. Willie doesn't know that. If she repeats it when she gets up, we'll just have to deal with it, but at least you'll be gone."

"Lila, I swear, I never did. Why would she say that?"

"Shhh, I believe you, but I won't guarantee I can control Willie. Maybe she wanted to give me a scare. Wish fulfillment. Whatever it is, it has to wait until you're not here."

There was another break in the conversation while Elliott's eggs were put in front of him.

"So why are you so mad at me, if you believe me? Aren't we good buddies?"

Because I'm hurt and scared, thought Lila, but she heard herself answer "We're <u>friends</u>, and we're adults. If you'd behaved more responsibly, this wouldn't have happened."

The room darkened. Elliott took a last forkful of eggs, a last mouthful of coffee and got up from the table. His tone was subdued "I'm truly sorry, Lila. I'll go pack."

Lila stared down at her napkin as he passed behind her. Good-bye, good buddy.

A half-hour later, Elliott was on his way to the airport and Willie on his way to the club. Lila went into the study to wait for Gloria to wake up. She sat down at her desk with her checkbook and shuffled some bills aimlessly, her mind on Gloria and Elliott.

The cooperative, friendly Gloria of a week ago was gone; the war had begun again and with a new weapon: the threat of sexual activity. How was Lila going to keep Gloria from using real instead of fictional adventures for that purpose?

Damn Elliott, acting like a sixteen-year-old, himself, like any of Gloria's high school classmates, with his schoolboy crush on Lila. At the same time, he encouraged Gloria's crush on him, horsing around with her in the pool, hugging and petting her developing body as though she were still nine years old. He was a big contributor to the current mess, and now, would you believe it, he was hurt and angry with Lila as though it was all her fault. Willie blamed her too, as, of course did Gloria. The whole pack of them blamed everything on her. As they always did.

"Mum?"Mary stood in the open doorway to the study. She held something in her hands.

"Yes, Mary?"

It was pair of flowered panties. Gloria's.

Mary's face was almost in tears, but her voice was firm. "Excuse me, Mum. Sarah was cleaning up Mr. Zinn's room and found these and didn't know whether it was her place to say anything, so she gave them to me. I thought you should know. They was down at the bottom of the bed, Mum, under the covers," Mary said indignantly.

Lila fought panic. Was it possible, after all, that Elliott—? She thought back over the years since Gloria had first walked into the New York living room while Elliott was giving Lila a lesson. Every memory testified that he was not capable of the terrible act Gloria had accused him of. She looked up at Mary who was standing patiently. Mary had been with her from the day of Gloria's arrival and had become Gloria's closest friend. She was owed an explanation.

"Please shut the door, Mary, and sit down. I need to talk to you."

Lila went through the events of the night and morning, omitting nothing. Mary listened quietly, occasionally nodding or shaking her head, making no other comment. At the end, she got up, leaned over the desk and put her hand over Lila's.

"It'll come out all right, Mum. Just be patient with her, like you've been. I'll just put these in the laundry." She picked up the panties and went to the door, then suddenly stopped and turned around. "Would you want me, Mum, to—?" She faltered.

"Want you to do what, Mary?"

"To—to look at the sheets?"

"No, no Mary, I don't think we should do that. But thank you."

The idea was repulsive. Also, Lila realized, unnecessary. If there had been blood on the sheets, Sarah would have seen it and told Mary. Not that unsoiled sheets proved anything. Virginity was often lost to exercise. Maybe there was still time to take Gloria to a doctor for an examination. But what was the point of detective work, anyway? The case was closed. Last night was over. What was going to happen now? That was what was important.

It was almost noon before Gloria's heavy tread was heard on the stairs, sounding as though she were jumping down them, one at a time, as she sometimes did as a child. Why she wanted to clump around exaggerating her bulkiness was a mystery to Lila. Lila had asked her once, and Gloria had merely answered "I like to," permanently closing the subject.

Lila set herself. Be cool. Let her come to me.

The clumping reached the bottom of the stairs and halted. "Hey, where is everybody?"

"In here, darling."

Gloria stuck her head in the door. Her hair was pulled back into a ponytail, with a few loose wisps over her ears. The angles of her face showed traces of her old elfin look, and Lila yearned to sweep her up in a giant hug.

"Is there any breakfast left? Where's Elliott?" Cheerful, innocent. She stepped into the room. She was wearing faded cut-off dungarees and an old shirt of Willie's, tied behind her, penny loafers on her bare feet, ready to pose for a Norman Rockwell painting of a kid sister. Had Lila imagined the scene they had gone through a mere five hours ago?

Lila took her lead from Gloria. "No breakfast, but I'll have lunch with you if you want. Elliott's gone back to New York and Willie's playing golf."

"New York? What do you mean he's gone back to New York? What did you do to him? Did Willie do something?"

"Calm down, Gloria. Nobody did anything to anybody. We had a little talk, that's all. Elliott told us what actually happened, and we all agreed that it was better if he left today."

Gloria froze. "'What actually happened?' He denied it? You're lying, Lila." Her voice rose.

"No, darling. Of course, he denied it. It never happened. We all know that, although you almost frightened me to death. And if Willie had heard you—"

"He said we didn't make love?" Her voice broke and her face contorted.

"Of course, darling. He wouldn't do that, no matter how foolish you were. You're still a child and my daughter and—"

"Stop it!" Gloria shouted. "You think that because he fucked you he wouldn't fuck me. Well, he did, no matter what you did to make him deny it."

Lila jumped from her chair. Her voice was even louder than Gloria's. "I never slept with Elliott, and neither did you and neither of us ever will, and that's the end of it." She stormed out of the room past Gloria through the hall where Sarah stood open-mouthed, then up the stairs to her room, and slammed the door. A moment later there was an echoing slam down the hall.

Lila lay motionless for over an hour, too worked up to sleep. As she came out of her room, she was encouraged by the sound of Gloria's radio. Downstairs, Mary reported that Gloria had eaten in the kitchen and had asked that dinner be brought to her room on a tray so she could finish her vacation homework. Lila gratefully gave her approval. Gloria had spoken, Mary told Lila, in her ordinary manner as though nothing unusual had occurred.

When Willie returned, Lila told him of Gloria's original accusation and then their conversation after Elliott's departure. She didn't tell him about the panties; Mary wouldn't want to say anything to him, and Sarah would be afraid to. Willie had been calmed by a good round of golf followed by a nice lunch and a few games of backgammon and took the news well, agreeing with Lila that Elliott was telling the truth and that Gloria had lied to hurt Lila.

Let Willie get back to New York and give her a chance to work with Gloria. It was going to be a difficult week at best. First, she had to get Gloria to school tomorrow. Then, of course, everyone would know all about the pool party. What repercussions would that bring?

Gloria stayed in her room all evening. Her dinner tray was brought up and, scoured of food, was put back outside her door. At ten, Willie went up to say good night, since he would be leaving on the early plane. He reported that she had been immersed in her homework, had barely raised her head to allow him a good-bye kiss on the cheek and had grunted an unintelligible farewell as she returned her attention to the book in front of her. All normal.

The next morning, Willie safely off to the airport, Lila was sitting in the dining room picking at a bowl of corn flakes, when, five minutes before the school bus was due, Gloria came storming down the stairs, through the dining room and out into the kitchen. "Shit!" she exclaimed, as her over-stuffed bookbag smashed against the Louis XVI commode. The refrigerator door opened then shut with a bang. A moment later, the back door did the same. Lila walked to the window and saw Gloria weaving towards South Ocean Boulevard, trying to manage the bookbag, a glass of orange juice and a piece of last night's pie. Normal again.

Lila sat back down. The sense of relief felt so good that she allowed a little optimism to creep into her mind. Maybe she could call a truce with Gloria. Maybe Gloria's coming maturity would cool her anger and allow a calmer relationship. In another two years, Gloria would be going away to college. Maybe those two years could be years of peace, their home no longer a field strewn with slaughtered hopes. Lila didn't have the strength for much more.

Strength. Was it possible that Gloria, over time, had become stronger than she? Time was Lila's enemy. She was starting to lose the tough tennis matches against younger players. Soon, she wouldn't be able to get away with pulling out the occasional gray hair but would have to decide whether to accept them or start coloring. She was realistic about these matters; maybe she could become the same way about Gloria.

No. It wasn't just a question of strength. She had not had the strength to battle her brother, lawyers, judges, teachers, often Willie and always Gloria, but she had done so. Her love was stronger than Gloria's hate; ultimately, she would win that battle. So she had promised Mrs. Warren years ago, and so she promised herself, now. Someday Gloria would accept her love and let Lila be all a mother should be.

She decided to go into West Palm Beach to run a few errands. She needed to get away from the house a bit, distract herself with the mundane duties of getting cash from the bank, dropping off a pair of shoes that needed new heels and getting her car serviced. She would have lunch by herself at the diner north on Route 1 where there would be nobody who knew her.

•　　　　　•　　　　　•

Lila walks Mr. Harris out to his car. After he drives off, she follows down the short drive through the gate to Via Amalfi. Outside her walls, she can feel the wind coming up. It flutters the palm trees and makes the water in Lake Worth slap against the concrete wall where the street ends. Across, in West Palm Beach, traffic is starting to clog the drive. It's after five and still a long way from sunset. How soon the winter ended this year. It seems as if the stores had just shed their Christmas decorations.

She returns to the drawing room just as Jeffrey enters with her afternoon tray. He pauses until Lila nods toward the card table. He has never spoken much and now, a little deaf, prefers alternative communication whenever possible. There are times when they look like Mafiosi transacting business in a room known to be bugged by the F.B.I.

Lila goes to the tray. Cook has sent her the white of a hard-boiled egg, cut in half longitudinally, with a dollop of salt-free, low-fat Russian dressing nestling in each half, three carrot sticks with tasseled ends and four Carr's Water Crackers. Lila sighs. It would be nice if just once Cook would forget and give her something not on the doctor's approved list: a strip of pimento, for decoration, maybe, or a cocktail onion. Jeffrey goes to the sideboard and makes her daily half-strength Canadian Club with ginger ale, all that she has allowed herself since Willie's death. They're all so efficient, she thinks, the place runs like an attraction at Disney World and would still do so if she never said a word.

"How do you do it?" a rather vulgar cousin of Willie's had once asked her at the conclusion of a trying weekend. "With servants the way they are these days and all?"

Lila's reply made the pages of the New Yorker: "Just teach them exactly how you want everything done and have them practice it for twenty years."

Lila was being truthful, not clever. Jeffrey, twenty years, Jane, the housemaid, formerly Jeffrey's wife, twenty-two. Willie had questioned keeping them both when they divorced, but shut up when Lila offered to fly up to New York to take over his construction business. Cook, thirty-one and Mary, Lila's personal maid, almost fifty years. Ernesto, the head gardener, was a newcomer, but his father, whom he replaced, had worked there for over thirty years.

It wasn't just the pay, which was always near the top of the Palm Beach scale. The Burkes respected their employees. After all, anyone who could meet their demanding standards was entitled to respect. The unsatisfactory left; the best stayed as long as they could and were afterward remembered with phone calls on their birthdays and fat checks every Christmas.

•   •   •

Lila drove back to the house in excellent spirits feeling a trifle guilty at having indulged herself with a greasy cheeseburger and french fries. As she pulled into the circular drive, she was alarmed to see a white police car parked near the front door. The alarm subsided when she pulled up and saw the gold "CHIEF" on the car door. Chief Tighe would not be the one to answer an emergency call. But why was he here? Was it possible that one of the parents had complained to the police about Saturday night's pool incident? That would be an extreme reaction even for stodgy Palm Beach.

A devastated Mary opened the front door even before Lila could get to it. "Thank God you're here, Mum. I didn't know what to do."

"What's happened, Mary? Is Gloria—"

"Nobody's hurt, Mum. That's all they would tell me. Then they started asking questions, and the Chief said I had to answer and the other fella's been going all over the house for an hour poking at things and after the other servants and I couldn't stop them. I'm sorry, Mum, but I couldn't do nothing about it." Mary, even-tempered, self-controlled Mary, began to sob.

Lila put her arms around Mary trying to steady them both. "It's all right, Mary. I'm sure you did the right thing. We have to cooperate with the police. But think a moment. Chief said nothing about what this was all about?"

"No, Mum," Mary gulped.

"All right, where are they, now?"

"In the drawing room. They have George in there now. He's the last."

"Bring us a pitcher of iced tea." Lila had learned the lessons of Southern hospitality. Even in crisis, there must be a cold glass to hold on to. As she approached the closed doors to the drawing room, they opened, and George came out. It was his day off, and he wore a flowered sports shirt, shorts and sandals, He stopped for a moment when he saw Lila, gave a puzzled shrug and walked past her toward the kitchen.

Lila steadied herself for a moment, then entered warily.

"What's happened, Chief Tighe?"

The Chief was standing by the piano, studying one of the framed pictures. At Lila's distraught voice, he started and turned and came to her. "Now, Miz Burke, don't y'all get too het up. I'm sure we'll sort all this out right smartly." He took both her hands in his. He was good at reassurance, a big, athletic man of sixty, with silky gray hair over a smooth, ruddy face.

"Sort what out, Chief? Has there been an accident? Is Gloria—?"

"No, Miz Burke, no accident, and Gloria's just fine." He gave her hands a little squeeze, then loosened his grip.

She kept her hands in his as she said, "But it has to do with her?" Over the years she had been in Palm Beach, the Chief had discreetly indicated that he would be delighted to squeeze more than Lila's hands, and she sensed she could use any ally she could muster.

"Actually, Miz Burke—" he was interrupted by a cough from across the room.

A tall, thin man she didn't know, wearing a brown suit, arose from his seat at the escritoire.

The Chief continued. "Excuse me, Miz Burke, this is Detective Hendricks."

Hendicks nodded. "Afternoon, Mrs. Burke. We just need to ask you a few questions."

Lila ignored him. "Chief, you have to tell me what's going on. Where's Gloria? I want to see her now. Then I'll answer all the questions you want. Please."

The Chief flashed an apologetic glance at the detective. "Gloria's downtown at the Courthouse, Miz Burke. She's not hurt, and she's not under arrest. So just set yourself on the couch for a few minutes and we'll tell what we know, and then you can tell us the rest, and maybe we can, like I said, sort it all out. Then y'all can go downtown."

Lila sat down and clasped her hands in her lap. What on earth could it be? Chief Tighe smiled benevolently at her, then addressed the detective. "You've got it all wrote down, Hendricks. Tell her what we have." Then, as Hendricks hesitated, "Gw'on, now. I don't care what the book says. These are good folks."

Hendricks returned to the escritoire and began to read from a notebook lying on it. "At 8: 15 A.M. a white female, aged approximately sixteen, entered the station by herself. Officer Wilson, who was at the desk, stated her manner was highly agitated. She told him that her name was Gloria Granatelli and that she lived at 15 Via Amalfi with Mrs. Lila Burke, whom she called her 'court mother.' She said she could not go to her home and asked to be sent to her 'real mother' Mrs. Catherine Granatelli, in St. Louis. She said that Saturday night, one Elliott Zinn had taken her and eight of her friends to a concert at the Orange Bowl. She described Zinn as Mrs. Burke's 'lover' and a guest in the house. On their return, at approximately 2 A.M. they had all gone swimming in the Burke pool partially or completely nude. Zinn had watched from the changing room. Mrs. Burke came down from the house, became enraged, struck her in the face and then struck Zinn, knocking him into the pool. Mrs. Burke then drove the other children home. Miss Granatelli said she went to Zinn's room to ask for help in dealing with Mrs. Burke. She stated that, under the pretense of comforting her, he seduced her. She further stated that she told Mrs. Burke of this at approximately 7 A.M. and that Mrs. Burke said she refused to believe her and again struck her, ordering her not to tell anyone else the story. She said she went to bed and when she awoke at approximately noon, Zinn had returned to New York. When she again approached Mrs. Burke, Mrs. Burke told her not to speak of it again and threatened her with punishment if she did. She spent all of Sunday in her room, went to the school bus early Monday and had the driver stop at the station on the way." Hendricks clapped the notebook shut and, holding it in one hand, crossed his arms, cocked his head, and looked across the room at Lila.

Lila felt as though she were watching a movie. How terrible must the woman be who had done this to a poor young girl? But what had this story to do with her and Gloria? Mary entered carrying a pitcher of iced tea and glasses. When Hendricks finished, Lila nodded to her, and she took the tray first to the Chief, then to Hendricks. When the tray came to Lila, the spell broke, and she reached for the glass and poured deliberately from the pitcher while she tried to think. She glanced at the Chief; at least he was still smiling while waiting for her response.

"That's not exactly what happened," she said without thinking, and saw the smile disappear with the word "exactly." But he said nothing, and it was Hendricks who replied.

"Would you tell us 'exactly' what did happen, Mrs. Burke?" He reopened the notebook.

She gladly told them so they would know she was not the terrible woman described in Hendricks's report, but a loving mother dealing with a difficult daughter under trying circumstances. She guessed she was doing it well since neither interrupted her, but their faces were impassive. There was a pause at the end while Hendricks went back over his notes.

"So you only struck her once, down at the pool, and not later in the morning?"

"Absolutely."

"And you didn't threaten her if she talked about Zinn?"

"Threaten her? I've never threatened her. I knew it wasn't true and I told her to stop repeating it, that's all."

"How could you be so sure he was telling the truth, and she was lying?"

"Elliott wouldn't do that. He's been a friend of the family and Gloria's friend and piano teacher since she was eight years old. He wouldn't take advantage of that situation. My husband and I talked to Elliott; we agree that Gloria was just trying to upset me. Just like she's doing today. I'm sorry she's wasted your time getting you into this." She jumped to her feet. "Let me go bring her home now. I'm sure I can get her to withdraw this silly accusation."

"Silly, Miz Burke?" the Chief interjected. "The law says intercourse with a sixteen-year-old is rape, even if she begged him to do it. That's ten years hard at Raiford. I doubt Mr. Zinn would find that silly. And the State might charge you with bein' some kind of accessory if you try to cover up for him. You heard the report; your daughter said you two had somepin' goin'."

"That's nonsense. Ask anybody who knows us. Ask my husband."

"Uh uh." The Chief grinned. "Miz Burke, the husband is the last person to ask. We're all either crazy jealous or totally blind, nothing in between."

"So your daughter is lying about that, too," said Hendricks. "These are pretty terrible lies. Is she some kind of compulsive liar?"

"No, only now."

"She has now accused Zinn at least five times. Once to you at seven, Sunday morning, again to you around noon, Sunday, and this morning to Officer Wilson at the desk and to me alone and then to me and to Chief Tighe. And, as far as I know, she's repeated it again to the County Juvenile people where we took her on the way out here. You're telling us that she's lying each time but that she's not a liar. Isn't it possible that she's telling the truth, at least about what Zinn did to her? How can you be so sure?"

Without hesitation, "Because I know Elliott wouldn't do it. And Gloria wouldn't either. She hasn't even had her first boyfriend yet. It just didn't happen."

Hendricks came closer to Lila. "So it's her word against his, and you chose to believe him. Did you do anything to check it out, try to have her examined by a doctor or anything?"

"No, there was no need. It didn't happen. I want to go get my daughter, now, Chief."

The Chief had picked up another picture from the piano and came toward her holding it out. It showed Elliott seated at the piano, mugging, while Lila and Gloria stood on either side, their hands covering his sheet music.

"Room 315 at the Courthouse: that's Juvenile. I can't say what they'll do. I've no authority at County. Mind if I borrow this, Miz Burke? The servants tell me that fella in the middle is Mr. Zinn. Unless your daughter decides to tell us it's all a big joke, we're goin' to have to charge him with rape."

"But Chief, you can't do that. It's not true."

"Well, I wouldn't worry too much about him. Even if we can get him back down here from New York, I doubt we can get a conviction if it's just your daughter's word against his. Reasonable doubt and all that legal stuff. Let's go, Hendricks. I sure wish you had found some hard evidence that would make it clearer one way or another."

Go on, you bastard, thought Lila. Get out of here. You know she was lying. You're just torturing me because I wouldn't sleep with you. You, too, wise guy, what are you fiddling with your briefcase for?

"Wait a minute," said Hendricks. "What about this?" And he reached into the briefcase and held up Gloria's flowered panties.

"God damn!" Chief Tighe whacked the side of his leg like a cowboy on a horse. "Sorry, Miz Burke, forgive the profanity. I forgot all about those things. Must be getting too old for the job. Can you identify them?"

"They're Gloria's." She couldn't keep her voice from dropping.

"Any idea where they were Sunday mornin'?"

"I know where Sarah said she found them." Even lower.

"Well, that's somepin', anyway, idn't it Hendricks? By the way, did you happen to look at the sheets? Sorry, Miz Burke, sometimes we have to go pokin' around where we'd rather not."

"All clean from the laundry, Chief. They did it yesterday. Even though it was a Sunday." Hendricks stood for a moment as though expecting applause, then put back the panties, picked up his briefcase and walked to the door.

Chief Tighe stood aside and let him exit, then spoke hurriedly to Lila. "That show was for Hendricks, or he'd tell people I was trying to whitewash you. This is a real mess, Lila, whatever the truth is. Get yourself a lawyer who knows his way around here. The quiet way. If this comes out in the newspapers, the State's Attorney will have to prosecute someone."

So she had been wrong about Chief Tighe; he was an ally after all. He had let her know what evidence he had and what the State's Attorney might do with it. But he'd made it quite clear there was little more he could do to help her. Like he said, she would need a lawyer who knew his way around locally. Cutler couldn't help here. It would have to be Alistair McKenzie, who had gotten Willie all the permits for his Palm Beach apartment houses. She should call him right away, or maybe she should call Willie first and have him call Alistair. And she should warn Elliott. But all that would take time, and she had to go get Gloria and bring her home. County Juvenile? It made Lila think of teenage car thieves with ducktail haircuts and switchblades and high school girls abandoning babies in bus stations. She had to get Gloria out of there now.

Driving across the bridge to West Palm Beach, Lila tried to come up with a plan. Sooner or later Gloria would give up on her story. She was not going to lie Elliott into prison, hadn't known that what she had accused him of was so serious. Could they arrest Elliott in New York and bring him down to Florida for trial? Chief Tighe had sounded doubtful. The Chief had also suggested that action might be taken against Lila herself; was that possible? Gloria had to come to her senses and tell the truth. And soon, before the word became public. Besides, the longer Gloria held to her story, the more trouble she might get into for lying.

•   •   •

The courthouse hallways were dimly lit, and Lila missed the sign for Room 315. She had to make a whole circuit around the third floor before finding the room on the second sweep. Inside she found three battered desks, a table and some chairs behind an oak counter. A man wearing the gray of the sheriff's office sat at the closest desk, his face in his hands, peering into an oaktag folder filled with official-looking documents. He didn't look up as Lila closed the door behind her. She waited about thirty seconds before she realized he was asleep.

"Excuse me, Officer." His head snapped up, looked around for a moment then focused on Lila. He pulled himself to his feet and came to the counter.

"Help you, Ma'am?"

"I'm Lila Burke. I've come to pick up my daughter, Gloria Granatelli. Chief Tighe told me she was here."

The man hesitated. "I can't help ya with that, Miz Burke. Y'all have to talk to the court worker. She'll be back in a while. Wy'ncha set yourself at that empty desk, there's a couple 'a magazines on the table, an' the water cooler's in the corner there." He pointed out the features of the room like a tour guide.

"Why do I have to wait? Isn't Gloria here?"

"Oh, yessum', she's rightly here." This time he pointed back to the closed door.

"Well, at least let me see her."

"I'm sorry, Ma'am, I'd sure like to oblige y'all, but I can't do that without Miz Leach's OK or the Judge's."

"Then let me see the Judge." Lila heard her voice growing shrill and made an effort to lower it. "Please, I'd greatly appreciate it."

He was patient. "He's not goin' to want to see you, least not until after you've talked to Miz Leach. Jes' set a bit. She won't be long."

Lila nodded. Making a scene here wasn't going to get her anywhere. She came around the counter to the water cooler and filled a paper cup, then sat down where she had been told. The officer smiled benevolently at her and went back to his desk and reopened the file. The room became silent except for the rustle of the pages of Lila's magazine. She heard the faint sound of music from behind the door in the back of the room. Was it Gloria who had turned on the radio?

After about ten minutes, the door to the hallway opened, and a woman entered carrying a shopping bag stuffed with files. She stepped around the counter, then, spotting Lila, paused.

"This here's Miz Burke, Alice." The officer spoke without getting up. "She wants to pick up the girl. Told her she'd have to talk to you."

"Thanks, Barney." The woman came over to Lila, depositing the shopping bag on the third desk as she passed it. She was younger than Lila, no more than thirty, dressed in a gray skirt and jacket over a plain white blouse.

Lila stood up. "Lila Burke, Miss Leach. I'm Gloria's mother. I'd like to take her home."

The woman's handshake was firm and brief. "That's Mrs. Leach, Mrs. Burke, Alice Leach. I'm glad you're here. We have a lot to talk about. Why don't you pull a chair up to my desk and I'll get out her file."

"I'll be happy to talk with you, Mrs. Leach, as much as you'd like, but right now, I think we need to get Gloria out of this place and back home where she belongs."

Mrs. Leach frowned. "I don't think we can do that, just now, Mrs. Burke. I don't know if you're aware that Gloria has told us a very disturbing story."

"I know what she's said. Chief Tighe and one of his men were just at my house, and they read me the report. It's not true, I mean the sex part, and the rest of it is exaggerated. I have to find out why she's doing this and stop it. It's crazy. She's hurting a number of people, herself included, no, mostly herself, when the truth comes out. You see that, don't you?"

"Please sit down, Mrs. Burke." Mrs. Leach now pointed to the desk where Lila had been sitting. Reluctantly, Lila reseated herself in the desk chair while Mrs. Leach sat in a straight-backed chair next to it. "I've heard Gloria's story. If it's substantially true, there may be serious consequences to several people. If not, yes, it will, at the least, create great embarrassment for her. But we have to investigate. We can't just allow you to take her home and get her to drop her charges. She says you've struck her twice in connection with these matters and threatened more violence to try to keep her quiet. We can't ignore that."

Lila's voice rose in response to the smugness in Mrs. Leach's tone. "Once. I lost my temper, and I slapped her once. I'd do anything to take it back, but I can't. But it was only once, for Christ's sake, in eight years. I swear it. Go ask Chief Tighe what the servants said when what's-his-name, the detective, interrogated them."

"We will do that, Mrs. Burke. I may want to talk to them myself. That will be part of the investigation in this case. You'll have a full chance to tell your version of the events before the hearing. But for now—"

"Hearing?" Lila exclaimed. "What hearing, Mrs. Leach? Has the State's Attorney already decided to prosecute Mr. Zinn?"

Mrs. Leach frowned and began to speak, enunciating distinctly. "Gloria has come to the State of Florida asking for help. She has told us that in your home and, through your negligence, she has been raped and that you have physically abused and terrorized her."

"No, no—." Lila was frantic to protest, but the stone-faced woman shook her head.

"Let me finish, Mrs. Burke. The Palm Beach police are investigating these events, and the State's Attorney will decide whether to prosecute one or more persons under the criminal statutes. That's his job, and any involvement you may have with his decision or any prosecution he may decide to bring should be discussed with his office, not with me. My job is to protect Gloria, and, from what she's told me, she is badly in need of such protection."

"Protection from me? I'd give my life to protect her. I'm her mother. Maybe you don't understand, because she has my maiden name."

"No, we know that, and we know the rest of her history. We know that you gave her up for seven years." Smug, condescending, contemptuous.

"Then you know that the judge in St. Louis gave her back to me and they followed up for years and found me a good mother. What do you want of me? I'll do anything. I'll talk to you. I'll come in with Gloria. I'll send her to a psychiatrist. I don't know why she is doing this. It can't be just her old anger. We're not as close as I'd like, but she's where she belongs."

This time, Mrs. Leach let Lila finish, then excused herself and went to her own desk. Lila gripped the sides of her chair with her hands to keep from jumping up and running through the door in the back of the room. Mrs. Leach returned with a file and placed it on the desk in front of Lila. Lila could read Gloria's name and a file number upside down. Mrs. Leach removed two copies of an official-looking document and handed them to Lila.

"This is an order of the Juvenile Court initiating a PINS proceeding for Gloria Granatelli. PINS stands for a Person In Need of Supervision. There's a preliminary hearing Thursday morning at 10 in Room 201 of this building. Would you please acknowledge receipt of a copy? Date and sign here." She handed Lila a pen. Lila signed one copy and gave the other back to Mrs. Leach who put it into the folder then steepled her hands on the desk.

"Mrs. Burke, I don't know what you are thinking, but you don't seem to understand what's happening. I'm going to have to ask Officer Cogwell to join us for a moment. Barney, could you come over, please?"

What was it that Lila didn't understand? These people were sticking their noses into her relationship with Gloria. She didn't like it, but maybe it would prove a good thing. Maybe some court-appointed counselor could get through Gloria to see how self-destructively she was behaving. And if Lila were doing something wrong, maybe that person could show her the right way. She wouldn't be too proud to accept help from any source.

The officer stood by the side of the desk, waiting for instructions.

"Mrs. Burke, this is Officer Cogwell."

What was this about? Lila stuck her hand out, and they shook awkwardly.

"I'm going to tell Mrs. Burke something, Barney, and I want you to make sure I say it clearly. I don't want any mix-up. O.K?"

"Sure, Alice."

"Mrs. Burke, your daughter Gloria does not accept that she ought to be living here in Palm Beach, with you. She has asked me, begged me, in fact, to get the Court to reverse the custody order, to permit her to live once again with your sister-in-law. Do you understand that?"

"Mrs. Leach, Gloria has said that a number of times over the eight years she's lived with me. But after the first couple of years, she only said it when we would have a disagreement, and I wouldn't let her do something she wanted. It was something to hurt me with when she was angry, that's all. She knew it wasn't going to happen."

"That may have been the case in the past. But this time it could very well happen. If Judge Constable believes most of what Gloria has told us, not necessarily every detail, he may decide that your home is not a suitable place for her to live in and that counseling and follow-up won't help enough. Based upon what I've heard so far, there's a good chance of that."

Lila stared blankly at Mrs. Leach. The woman hadn't heard a thing Lila had told her. Why was she getting poor Cath involved? This was between her and Gloria, and they would work it out if these stupid people would only leave them alone.

Mrs. Leach, shook her head wearily. "Officer Cogwell, what did I just tell Mrs. Burke?"

Barney squirmed like a child who's been watching the teacher go at another student and finds himself called on without any warning. She shouldn't do that to him, thought Lila.

"I'm sorry, Mrs. Burke. Mrs. Leach said that Judge Constable might take your daughter away from you."

"Thank you, Barney. Is that clear, Mrs. Burke? Do you understand what's involved here?"

Lila had dreamed this many times. Someone was taking something important from her, sometimes a person, Gloria or Lila's mother or father, sometimes something unknown but of inestimable value. There was always something she could do to stop them, but she could never remember what it was until it was too late, and she would desperately shout "NO! NO!" and Willie would grab her and shake her awake and then hold her until she was calm enough to go back to sleep. And sometimes, like now, she would be so close to finding the right thing to say. It was on the tip of her tongue, but there was no more time, no more—"NO! NO!"

Then someone was shaking her, but it wasn't Willie; it was the officer who had come around the desk and taken hold of her shoulders. Mrs. Leach was backing away holding her chair as though she were a lion tamer in a circus. So, this time, it wasn't a dream. She must find out how to stop them. Lila made herself go limp.

"It's OK, Officer Cogwell. Sorry, Mrs. Leach, I'm all right, now."

The door at the back of the room opened. "What's going on out here?" It was Gloria. "Oh, my God, Lila. That was you? What happened?" For a moment Lila was certain she heard real concern in Gloria's voice, but it was gone in a moment, replaced by mockery. "Barney, are you molesting my mother?"

Cogwell dropped his hands. "No, no, I just—now, you 'git back in there, Missy, you know you're not supposed to come out here."

Gloria ignored him. "What's going on, Mrs. Leach."

Lila spoke before Mrs. Leach could answer. "I came to bring you home, darling, and Mrs. Leach just told me that they won't let me and that, in fact, they are going to try to take you away from me altogether. That upset me a great deal, and when I tried to tell her that they couldn't do that, it came out the way you heard it. I'm sorry to have startled everybody, but I mean it, Mrs. Leach. I will not let you take my child from me. Gloria, I know I let them do it once. I have regretted that every day of my life since then, and I promise you I will not let them do it again. Come, let's go home. We can talk this out."

Gloria looked frightened. "No. I'm not going. You can't make me. Mrs. Leach? You promised."

"Mrs. Burke." Mrs. Leach had put the chair down and now went to Gloria and stood between her and Lila. "Gloria will not be returned to your custody unless the Judge so decides. You can see she doesn't want to go with you, now. Gloria, please go back into the other room and let me finish talking to your mother. Did you make your list?"

"What list?" demanded Lila.

"The things she'll need for the next few days. Someone can pick them up later. Gloria?"

"Pretty much. I'll go get it."

"No, Officer Cogwell will go with you and bring it out. And please show him proper respect. This is serious business."

"Yes, ma'am," Gloria ducked her head respectfully and turned back to the open doorway.

"Gloria!" Lila tried to rise, but Cogwell gripped her shoulders. In a moment he released her and followed Gloria through the door.

Mrs. Leach tidied her papers for a moment. "Gloria will be staying with the family of one of the County officers. They'll take good care of her. She'll miss three more days of school, but that can't be helped. You don't want me to interview you now, do you?"

Lila spread her hands. "I don't know." She needed time to think. "I guess not."

"I think you could use a night's sleep to pull yourself together. There's a lot of information I'd like to get, and you should have the chance to bring up anything you want."

Lila looked searchingly at this cold, impersonal woman, so different from Mrs. Warren. "Will you listen to me, or have you already made up your mind?"

"Look, Mrs. Burke. I've heard Gloria's story, and it's a bad one. You came in here this afternoon asking us to pay no attention to it but to do exactly what you tell us to. I think you now understand that we won't do that. If you conclude from that that we won't listen to you at all, you're wrong. I'll listen to anything you'd like to tell me and try to put it all into my report to the Judge. How's tomorrow morning at nine at your house?"

Lila assented and stood up. They shook hands. Officer Cogwell came out of the other room and handed Lila a sheet of paper covered with Gloria's illegible scrawl. As Lila left, she rapidly scanned the list. Blinky was not on it.

•　　　　　•　　　　　•

Across the street from the courthouse was a battered bar and grill called "The Jury Box," so advantaged by its location that its owner had found it unnecessary to renovate any of its original 1920's fixtures. But it had two pay telephones on the wall near the end of the bar. At four o'clock, long after the morning calendar calls and a half-hour before the official court day ended, Lila found the dingy room full and both phones in use. She needed to talk to Alistair McKenzie, right away, and to Willie, who was going directly to his office from the plane.

"Kin ah offer you a seat, Ma'am?" A white-haired, white-mustached man in a rumpled white suit pulled himself off a stool at the end of the bar and pointed toward it with an exaggerated bow.

Lila seated herself without speaking. Her benefactor picked up his glass with his left hand, bowed again and drifted to the other end of the crowded bar to an opening between two patrons. He set his glass down and engaged the man on his left in conversation. They both glanced her way, then focused their attention on their drinks.

Wonderful, thought Lila. I've been recognized. Another crime on my record. It was not that The Jury Box was a disreputable place; every judge in Palm Beach County ate and drank there. But none of the few women in the room appeared of Lila's social standing or sat at the bar. When the bartender came over to her, she ordered coffee although she would have much preferred a drink. She knew how easily gossip could exaggerate one drink into a binge. Even iced tea could be misidentified. At least the big white china cup advertised innocence.

The men at the telephones kept talking, so Lila made herself relax as she sipped her coffee and watched the endless belt that turned the ancient ceiling fans. Crazy as it was, she now recognized the danger in the situation. If Gloria stuck to her story, Lila would come across as negligent, at best. Lila couldn't blame the police and Mrs. Leach for taking Gloria seriously; Gloria was proving herself a superb actress.

A telephone was freed, and Lila sprang from her stool to capture it, a handful of coins ready. As she started to dial, half of them slipped from her hand and spilled around her, and several men jumped from their chairs to retrieve them. Finally, she placed the call, and the familiar voice of Willie's receptionist came on the line. A moment later, Willie, himself, was on.

"Lila, what's the matter? Laraine said—"

"Help me, Willie, for God's sake. They've taken Gloria."

The men at the nearest table were staring at her, and she forced herself to lower her voice to a desperate whisper. "She went to the police, and the Juvenile Court people have her. She's trying to get them to send her back to Catherine."

"Calm yourself, Lila. It can't be that bad."

She had to make Willie understand. "It is. She's told them terrible lies, and they believe her. There's a hearing Thursday. The Judge might—" The words wouldn't come out.

Willie's voice changed. "I'll be on the first plane tomorrow. We need Alistair, for this."

"Yes, and I need to see him tonight. The court worker is coming tomorrow at nine."

"Where are you? I'll find him and call you right back."

She gave Willie the number of the pay phone and guarded it grimly until he called back. He had located Alistair and arranged for him to meet Lila at his office at six.

"Stay calm, darling girl. You've been a wonderful mother, and everybody knows it."

"Who's going to say that?"

"I will. Mary will. The Russells, the Johnsons, her teachers. Lots of people. Doctor Spence tells everyone how well you take care of Gloria."

"Will they come into Court?"

"Of course, after it's all explained to them. But it won't be necessary. Gloria will give up this nonsense before it comes to that."

"I don't know, Willie. You wouldn't believe how she sounded—it was as though I were threatening her life."

"Don't let her get to you, Lila. She's not going to go through with it. And my partners down there have a lot of pull. One of them must be able to talk sense to the State's Attorney and the head of the Juvenile Division. They're not going to take her away from you. Believe me."

More people had crowded around the bar, and frantic lawyers stood glaring at Lila and jingling change in their pockets. It became too noisy; she could no longer make out what Willie was saying, so she thanked him and hung up. She didn't have the strength to fight through the crowd to the bar to pay for her coffee, so she left, feeling guilty. But not as desperate.

Since she was a half-hour early for her meeting with Alistair, she stopped at the house, where she brought Mary up to date and gave her Gloria's list of things to assemble and hand over to whichever officer might come.

Mary was aghast at hearing what was happening. "The child is after goin' to law 'gainst her own mother?" But this was nothing to her reaction when Lila told her to be prepared to be a character witness. Mary burst into tears. "Mum, no, please Mum," she sobbed. "I've not said one word about this house from the day you took me on. I could never do it before a judge and *thim* lawyers and all, not knowin' if I might get it wrong and they be takin' our little girl from us because of it. No, Mum, please. Tell *thim* I took a crack on me head and haven't the memory."

Lila put her arms around Mary. "We have to do what we have to do, Mary. Just tell the truth and leave the rest to God." That seemed to comfort Mary if it did little for Lila.

Alistair was late, "delayed at a meeting," said his secretary in a snippy tone, without lifting her eyes from her compact mirror, as she applied powder to her face. Lila sat down in a chair by the door, selected a year-old issue of Field and Stream and tried to interest herself in an article matching breeds of bird dogs to different hunting conditions. A heavy mahogany grandfather's clock standing next to the door to Alistair's private office showed five minutes past the hour. The secretary finished with the powder, removed tweezers from a huge handbag sitting on the floor next to her desk and began plucking her eyebrows. Lila turned pages admiring the handsome dogs. How much she owed to poor little Pinto, run over three years ago. The secretary finished with the tweezers, replaced them in the handbag, checked the clock and glared at Lila.

Still another crime, thought Lila. I'm making her late for her boyfriend.

At 6:15, Alistair arrived. He was slim and dark, haughty and taciturn. Willie once said that he was the only man in the county who could keep his mouth shut. People might not like him, but they trusted him, which was more important. With one nod he sent the secretary out the front door, with another, Lila to a chair in his private office. He took two Coca-Colas from a small refrigerator, opened them, handed one with a glass to Lila and gestured for her to begin.

She started with the return of the station wagon from the concert, but Alistair stopped her with his first words. "No, from the beginning."

"You mean with Gloria's father?" Alistair smiled encouragement, and she continued, uninterrupted, for forty minutes, while he furiously scribbled notes on a yellow legal pad. There was a long silence after she finished.

"Well, what do you think? Can they possibly take her?"

"Possibly."

The hysteria of fear returned, but she couldn't give in to it. "How likely, do you think?"

"I don't know enough, yet. Again, from your mother's death. I'll be Judge Constable."

This time he frequently interrupted with questions. Some were intelligent, but others seemed to have little to do with the issues and only to be asked to make her look careless or insensitive. Finally, she stopped and said, "Hey, I thought you were being the judge. Isn't this sort of thing cross-examination that the State's Attorney might try and you could object to?"

"The State's Attorney won't be involved in this."

"Then who tries the case against me? Mrs. Leach isn't a lawyer, is she?"

He looked at her strangely. "They didn't tell you? No lawyers in Juvenile Court. Nobody's on trial, so you don't need lawyers or cross-examination. Mrs. Leach investigates and reports. The judge conducts the hearing and decides what he thinks is best for the child."

Lila was stunned. "I can't have a lawyer either?" Alistair shook his head. "But, Alistair, we had lawyers when I won her back."

"Well I'm not familiar with the practice in Missouri, but it sounds like that was a straight family court custody case. This is a PINS case, in Juvenile Court, brought on only because Gloria may need court intervention to protect her. No lawyers."

"What am I going to do with no one there to help me?" Lila pleaded. "What if Gloria keeps lying, and people believe her like Mrs. Leach does. Will the judge cross-examine her?"

"I don't know, Lila."

"Alistair! You've got to know. You're the lawyer, not me. Wait. Can you teach me how to cross-examine?"

"You won't get a chance. The Judge examines the child alone in closed session."

"I can't be there? When my own child is talking about me? That's not fair."

"Believe me, Lila. That's the way it's done."

Lila fought to keep her voice calm. "We have to do something. I'm sure I could stop this if I could talk to her, but they wouldn't let me this afternoon. Can you get them to let me?"

Alistair shrugged. "I'll try."

"There must be more. Please. We can't just sit and do nothing." She was ready to run around his desk and shake him, hit him, anything to get him engaged.

`He put his hands on the edge of his desk and spoke in his measured voice. "The best thing you can do is make a good presentation of yourself and bring in some people who will tell Mrs. Leach what a devoted mother you are. Do you have any friends down here who could do that? Go beyond Willie and the help."

The tension slackened as she considered his question. "I'll have to think that over. Should I try to get Elliott to come down?"

Alistair gave a peculiar snort that she recognized as the closest sound he had to a laugh. His accent broadened. "Even if the sumbitch was dumb enough to set foot in this state an' frisky enough to git one hand in the air an' the other on the Bible wearin' handcuffs, which is the only way he'd git into the courtroom. I don't hardly reckon ol' Jedge Connie'd believe he'd' jes' been too sleepy to figger out it weren't the cat, but a gal in his bed takin' off her panties and stuffin' them down by his feet." He looked embarrassed. "Sorry, Lila, but that's how people will look at it: that his claim of innocence is a joke. But the other way is a joke, too. The carpetbagger's daughter got bagged. You know," a thin smile flickered across his face, "Judge Constable likes to swap dirty jokes with the boys. He could easily decide that this case is a comedy and not a tragedy and just tell you to take Gloria home and watch her."

So her best chance was that some hick judge would laugh the whole thing off. That was a thin straw. "So you think I'm going to lose?"

Alistair frowned. "Not necessarily. It depends on who says what and how the Judge is going to feel about it Thursday morning. I'll have to poke around tomorrow. Meet me here at five with Willie. Tell your story to Mrs. Leach just like you did to me. Become her friend."

●   ●   ●

Mr. Harris's tardiness hasn't left Lila much time to try the piano. It's not necessary; she would trust Mr. Goetz even if she hadn't heard him demonstrate its tuning for her. She does it for another reason: validation. She would be demeaning both his work and her sensibility if she didn't reserve her final judgment until she played herself. Of course, that's silly. It's just a ritual that doesn't make a bit of difference. She knows that. Her whole day is taken up with such silly rituals; together with her love for Gloria, they are all that keep her alive.

First, she closes the door to the hallway for privacy. That's silly, too. The servants can hear her clearly through the closed door. But that's not the same thing as being in the same room. She could never stand anyone in the room with her when she played except Elliott, who, as her teacher, belonged there. She wonders if Elliott is still in a Buddhist temple somewhere in India where he went to study music and meditation many years ago. If so, he would be the only one of her old friends still alive.

She sits and starts one of her old exercises. There was no one moment when she stopped playing. She just let it slip bit by bit, as she did with much of her life. The difficulty of setting aside an hour every day and the effort in concentrating for that hour were sometimes too much, particularly if she had been drinking the night before. Diminished diligence was naturally followed by diminished proficiency. Periodically, she would rally herself, but less and less as the years went by. By now, she hardly plays at all, except on the day the piano is tuned.

After the exercise, Lila begins a Chopin etude. The fingers remember, and she is doing fine until she starts to think of what comes next and falters. She is annoyed for forgetting and, determined to concentrate, begins to play "Smoke Gets in Your Eyes," not the standard solo version, which she used to play, nor Elliott's searching version, which she could never master, but her old accompaniment. After a while, she begins to sing softly. She shuts her eyes and sees the rows of sailors staring at her, hungrily. Willie is there, too, in the last row, where he always sat, his eyes fixed on her. People are standing behind the seats, but she can't make out their faces. Suddenly the lights go up, and she can see Elliott, his arm around Margo and next to them John and Cath, smiling at Lila, and her mother and, right behind Willie, it's Gloria, waving for Lila's attention, and when she catches Lila's eye, her mouth forms the words "I love you."

She finishes the song, wipes her eyes on her sleeve and goes to look in the mirror over the bar. The face she sees doesn't look much worse than it did before her little crying jag. Good. She needn't stop off in the powder room on the way to dinner. It's 6:29 and Cook must be ladling the soup into the tureen.

•   •   •

Mechanically, she left Alistair's office and drove home. An officer had already picked up Gloria's things. Lila declined dinner, waved off all questions and went up to her room. She forced herself to call Willie, in New York, reported her meeting with Alistair, then cut short the conversation, hung up and pulled the phone cord out of the jack. She needed to be alone to think. What should she say to Mrs. Leach? "Make her your friend," Alistair had said. How on earth was she supposed to do that? Play tennis with her? Stupid. Find a common ground, Lila supposed. If Mrs. Leach had a child, it would be young, and she wouldn't be working. Unless she, too, had been forced to give it up. Stupid, stupider, stupidest.

Was the case that bad, Lila asked herself. She pulled a pencil and pad out of the sewing table and started to list the points that would be brought out against her. After a few minutes, feeling thirsty, she went to the little bar and refrigerator and took ice and ginger ale. She went over the list, tore it off the pad and scotch-taped it to the left side of the mirror over her dresser. She went back to the pad and made a list of points in her favor, then taped it to the right side of the mirror and stepped back and looked.

The list on the left was a long one. Weakness, abandonment, deception, stupidity, impatience, anger, carelessness. Lila didn't need Mrs. Leach to indict her; she was guilty of them all, and Gloria had suffered for it. On the right just two: love and determination. Hoping to find some idea that might help, Lila went down the hall into Gloria's rooms. She wandered about, leafing through a school notebook, pulling out drawers, peering behind the hanging clothes in the closets, finding nothing. On the top shelf of the closet in Gloria's bedroom, Lila came upon Gloria's photo albums and pulled down the very first, which Lila had begun for Gloria shortly after bringing her home from St. Louis. There was Gloria alone and Gloria with Margo and with little Julia and with Mary and, of course, over and over with Pinto.

Life was very hard in those days; Lila would never forget the terrible struggle just to get Gloria to speak to her at first, and then the lesser battles to get Gloria dressed and to school some mornings. But there had been hope and, however slow, there had been progress. Lila didn't need photographs to remember the shy smile with which Gloria would acknowledge something new that brought her joy even if she refused to acknowledge it in words. Rare even then, it seemed now extinct. Lila began to cry softly. Progress had long since stopped, and there seemed to be no hope left for her poor, clunky, unhappy child, whose life was so driven by hatred for her own mother that she would lie to the world and put Elliott, whom she adored, in jeopardy of prison.

Lila turned back the album to the first page and sees the tear in the stiff, black paper. She had pasted in it her only saved picture of herself holding Gloria as a baby. Shortly thereafter, in a rage over something Lila no longer remembered, Gloria had pulled out the picture, torn it to pieces and flushed it down the toilet. Now she was pulling herself out of Lila's life altogether. Did she know how much pain she would cause? A voice inside Lila, kept silent for eight years, answered with another question. "As much as you caused her?"

She jumped up and ran from Gloria's bedroom. She crashed into a chair in the sitting room, then staggered out of the door and back to her own room. She tore open the liquor cabinet, pulled out a bottle of Canadian Club, filled her half-empty glass of ginger ale and gulped it down. Coughing and spluttering, she flung herself onto the bed, gripped the headboard tightly with both hands and braced herself for the takeoff that would fly her away from the insupportable reality. The next thing she was conscious of was Mary calling softly as she knocked on the locked door.

"Mrs. Burke, you have to get up, the woman's here, now."

Lila came fully awake. She didn't need to look at her watch to know that it must be nine o'clock and that the woman must be Mrs. Leach. She started to get up, but the room spun around, so she fell back. She had a terrible headache. She couldn't tell how much she had drunk; she had spilled a lot from the bottles strewn around the room. She thought she had slept, woke up to vomit, drunk more and vomited again; there were messes in two places, and the clothes she had been wearing were soiled. She couldn't possibly get clean and dressed and in shape to be seen in less than a half-hour, and, even then, would be incapable of a rational conversation.

"Tell her I'm sick, Mary. I'll call her when I can get up." It was a disaster, but trying to see Mrs. Leach in this condition could only make it worse. She lay back until the room stopped turning around, then very gingerly got up and went to the bathroom for an Alka-Seltzer. She paused for a moment in front of her dresser and looked again at the lists. During the night, "Determination" had been crossed off the right-hand list; all that was left was "Love."

By the time Willie's plane landed, Lila was back under control. She had called a cleaning service and, by doubling their usual rate, induced them to pull two people from another job to come immediately to restore her room. The staff was mystified at their arrival, but that was better than allowing them into the room to see what had happened; Sarah had done enough talking already. Next, Lila addressed restoring herself. A long hot bath was followed by a light breakfast. She kept her mind focused on the moment, determined not to think about Gloria or Mrs. Leach until she felt in condition to function properly. After breakfast, she inspected the tennis court and the grounds, making a few notes of things that needed attention. Back at the house, she found her room in its customary immaculate condition, the cleaning people ready to leave, taking the empty bottles and other evidence with them in a big black garbage bag. She opened the windows to dissipate the smell of the carpet shampoo.

It was not until Lila got into her car to drive to the airport, that the answer came to her. She should ask Mrs. Leach for the benefit of her experience with children in difficult family situations, how to speak with Gloria, how to handle problems after Gloria came home. If Mrs. Leach could be persuaded to become her counselor, she could hardly continue to press for Gloria's removal.

At the airport, she called, but Mrs. Leach was out. Lila picked up Willie, and they drove to the Club for lunch. Lila ate little because of her "stomach virus," but Willie made up for it. He had brought with him copies of papers sent by Cutler and was preparing to fight the case. He disagreed with Lila's new plan.

"What if you don't put it to her as well as you might and she takes it as an admission that you're incapable of dealing with Gloria yourself. I thought you were doing fine with Gloria until that asshole came down last week. Are you sure—?"

She wasn't sure at all. How could she be? Alistair had said to make Mrs. Leach her friend, and this seemed the best way to do that. But Willie might be right. If she could only get to talk to Gloria. But from yesterday's scene at the Courthouse, it was clear she wasn't going to be allowed to do that. How can they keep a mother from talking to her own daughter? They finished their lunch undecided pending their meeting with Alistair, and Lila left a message at the Courthouse that she would call Mrs. Leach the next morning. On their way out, they met Clarice Johnson, Sally's mother, with another woman, coming in from the ninth hole for lunch.

"Hey, Clarice, how're you hitting them?" Lila asked casually, as they passed.

Clarice stopped short while her friend continued towards the dining room. She reached for Lila's arm to slow her. "You've got to stop this thing, Lila," she said, then, seeing her friend turn back for her, let Lila go and went on.

"So she's heard about the pool party." Lila shrugged. "We expected that. But what was she telling me to stop?"

"I have no idea," replied Willie. "Maybe Alistair does."

They knocked on Alistair's door promptly at five. Alistair opened it, himself. "Willie, you old son. You're getting fat as a pig." He gave Willie a whack across the shoulders, and they shook hands. "Lila, are you going to enter him at the county fair this year?"

Without waiting for an answer, he took her hand and started her toward his private office as though he were passing her down the line in a country dance, completing the maneuver by grabbing Willie's elbow and steering him into the room as well. They sat, and Alistair poured Cokes after Willie declined the offer of something stronger. Alistair sat behind his desk, tilted his chair back, looked first at Willie and then at Lila, and, when neither said anything, began.

"How are you feeling, Lila? I heard you were sick."

"A little better, thank you. I must have picked up a stomach bug. I had a bad night with it. Did you speak to Mrs. Leach?"

"Not directly. But I heard a bit here and there." He paused.

"Well, what did you hear?" Willie prompted.

"First, there are a few people around who would like not to have to hear anything about this affair again."

"Like Clarice Johnson?" asked Lila.

"Yup. Harold and Clarice are definitely in that group. Neither Harold's chances for the Circuit Court nor Clarice's standing in her church group would be advanced by the story, however much denied, that Sally forgot her bathing suit when she went swimming in your pool."

In spite of herself, Lila laughed. "You should have seen her jackknife off the board."

Alistair grinned. "That lovely young girl? I surely wish I had. Well, Chief Tighe has stirred up a hornets' nest by going around interviewing the kids. The parents would like the story to go no further, and, among them, they carry considerable clout. If an indictment is brought on, the case will make the newspapers and the swimming party with it. So we can imagine some friend of the State's Attorney suggesting that he bury the file since he'll never get Zinn down here for trial, anyway."

"Good idea," Willie interjected. "You know, don't you, that we believe he's innocent?"

"Yes, Lila told me. And, the State's Attorney knows that. So he knows that Gloria's family won't object if he doesn't indict. But he would have told his friend that the complaining witness is sticking to her story and is planning to tell it in detail in Juvenile Court Thursday."

"So what?" asked Willie. "That proceeding is in a closed courtroom, no reporters."

"But Judge Constable is going to hear it. If he finds that a crime may have been committed against the juvenile before him, he's required to report that finding to the State's Attorney who's obliged to investigate and either indict or report back that there aren't grounds.."

"So, let Judge Constable decide he doesn't believe it happened."

"Willie, it's not so easy. With Zinn not there, the only testimony is Gloria's."

Lila broke in. "Alistair, if the Judge, if someone, cross-examines Gloria the truth will come out. I told you yesterday."

"I wouldn't count on it. The people she's told the story to already, seem to have believed her. And, by now, she's had lots of practice. Alice Leach is totally behind her, and Alice has the reputation of being very determined. Besides, they're all afraid that if the Judge decides you can keep Gloria here, she's going to continue to squawk and sooner or later it will get to the papers."

"That's too bad," said Lila, "I'm not looking to embarrass anybody, but there's no way out of it, not from what you say."

There was a long silence, then Alistair looked at Willie who nodded.

"What was that about?" Lila's voice rose. "Willie, have you cooked something up with Alistair?" Again, it was the whole world against her.

"We've not had a word, Lila. I swear to God. But I think I know what he's going to tell you." Willie stood up. "I'm going outside. Alistair's your lawyer, today. You talk to him. I'll sit in the car until you want me." He was out of the room before Lila could stop him.

Lila took a deep breath. "All right, counselor, tell me."

Alistair went to the refrigerator and opened another coke and poured half in Lila's glass and half in his own. "Lila, you can get someone else. I won't be offended."

"Come on, Alistair, we haven't time for that, now. Who am I going to call, Harold Johnson? As long as you're representing me, not Willie or a bunch of parents, it's fine."

"Thank you. And you are my only client, here, Lila. All right, it has been suggested to me that there is one way to avoid a public scandal. If you agree to transfer Gloria's custody to your sister-in-law, Judge Constable will make that his ruling without an evidentiary hearing. The State's Attorney will close the file on the rape case, and it will be forgotten in a month."

"I won't forget it in a month," she said with only the hint of reproach in her voice.

"I'm sorry, Lila. I didn't mean it that way."

"I told you the story, Alistair. I was talked into giving her up once, and neither of us has forgiven me for it yet. Not again. What happens in court?"

"That depends on who's been talking to whom. You see, Judge Constable might be aware that some influential people think it would be much better for them, as well as for Gloria, if she were out in St. Louis, rather than in Palm Beach."

"So the case is fixed?"

"Let's just say that your chances are not good if there is any doubt on the merits of the case. And unless Gloria changes her story, there's plenty of doubt."

"But at least I'll have a chance. The other way I would give up without a fight." Lila got up from her chair and started to pace back and forth across the room. "Why would you think I might do that? To keep Harold and Clarice from being embarrassed?" She wondered what Alistair's answer would be. It would sound persuasive.

"No, Lila, to keep Elliott Zinn from being indicted for rape—and to keep yourself from being indicted for attempted obstruction of justice."

"Are you serious?"

Alistair ticked off on his fingers "One, you sent Zinn back to New York, , two, you tried to prevent Gloria from reporting the incident to the police, three you may have destroyed evidence by having the sheets laundered a day early and four, you failed to tell Chief Tighe about Gloria's panties being found in Zinn's bed. It's not much of a case, but charging you would show they were doing what they could, considering they won't be able to extradite Zinn."

Lila thought for a moment. "What you're saying is, they would punish me this way for not cooperating in the cover-up. Right?"

Alistair winced. "I'm not saying it, but that's the way it is."

"What if they were told that, if they let me keep Gloria, I would take her back to New York so they wouldn't have to worry about her talking?"

Alistair's eyebrows raised. "That's interesting. Let's see. Johnson and the other parents would be satisfied, and that would satisfy the State's Attorney. But Judge Constable isn't going to send Gloria off kicking and screaming without a hearing unless Mrs. Leach recommends it."

"So my worst enemy is Mrs. Leach, the only one in the bunch who cares about doing the right thing. That's why you told me to try to make a friend of her. And I broke our appointment this morning. No, I'm my worst enemy, not her." Rage flared. Once again, she had blundered, and there was nothing she could do to save Gloria. She stood still, her eyes searching the room for an object to wield or to destroy. But something held her back. Wait. Think. She sat back down. There was one way to stop them. It had always been the best way; now it was the only way. Gloria had to realize she wanted to stay with Lila.

It had to happen sooner or later. Gloria could not hold out forever against the constant, unceasing force of Lila's love. Lila had assumed that Gloria would come to her bit by bit, over time, But maybe bit by bit was not the way. Maybe Gloria's walls had been so weakened that they could now be brought down by one determined assault. Maybe Gloria sensed what was happening and was trying to escape from Lila before they fell altogether.

She looked at Alistair. He sat patiently, hands clasped in front of him, his only motion an occasional blink. But she could sense his anticipation, like a lizard waiting for its meal to come a little closer. Their little exchange had been a charade; his first loyalty was still to his own people. That was all right, though; what she was going to do wouldn't threaten them.

"I'll agree to what they want, on one condition."

She paused just to watch Alistair's face. Was it her imagination or did the lips start to open for the lightning tongue, then close again?

"I have to talk to Gloria first. Just the two of us. If she changes her mind, this whole thing is over, and she comes home with me. They drop this PINS proceeding, there are no indictments, no reprisals, nothing."

Alistair started taking notes as Lila spoke. He looked up when she finished. "How about taking Gloria up to New York, like you said before?"

"All right, we can go up now and stay up for the summer. That should do it. But they have to promote her with her class, and she goes back with the class in September."

"So you wouldn't leave permanently?"

"I don't see why we should. We like it here. We've put a lot into our home and the community; you know Willie's business commitments. Do it this way, and we can all forget about it. Don't you think that's possible?"

He looked up at the ceiling, then back at her. "Could be. Folks get what they want, they forget the rest. You think you can persuade Gloria? You'll have to sign a complete release, and I'll have to hand it over five minutes after your meeting if she hasn't changed her mind."

Lila took a deep breath. "She will change her mind, Alistair, I know she will. But no funny business. You get someone to tell Mrs. Leach to stop pushing Gloria away from me. And no hints that it's too late to change her mind or her story, if she's ready to admit the truth."

Alistair put down his pencil. "That won't be a problem. This is far and away the best solution for everybody if Gloria acts voluntarily. Shall we tell Willie?"

•   •   •

The next afternoon, shortly before 4 o'clock, Lila sat on a bench overlooking South Ocean Drive, across from the entrance to Via Amalfi. A few hundred feet away, Willie and Alistair sat at another bench. They seemed to be arguing, and Lila could occasionally hear the sound of a raised voice, but the noise of the ocean and the wind made any words indistinguishable. She got up from the bench and walked to them. The argument stopped.

"That's fine," Lila said. "I couldn't hear a word. Go on home, Willie. If Mrs. Leach sees you here, she may decide it's a kidnap attempt and drive right past."

"If you say so, darling girl. I just thought it might help a bit, my being here. Like to show I care about Gloria, too."

"That's sweet, Willie. But it's all come down to her and me. Anyone else, even you, is either a weapon or a distraction. Poor Elliott became a weapon. I'm afraid you'd be just a distraction, and we need to concentrate." Lila kissed his cheek and sent him back to their house. She sat down next to Alistair and peered out to sea to avoid looking at the thin Manila envelope, which lay on the bench between them and which contained the stipulation releasing custody of Gloria. Her hand had been shaking when she signed it, but there was no other way.

The morning had been spent either on the telephone or waiting by it for Alistair's calls reporting progress in the negotiations. Lila went through them cheerfully as soon as she was told that Gloria had agreed to the meeting. Alistair persuaded Mrs. Leach to drop her initial demand that the meeting be held at her office with an officer present for protection against possible violence from Lila. Here, at the beach, she could watch from close at hand but not hear what was said. Then the high school demurred at promoting Gloria

BABY GRAND

if she missed the rest of the semester until Lila agreed to hire a tutor who would supervise the completion of the curriculum by mail.

The more Lila had thought about it, the more certain had been her conclusion that no planning, no maneuvering would affect the outcome. The severed emotional cord between them would reconnect, and restorative love would flow through it again. Whatever else was necessary would follow from that connection. She had prepared no speeches, planned no appeals, worked no arguments. When she had visualized this meeting over and over, she had not gotten past the picture of a car door opening and a smiling Gloria climbing out. As she had pictured it, a battered Honda pulled up, and Gloria emerged from the passenger seat and walked toward her, while Mrs. Leach came around the car from the driver's side.

"What's up, Lila?" Gloria asked, cheerfully. She was wearing a white blouse and a burgundy skirt Lila had picked out for her just a few days ago. Her hair looked newly washed, and glints of copper showed among the brown. Her back was straight, and she walked gracefully. Lila marveled at how much better her daughter looked with a little effort.

"You look very nice, darling." Lila got up from the bench. "You've met Mr. McKenzie at the house, I think." They all stood awkwardly, like boxers being given instructions in the center of the ring, then Alistair and Mrs. Leach sat down on the bench while Lila and Gloria walked down the road to the other bench. Lila sat down, but Gloria perched on the iron railing, her back to the ocean, swinging one foot below her.

Gloria spoke first. "Mrs. Leach says that you're going to sign a piece of paper letting me go. Are you?"

Here we go, thought Lila. Her voice was steady. "If that's what you believe will make you happy."

"Happy? You're asking me what will make me happy? That's very funny, Lila. You've always been so sure about what was going to make me happy, you never bothered to ask me."

"I'm still sure, darling, but you're almost an adult, now. You can think about what's good and what's bad for you and you can explain your reasons, and we can discuss them intelligently. We couldn't do that when you were a little girl. I know that something has you terribly upset, so upset that you've turned the whole town upside down. They're ready to throw Elliott in jail and maybe me, too. Did you know that?"

"Yes, they told me."

"Well. If you wanted to show that you were serious, you certainly have. I think you could have gotten my attention without all this. But here we are. What's upsetting you and what can I do to help?"

Gloria started to speak, then stopped herself and was silent for a few seconds before replying, "Just sign the paper, Lila."

"But what's happened to make you want to do this now, darling? Something I've done, or something I haven't done? Maybe we can fix it. Does it have to do with Elliott? He didn't actually—do it, did he? The truth. This is no day for lies."

Gloria hesitated, then shrugged. "Poor Elliott. Of course, he didn't. I just said he did, at first, to get under your skin. And I left my panties in his bed to embarrass him as revenge for his falling asleep when I was talking to him. But when you told me you had sent him back to New York, I suddenly realized that people might believe me if I stuck with the story and anything might happen. Now everybody believes me. And if you tell them I confessed I'll deny it unless you sign the paper; then it won't matter. I wouldn't let them put him in jail, though."

Somehow, Lila felt more relieved than angry. "Why did you tell such a terrible story?"

"It's obvious. So I can get away from you. And it's worked."

"But why would you decide to do this now?"

"Now, Lila? You think it's only now? It was last month and last year and the year before that and the day you dragged me away." As she spoke, she swung her foot harder and harder until she was smashing her heel into the lower railing with each swing. "I've always wanted to get away from you. You knew it, too, but wouldn't admit it."

"I admit that you did, at first. I can understand that. But not after a while. Why would you want to? I'm your mother, and I love you; you can't deny that. I've given you all the love and patience and understanding I possibly could. You've had a good home, the best of everything. Willie and I are prepared to do anything for you. Why would you want to go to St. Louis now? My brother is gone. Catherine has accepted what happened. She's not your mother; you call her by her first name, too. Why go?"

Gloria jumped down, then put her hands behind her to grip the railing. "Because she is my mother, no matter what I call her just like you're not my mother, no matter what I call you."

"Gloria, my own darling child, my baby. Can't you forgive me just a little? I wasn't so much older than you are now, and I didn't know what I was doing. I've been punished for it over and over. I've tried to at least make it up to you a little, and I'll keep trying the rest of my life. Just forgive me a little, just enough to stay with me."

Lila got up from the bench and stretched her hands towards Gloria, who spun away from her and faced the ocean, again gripping the rail as though she feared being blown away by the wind. Her shoulders began to shake and Lila, realizing that she was sobbing, went to her and put her hands on Gloria's shoulders to comfort her. Was this the signal of capitulation?

"Hey!" Lila looked to see Mrs. Leach standing and starting to run towards them. Lila dropped her hands then Gloria turned and waved reassuringly. Mrs. Leach stopped, and Alistair took her arm and pulled her back to the bench.

"You're not going to push me over, are you Lila?" Gloria was half-laughing and half-crying. "I'd just fall onto the sand. My friends and I jump from here all the time."

"What's the matter, darling, why were you crying?"

Gloria sat down on the bench and looked searchingly at Lila. "You are so out of it, Lila, it's hard to hate you. Someone tells you something, it gets turned around in your head, and you remember it as something else. For the last time, I can forgive you for giving me up when I was one year old. You shouldn't have done it, but you gave me to wonderful people who really wanted me, but—" her voice started to break, "but then you took me away from them and broke their hearts and—" Gloria was sobbing so hard that Lila could hardly make out the words, "and killed—my poor Daddy—." Her head dropped to her knees, and she began to rock back and forth making barely audible sounds more terrible than any scream.

Lila ran. Away from her child, she ran, no thought at all in her head to distract her from the overwhelming need to escape. At the intersection of Via Amalfi with South Ocean Drive, she didn't even look for traffic before crossing. Off to her left, from where she had come, Mrs. Leach was nearing Gloria while Alistair stood motionless, the envelope in his hand.

Gloria couldn't have said those things; it was impossible. And each time memory repeated, Lila's mind rejected. "No," it said, over and over. Lila's pace slowed as she neared the house, and she began to mark each footstep with the comforting word, saying softly, "No, no, no, no, no," until the memory was silenced.

She stopped at the gate to her house and leaned against one of the pink, concrete posts until her breathing slowed to normal. She entered the house and, hearing the rattle of dice, went into the game room. Willie was sitting at the table, a backgammon board in front of him. He looked at Lila, then at the empty doorway behind her, and the strong planes of his face softened.

He's getting old, thought Lila. She knelt by Willie's side, put her head on his knee, her arms around his waist. "Don't cry, darling," she said. "She'll be back."

●   ●   ●

It's a Wednesday, so Lila goes upstairs directly after dinner. Tonight she has to rest twice on the way up. She senses Jeffrey watching her from the door of the dining room, ready to dash to her rescue if he sees her falter. He'd probably break both their necks if he tried it, but it's the thought that counts. At this moment, contemplating another dozen steps, the gizmo on a track doesn't seem quite as impossible as she told Mr. Harris it was. But she makes it to the top and dismisses the idea again.

When Lila gets to her sitting room, she sits at the little French sewing table she still uses for writing her personal letters. Her business correspondence is maintained in the office, downstairs. She used to spend a lot of time at this table keeping up with their Navy friends, but there are none left and, now, she uses it only for her weekly letters to Gloria. She started writing them eight years ago after she learned from a cousin that Catherine had died.

Lila has not seen Gloria in forty years. Alistair had reserved visitation rights in the stipulation Lila had signed, but Gloria refused to see her. Lila didn't try to enforce her rights; her child would come to her of her own will.

Nor has she spoken with Gloria in all that time. Willie called St. Louis a few days after Gloria had left. Gloria had said good-bye to him. She had not wanted to speak to Lila. When he called again, two weeks later, Catherine told him Gloria wouldn't speak to him, either. After that, Willie called Catherine every few months. Lila would listen attentively to his reports.

After Catherine's death, Lila retained the St. Louis detective agency Gerry had hired so many years before; she still has their original report with the photostat of Gloria's forged birth certificate. They check on Gloria three or four times a year and tell Lila how she is doing. Sometimes they are able to take a snapshot without being seen.

That first letter was the hardest. Somehow, Lila took her own self-pity and purged it of self so that it spoke to Catherine gone and Gloria left behind. Lila had never forgiven Catherine for the love with which she had twice enfolded Gloria when taken from Lila, even though Catherine's was the least part in the taking. Lila forgave her now and John, too. Then, once and for all time, she forgave poor Willie, who, from stupidity, not malice, brought devastation to their lives and was punished so dreadfully for it.

When she had forgiven them all, she realized that she could forgive herself as well and, shriving and shriven, could rightly take up the task of consoling her wounded child. Cleansed of all rancor, she felt as though she were again rocking that squalling baby with the little cap of black hair. She wrote page after page, sometimes humming wordlessly or crooning a snatch of the lullabies, learned from her own mother, she used to sing to Gloria in that first year of motherhood. When she finished at 2 A.M., she hurried to the garage to drive to the Post Office to mail the letter. She hadn't wanted to wake Jeffrey to do it, but he heard the garage door open and, as she pulled out, he ran down the stairs with his shotgun and came near to scattering her brains all over the Bentley.

That had been a Wednesday night. For the next week, she never left the house, fearing Gloria might telephone while she was out. Each morning, without telling him why, she would send Jeffrey down to wait while the workers sorted the day's mail. As soon as she heard the car in the drive, she would come to the front door to take the packet from him. On the following Wednesday, he hesitated just a beat before handing it to her, and she knew. At the bottom of the pile was her letter, unopened, marked in Gloria's hand, "RETURN TO SENDER."

That night, Lila wrote again and has every Wednesday since. They have all been returned the same way. A few months after she started, a letter didn't come back in the usual week, and she oscillated between fear and hope until two came back together. "I hope you enjoyed your vacation," she put in her next letter. A few weeks later there was another delay, and she noticed the letter had been forwarded from Gloria's apartment building to John and Catherine's house. She congratulated Gloria on the move; it was a house that had seen much happiness and should do so again. She enclosed a check to help with painting or whatever. That letter came back, too, and, check still inside, was placed with the others in a shoebox in Lila's closet.

A report from the detectives has just come with a wonderful surprise: a newspaper article on the selection of Gloria as the recipient of this years S. L. Mantell award for fostering advancement in the arts among the children of St. Louis. It describes, in detail, the after-school music programs developed by Gloria, and Lila reads it twice before starting her letter.

"My Darling Gloria, I can't tell you how proud I am of you. Helping children is the best thing anyone can do with her life. To have done this so successfully in the field of music must bring you great satisfaction." Lila picks up the article and looks closely at the picture of Gloria receiving the award. Yes, there are new lines in Gloria's face, and she is thinner. "I hope you're not working too hard. Everybody needs a rest once in a while, even from the best of causes. If you'd like to come down, your old room is always ready for you, and there's a car you can use whenever you want. I even had the piano tuned today. It made me think of the first time you walked into the living-room while Elliott was giving me a lesson. Was that the beginning of your career? I'd like to think so. I love you always. Mama."

She reads the letter to herself, puts it in an envelope, addresses it and rings Mary on the intercom to come up and prepare her for bed. Mary will give the letter to Jeffrey who will mail it first thing in the morning. Lila yawns. She is too tired, tonight, but tomorrow she must tell Mary about Gloria's award.

THE END

ABOUT THE AUTHOR

Bob Bachner practices real estate law in New York City. He was educated at Phillips Academy, Andover, Harvard College and Harvard Law School. His first novel, Last Clear Chance, was a finalist in the Faulkner-Wisdom Competition. His wife, Barbara Bachner, is a multi-media artist, and his daughter, Suzanne Bachner, is a playwright and director.

Thank you so much for reading one of our **Historical Romance** novels.

If you enjoyed our book, please check out our recommended title for your next great read!

Fateful Decisions by Trevor D'Silva

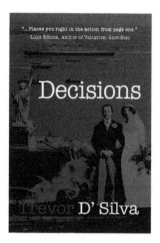

"...Places you right in the action from page one."

-Luke Edison, author of Valcarion: Sacrifices

CPSIA information can be obtained
at www.ICGtesting.com
Printed in the USA
LVHW031823270819
629113LV00002B/231/P